THIS TIME NEXT YEAR

Also by Evelyn Hood

A Pride of Sisters
The Damask Days
A Stranger to the Town
The Silken Thread
A Matter of Mischief

THIS TIME
NEXT YEAR

Evelyn Hood

BCA

LONDON · NEW YORK · SYDNEY · TORONTO

This edition published 1992
by BCA
by arrangement with
HEADLINE BOOK PUBLISHING PLC

CN 2559

First published in 1992
by HEADLINE BOOK PUBLISHING PLC

10 9 8 7 6 5 4 3 2 1

Printed and bound in Great Britain by
Richard Clay Ltd, Bungay, Suffolk

Some Greenock geographical and historical facts have been slightly altered to suit the needs of the story line.

My gratitude goes to Alice Robertson for generously giving me access to her research material into the history of Greenock's sugar refiners.

E.H.

1

'I think he's dead.'

A steamer out on the River Clyde bellowed mournfully as though in agreement and a chill draught breathed against Lessie's cheek as she straightened, stepping back from the bed, the fingers that had brushed the cooling grey face automatically rubbing at her skirt to rid themselves of the touch of death. Rain had started pattering against the small ill-fitting window that lit the room.

Incongruously, she smelled roses, and realised that it was Anna McCauley's scent. Cheap and sharp though it was, it made a pleasant alternative to the smell of damp and decay and generations of human residence that permeated the weary old tenement building.

'Oh Jesus,' moaned Anna, one fist clenched against her chin to stop its trembling. 'Don't say that!'

'What d'you want me to say?' Lessie snapped, her own nerves in shreds as she held the small mirror, innocent of any clouding, out to the other girl. 'The man's not breathing, is he? Where's the sense in saying he's fine when he's not?'

'What the hell's he doing dying in my bed?'

Lessie's voice was tart when she said, 'You know that better than I do.' But Anna was deaf to sarcasm or criticism. She stood on the broken blackened linoleum, swaying back and forth, moaning.

Lessie, fighting back the urge to slap her, stared round the room, wondering what in God's name was to be done. A portrait of the ageing Queen Victoria as a young woman, neat beneath a coronet, incongruous as the smell of roses in the bare room, looked back at her from behind Anna's tangled red curls. The royal eyes were disapproving. And no wonder, Lessie thought. The poor woman must have witnessed sights in this place that no personage of blue blood should ever witness. But surely this was the worst scene of all.

'How could he no' have waited till he was out in the street afore he did it? How could he no' have—' Anna managed to bite back the self-pitying tirade, then said in a rush of panicky words, 'They'll say it was me that killed him. They'll take me to the Bridewell and h-hang me.'

Her own panic honed Lessie's voice to an edge that would have sliced through iron. 'They'll not hang you! It'll have been his heart that did it.' His heart, and over-strenuous exercise on the narrow, grimy, tumbled bed, she thought, but kept that to herself, saying only, 'I'll have to get back. The wean's on his own.'

'You'll no' leave me?' In her agitation Anna snatched at Lessie's arm. The movement dislodged the coat she had hurriedly wrapped about herself before rushing out onto the tiny landing in search of help when her bed companion had suddenly departed – in spirit though not, unfortunately, in body.

There was a flash of long slender limbs, the curve of a perfect pink-tipped breast before the coat was scooped back into place.

'I've got tae see that Ian's all right.'

'But you'll come back?'

Lessie would have given anything she had, except Ian, to stay away, but it was clear that her neighbour wasn't going to let her escape easily. Donald, she silently asked the memory of her dead husband, Donald, what did you think you were doing, bringing me to this street, then dying and leaving me alone to deal with the likes of Anna McCauley?

Aloud she said as she moved to the door, 'Get yourself dressed. I'll be back in a minute, then we can decide what to do about – ' she paused, then flapped a hand at the still figure in the bed, ' – him.'

'You're sure you'll be back? I couldnae—'

'I'm sure!' Lessie snapped and closed the door of Anna's flat behind her to the sound of a low moan of anguish from its living occupant. For a moment she leaned against its panels and drew a deep, shaky breath.

The basket of still-damp washing she had been bringing up from the crowded little back yard stood by her own door on the other side of the landing. She had dumped it there when Anna, wild-eyed and wrapped in the coat, rushed from her flat just as Lessie reached the top step. Picking it up she went into her own living quarters, suddenly anxious about the silence. By this time Ian, fretful after a bad night, should surely have been bellowing out his loneliness and his fear of being deserted.

To her relief he was asleep, still tied firmly into the fireside chair with a long woollen scarf. His head had sagged against one shoulder, his small pale face was streaked and dirty round the mouth, and a fist still clutched the well-chewed remains of the sugared crust she had put into it to keep him happy for long enough to let her hurry down to the back yard before the threatening rain started. There was a sharp tang of urine hanging in the air around him and she was glad she had thought to put a napkin on him. Ian, not long past his first birthday, was learning how to use a chamber pot and learning well, but ill health had caused a reversion.

At the sight of him, all thought of the dead man in Anna McCauley's bed vanished from Lessie's mind, swept away by her burning, over-whelming love for this sickly scrap of humanity, this living proof of the happiness she and Donald had shared for one brief year before pneumonia took her young husband from her.

She bent over the baby, careful not to wake him, and listened anx-iously. His bout of whooping cough had given them both disturbed nights for weeks but now, thank God, he was breathing easily. Better to leave him where he was, wet backside and all, than to disturb him by moving him to the shabby cot against the inner wall of the room,

2

as far away as possible from the draughts that always found their way in, no matter how much she tried to plug the gaps in the window frame.

In the meantime – Lessie's heart sank at the thought – Anna McCauley was waiting for her. If only she had been two minutes earlier bringing in the washing she might have been safely inside her own door by the time Anna, violet-blue eyes wide with horror, had burst out onto the landing. Instead she had been right there, to be caught by the wrist and dragged into the woman's flat and into her problem.

The whole building – the whole of the Vennel, come to that – knew how Anna McCauley made her money. Lessie had been shocked to the core, once she worked out why there were so many men coming and going up and down the hollowed-out stone stairs, to realise that she was living on the same landing as a prostitute. Her husband had promised her that as soon as he was made up to foreman in the shipyard they would move out of the Vennel and find somewhere better to live. Poor Donald had not lived to keep his promise.

Lessie, a respectably married woman, had always carefully avoided contact with Anna apart from the occasional word of acknowledgement if they happened to meet on the stairs or in the close leading to the street. But now it seemed that she was burdened with Anna and the wages of her sins, for the moment at least. If she didn't go back across the landing now, the woman would no doubt come banging on her door and then Ian would be wakened.

With a sigh dragged up from the soles of her cracked shoes, Lessie gave one last glance at her son and crept from the room.

Anna was waiting anxiously, one bright eye peering through a crack in the barely opened door. As Lessie appeared, the door opened wider and she was almost hauled through it. It shut behind her with a firm click and Anna, her voice still tremulous, said, 'Now what are we to do?'

'You must fetch a policeman and let him deal with it.'

'And have myself taken off tae the polis station and questioned till I don't know what I'm sayin'?' In a panic Anna seized at Lessie again with a grip that would raise bruises by nightfall. While waiting for Lessie's return she had dressed herself and pinned up her hair. It glowed a vibrant russet colour in the dim grey room.

'What else can you do? A man's dead in your bed; either you have him taken away or you let him be. It's up to you.'

'D'you no' know who he is?' Anna waved a hand towards the bed and Lessie took advantage of the movement to prise herself loose from the other's grip.

'How should I know him? He's nothin' tae do wi' me.' She had looked at the dead man as little as possible. All she knew was that he was middle-aged, scrawny and unattractive, probably in life as well as in death.

'I thought everyone did. It's Frank Warren!'

Lessie gaped at the bluish sunken face on the shabby pillow, then at Anna. 'One of the sugar folk?' Her sister Edith was a maid in the

3

elderly Warren brothers' house, and to hear Edith talk, Mr Frank and Mr James were on nodding terms with God. Lessie had occasionally glimpsed one or other of them walking or driving in the town, on their way to or from their successful refinery, but that was the nearest she had ever come to them, until now.

'Aye, one o' the sugar folk!'

'What's a man like that doing here?' The question was blunt, but Anna was too upset to take umbrage.

'He liked coming here,' she said simply. 'We could have taken a room at one of the hotels or even gone out of the town tae somewhere like Glasgow.' She gave a sniff and a gulp and scrubbed the back of one arm over her face. 'But he liked tae come here wi' a scarf over his face so that nob'dy would recognise him – the selfish bastard,' she added, glaring at her dead lover.

Lessie could see now why Anna could scarcely tell the police that the man had died in her bed. God knew what the townsfolk would say if they found out. Although the Warrens meant nothing to her, the sense of duty towards her betters that had been instilled into her at school wouldn't allow her to see them humiliated.

She bit her lip in thought for a moment. 'We could dress him and sit him in the chair.' The idea developed in her mind as she went along. 'Then you could fetch a policeman and tell him that – that Mr Warren took ill in the street and you saw him there and brought him in tae rest for a minute. And he just up and died before you could fetch help.'

Anna was looking at her as though she had just come down from a mountain carrying God's words carved on tablets. 'Aye! They'd think he was just goin' through the street on his way tae the sugar warehouses on the harbour, wouldn't they? Here, help me!' Spurred into action now that a plan had been formed, Anna scooped up the clothing lying over her one and only chair, dumped it on the floor by the bed, then pulled back the sheet that covered the dead man. Her nose wrinkled and she reeled back. 'Christ, he's fouled my bed, the dirty bugger that he is!'

'He can't help that, can he? It happens when folks die.' In the days before her withdrawal from the world, Lessie's mother had done her share of laying-out. Lessie had helped her on a few occasions. 'You can wash your sheets afterwards,' she told Anna brusquely, anxious to get out of the place as soon as she could and get back to Ian. 'Come on, the sooner we get it done the better. He'll stiffen up if we waste any more time and then we'll not be able tae dress him.'

It was a long and difficult task. Frank Warren, naked as the day of his birth, wasn't a big man, but in death it seemed that every limb had doubled its natural weight. It was like coping with a huge, unwieldy rag doll. Both women were slender and, in Lessie's case at least, undernourished, but they were young and used to hard work. Even so, they were breathless by the time they had dragged the dead man from the bed, dressed him on the floor to the accompaniment of a flow of muttered curses from Anna, then heaved him into the chair, a sagging piece of furniture with broken springs that twanged their protest as the body was dumped on them. All the time Lessie kept one ear open for a sound from her own flat. If Ian should waken before they were finished she might have to fetch him in, and she had no wish to let him see what his mother was up to, even though he was still too young to ask questions or to talk about what he saw.

'Thank God,' Anna panted when they finally got the corpse settled and had stripped the bed, covered it with the old stained coverlet and put the sheets to soak in a bucket of cold water brought from the sink on the landing. Most of her hair had escaped from the pins to lie in tendrils about her neck and her lovely face was red with exertion. Lessie knew that she herself must look just as hot and exhausted.

'Now you'll have tae run down and fetch a policeman,' she started to say, but Anna interrupted her, dropping to her knees to reach beneath the bed.

'His wallet.' She waved it as she got up again. 'Lucky I saw the corner of it peeping out. They'd have had me for theft if I hadnae.'

She flipped open the leather wallet, riffled through it, and extracted more crisp notes than Lessie had ever seen at one time. Dampening one fingertip on her tongue, Anna removed two of them with decisive flicks of the finger and held one out. 'Here, take this for your trouble.'

'I'll do nothing of the sort!'

'Och, go on!' Anna pushed the money into Lessie's hand and stuffed the remaining note down the bodice of her own blouse. Putting the rest back and stowing the wallet into the dead man's breast pocket, she said over her shoulder, 'It's only what he owed me. He'd finished when he went an' died so it's mine by rights. An' God knows you're entitled tae half o' it.'

'I don't want it.' Lessie put the money down on the table.

'Don't be daft! You're no' goin' tae tell me that you don't need it, an' you wi' a bairn to raise.' Anna tried to push the money back into Lessie's hand and for a moment there was a brief struggle which ended with Lessie spinning away towards the door, leaving the crumpled, rejected note on the cracked oilcloth.

'I don't want it! Now go and fetch a policeman,' she said over her shoulder, and left the room.

Anna caught up with her in the gloom of the tiny landing, clutching at her once again. 'Lessie, come wi' me tae speak tae the polisman; he'll believe you more than me.'

'It's got nothing to do with me!'

'It wis your idea to—'

A wail followed by an ominous bout of coughing from her own flat gave Lessie the strength to wrench herself free of Anna's clinging fingers, her mind filled with thoughts of Ian. 'It'll look suspicious if there's two of us. Go on now, I've my bairn tae see tae!'

Ian, his small face purpling, was struggling against the scarf that held him in the chair while choking sounds tore their way out of his chest and his lungs laboured to suck in air. Lessie jerked the ends of

5

the scarf apart and lifted him into her arms, carrying him to the window. His fists beat at her in misery and fear, then the first terrible crowing whoop came and he stiffened in her arms, pulling away from her so that she had to put one hand on the small of his back to prevent him from toppling from her arms. The veins in his neck stood out with the strain of trying to breathe. His blue eyes, the same vivid, far-seeing blue as Donald's, were bulging, suffused with tears. His nose began to run and still the attack went on.

'Dear God . . . ' She felt so helpless, guilty because her own lungs were drawing in life-giving air while her child suffocated. Then suddenly, when she felt that he could stand it no longer and she could bear it no longer, Ian sucked in air again, falling against her and vomiting the half-digested crust he had so enjoyed earlier down the front of her blouse.

'There, my wee dove, you're all right now, Mammy's got you safe,' she whispered, pacing the small room with him, rocking him while the panic-stricken weeping that always followed an attack shook his small body. How could you tell such a tiny bairn what was wrong with him? How could you assure him that in two weeks, three, six maybe, he would recover?

'As long as his lungs stay clear,' young Dr Miller had told her when she first took Ian to him. 'Keep him warm and away from draughts. And see that he gets nourishing food. A spoonful of tonic wine once a day, perhaps, and cod-liver oil to build up his strength.'

Looking at the thin fair young woman before him, seeing the little frown lines that worry had already engraved between her brows, knowing full well how hollow his words were to the likes of her, he had added, without hope but bound to say it, 'Chicken soup, if you can afford it.'

Lessie hadn't known whether to laugh or cry. It was hard enough just feeding the two of them and her brother Davie, who had been sent by their father to live with her after Donald's death so that there would be a wage coming in. Not that a young laddie like Davie earned much. Certainly not enough to buy chicken soup and tonic wine and cod-liver oil. Unless, she thought ironically as she wiped Ian's sticky tear-stained face with the wetted corner of a towel and put him back in the chair, she used the rent money and risked eviction. At least Ian would be the best-nourished child in the gutter.

'It's all right, Mammy's no' goin' away,' she reassured him as he whimpered and held his arms out to her. 'She's just getting you somethin' tae eat.'

She had saved the last few spoonfuls of a pot of broth made the day before with a good piece of bone she'd coaxed from the butcher. She heated it now, wishing as she stirred at it that Davie hadn't eaten so much of it the night before. But he put almost all of his wages into the house and he was a husky, growing lad. It would be wrong to ask him to deny himself nourishment when he had such hard work to do on the docks. It was different for her – women in Lessie's world were used to going without so that their menfolk and children could eat.

6

When the broth was at the right temperature for Ian she put a little into a bowl and coaxed it into his mouth, drop by drop. By the time he had finished his eyelids were drooping.

'Poor wee scrap, you're worn out wi' all that nasty coughing.' She changed his napkin, ignoring his girning and his fretful, irritated swipes at her busy hands, and laid him down in his cot. Then she found a clean blouse for herself. As she took the soiled blouse off, something fell to the ground. Lessie, who had a hatred of the cockroaches that infested the old building, choked back a scream and shied away. But the object on the floor didn't scurry away to the safety of the ill-fitting skirting board. Cautiously she picked it up and found herself holding the pound note Anna McCauley had tried to force on her earlier, folded into a tiny square.

'That besom!' She remembered how the girl had followed her out onto the landing and clutched at her – in a panic, Lessie had thought at the time. But instead Anna had been making sure that the money she took from the dead man was shared between them, making them partners in conspiracy.

'I'll show her!' Lessie said to a drowsy Ian as she struggled into the clean blouse. She wrenched open the door then closed it again at once. The door of Anna's flat was half open and a man's voice was rumbling in the room beyond. A second man was on his way in, his back to her, a small black bag in one hand.

Quietly, like a thief in her own house, Lessie tiptoed away from the door, back into the centre of the room. She opened her fist and smoothed out the note. The very look of it was opulent, with its crests and whirls. The words 'Pay on Demand' jumped off the paper at her. She closed her fist, feeling the money crinkle and rustle in her palm. Twenty whole shillings. Biting her lip, she glanced at Ian, who was breathing easily now. With the money she held she could buy the cod-liver oil the doctor had recommended, another bottle of cough mixture, and a small boiling fowl to make more broth and provide at least two dinners for the three of them. Ian needed the nourishment.

She laid the note down on the table then picked it up again and smoothed it out. She wouldn't be keeping the money for herself, but for her bairn, poor wee fatherless morsel that he was. It wasn't his fault that he had been born in the oldest and shabbiest part of Greenock instead of in one of the better tenements, or even one of the villas along the shore with his own nurse and everything his little heart could want.

Lessie chewed at her lip again; she knew that she wouldn't return the money. Not now, at any rate. Later, when Ian was well again, she would repay every penny, no matter how many stairs she had to scrub or how many floors she had to wash to earn it.

She would have to pay it back, because until she did, the money forged a silent, sisterly bond between herself and Anna. And Lessie Hamilton was an independent woman. She always had been independent, even as a child. She wanted a bond with no one, especially the likes of Anna McCauley.

2

Not many of the men crowding the streets on their way home from the docks were given to talking, mainly because after a day's work they were too tired. The predominant sound was the clatter of nailed boots on the cobbles and paving stones, with the occasional farewell grunt as this man and that peeled off to vanish into dwelling houses or along narrow side streets. Larger groups turned into one or other of the public houses, where drink would help to ease tired muscles and loosen tongues.

Archie Kirkwood and his younger son Davie, walking almost shoulder to shoulder, said nothing because they rarely had anything to say to each other. Stealing a sidelong glance at Davie, Archie saw the tired droop of mouth and shoulders, the way the boy's booted feet scuffed along. He didn't have the stamina needed for a docker, this one. Didn't have the muscle and gumption. Too fond of reading and thinking. Engineering, for Christ's sake! A man never knew what was going on in that dark head, or behind the cool grey eyes. Archie felt much more comfortable with Joseph, his firstborn. He was a real chip off the old block, was Joseph, never out of mischief and trouble. It was a pity he'd refused to become a docker. He was strong, like his father.

When they reached Dalrymple Street, the parting of the ways, Davie would have swung off towards the tangled knot of crowded old streets where Lessie lived with no more than a murmur of farewell, but the older man said gruffly, 'Is our Lessie goin' out tonight?'

'No.' Davie hesitated then said, his voice defensive, 'It's my night-school night.'

Archie's mouth gave an involuntary downward twist of derision, but he only said, 'Tell her I'll mebbe look in later.'

'Aye.' Davie loped off, his step quickening now that he was moving away from his father.

'God,' thought Archie Kirkwood in disgust as he walked on, turning away from the Clyde and moving deeper into the town. 'Night school!' That was no place for a man. In his own young day he would have been one of those marching into the pub, or gathering on a street corner, but not now. Not since—

He pushed the memory out of his mind but it came creeping back, as it always did, to haunt him as he turned in at the mouth of the close, climbed the stairs to the first floor, and opened the door of his home. The smell of cooking and polish, the smell at once both warm

9

and cold that meant home, enfolded him as he stepped across the lintel.

'Dadda!' Thomasina, dark like him, just past her twelfth birthday, came skipping to meet him at the kitchen door, trailing the shabby rag doll her eldest sister Edith had made for her when she was a toddler. She beamed up at him, clutching at his jacket then pushing her short stubby fingers into the pockets in a way that the others had never dared. Thomasina wasn't afraid of him as her brothers and sisters had been at her age. She loved everybody and expected everybody to love her. With a squawk of delight she found the orange he had brought for her and ran to show it to her mother.

'There wis a fruit ship in,' said Archie, and at once hated himself for trying to make conversation with his wife. He was always trying, and always being rebuffed.

'Give it to me, lovey, and I'll cut it for you,' Barbara told her daughter gently, then with a change of voice she said over her shoulder to her husband, 'Wash your hands then sit at the table. Your food's ready.'

One knife, one fork, and one spoon awaited him on the scrubbed table. He always ate alone these days. Barbara and Thomasina ate when he was out of the house, as though taking nourishment was something shameful, to be done in secrecy.

As his wife brought the steaming soup plate to the table, Archie caught the faint smell of whisky. Ironically, while he had never touched a drop in years, Barbara, a strict teetotaller through all the years of his intoxication, couldn't get through the day now without drink. There was always a bottle hidden about the place.

A plate of meat and potatoes, also steaming, followed the soup. While he ate in silence, Barbara moved about the kitchen, rubbing at spotless surfaces, washing his soup plate and spoon the moment he had finished with them, always busy. Thomasina sucked and chewed noisily on her orange. Juice glistened on her chin and Barbara swooped on her, crooning, to wipe it off.

Archie cleared his plate and pushed it away. It, too, was immediately claimed and washed while he moved to his fireside chair and opened the newspaper he had brought in with him. Home was the loneliest place in the world. In the past twelve years Barbara had only spoken to him when it was necessary. When Edith and Lessie married and moved out, Barbara had left the marriage bed and taken over their room. She slept there now with Thomasina. Joseph still used the wall bed when he was home, but more often than not he was out God knew where with his cronies or some woman or other, or in the jail. As soon as he was old enough, Joseph had taken up his father's abandoned mantle of drinker and fighter.

Thomasina, sitting in her relaxed, boneless way on the rug before the range, discarded the last sucked-out quarter of orange peel and scrambled to her feet to claim her place on her father's lap. None of his other children had ever tried to sit on his knee but Thomasina always did and Archie, aware of Barbara's eye on him, didn't dare reject the girl.

Christ, he thought as she wriggled into a comfortable position, pushing the paper aside, her head bumping painfully against his lip, the faint smell of orange juice mingling with the scented soap that Barbara washed her with every day, it was embarrassing for a man, so it was, to see a near-grown lassie behaving like a wee bairn.

He caught Barbara's eye and saw by the chill look in it that she was reading his thoughts. Thomasina wasn't going to change because Thomasina, through no fault of her own, was simple. Guiltily, carefully, he rearranged the newspaper so that he could hold it and support the girl's body at the same time, narrowing his eyes to squint at the newsprint across the silky head that nestled confidingly on his shoulder.

'What's going on across the landing?' Davie wanted to know as soon as he walked into the house. His voice was anxious. 'A polisman was coming out just now. Is there something wrong with Anna?'

'How should I know?' Lessie asked tartly. Davie had been fascinated by Anna McCauley since the moment he had first set eyes on her, and Lessie sometimes had nightmares about what might happen if she didn't do all she could to keep him away from the woman. Anna was a man-eater and Davie was only seventeen. She felt responsible for his welfare.

'For God's sake, Lessie, you don't have the polis visitin' for nothin', ye know that. They were at our house often enough after our father, then Joseph.' He half turned towards the door. 'Mebbe I should go an'—'

'You'll do nothing of the kind! Anna's fine, I saw her myself earlier. Anyway, we should mind our own business.' Lessie stirred hard at the pot on the stove then tutted as a splash of broth flew out and landed on the cuff of her clean blouse. 'Now look what you've made me do!'

'Your mammy's in a terrible mood, young Ian,' Davie told his nephew, picking him up and nuzzling into his midriff. Ian, who was tickly, gave a screech of laughter and wriggled.

'Here, is that chicken I can smell?' Davie suddenly forgot about the policeman. Working on the docks, out in the open most of the time, he had a hearty appetite.

'I did a bit of extra cleaning for Mrs Hansen today,' Lessie lied. 'I thought we'd have a treat, for once.'

'Chicken!' He put the little boy down. He took his jacket off and hung it neatly on the nail in the back of the door.

'Och, I forgot tae fetch the water for you.' Lessie left the stove and picked up the bucket.

'I'll do it.' Davie took it from her. 'You look tired out.'

'So do you.' He always looked exhausted after a day at the docks.

He grinned at her, elated at the prospect of the meal ahead. 'I can manage to carry a pail of water.' She heard him whistling as he went out to the stone sink on the landing. Davie was good company and she didn't know how she would have managed without him. Quiet

11

and withdrawn at home, where his mother had no time for anyone but Thomasina and his father thought him a weakling, Davie had blossomed since he came to live with her in the Vennel.

To the accompaniment of the clanking of ancient protesting pipes and the gush of water from the landing, Lessie set out bowls on the table then ladled broth into them, carefully stepping over Ian, who was sitting on the rug, poring over a battered rag book someone had given him and telling himself a story in a singsong nonsensical babble. The fine wispy red hair at the nape of his neck, hair the colour of his father's, made her heart turn over with love.

She cut some thick slices from half a loaf and arranged them on a plate, then suddenly realised that Davie was taking his time about coming back inside. Hurriedly she went to the door and her heart sank as she saw Anna by the sink with a pot in her hand, one shoulder leaning against the scarred streaked wall, her hip jutting. Davie had filled his bucket and turned the stiff old tap off; his hand still rested on it and his attention was given over entirely to Anna.

'I don't know what I'd have done without your sister,' she was saying as Lessie got to the door.

'Lessie?'

'Aye, did she no' tell ye? I ran oot screamin' like a lost hen.' Anna's clear laugh rippled out; she had turned her earlier terror into an amusing story for Davie's benefit and even in the gloom of the landing Lessie could see her eyes sparkling up at him. 'An' it was Lessie who—'

'Davie, your food's spoiling!'

He jumped at the interruption and looked round at Lessie guiltily. Anna laughed, then moved to take her own place at the sink as he hefted the battered bucket.

'Ye're a strong lad, Davie Kirkwood. Lessie's fortunate tae have someone tae lift full buckets for her.'

Davie glanced at his sister then said quickly, 'I could fill a bucket as easy for you as for Lessie if you left it outside your door each evening.'

Anna's eyes, slightly tilted at the outer corners, moved over him, then rested lightly on Lessie, standing watchfully at her door. 'Och, I'm strong enough tae dae my own carryin'. I've aye had tae fend for myself. But thanks for the kind offer.'

She turned on the tap and held the pot under it. Her sleeves were folded back and her arms, bare to above the elbow, were smooth and slender. Lessie saw Davie's eyes linger on them and wished that she could dip a hand into her apron pocket and take out Anna's pound note and hand it back. But she had already spent it on a bottle of tonic wine and a large bottle of cough syrup, not to mention the chicken.

'Davie!'

He came at last, with one final glance at Anna, who smiled back at him.

'Why did you no' tell me what had been going on?' he wanted to know when the door was at last closed, leaving Anna outside.

'It wasnae something I'd want tae talk about, least of all tae you,' she snapped. Ian had come toddling to the door to find out where everyone was and she shooed him ahead of her into the kitchen. 'Get yourself washed or you'll never finish your meal in time to go tae the night school.'

'God, Lessie, anyone'd think I was the same age as wee Ian here,' her brother burst out, pouring water into the basin and stripping off his shirt. He reached for the harsh yellow soap. 'I know fine how Anna earns her keep.'

'Then you'll know why I'm not interested in talking about her. D'you think I like living in the same building as a . . . a . . .'

Davie lifted cupped handfuls of water to rinse his face. Watching him, Lessie realised that her little brother was a man now. Healthy though he was, Davie, when matched with his father and brother, had always seemed slight and frail. But six months' hard work on the docks had added muscle to his arms and shoulders.

'Folk have tae feed an' clothe themselves, an' pay the rent.' He spoke indistinctly, bent low over the basin to prevent the water splashing everywhere, but even so she could hear every word. 'Anna has nobody tae fend for her.'

'There are better ways of earning money.'

Davie reached for the towel and buried his face in it, then emerged to say bitingly, 'You're great at moralising, Lessie. Mebbe if you hadnae been fortunate enough tae find a good man like Donald you'd be more understanding.'

'Understanding?' She stared at him, deeply hurt by his criticism. 'How can you try tae defend someone like Anna McCauley?'

Davie gave his arms a final rub, ran his fingers through his hair and went into the tiny narrow room where he slept. He came back almost at once, pushing his arms into the sleeves of the clean shirt she had left hanging on the back of the door for him. 'Someone has to. You helped her this afternoon, from what she told me.'

'I'd no choice. She caught me on the landing, else I'd not have had anything to do with what was going on.' Lessie became aware that Ian was listening, his small face turning from one to the other, his brow furrowed. He was used to laughter and harmony, for Lessie and Davie got on better together than any other members of the Kirkwood family.

'I'll just say this, Davie, before we sit down at the table. If you ever take up with Anna McCauley you're out of this house.'

He smiled without humour. 'I couldnae afford Anna, an' you know it.' Then he pulled his chair out and sat down, picking up his soup spoon. Lessie stared down at him, chewing her underlip. She loved Davie, loved his quick smile, his warmth and compassion. She fretted for him because she knew how much he hated working on the docks. She was proud of the way he had started night school in the face of jeers and taunts from his father and brother. She desperately wanted him to do well in life, to be happy, to have all the good things that he deserved. And at that moment she also wanted to slap him, to shake him, to force him to promise that he would never, ever lie with the likes of Anna McCauley. Davie deserved a good woman, a woman he could be proud of. Slowly, unable to say all these things, she sat down opposite him and picked up her own spoon.

The soup was good, the chicken was tender and succulent, the potatoes were served in their jackets the way Davie liked. But the meal had been spoiled for them both by their quarrel and they ate in unaccustomed silence. Pushing pieces of chicken around her plate, tasting them without pleasure, Lessie reminded herself bitterly that the food had been bought with ill-gotten money. Everything to do with Anna McCauley was defiled, even the chicken.

Once or twice she sensed Davie glancing at her, but when she looked up, ready to smile, his eyes hurriedly slipped away. He spoke now and again to Ian, feeding the little boy chicken from his plate. When Lessie protested half-heartedly that he'd had his share, Davie shrugged and said, 'The laddie needs it. He's got a lot o' growin' tae dae yet.'

When they had finished, he went into the tiny hallway to fetch his jacket and came back. 'Here's my wages. An' I brought this for the wean. I thought it would help tae ease his cough.'

The orange lay on his palm, round and golden, a captive sun.

'Och, Davie!' Lessie felt tears pricking at the backs of her eyes. She knew how much he hated the way his father and the other dockers looked on a percentage of any cargo they unloaded as their rightful due. The big hooks they used in their work might, by accident, breach a barrel or damage a crate and the contents find their way into pockets or empty bottles. One crate or barrel out of hundreds was never missed, but Davie, who, as his father scornfully told him, had been born with enough of a conscience to do for the whole world, would never take part in sharing out the spoils. Lessie knew how much it must have cost him to take that one orange.

Ian, wide-eyed, reached up with both hands and took the fruit from his uncle, lifting it at once to his mouth. He bit into the skin then blinked rapidly and dropped it, rubbing at his lips and grimacing.

Davie laughed and scooped him up. 'Ye're supposed tae take the skin off first, daftie!'

'I'll give it to him tomorrow.' Lessie retrieved the orange, then said softly, 'Thanks, Davie.'

He grinned at her and suddenly the quarrel was over. Davie wasn't one to nurse his anger. He glanced at the clock on the wall and picked up the books that were always kept at one end of the mantelshelf. 'I'd better go or I'll be late. My father said he'd mebbe look in on you.' Davie didn't refer to his parents as Mam and Da like the others. He made them sound as though they were distant beings, and for years – ever since Thomasina's birth had changed both his parents – he had managed to avoid giving them any title when speaking to them.

Archie Kirkwood arrived an hour later, when Ian, rosy and clean after a good going over with cloth and soap, was being dressed in the tattered jersey and trousers kept for night-time wear. Lessie heard his heavy footsteps on the stairs and was at the door, the baby riding comfortably on one hip, by the time Archie reached the landing.

He didn't hear the door opening; he curled one big scarred hand round the corner at the top of the stairs for support and paused, head down, drawing a deep breath. He looked, Lessie thought with compassion, like an old man. Then he lifted his head, saw her, straightened his shoulders, and became his usual self.

It was raining outside; his jacket was black with moisture but he shook his head when she told him to take it off. 'I'm used tae a drop o' rain. This past winter I've worked in it day in an' day oot. Whit is it they say?' A creaky, little-used smile tugged at the corners of his mouth. 'April showers? By God an' they seem jist as harsh as they were in January an' February an' March.'

His voice filled the small room. As a child Archie had been regularly beaten by a violent stepfather and by the time he was old enough to fight back, the hearing had completely gone in one ear and was impaired in the other. He hated his disability and did all he could to hide it from others. His loud voice and his way of staring intently into the faces of those speaking to him so that the movement of their lips helped him to grasp what they were saying intimidated people who had no knowledge of his deafness. The hidden impediment had also run him into many a fight in his younger days, for if men spoke and laughed with their faces turned from him he was quick to suspect that they were making mock of him.

Lessie made strong black tea and he drank it thirstily, the cup almost hidden in his fist, and nodded when she questioningly lifted the teapot. 'Aye, lass, I've a thirst on me tonight. How's the wean?'

'He's doin' fine.' Out of habit she spoke clearly, shaping the words so that he could read as well as hear them.

'An' yersel'?'

She refilled her own cup and sat down opposite. 'I'm fine too.'

He nodded, then stared into the glowing embers in the grate. Used to his silences, Lessie picked up her sewing basket and started darning a shirt of Ian's. Ian himself squatted contentedly on the rag rug between their feet, staring like his grandfather into the fire, picking at the little balls of fluff that bobbled his faded, too-tight jersey.

Archie visited every two weeks or so now, visits that had started not long after Donald's death. At first Lessie, unused to attention of any sort from her father other than a fair number of slaps when she was younger, had been uncomfortable when he came into her home; but gradually she came to realise that it was his way of conveying sympathy over her early widowhood. He never spoke much, and he never called when there was a chance that Davie might be in.

She put down her sewing, stooped to gather up the neat little pile of fluff balls Ian had amassed, then picked up the baby, who was beginning to nod drowsily.

'Say goodnight to your granda.'

Ian tucked his head into her neck, overcome with sudden shyness, and she carried him to the cot that Donald had worked hard to earn, noting as she tucked him in that he was getting too long for it. She would have to look round for something more suitable soon.

By the time the teapot was empty, Ian was sound asleep. The medicinal syrup she had bought that day seemed to have done the trick, for apart from one chesty bout of coughing that didn't, mercifully, turn into gasping and whooping, he had had a good evening. Lessie prayed that it would stretch into a good night; being startled awake at frequent intervals wasn't fair on Davie, who had a long hard day ahead of him. Not that he had complained; that wasn't Davie's way.

'I'll make more tea.'

'No, I'd best get back.' Archie levered himself to his feet then dipped a hand into his jacket, which had added its drying aroma to the mixture of smells in the house – dampness, the disinfectant Lessie scrubbed the floor with in an attempt to deter the cockroaches, the general smell of an old, uncared-for building – and brought out an orange. 'This is for the wee fella.'

'Oh Da, that's good of you!' She took the fruit from him, thankful that she had put Davie's orange away, out of Ian's sight. It wouldn't do to have Archie finding out that his wasn't the first gift.

'Tell Mam I'll look in on her soon,' she said as she stood at the open door watching him pull his cap down over his bristly grey hair before stepping onto the landing. The tap was dripping as usual; Archie gave it a wrench as he passed the sink and the dripping stopped. Lessie knew that she was going to have a struggle to get it on again.

As he paused at the top of the stairs to accustom his eyes to the poor light of the flickering gas mantle on the landing, his shoulders slumped again and his first tentative step looked like the tottering of an old man.

Watching, she felt pity for him. It was a disturbing emotion. All her life she had feared him; if there was love there, it was hidden so deep that she was unaware of it. True, a strange rapport had grown up between them since his visits began, but she had thought of it as a grudging, unvoiced mutual respect.

It saddened her to realise that on her side it was only pity.

3

The corner shop was busy. Shoulder to shoulder, Mr and Mrs McKay worked hard weighing and parcelling, calculating totals with brows knotted and fingers scribbling invisible sums on the scarred old counter.

Waiting in line, Lessie noted that Mr McKay's face was grey with fatigue, though it wasn't yet midday, and his lips had a blue tinge to them. His wife kept darting anxious glances in his direction. When it was Lessie's turn to be served and the old woman was dropping broken biscuits, cheaper than whole ones, into a paper bag on the scales, she said below her breath, 'Could ye mebbe gie me an hour or two this afternoon, lass?'

'I'd need tae bring Ian with me.'

'Och, he's not trouble at all. Geordie had a bad night,' the wrinkled bloodless lips mouthed the words so that there was no danger of Mr McKay overhearing, 'an' I'd like him tae have a bit o' a rest after his dinner.'

'I'll be here by two o'clock.' Lessie dug into her purse and offered her halfpence in payment for the biscuits, but Mrs McKay said, 'Tuts, lassie, put your money away,' and shooed her from the shop.

Ian, strapped into a battered old perambulator that someone had given Lessie in exchange for a few days' housework, was waiting outside, thumb in mouth, watching the people around him. The Vennel was a noisy, busy place at all times. By day the street echoed to the clamour of voices, children's shrill yells, and the incessant clop of hooves on cobbles and the rumbling of iron-bound cart wheels; by night, when the carthorses were in their stables and the children in their beds, drunks cursed and shouted and quarrelled their way up and down the footpaths.

Lessie tucked the biscuits, a special treat for her mother and Thomasina, into a pocket where Ian's busy fingers couldn't get at them, and began to bump the perambulator carefully over the uneven pavement. The pram had been shabby when she first got it, but Davie had mended the broken wheels for her and lashed the handle back together with string; Lessie dreaded the day it disintegrated for good, because Ian was getting heavier and she was fortunate to have transport for him.

For a few hours' work in the shop this afternoon she would get the biscuits and perhaps a bag of barley and split peas for soup, or porridge oats. In return for scrubbing stairs and doing housework she was very often given some child's cast-off clothes for Ian, or

17

something for herself. Bartering was popular in the world she inhabited, and at times it was a more sensible method of payment than money.

Before going to her mother's house she had work to do, scrubbing the stairs in a tenement in Cathcart Street. She hurried there, the pram wheels squeaking with every turn. The bobble on Ian's woollen hat, knitted from a ripped-down shrunken jersey that had once belonged to Davie, bounced cheerfully as she bumped the baby carriage up the step into the close. She knocked on the door of one of the ground-floor flats and it opened almost at once.

'I was watching out for you.' Miss Peden, erect as ever in spite of her snowy hair and her wrinkled-apple little face, backed along the hallway before the pram. 'Come in, come in.' Her kitchen, spotless as usual, was warm and smelled of baking. 'You'll take a cup of tea, my dear.'

'I'd best get on. I've to visit my mam and I promised to go into the shop this afternoon.' Lessie squatted to unfasten Ian. The pram's leather straps had long since broken and he was tied in with the woollen scarf she used for him at home. She lifted him out and set him down on his feet, then began to unfasten his knitted coat.

'I'll do that, since you're in a hurry. Off you go and the tea will be waiting for you when you've finished.'

Lessie stripped off her outer clothes and dug into her worn shopping bag for the sacking apron she wore for heavy work. 'Be a good boy, Ian.'

'He's always a good boy,' Miss Peden told her briskly. 'Go on now, girl. Sooner gone, sooner back!'

The note of crisp command in her voice made Lessie smile as she hurried up to the top floor of the building. Once a teacher, always a teacher. Miss Peden had taught all the Kirkwood family and Lessie had been a special favourite of hers. The two of them had built up a friendship as Lessie grew into maturity, for the retired schoolteacher had no family of her own. It was Miss Peden who had helped to get Davie into night school, giving him extra tutoring when he needed it. It was Miss Peden, still well thought of in the town, who recommended Lessie to ladies who could afford someone to do their heavier housework for them when Donald died and his widow and child were left to fend for themselves.

'Ye're late,' a grating voice said as Lessie topped the final flight of stairs.

'I'm sorry, Mrs Kincaid.'

'Aye, so ye should be. The water's near cold.'

Lessie bit back the suggestion that Mrs Kincaid could easily have waited until she arrived before filling the bucket. In the old woman's view, she knew, tepid water was a fitting punishment for tardiness. Instead, she forced a smile to her lips as she took the bucket that had been waiting by Mrs Kincaid's door, together with a scrubbing brush, a cloth, and bar of soap. Mrs Kincaid stood and watched her work for a few minutes before retiring into her own flat and shutting her polished door.

18

Outside, the day was grey and chill in spite of the fact that it was May; the River Clyde was sullen, the far shore hidden behind a misty screen. Although she had tied a shawl over her thin coat, Lessie had been chilled on her way from the Vennel. She was glad to work hard now, for scrubbing was a fine way to set the blood coursing warmly through her veins.

The building consisted of eleven flats in all; two on the ground floor, and three on each of the three other floors. There were six flights of stairs, with a half-landing between each floor. This type of tenement was similar to the home in which Lessie's parents lived. She dreamed of having a place of her own in such a building one day, for each flat had its own sink in the kitchen and there was a water closet on each half-landing. In the Vennel, the water closets were out in the back yards, one to each building. If one was out of order, the residents in that building used the nearest. More often than not there were two dozen families using one water closet.

Scrubbing stairs was an occupation Lessie quite enjoyed, physically exhausting though it was. It freed her mind to wander over the precious months she and Donald had known together, to daydream a little, and to fret over Davie's future and the mysterious estrangement between her parents. No matter how hard she tried not to concern herself, the worrying thoughts kept coming back to nag at her. Lessie cared about her family, she wanted them all to be happy, and she suffered more grief over their hardships than over her own.

When she reached the ground floor she worked her way out to the closemouth, knelt on the pavement to scrub the final step, then tipped her pail into the gutter, her back creaking when she finally stood upright. She swilled some of the dark grey water round vigorously in the bucket to catch up the sediment at the bottom then poured it all out with one final triumphant flourish before making her way back to the top floor, walking carefully to avoid leaving marks on the newly scrubbed surfaces.

Mrs Kincaid studied the soap closely to establish how much of it had been used, then dipped into her apron pocket and counted ten pennies into Lessie's palm. 'That auld miser McAllister didnae answer his door when I went chappin' on it for the money. Ye'll hae tae see him yersel',' she said, and withdrew, shutting her door in Lessie's face.

Nobody answered the middle door on the landing below when Lessie knocked, though it seemed to her that there was a waiting silence on the other side of the wooden panels. She sighed, and trudged down to Miss Peden's flat.

'I'll see to McAllister,' the retired schoolteacher said briskly when Lessie told her.

'I feel bad about it. Mr McAllister's a poor old soul.'

Miss Peden snorted. 'He has to pay his way the same as the rest of us, lassie, and you need the money you earn. You don't scrub stairs for the pleasure of it. Now take that apron off and sit down by the fire. You'll have a fresh-baked scone with your tea,' she added. With

Miss Peden it was sometimes hard to tell the difference between a question and a command. The old lady busied herself at the gleaming range, blackleaded every morning except Sundays, and Lessie sat down on one of the two comfortable fireside chairs. She looked with pleasure at the crisp white netting across the window, the heavy red chenille curtains, looped back by day, the matching chenille table cover weighted down by a blue and white bowl of wax fruit. By her feet the companion-set holding poker, brush and shovel glittered brassily in the firelight, and above her head two 'wally dugs' – matching golden-brown, long-eared china dogs – looked down with blank brown eyes. Miss Peden's house was large by Lessie's standards, with two bedrooms and a shared wash-house and little patch of garden at the back. Miss Peden grew vegetables and a few flowers in her section of the garden.

As she handed her guest a cup of tea, the old woman asked, 'How's David's studying coming along?' She always gave Davie his proper name.

'He's doing fine.' Lessie sipped at the hot, well-sugared tea and felt herself relaxing into the soft cushions that Miss Peden had made herself. Ian, already filled to the brim with scones, sat on the floor, playing with a wooden horse kept specially for him.

'Tell him if he's got any problems to mind and come to me. I might not be an engineer but books are books and between us we'll puzzle it out.'

'I wish,' said Lessie, 'that he could be put onto working one of the cranes at the docks instead of loading and unloading the ships. He'd be a lot happier, and that would be more in the engineering line. My da could arrange it for him, but he won't, for all that he knows how much Davie hates the work he's doing.'

'Archie Kirkwood's a stubborn man, one of those folk who believe that it only softens people to give them what they want. But mind you, David's fortunate that his father's an overseer. At least it means that the laddie gets work every day.'

'That bothers him too, being picked out before other men who wait alongside him morning after morning.'

The dock system was a harsh one. Early every morning men hoping for a day or half-day's work gathered at the gate and the overseers of each gang picked out those they wanted. The others usually waited on, enviously watching fortunate workers who had been chosen, hoping against hope that extra hands might be needed. Lessie knew that being picked out every day by his father over men who were desperate for work and might be more skilful dockers than he was, was a humiliating experience for Davie. He had come home with a bloodied nose more than once from a street fight over it.

'Tuts, girl, your heart's far too soft. Someone has to be taken on and it makes sense for your father to favour his own. Besides, if David didn't bring in money, you'd be in an even sorrier state than you are.'

'Ian and me manage fine!' Lessie was stung into answering sharply, and the older woman gave a bark of laughter.

'No need to fly at me. I know you manage very well, but you have to work far too hard for what you get. You look tired – even when you first came in you looked tired. Is it the bairn? Is his whooping cough troubling him at nights again?'

'It's a lot better. I think it's almost gone.' Lessie leaned forward to put a hand lightly, thankfully, on Ian's red-gold head. 'Mebbe I'm just getting old.'

'Away with you! You're not much more than a bairn yourself.'

'I'm twenty now.'

'Imagine!' said Miss Peden dryly, then, 'No, no, lassie, you've not lost that bright glow that always set you apart from the rest of them in the classroom. It's just dimmed, that's all, with the worry you've had. It'll come back.'

'You think so?'

'I know so. There are some who never lose it and you're one of them. Mebbe,' said the old woman thoughtfully, 'this new century'll be your turning point.'

'It's strange to think that we're living in nineteen hundred now.' Lessie touched Ian's head again. 'A new century. I wonder what it'll bring to him – to all of us.'

'A better way of life, surely, for you and your bairn. Mebbe it's time for all of Britain to have some sort of a change. As for me – well, I belong to the last century. Me and the old Queen, God bless her. I wonder if the two of us'll see many more years out.'

The maudlin turn the conversation had taken upset Lessie and robbed her of her brief contentment. She cared little for Queen Victoria, but the thought of being without Miss Peden worried her more than the old lady knew. She glanced at the pretty little enamelled clock on the mantelshelf, finished her tea, and began to bundle Ian into his coat and hat. He gave up the wooden horse placidly, having learned by now that it would be waiting for his next visit. 'If I don't go now I'll not have time to visit my mother and get back to the shop.'

'Here, take a few scones to your mother.' Miss Peden wrapped the scones up in a spotlessly clean dish towel and handed them over. 'You can return the cloth next time. Look after yourself, lassie.'

Edith Fisher, Lessie's older sister, was already in her mother's house with her son Peter when Lessie and Ian arrived. Thomasina greeted the newcomers with her usual cries of joy and Lessie hugged her close. She loved this little sister, the prettiest of the three Kirkwood girls with her soft, dark, curly hair. Thomasina returned the hug affectionately then set about clumsily helping to get Ian out of his outdoor clothes. Barbara watched with a slight softening of her expressionless face, and said when Lessie handed her gifts over, 'You shouldnae go spendin' your money on us.'

'It's only a few wee biscuits for Thomasina, and the scones are from Miss Peden. Fresh-baked this morning.' Lessie sat down and watched her mother put the biscuits carefully in a cupboard then give her hair a nervous, automatic pat and head for the bedroom, murmuring, 'I'll just give my hair a tidy up.'

21

'That's the third time since I arrived that she's gone to tidy her hair,' Edith hissed as soon as their mother had left the room. 'I don't know why I come here to be disgraced like this! It was bad enough Da being a drunkard without Ma turning to it as well!'

'She only takes a mouthful each time.'

'Mebbe so, but she can't even let an hour pass without at least one of her mouthfuls.' Edith's voice was accusing. 'You should do something about it.'

'Why me? You and Joseph are older than I am.'

'Joseph!' Edith almost spat the name out. 'In the Bridewell more often than out of it. And it's probably him she's hiding her drink from – he'd have the lot if he could find it. Anyway, you see more of her than I do.'

'What can I do? I can scarcely ask Da to try to stop her, can I? I'd get my ear slapped and you know it.'

'It's not good for Thomasina.' Edith mouthed the final word so that the girl, now on the floor with Peter and Ian, didn't hear her. Her thin colourless lips, so like Barbara's, writhed over the name. Edith, with her pale blue eyes and straight fair hair, was going to look just like her mother in twenty years' time.

Lessie looked round the room. It was spotless, but unlike Miss Peden's little flat it was cheerless, unwelcoming, lacking soul.

'Thomasina and the house are as clean as they can be,' she said.

'Now, mebbe. But what if she gets worse? What if—'

'What if she doesnae get worse?' Lessie interrupted, unwilling to take on any more worry. Edith glared, and would have argued on, but Barbara came back in, bringing with her the unmistakable smell of whisky. She smiled at her daughters with an air of relief.

'I'll make some tea an' we'll toast some bread wi' a wee bit o' cheese, eh? Lessie, you take the toasting fork. I've cut the bread ready.'

'I can't stay long,' Edith told her grimly and Barbara's face fell.

'Och, Edith, I scarce see you these days. You can stay long enough for a cup of tea and some toast, surely?'

'Please, Mama.' Peter's voice was eager. Lessie smiled at him and he flushed and ducked his head shyly.

'Peter, when your grandma's talking to you I'll let you know,' Edith snapped. Deserted by her husband four years earlier when her son was a toddler, she had gone into domestic service at the Warren family's mansion in Gourock, the neighbouring town. She and Peter stayed with Barbara's sister Marion, a childless widow who had had little to do with Barbara since her marriage to Archie Kirkwood, looked on by Marion from the first as unworthy of Barbara. Edith, who had seen how the 'posh' folk raise their children, was determined that her son would grow up to be a little gentleman. Her aunt fully agreed, and between them, in Lessie's opinion, they had turned poor little Peter into a well-dressed miniature adult.

'Besides,' Barbara coaxed, putting the kettle on the range, 'I doubt if Lessie's heard about the new Mr and Mrs Warren arriving from Jamaica.'

22

Lessie looked up sharply. The name immediately conjured up a picture of a dead face on a dirty pillow, Anna McCauley's hands clutching at her, the money that she had accepted, knowing full well that it was tainted.

The Warrens' Gourock mansion where Edith worked had smooth lawns and huge windows overlooking the broad rivermouth and the lush, wooded shore opposite. For several years now there had been only two elderly brothers living in the house. Now that Frank Warren had succumbed in Anna McCauley's bed, Lessie had assumed that his brother would live on in the family house on his own.

'One day,' Donald had been in the habit of saying when they walked past the Warren gates, Donald carrying Ian, Lessie with her hand tucked proudly into the curve of her man's elbow, 'One day, lass, I'll buy you a house like that. Mebbe this time next year, eh?'

But when this time next year had arrived, Donald was dead, his sparkling blue eyes that could set her heart thumping with just one look closed for ever. Lessie thrust the memories away and asked, 'What new Mr and Mrs Warren?'

Edith smirked, pleased to be the centre of attention. 'The nephew. You'll have heard that Mr Frank died several weeks back—' She broke off, then said, 'It was down your way it happened. Did you not hear about it?'

'I heard something.' Lessie reached down to tug Ian's jersey down at the back, hiding the sudden colour that rose in her cheeks.

'Did you not go to see the funeral procession? A lovely funeral we had. The procession was so long, and we'd to bring in extra staff to see to the meal afterwards. The house was full to the brim.' Edith was smug, as though she had organised it all herself. 'We all thought that that only left Mr James, but not a bit of it. Two weeks after the funeral, who should arrive but Mr Andrew, son of Mr George that died years ago. Brown as a berry he is, for he's been out in Jamaica for years seeing to the family business out there.'

Her voice rattled on about Mr Andrew and the wife he had married out in Jamaica and their twin son and daughter and the house being filled and Mrs Andrew being cold in the Scottish climate. Barbara slipped in murmurs of admiring surprise at the right moments, but Lessie let the long recitation flow by her. She wished that her mother wouldn't feed Edith's vanity by fawning so openly on her elder daughter. Barbara was well aware that it was poor Thomasina and her own supposedly secret tippling that kept Edith from spending much time in her old family home. And Barbara was never invited to call at the Gourock house that Edith and Peter shared with her sister. But instead of being insulted, as Lessie was on her behalf, Barbara worked hard to flatter Edith whenever she did condescend to visit her old home.

Thomasina gave one of her excited shrieks, holding her hands out greedily for a piece of the cheese her mother was cutting, and Lessie was startled out of her private thoughts.

'Sit up at the table, there's a good girl,' Barbara said. 'See, Peter's going to sit nice at the table.'

'Beautiful, she is,' Edith burbled on, raising her voice slightly so that she could be heard above her mother and Thomasina as they all took their places round the kitchen table. 'Every inch a lady. So now we've had to take on more staff – a nurse and nurserymaid for the children, of course, and a lady's maid for Mrs Andrew. The housekeeper says it's like the old days, when Mr James's parents were still alive. She was the housemaid then, in the post I hold now. Peter, smaller bites if you please. Only starving paupers stuff their mouths like that.' She nibbled a few crumbs from her own toast.

Lessie broke off a piece of cheese, popped it into Ian's mouth, open and ready like a fledgling's beak in spite of the scones he had had at Miss Peden's, and wondered how soon she could get away. Draughty though the shop was, it was full of life and interest, free of Edith's sickening snobbishness and her mother's fawning.

Three days later Lessie was washing clothes in the stone sink on the landing, elbow-deep in water patiently heated in a tin bucket on the range. The weather had relented and a glimmer of sunlight had managed to find its way in through the landing window above the sink. She cleaned the window frequently, but as some of the panes were missing and the gaps had been covered with bits of board, not much daylight filtered through.

Ian sat on the floor just inside the open door of her flat, chewing at the last piece of orange. The cough syrup and tonic she had bought with Anna McCauley's money had made a difference to him and the whooping, strangling coughs had almost disappeared. Anna herself had become a nuisance, though. She insisted on assuming that they were now friends, and it seemed to Lessie that almost every time she set foot out of her own door Anna appeared, arms tucked beneath her rounded bosom, ready for a gossip. Today, Anna was out and Lessie was making the most of her absence.

She scrubbed hard at Davie's shirt with a scrap of rough grainy soap, then fisted her hands and used her knuckles to rub one piece of material hard against another. Her washing board, left out in the back yard for a thoughtless moment several weeks earlier, had promptly disappeared and she couldn't afford another. As she plunged the shirt under the surface of the cooling, scumming water, someone came up the stairs at her back and a well-educated male voice asked, 'Are you Anna McCauley?'

Lessie whipped round, wiping her hands on her sacking apron.

'Indeed I am not!' she said indignantly, scandalised to think that one of Anna's clients should mistake her for a prostitute. The shirt slid into the sink. 'She's my neighbour,' Lessie went on, nodding at Anna's door, then she added, as he rapped on it with the handle of his cane, 'She's not in.'

'When will she be back?'

Lessie rubbed a damp forearm over her hot face, tucked a loose strand of hair behind her ear, and saw, in the dim light, that Anna's visitor was far superior to the men who usually came calling on her.

24

This one was immaculately dressed in a suit of dark material, so well fitted to his tall body that it must have been made for him. His bow tie had been tied with casual, careless elegance and atop his high snowy collar, piercing grey eyes surveyed her from a dark square face. A curly-brimmed bowler hat and a silver-handled cane grasped in a gloved hand completed an outfit that must have cost several times as much as all the clothes she and Davie and Ian possessed between them.

'When,' he repeated with a hint of impatience, 'do you expect her back?'

'I've no idea,' Lessie told him, determined not to be drawn into conversation with one of Anna's clients. 'I'm her neighbour, not her mother.'

He blinked, and she had a feeling that his mouth trembled slightly beneath his dark, well-kept moustache. But instead of leaving, he stood for a moment, tapping the head of his cane against the palm of his other hand, then said, 'Who owns this building?'

'The factor's Lindsay and Ross.'

'How much rent do they charge you?'

He was obviously used to having his questions answered without delay, and she found herself beginning, 'Three shilling a w—' before she stopped herself and said instead, haughtily, 'If you're looking for a place to rent I'd advise you to go to the factor's office. They'll give you the details.'

This time he did smile; she caught it in a sidelong glance. Then the smile was gone as he said, 'It's a slum. How can you live in such a place – and bring up a child?' he added as Ian, covered with sticky orange juice, toddled out to grasp Lessie's skirt and stare, finger in mouth.

The man's impudence infuriated Lessie. 'I don't choose tae live here – nobody would choose tae live here. But some folk have no other place tae—'

Footsteps, light and swift, came up from the close below and Anna McCauley, face rosy from being out of doors, skirt swinging round trim ankles, feathered bonnet set at a jaunty angle on her auburn head, arrived on the landing, her eyes bright as they took in the man standing by her door.

'Are you Miss Anna McCauley?'

She beamed at him. 'I am.'

'My name's Warren. Andrew Warren. I'd like to speak to you.'

The colour drained from Anna's face and Lessie swallowed hard. She might have known the incident of the dead man in Anna's bed wasn't over.

'I came to thank you on the family's behalf for taking my uncle in when he fell ill,' Andrew Warren was saying, and Anna bloomed again, taking her key from her bag, opening her door, ushering him in. She winked at Lessie behind his back, then swept after him and shut the door.

Lessie, left alone, bent and picked Ian up, hugging him tight in her relief. Retribution wasn't about to sweep down on them after all. As

25

she put the little boy down and urged him back inside the flat so that she could get on with her washing, she recalled the sudden widening of Andrew Warren's eyes when he looked down and saw Anna, pretty as a picture, emerging from the dark well of the stairs.

'I just did what anyone would have done,' Anna was saying expansively in her flat, sweeping her hat off, motioning Andrew Warren to the only chair. As she slipped off her shawl and hung it on the nail hammered into the door she glanced at him out of the corner of her eye. He was good-looking, this young member of the Warren family. She wondered what it would be like to lie in bed with him.

He was glancing round the room, taking in every stick of furniture, the black damp patches on the walls, the portrait of Queen Victoria. 'D'you live here on your own?'

She sat down on a stool opposite him, moving gracefully for his benefit, arranging her skirt carefully so that her slender ankles peeped from beneath the hem. 'I've no man living here with me, if that's your meaning.'

'It's an ugly building.'

Unlike Lessie, Anna didn't take offence. 'The factor's a bastard – quick to collect the rent but slow to do anything to help us. If you complain you're put out.' Her voice was cheerful, matter-of-fact. 'But at least I've a roof over my head and that's more than some poor souls in this town can say.'

He glanced up at the ceiling, cracked and dirty and sagging, then reached into his pocket. 'I'm sorry we've taken so long to express our gratitude, but my uncle's an old man and his brother's death has been hard on him. I myself only arrived in Greenock a week or two ago. My uncle and I would like to express our gratitude with this.'

Anna's heart leapt as she saw the notes in his hand. It was all she could do to stop herself from snatching them. With an effort she managed to take them as casually as they were offered, thank him in her softest, most feminine voice and hold his gaze with her own for a few seconds before he got to his feet abruptly, picked up his hat and said that he must go.

At the door he shook her hand, thanked her again, then went, with a nod to Lessie, still working at the sink. Anna watched him descend the stairs, thinking of the crisp notes lying on the dresser behind her, but thinking even more of the man who had given them to her.

4

The big house overlooking the Firth of Clyde was far too hot. Andrew Warren, returning home for his midday meal, felt as though he was smothering as soon as he stepped inside the front door.

His wife and his uncle were already at the table and as Andrew entered, Madeleine's dark eyes swept up towards him reproachfully. He bent to kiss the cheek that she offered to him. 'Sorry, my dear, I had to attend to something at the refinery. How are you today, Uncle James?'

'Still out of sorts, my boy,' said the elder Mr Warren feebly, although he was making good work of putting his food away, Andrew noticed. James and Frank had been twins; they had never married and had lived all their lives in quiet harmony in the house their father had built when his sugar refinery began to make his fortune. James had been badly shaken by Frank's death and hadn't set foot in the refinery since, leaving all the business to his nephew.

'You should come to the refinery with me this afternoon,' Andrew suggested, taking his place opposite Madeleine. 'We could do with your advice on a few matters.'

'Perhaps next week.'

'At least go out and walk about, or send for a cab and take a ride along the coastline. You could take Madeleine with you.'

Madeleine's elegant shoulders rippled in a shiver. 'It's far too cold to go out, Andrew.' Her voice was petulant and even her attractive French accent sounded sullen. 'This country of yours is the coldest place I have ever known. We will all die of it, my babies and I.'

'If you insist on staying inside all the time and mollycoddling your-self, you're quite likely to die of boredom if nothing else,' Andrew told her, an edge creeping into his voice. 'You can't expect Scotland to be as warm as Jamaica, my dear. You'll become acclimatised.'

'Never!' Her shoulders rippled again, this time in one of the feminine little shrugs that had so captivated him a few short years ago when they first met and he knew at once that he wanted her to be his wife. Today she wore a soft woollen lilac gown decorated from neck to hem with violet bows. The colours suited her rich dark beauty, but the shade of the bows reminded Andrew of the girl in the slum down in the Vennel, the girl with tumbled red hair and wide, long-lashed violet eyes.

He had been thinking of her a great deal in the six days since he had visited her. Aware that it was unseemly to be thinking of another

27

woman in his wife's presence, he put the girl from his mind and said, 'Have the children been out this morning?'

'I said no. The air is too chilled.'

'My dear, we're into June now, this is our summer. You must tell their nursemaid to take them for a walk this afternoon.' Then, seeing the mutinous set of her mouth – a small neat mouth, quite unlike the generous full curve of Anna McCauley's lips – he added, 'I shall tell her myself when I visit the nursery.'

Madeleine glared, but said nothing. When the meal was finished, she rose and left the dining room, followed by James, who muttered something about forty winks in his room. Left alone, Andrew folded his napkin and replaced it carefully in its heavy silver ring, head bent over the task.

It had been a mistake to bring Madeleine to Scotland. He himself would far rather have stayed in Jamaica's sunshine, but someone had to run the refinery and with Frank dead and James apparently sliding comfortably into self-imposed retirement, Andrew had no choice but to stay in Greenock. He got to his feet, telling himself grimly that Madeleine would get used to it. She would have to get used to it.

He yearned for the early months of their marriage, days filled with pleasurable companionship, warm, flower-scented nights of passion. It had all begun to fade with Madeleine's pregnancy, and the shock of producing not one baby but two had put an end to the carefree joy of their marriage. To Madeleine, motherhood was allied with ageing, a fear that dragged her down, and she made no secret of her determination not to have any more children. At first Andrew had been patient with her, finding outlets for his own needs with other women, but six months after the birth of the twins he had requested, then demanded, his marital rights. Although Madeleine remained indifferent to his argument that she was his wife, the woman he loved and wanted, he nonetheless finally availed himself of her body, and had continued to do so, once a week.

It was a cold, unhappy coupling. Madeleine's indifference, her sullen passive acceptance of him, made him feel like an assailant instead of a lover. But having claimed her he could not retreat, although their unloving physical union had become as distasteful to him as it was to her.

The three-year-old twins, supervised by their nursemaid, were messily spooning lunch into themselves. They greeted him with screams of pleasure, for Andrew liked children and he made a point of seeing his son and daughter several times each day.

They were beautiful children, dark-haired and dark-eyed like their mother. Andrew's hair was also dark, but Martin and Helene both had Madeleine's blue-black tresses. Martin was the heavier, Helene small and dainty.

'Take them out this afternoon,' he told the nurse.

'Mrs Warren—'

'Never mind that, I want them to get some fresh air,' Andrew interrupted, the edge creeping back into his voice.

28

The woman flushed and said flatly, 'Very good, sir.' He knew very well that she disapproved of fathers visiting the nursery, and preferred to take her orders from Madeleine. Who paid her wages? he asked himself angrily as he left the room and went downstairs again. It was time the nurse – and Madeleine – learned that his orders were to be obeyed.

His wife was lying on the chaise longue in the drawing room, her eyes closed. They opened as he bent to kiss her and a brief frown drifted across her lovely face. 'You'll be back in good time for dinner, Andrew?'

'Of course. I've told nurse to take the children out, and please do as I suggest, Madeleine, and drive out yourself.'

'I have a headache.' The diamond ring he had put on her finger when she agreed to marry him flashed at him as she drew white fingers across her forehead.

'It's little wonder. This house is like a furnace.'

'Your children and I must surely be warm!'

'For God's sake, Madeleine, there are some folk not far from here who have to do without a fraction of the heat you need, even in the winter.' He was on the verge of telling her about the cold clammy tenement slum he had visited in his search for the woman who had taken his uncle into her house, the high cheekbones and fragile, hollowed pale face of the girl washing clothes in a big chipped stone sink on the landing, but her sullenness stopped him.

'This is such an ugly country,' she said. 'Cold and ugly.'

He walked to the window and looked out over the river to the hills beyond. The sky above them was eggshell blue, the sun blessing the water and turning it into diamonds. 'On the contrary, my dear, this part of the Clyde must be one of the most beautiful spots in the world. It is man who makes the ugliness with his factories and mills and slums.' Then he added with a smile, crossing to kiss her, 'Though I must admit that in my eyes the Warren refinery has its own beauty.'

She twitched herself round, away from him, and the rug that lay over her slid to the floor. Andrew picked it up and put it back. His hand brushed against the softness of a breast beneath the wool dress as he did so and she twitched again, almost burrowing into the chaise longue. Madeleine had a beautiful body, satin-smooth hills and softly shaded hollows; at one time he had known it as well as his own. Now it was a strange and alien land that he visited regularly, briefly, with no pleasure other than physical satisfaction.

As he left the house, breathing in the cool air with relief, and climbed into the waiting carriage, he thought of another body, one that he didn't know but could guess at, a promising ripeness beneath a shabby blouse and a skirt with an uneven hem. Every movement Anna McCauley had made had spoken to the sensual side of his nature. He wondered, as he had wondered from the moment he first set eyes on her, if Uncle Frank had really collapsed in the street or if he had collapsed in her sordid, cheerless room. He couldn't blame the old man for seeking a bit of pleasure out of life, and there was something about

29

the confident way the girl had taken the proferred money that made Andrew feel that she was used to being given money by men. All the same, the thought of her sent a pleasurable frisson through his muscles and sinews.

The hooter marking the end of the midday break sounded just as he dismounted from the carriage at the Warren sugar refinery in Bank Street. The row of carthorses outside the loading bay jingled their harnesses and tossed their heads, turning to watch the carters straggling out of the warehouse. The horses knew the routine well and could be trusted to pull their carts down to the docks by themselves then back up to the refinery once they were loaded with great sacks of raw sugar from the ships. The carters could afford to walk in a chattering group behind them.

Andrew crossed the cobbled yard and went into the warm, sweet-smelling world of sugar refining. There was plenty of work for him to see to, for his uncles had not kept up with modern trends and he had a great many plans for the refinery. It was one of several in Greenock; many more had gone to the wall in the past decade or so, and Andrew had no intention of letting the same thing happen to the Bank Street refinery.

But halfway through the afternoon the work palled. His mind wasn't on it today. He put down his pen, stared at it for a long moment, then got briskly to his feet and with a curt word to his clerk left the refinery.

Scorning his carriage, he walked down towards the river, turning left along Dalrymple Street then left again into the Vennel. The landing was vacant this time, the sink empty, its greened brass tap dripping steadily. Anna McCauley opened the door to his knock. Her violet eyes, as lovely as he had remembered them, widened at sight of him, then a small knowing smile curved her full mouth and she tilted her head to one side. 'Mr Warren.'

The wanting that had been flickering through Andrew since he first set eyes on her strengthened as he stood looking at her. There was no need to think of an excuse, he realised that now. So he simply said, 'I had to come back.'

'Yes.' She moved aside, opening the door wide, and he stepped past her into the tiny cold room.

Edith waited impatiently until the corner shop emptied of customers and her sister was free.

'I called in at the house but you weren't there,' she said. Lessie controlled an impulse to inform her solemnly that she'd been here, in the shop. Sometimes Edith's humourlessness and bizarre logic could be amusing, at other times it could be infuriating. Lessie often wondered what it would be like to hear a conversation between two Ediths. They would never get to the point.

'I should be finished in a moment, then we can go and have a cup of tea,' she promised.

'I've not got all day,' Edith protested, then tutted with vexation as

30

a ragged barefoot lad pushed past her to claim Lessie's attention. The boy had the face of an angel that had fallen from Heaven straight into a mud puddle.

'Ha'p'nny o' broken biscuits,' he said gruffly, dumping his coin onto the counter, having to reach up to do so.

'A ha'penny of broken biscuits. You're in luck – we just happen to have some,' Lessie told him pleasantly, picking up a scoop and walking round the end of the counter to the shop door. The place was so small that its goods spilled out onto the footpath and a box of broken biscuits sat outside, perched on a sack of barley and covered with a piece of board to protect its contents from dirt and flies. The child watched greedily as she weighed the biscuit fragments then poured them from the scales into a bag. He took it and did a thoughtful circuit of the small shop before leaving, his blue eyes flickering between the goods and Mrs McKay, who was serving another customer.

'Lessie, I said I've not got all—'

Lessie fluttered the fingers of one hand at her sister, her eyes on the child. 'Just a minute, Edith.'

Near a jar of sweets he stopped, shifted the bag of biscuits from one grimy fist to the other, and looked at the shopkeeper, then at Lessie, who gazed back calmly until his eyes dropped before hers. The corners of his mouth turning down, he humped his shoulders and stamped out, clutching his purchase.

Edith had watched the scene with growing confusion. 'What was all that about?'

'He had it in mind to steal some sweeties. You've to keep your eyes on some of them.'

'The wee rascal!'

'Och, it's probably the only way he has of getting them, poor mite. Even so, he'll have to learn that being poor doesnae mean he has the right to be a thief as well. Anyway,' Lessie finished briskly, knowing full well that if she started fretting over every child that longed for the money to buy a sweet her heart would soon be broken, 'he'd already used up his criminal tendencies for one day.'

'Eh?'

'The biscuits he bought were broken half an hour ago when his elder brother and some friends of his just happened to knock the box over as they were running by,' Lessie explained. 'Broken biscuits cost less and they know it. They break them, then they get one of the wee ones to come in and buy them cheap.'

'I've never heard the like!' Edith's mouth hardened into a thin line.

'No? You'd have heard it long before now if you lived in this part of the town.'

'You should send for the police!'

'Their lives are hard enough without that,' Lessie began to say as Mrs McKay finished with her customer and turned to her.

'Thanks for helpin' me out, hen. Off you go now, you look tired out,' said the old woman, her own face paper-white with exhaustion. Lessie felt bad at leaving her on her own, but Ian would soon be clamouring for food and Edith was impatiently tapping her foot at the shop door.

Mr McKay, a woollen scarf wound round his neck over a shabby jacket, was in bed in the inner room, sound asleep and snoring. Beside him Ian, who had been tucked between the old man and the wall for safety, also snored slightly, lying on his back with his mouth drooping open. His eyelids lifted as soon as Lessie touched him and he beamed a welcome and held his arms out to her. His small body, warm from the bed, nestled against hers and she lowered him into his pram reluctantly.

'I'm worried about the McKays,' she said to Edith as they walked the short distance to Lessie's house. 'His heart's getting worse and she's half-killing herself trying to run that shop on her own and look after him. I'm helping out more and more.'

'I hope they pay you for it.'

'Of course they do. But what'll happen if they decide to give it up? I need the money. Besides, it's handy for me and the work's not as hard as scrubbing stairs. And they let me take Ian with me too.'

'Somebody else'll take it over and they'll still need help.'

'It might be a couple with a family. They might have their own help.' But a sidelong glance at her sister's tense face told Lessie that at the moment Edith was uninterested in her problems. 'What was it you came about?'

'I'll tell you when we're behind closed doors,' Edith said primly as she followed Lessie into the narrow close. She seldom ventured into the Vennel, terrified of meeting the thieves and vagabonds she was certain inhabited the place. She preferred to meet Lessie in their mother's house.

'It sounds important.'

'It is.'

Lessie sighed inwardly as she lifted Ian from the pram, hoping that she wasn't in for another burst of complaints about their parents. Edith would not accept the fact that whatever had happened to estrange Archie and Barbara was none of her business, or Lessie's.

'You carry Ian and I'll take the pram,' she said, adding dryly when Edith shied back from the baby, 'He's over the whooping cough now. You'll not catch anything from the wee soul.'

'It's not that.' Edith glanced down at her smart brown jacket and skirt, vulnerable to sticky little fingers and teething dribbles, and said reluctantly, 'I'll see to the perambulator. He'll mebbe cry if I take him.'

Lessie began to mount the stairs, keeping her tongue between her teeth. Edith didn't care for children and lived in constant fear of having her clothing dirtied or crumpled by small clutching hands. Poor little Peter was quite unused to being cuddled and whenever Lessie put her arms about him, even when he had been Ian's age, he stiffened and flinched away just as his mother had done at the thought of carrying Ian. Lessie held her small son closer and decided that Edith wasn't worth fretting over.

They had almost reached the landing, Lessie several steps ahead, Edith struggling with the pram, when a door opened and shut above their heads and light steps began to descend swiftly, almost skimming down.

'It's yourself, Lessie.' Anna McCauley came to a stop and reached out to tickle Ian under the chin. 'Hello, wee man!' She beamed down at Edith, who was getting red in the face because the pram had jammed itself across the stairway and refused to move. 'Here, I'll see to it.'

'I'm quite able to—' Edith began coldly, but the pram was whisked from her hands, deftly disentangled, and handed back. Anna, pretty as a picture in a leaf-green coat with a bunch of darker green satin ribbons at the neck, beamed into Edith's set face.

'There you are. Just hold it straight and you'll be fine,' she said, and was gone.

'I see that . . . woman is still living here.' Edith grimly heaved the pram onto the landing and waited for her sister to open the flat door. 'Does she still have all sorts of men up and down the stairs, visiting her at all hours?'

'I've not seen all sorts of men on the stairs for the past month or more,' Lessie was able to answer truthfully. Andrew Warren could scarcely be described as 'all sorts of men'. Since she had met him, Anna had stopped entertaining anyone else.

'Hmm.' Edith followed her into the small lobby and put the pram into its corner by the wooden coal bunker with a final admonishing shake as though ordering it to stay there and behave itself. 'Don't tell me she's gone and got herself a decent job at last?'

'I've no idea. I've enough to do attending to my own business to worry about hers,' Lessie retorted, putting Ian down and straightening her back with a sigh of relief. He toddled ahead of her into the kitchen, where the kettle simmered on the range. She took her coat off and measured tea from the caddy into the pot, relishing her good fortune in having enough coal to keep the range going. If it hadn't been for Davie's wages she would have had to save what fuel she could afford for the evenings and do without hot food or drink during the day. She was fortunate in so many ways, compared to some of the poor souls who lived in the Vennel.

Edith had settled herself in a fireside chair. 'If she's not entertaining men for money she must have found some sort of work, for that coat cost a pretty penny, even though it's not new.' Edith liked nice clothes, and did her best to ape the gentry when it came to dressing herself and Peter. She and Lessie had been taught by their mother to be good with their needles and they knew all about skilful darning and turning worn garments to make use of the fresh material on the inside.

Lessie said nothing, and her sister waited until the tea was made and poured out before delving into her shopping bag and producing a copy of the *Greenock Telegraph*. 'Have you seen the paper?'

'I can't afford to buy newspapers, Edith. Davie brings one in sometimes.'

'Read that!' Edith thrust the newspaper into her hands, a bony finger tapping a short item near the bottom of one page. Lessie put down her cup, making sure it was well away from Ian's inquisitive fingers, and went to the window to catch what light she could.

Edith waited with pursed lips, and looked scandalised when her sister began to laugh. 'It's not funny.'

'It is! Who else but our Joseph would get into that sort of trouble? Who else would meet a soldier, a complete stranger, in a public house then get so drunk that he agreed when the soldier suggested changing clothes for a lark?'

'You'd think even Joseph would have realised that the soldier was a deserter.' Edith's voice was sour.

'I wish I'd seen him and his cronies waiting in that back room in the pub for the man to come back from his walk, then realising he wasn't going to.' Lessie giggled again, and this time Edith's mouth twitched, then broadened into a smile.

'Then going into the street to look for the man and meeting a policeman instead. I can't imagine our Joseph in uniform – except a prison uniform,' Edith finished, grim again, the amusement stifled almost at birth. 'Seven shillings and sixpence he was fined for receiving the uniform. Seven shillings and sixpence – a good week's wages to most. And him never in work! Where's he going to find that sort of money?'

'He'll get it from somewhere. He's been fined before.' Lessie sobered up and went back to the newspaper. 'I see that the deserter was caught, so at least Joseph'll have got his own clothes back. That poor soul, waiting in prison for men from the War Office to take him back to his regiment in disgrace. I wonder what they'll do to him, and what made his life so bad that he had to run away. P'raps his regiment was going to be sent to South Africa to fight the Boers.'

'You're too soft, Lessie. We all have to face up to the life we choose, even when we didnae choose it o' our own free will. And a soldier has to go where he's sent. Mrs Warren attended a ladies' tea party last week for the soldiers.'

'Oh? Were there many soldiers there?'

'Sometimes, Lessie Hamilton, I don't know whether you're making fun of me or just plain daft! It wasnae for the soldiers themselves and well you know it. The ladies were all stitching clothes to send to South Africa for the men. Mrs Warren came home exhausted.' Edith's mouth suddenly tightened again. 'I saw Mother staggering in the street yesterday.'

'You did not!' Lessie was scandalised on her mother's behalf. Barbara was and always had been a proud woman who had dinned her belief in self-respect into her children – not that Joseph had paid any notice. 'She'd never go out while she was . . . like that!'

'She did so stagger – a wee bit, anyway. I was appalled.'

'What was her speech like when you spoke to her?'

'Spoke to her?' Edith was outraged. 'I crossed the street and managed to get into a shop before she saw me. D'ye think I'd stand talking in the street to her after everyone had seen her near falling against a lamppost?'

'Och, the pavements in this town are a disgrace. She'll have tripped over a paving stone. I've done it often enough myself – and so have you, no doubt.'

Edith took evasive action. 'Why does she have to drink like that?'

'I don't know any more than you do.'

'It started about the time Thomasina was born. It's something to do with her, I'll be bound.'

'Mebbe so, but that's her business, not ours.'

'I don't think she tripped over a paving stone.'

'P'raps she's not well. Did you not think of that instead of running away from your own mother in the street, and her mebbe ill and in need of help and a bit of kindness?'

Edith flushed, and smoothed her skirt. 'She wasn't unwell, I know what I saw. D'you like my new coat?'

Lessie gave in and let the subject be changed. 'It's bonny.'

'Mrs Warren gave it to me. Her maid had the colic so I was sent for to help her to dress. She's got a lovely way of talking, Lessie. It comes from being French. Parisienne,' said Edith reverently. 'And you should see the furnishing in her bedchamber!' She cast a glance round the shabby room. 'The bed alone's near enough as large as this room.'

'It sounds large enough to hold the whole household, servants and all, instead of just two folk.' Lessie was getting tired of hearing about Mrs Andrew Warren.

'It's only for her. Mr Andrew has his own room.'

'They don't sleep in the same bed?'

'The gentry don't need to sleep in the same bed. They've got big houses.'

'Even so . . .' Lessie began, then let her voice die away. She reached for the teapot and refilled Edith's cup, thinking of Andrew Warren, now a regular visitor to the shabby building. The other men who had visited Anna McCauley had arrived and left furtively, heads down, caps or bowlers pulled down over their eyes. They would press themselves against the walls if they happened to encounter Lessie or any other resident, and meeting them always made her feel dirty and ashamed, almost as though it were she, not Anna, who plied a trade in flesh. But Andrew Warren walked into the close and up the stairs with his head high and his shoulders back. If he happened to meet Lessie, he greeted her calmly and civilly, and once he had helped her with Ian's pram. There was an air of strength and confidence about him, a masculinity that spoke of a virile man, surely not the sort to sleep apart from his wife. Did she know about his visits to the Vennel, or did his very openness save him from gossiping tongues?

'Does Mrs Warren keep well?'

'She has a lot of headaches,' said Edith. 'And she feels the cold a great deal after living in Jamaica. She told me herself that she wants to go back there.'

'Mebbe they will.'

'With Mr James turning himself into an invalid and refusing to go

35

to the refinery? Mr Andrew's got to stay here, unless he sells the refinery or gets a manager. Oh, Lessie, you should have seen the gown she wore the other night when they had guests! A crimson bodice and a rose-coloured skirt with a great long train. And golden-coloured lace round the shoulders and the skirt. Silk, the material was. I helped to dress her, and touching it was like dipping your hand into a burn in the summer, all cool and soft . . .'

Lessie let her sister's voice fade into the background. Once Edith started talking about her work and the Warrens, she could babble on happily without need of comment or interruption. Lessie wasn't interested in listening to a long description of fine gowns that she herself could never hope to own. She was far more intrigued by the puzzle of why a good-looking man like Andrew Warren didn't share his wife's bed. True, her own parents hadn't slept together for many years, not since Thomasina's birth, but Edith and Lessie, when they discussed the matter, thought that that might be because they had as many children as they could look after and wanted no more. Though it didn't explain their mother's coldness towards her husband.

But surely the fear of having more bairns than they could feed and clothe wasn't the reason why the Warrens chose to sleep apart? If her Donald had lived, she thought with sudden longing, lifting the teacup to her lips, she would never, ever, have slept alone again, no matter how many rooms they might have had.

5

The pounding on the door made Lessie jump and catch the tip of a finger in the bedspring she was carefully cleaning with paraffin and hot water. Irritated, she put down the cloth she had been using and went into the little hall, sucking at the stinging finger as she went and grimacing at the taste of paraffin from it. Anna McCauley leaned against the door frame, a coat clutched about her body, her hair bundled on top of her head, her face, on this pleasant late summer day, almost beet-red.

A hot, damp hand clutched at Lessie's arm and Anna said, her voice slurring, 'Lessie, ye'll have tae help me!'

It was so reminiscent of the scene several months earlier on the day when Frank Warren died in Anna's bed that Lessie's heart sank.

'Dear God, what have you done now?'

'Are ye alone?' Anna leaned forward to hiss the words and Lessie was surrounded by gin fumes. They clashed with the smell of paraffin and she felt her stomach churn.

'Ian's at my mother's. I'm cleaning the bedsprings to keep the bugs away and I couldna let him near the par—' The words were cut short as Anna pulled her out of her own doorway and started across the landing, her hand still clamped over Lessie's arm.

'What d'you think you're doing?'

'I need yer help.'

Lessie jerked herself free. 'Anna McCauley, if you've got yourself into more trouble, you can find someone else tae get you out of it this time. Away tae your bed and sleep the drink off!'

She turned towards her own open door but Anna, despite her drunkenness, managed to eel round her and get between her and the door. 'Lessie!' Two large tears rose in her lovely eyes and spilled over, followed by two more. 'Lessie, please! I have tae dae it, an' I cannae manage on my own.'

Lessie hesitated, biting her lip. Then she nodded, cursing herself for a fool as she did so. 'Let me shut my own door first, then I'll come across.'

Anna waited instead of going ahead and together they went into her flat. It was the first time Lessie had been in it since Frank Warren's death, and she saw at a glance that it was cleaner than before and more comfortably furnished. Thanks to Andrew Warren, no doubt. But the room was stiflingly hot and stank of gin. A half-empty bottle and a glass stood on the table, and the centre of the room was dominated by a battered tin bath half filled with water. Steam rose lazily from a large kettle on the hob, and two buckets of water stood against one wall.

Anna slipped her coat off. As before, on the day of Frank Warren's death, she was naked beneath it, but this time her soft, slender body was pink and damp. 'Lessie, I'm carryin' a bairn.'

'Andrew Warren's bairn?'

'There's been nobody else these past three months.'

'You've not just found out, surely?' Lessie noticed now that the girl's breasts were full and heavy, her belly beginning to take on a soft curve.

Anna hiccuped and poured a generous measure of gin into the glass. She swallowed, almost gagged, and made a face. 'God, it's terrible stuff! D'ye want some?'

'I do not.' Lessie waved away the proferred bottle and asked, 'How far on are you?'

'Three months. It must've been the first time we were together, or near enough then.' The tears came anew and dripped into the gin. 'If he finds out he'll leave me and I c-couldnae bear it!' Anna hiccuped again, then said, her drunken voice earnest, 'I love him, Lessie. I've tried everything but nothin'll shift it.'

Clumsily, so clumsily that Lessie feared for a minute that the tub would tip over and flood the place, Anna clambered into the water, balancing the glass in one hand. She eased herself down, drawing her breath in sharply as the hot water touched her tender skin, forced to sit in the small space with her knees pressed tightly against her breasts.

'I cannae keep climbin' out tae get more hot water,' she said tearfully, her voice slurring over the words. 'An' if I try tae lean ower tae get the kettle, the damned tub threatens tae tilt an' coup me out. I need ye tae pour more water in for me.'

'I'll not help anyone to get rid of a bairn,' Lessie said firmly.

'It's this or goin' tae the old wifie round the corner,' Anna told her grimly, and took another gulp of gin.

Lessie felt sick. She had heard terrible tales of the old wifie and her methods. Many a desperate young girl or a woman with more than enough children already had lost their lives after visiting the abortionist. 'You'd not do that. You'd not let her—'

'I would.' Anna's voice was suddenly clear and fierce, her gaze level. 'I'd do anythin' tae get rid o' it an' keep Andrew.'

'You'll be found out and sent tae the jail – if you're not already dead by that time.'

Anna splashed a petulant fist into the water, sending a small fountain over the edge onto the linoleum. 'I've got tae get rid of it!'

'Surely you of all folk knew how to prevent this?' Lessie snapped as she wrapped her apron round her hand, seized the kettle, and advanced on the tub. Anna's mind was clearly made up, and anything was better than letting her submit to an abortionist.

'I've always managed before. But that man's no' like other men. No won'er his wife had two instead o' just the one—' Anna broke off

38

with another sharp intake of breath as boiling water trickled into the tub. Steam rose into the air and perspiration ran freely down her face to drip into the water.

'I'll add some cold.'

'You'll not! It's to be as hot as I can bear it.'

'You can't bear it,' Lessie protested.

'I must.' The words were forced out through gritted teeth. 'It's the only way. Here.' She emptied the glass and held it out. 'Fill that up again.'

Lessie took it, filled it, handed it back, and at Anna's insistence trickled more boiling water into the tub. After a few more applications her own skin burned and stung in sympathy, and still Anna stayed where she was, refusing to give up. The level in the bottle dropped steadily and Lessie filled it willingly now, realising that the more Anna drank, the closer she came to lapsing into a stupor. The room was stiflingly hot and they were both perspiring freely. Filling the glass yet again, pouring more water into the tub and watching Anna's face contort as she forced herself to stay where she was, Lessie wondered if this was what Hell was like. If not, the Devil was missing out on a good form of eternal torture.

The ordeal finally ended in a flurry of water when Anna suddenly announced thickly, 'Gaun be—' and erupted from the tub, drenching Lessie with hot water. Anna reached the basin by the window just in time, and as she vomited into it, Lessie hurried to hold her head. The girl's body was lobster-red and almost too hot to touch. As the draught from the ill-fitting window got to her, she began to shiver. Weak as a kitten, she made no more than a token protest as Lessie dried her with a rough cloth and eased her towards the bed.

'Enough,' she said, collapsing onto the mattress. 'We mus've got rid o' the wee bugger by this time.'

Lessie covered her with the blanket and smoothed sweat-soaked hair back from her own forehead. 'Enough,' she agreed thankfully.

Anna mumbled something and was instantly asleep. Lessie went through the laborious process of emptying the tub with a bucket, carrying the water out to the sink on the landing. Then she emptied and cleaned the bowl and after a final glance at Anna hurried back to her own flat.

It was time to fetch Ian home and prepare the evening meal. She lugged Davie's bed, only half disinfected, back into place and dragged the thin mattress onto it. Then she tidied herself and hurried out of the building, wishing as she went that she had never set eyes on Anna McCauley. The woman was nothing but trouble. But Lessie still owed her money, and although Anna herself cared not a jot, to Lessie it was an obligation that bonded the two of them together in uneasy companionship.

As soon as Davie had clattered off to work on the following morning, Lessie fed Ian then settled him down on the rag rug while she filled a bucket with warm water and washed herself from head to toe. She didn't have the luxury of an old tin tub like Anna McCauley's; she and Davie had to make do with the bucket, Davie washing himself thoroughly in the evenings when Lessie was out scrubbing stairs or helping in the corner shop.

When she had dressed herself again she pulled a basin out from under the bed and plunged the contents, strips of cloth that had been left to soak in cold water, into the bucket, rubbing and scrubbing hard in an effort to remove every trace of blood.

What, she wondered as she worked on her knees by the bucket, did rich folk like Mrs Andrew Warren do when they had their monthly bleeding? She couldn't see wealthy women washing their own soiled cloths. Surely they didn't expect their servants to see to the business for them? Squeezing the cloths out, draping them over the range to dry quickly so that they would be out of sight before Davie got back, she decided that they probably just burned them and tore up fresh cloths when they were needed. Wealthy folk were fortunate.

Quiet though she was when she went onto the landing to empty the bucket, she wasn't quiet enough. Anna's door opened so suddenly that Lessie gave a guilty start and water splashed from the bucket onto her foot.

Anna looked ill. Her pretty face was small and waxy, her eyes heavily shadowed. Her hair was still tied up as it had been the day before, long matted red tendrils hanging to her shoulders.

'It's not come,' she said, and the tears welled up again. 'Oh Lessie, what am I to do?'

'Tell the man. It's his responsibility as well as yours.'

Anna blinked, sniffed, scrubbed the back of one hand across her face, and said without emotion, 'God, Lessie Hamilton, you're either daft or you're simple. Men don't have to take responsibilities, they only take their pleasure.'

Lessie tipped the bucket over the sink and saw Anna's envious gaze fixed on the telltale pink tinge of the water sluicing away down the drain.

'Surely he'd not want you to risk your life going to the old wifie.' At the thought, Lessie felt fear grip at the pit of her stomach, right where Ian had nestled trustingly for the nine months before his birth. 'You'll not do anything as daft as that?'

There was a flash of desperation in Anna's eyes, a tremor of sheer terror in her voice. 'What else can I do?'

'Give it a wee while longer. Mebbe the gin and the hot water'll work yet. Give it until tomorrow.' Put off your bairn's death, and as like as not your own death, a little longer, Lessie beseeched silently.

Perhaps it was that unspoken plea that made Anna say as she stepped back and began to close her door, 'Aye, mebbe you're right. Mebbe it'll work yet. But I'll only wait until tomorrow,' she added through the final crack in the door. Then it closed and Lessie was left standing on the landing, the empty bucket in her hand, the last trickle of bloodied water circling noisily into the drain.

She fretted about Anna McCauley all day as she scrubbed stairs then took tea with Miss Peden. She would have liked to ask the old woman's advice, but Miss Peden had never been married and it wouldn't be seemly to talk to her of childbirth, let alone abortion and prostitution. So Lessie carried her burden about with her, finding it much heavier than Ian, recalling over and over again the fear in Anna's eyes when she spoke of the old wifie with her filthy hands and her unspeakable practices.

In the Warren garden the roses were a riot of colour, the grass green and lush, the air rich with the smell of summer and the sound of bees humming round the flower beds. And yet a few miles away in the Vennel it was hard to know what season it was, Andrew Warren thought as he picked his way between the grimy house walls and the gutter with its rich harvest of rotting matter.

The sun had very little chance of finding its way between the buildings and into the dank, narrow street. The people were as pale and undernourished as always, though at this time of year they shivered less. And yet – his thoughts became uncharacteristically lyrical as he neared his goal – this rancid garden had its own blossom, a girl with red hair and violet eyes who, for the moment at least, held him captive. They hadn't arranged a meeting for that day but Andrew had suddenly felt the need to touch Anna, hold her, hear her voice. He hoped that she would be at home.

His step quickened as he turned in at the mouth of the close, almost colliding with Anna's pale, fair-haired little neighbour on her way out, her baby fastened against her body by means of a shawl knotted about them both. His hands went out to steady her and felt her thinness and fragility.

'Forgive me.' He set her safely on her feet, smiled, and went past her into the close, his mind filled with Anna. He was almost at the foot of the stairs when he heard the girl calling after him.

'Mr Warren?'

He swung round, impatient at the delay. 'Yes, what is it?'

She had stepped back into the close, her thin face ghostly in the dim light. 'Mr Warren, I must tell you something.'

He could tell by the quiver in her voice, the way her arms tightened about the child sleeping against her shoulder, that she was nervous. He pushed his impatience aside and said mildly, 'By all means. If there's anything I can do for you—'

'No' for me, for Anna. I'm feared for her.'

'Is she ill?'

'Not ill, but I'm feared that—' She stopped, took in a deep breath, then said swiftly, 'Mr Warren, I'd not talk of other folk's private business tae anyone, so you've no need tae fret about that. But Anna's goin' tae be hurt if she . . . She's carryin' your bairn, Mr Warren.'

For a moment Andrew could only gape at the girl. She moved a step back, as though unsure of his reaction, ready to run if he lifted a hand to her.

'What?' It was a stupid thing to say but it was all he could think of.

41

'She's carryin' your bairn,' she repeated patiently. 'She says it's yours and I believe her. And she's done everything she can think of tae put an end tae it. But nothing's worked and now she's talking about visiting an old woman who sees tae things like that, only most women who visit her die as well as their bairns an' I'm feared for—'

'Why didn't she tell me?' His voice was loud in the enclosed space and she took a second step back.

'She was frightened.'

'Of me?'

'You've already got bairns of your own. You'll not want this one, Anna says.' Then, her task completed, she fell silent, staring up at him.

'Thank you, Mrs – er-'

'Mrs Lessie Hamilton,' the girl said clearly, taking time over each word, proud of the title. Andrew was suddenly touched by her pride, her dignity.

'Thank you, Mrs Hamilton, for confiding in me. You've no need to worry about Anna. She's my responsibility.'

Lessie Hamilton smiled and her thin, solemn little face was suddenly transformed. 'I thought you'd say that,' she said with satisfaction, then dipped her head in brief acknowledgement and hurried on her way, the child's head bobbing on her shoulder, his body relaxed and boneless in sleep.

Andrew took the stairs three at a time, his feet sure now on the hollowed stone treads. He knocked on the door, waited for a while, then knocked again, insistently, certain that someone was inside. When the door finally opened Anna stared up at him, her hands going at once to her hair, which was loose about her shoulders like a fiery veil.

'Andrew. I didnae think tae see ye today.' She stepped back in confusion as he moved forward into the flat.

'I had a sudden notion to call on you.'

They were in the kitchen now. The place was untidy, clothes strewn about and some dirty crockery lying on the table. Anna turned to face him, her hands still fidgeting with her hair until he took them and imprisoned them in his. She wore a plain blouse and skirt and now that he could see her more clearly he noted the shadowed eyes, the trembling mouth with a bruised, hurt look to it that wrenched at his heart.

'Why didn't you tell me about the child, Anna?' he asked gently.

Her eyes widened, then fell before his gaze, but not before he had seen the apprehension in them. 'How do you know about that?'

'You should have told me.'

'I was feared,' Anna whispered. He had never seen her like this before, stripped of the bravado and the confidence that normally radiated from her. She seemed much younger now, helpless, vulnerable. Madeleine had never moved him as much as Anna did at that moment.

He drew her into his arms, held her close, and said into her hair, 'There's no need to be frightened ever again. And there'll be no more talk of killing my child, d'you hear me? I'll take you out of this place,

42

Anna. I'll find you a decent house where our baby can be born and raised. I'll look after you both. I promise you that.'

6

Beyond the tumble of decks and masts and funnels the river was a broad grey sullen ribbon beneath a grey sky. The bitterly cold January wind ruffled the water surface into flecks of white spume and reddened Davie Kirkwood's nose as he waited at the dock gates with a crowd of other men.

He was cold despite his warm jacket; others in the group, less warmly dressed, were blue and shivering, trying to find shelter in the press of bodies while at the same time remain near the front so that the foremen would see them when they came to pick out the gangs to unload that morning's ships.

'Here, Johnny, take my scarf.' Davie's hands went to his throat and started unknotting the scarf that Lessie had knitted as a Christmas gift but the man beside him shook his head.

'You keep it. I'll get warm enough when I'm working – God willing,' he added, and stamped his feet on the ground. Davie studied him with growing concern. Johnny Lachlan and he had been playmates in the same street for the first ten years of their lives, but Johnny's parents had long since died and his two sisters married and moved far from Greenock. Johnny now lived in a lodging house for men and until recently he had been employed in a small engineering factory as an unskilled worker, sweeping floors and running errands.

He and Davie hadn't seen each other for two years, and as a fresh blast of wind scoured the group by the dock gates, Davie, doing his best to edge between Johnny and the cutting edge of the wind, saw only too clearly how puny and undernourished the man was. He was unfit for the work he so desperately sought.

'Johnny, is there nothing else for you to do?'

His old friend's mouth twisted into a wry smile. 'D'ye think I've no' tried tae find somethin' else? Man, I've begged at every shop an' factory in the toon wi'oot ony luck. Naeb'dy wants an unskilled man. I wish I'd had the brains you have, then mebbe I'd've been able tae go in for the engineerin' tae.' The smile widened; it was genuine, though his eyes were watering with cold. 'Ye'll dae well as an engineer yince ye've got yer papers, Davie. Though mind ye, they've got their troubles tae. Old Mr Beattie that I worked for's findin' it hard tae make ends meet these days. That's why he had tae let me go. An' he cannae afford tae pay skilled men for the factory. I doot he'll hae tae close down soon.'

He stopped and clutched at Davie's arm. 'Here's yin o' them comin'.

Wish me luck, man. I need this work awful bad. It's no' the right time o' year tae be stuck for the money tae buy a bed in the lodgin' hoose.'

The muttered conversations around them died away as the men pressed against the gates, each jostling to be in the forefront. With a sinking heart Davie saw that the man striding along the dock in their direction was his father. He knew well enough that Archie, who didn't have an ounce of compassion in his entire body, only wanted able-bodied men. Johnny didn't stand a chance.

Even so, Davie pushed the other man firmly forward until he was against the gates, then tried to ease back himself. It angered and humiliated him to be picked out of the crowd each day by the man everyone knew to be his father. But Archie ignored him when he tried to insist that he be left to take his chances with one of the other foremen. 'Ye're a good worker an' I'll pick out who I please,' he growled each time. Now he walked up and down the cobbles before the gate, taking his time, eyeing the hopeful men who waited for his verdict. In his youth Archie had gone through this humiliation himself day after day and now it was his turn to be top dog. He saw nothing wrong with his attitude – some of the men eyeing him hopefully at that moment would, one day, be in his place and good luck to them.

'I'll hae you, an' you, an' you.' His thick forefinger stabbed at one man after another, moving relentlessly along until, inevitably, it pointed at Davie. 'An' you,' he said without a flicker of recognition, then moved on. 'An' you.'

When he had finished he nodded to the gateman to open the small side gate for the chosen gang. Johnny had not been one of them and Davie, shouldering his way through the crush, trying not to listen to the muttered comments from men who had, once again, watched the foreman's son being singled out while they themselves had been passed over, saw his former friend's head droop, his hands clutch at the bars of the gate before him in despair.

'Come on, man, don't stand there dreamin' when there's work tae be done.' On an impulse Davie caught at Johnny's arm and tugged him through the small gate by his side.

'But I wasnae picked!'

'You were so, I saw him lookin' at ye. Come on,' said Davie relentlessly, and then the two of them were standing on the dock and Archie, suddenly realising that he had one man too many, was swinging round on them, his mouth opening and his hand lifting to indicate Johnny's way back through the gate.

'Ye'll take him as well or ye'll do without me.' The other men picked for the gang were already hurrying towards the sugar ship where they were to work.

'I'll take the men I picked!'

'Ye picked him. I'm no' so sure about me. Mebbe I should go back outside an' wait for the next foreman,' Davie insisted, keeping Johnny by him with a grip on the sleeve of his thin jacket.

Archie's hand fell back to his side. His mouth closed, then tightened. Davie stared back at him, and saw his father waver. He knew that the older man was thinking of Lessie and Ian and their need for Davie's wages. Davie was thinking of them too, hoping that if his bluff was called and he had to go home empty-handed, Lessie would understand. Surely she would understand.

'Come on then, we've not got all day,' Archie said gruffly, swinging away from them, and Davie was free to breathe again. For once he had bested his father.

'Thanks, Davie,' Johnny muttered as they hurried to join the rest of the gang. On the dock by the sugar ship, a row of carts waited. They would take the first batch of unloaded bags to the Warren refinery and the rest of the load would go into the dock warehouses.

'Thanks for what? It was him that picked you, no' me. Stay close tae me, Johnny, I've worked the sugar ships many a time and I know what's tae be done.'

An hour later Johnny had tossed his jacket into a corner and sweat was streaming down his face. To Davie's dismay he was still clumsy in his handling of the large hooks every docker used, one in each hand. He stumbled and slipped over the jute bags that filled the hold, finding it hard to keep a footing on their uneven surface. He had gashed one of them with a hook as he helped to lift it and it had swung up out of the hold leaking brown Demerara sugar as it went. Archie's watchful eyes and his barked reprimands every time one of the men did something wrong were making Johnny nervous; he worked with one eye on the foreman instead of concentrating on what he was doing.

Skilfully, Davie seized another bag and lifted it about a foot off the ground, tensing his back, managing to balance its three hundredweight. 'The rope!' He grated the words at Johnny, who hurried to flip the rope sling under the bag. He fumbled the first time and Davie's back muscles gave a protesting twinge. Then the sling was in place and the dragging weight on Davie was eased. Between them, with Davie doing the lion's share of the work, they packed a dozen bags onto the sling.

The ship's derrick lowered a massive hook down and Davie stepped lightly onto the packed bags, balancing while he guided the hook into the sling. Then he sprang clear and signalled to the hatchman to start swinging the load up.

'You two – outside,' Archie ordered as the bags cleared the hold. 'Start loadin' the warehouse.'

Davie swore under his breath. The bags were taken to the warehouse manually and he doubted whether Johnny could manage. But there was nothing else for it. They handed their hooks over to another gang and clambered up the ladders, first to the deck, then to the quay, for the tide was low and the ship was now several feet beneath the quayside where a few horses and carts still waited. Davie reached down when he was on the harbour to give Johnny a hand; he scarcely had the energy left to haul himself up the final rungs. Archie watched with sour disapproval, but said nothing.

The cold wind chilled the sweat on their faces at once. Johnny huddled his jacket on and eyed the pile of heavy sacks doubtfully. Then

47

he gritted his teeth and said, 'Gie us a haun', will ye?'

'Take your time now, laddie. I'll balance the bag till you've got the feel of it.' Davie eased a heavy sack onto Johnny's back, steadied him, and watched the smaller, slighter man make his way slowly towards the warehouse, almost doubled under the weight of the bag, his knees buckling. Davie walked over to his father. 'He was doin' fine in the hold. You should've left him there.'

The dockside was noisy with voices and horses' hooves and the clatter of iron-bound cart wheels on cobbles, but a lifetime of experience made Davie shape his words well so that Archie could read his lips.

'It's you that should've left him at the gates. The man's nae use.'

'He's half starved! How can he build up any strength the way he's had tae live?'

'If he's workin' on my gang he'll dae his fair share,' Archie said implacably. 'An' so will you. Get on wi' your work or ye'll be turned away – an' I mean it!'

Seething with anger, Davie strode to the bags and swung one onto his back without waiting for help. He caught the twisted corners, steadied the load, and straightened to stare into his father's cold eyes. Then he turned and went towards the warehouse, passing Johnny on his way back for another bag. Johnny was moving slowly, working his shoulders to ease the pain in them. Catching Davie's anxious glance, he twisted his face into a grin, winked, and swung into an attempt at a jaunty walk.

Men waited inside the huge dim warehouse to take the sugar bag and heave it into its place. Davie hurried out with the intention of working twice as fast as usual so that he could ease Johnny's toil, and saw that the man helping Johnny to hoist a second bag onto his back had done it too quickly so that he was staggering. One or two of the dockers watched, grinning, as the little man reeled this way and that, trying desperately to master the crushing weight that threatened to topple from his back. It was a favourite prank on the docks, where men had to work hard and were only too aware of the dangers they faced every day, the ruptures and damaged joints, the burns from cargoes of salts and lime. But this time the joke was clearly going awry, for in his attempts to stay upright and hold onto the bag, Johnny was staggering back towards the edge of the harbour, his heel catching against a rusted iron ring protruding from the cobblestones.

As Davie sped towards him, his studded boots striking blue light from the cobblestones, he could see the momentum of the heavy sack Johnny carried pulling him back, back, and over the edge of the dock just as Davie's hand reached for him.

There was a double thud from below and a yell of alarm from the open hold.

'Johnny!' Davie threw himself down the ladder onto the deck, then past the burst sugar bag, its contents crunching beneath his feet, and down the second ladder into the hold where a group of men crouched over his friend.

'He caught his head on the edge of the hold as he came down, poor bugger,' someone said, turning a white face up towards the hatch above, ringed with staring men.

Davie took one look and knew the worst. Nobody could sprawl like a discarded cloth doll, head lolling at such a sickening, impossible angle over one shoulder, and still be alive. Davie didn't need to feel for a pulse or a heartbeat. Turning his back on the scene, he scrambled up the ladder again to where Archie had just arrived on the deck.

'He's dead. His neck's broken.'

A muscle jumped in Archie's cheek then he said over his shoulder to the staring men grouped round the open hold, some of them with hats hurriedly snatched off and clutched in their hands, 'Have him taken tae the warehouse an' fetch a doctor.'

'Is that all you've got to say?'

'Accidents happen all the time on the docks, you know that yourself. An' we've still got a ship tae unload.'

His jaw clenched, Davie took a step forward. His father shifted slightly so that his weight was poised properly and waited, his big hands by his sides, ready to curl into fists if need be. Someone touched Davie's arm; someone else said, 'For God's sake, man, he's yer faither!'

Davie hesitated, then hawked deep in his throat and spat, sending a great glob of phlegm onto the deck an inch from the toe of one of his father's boots. As he pulled away from the restraining hand on his sleeve and began to climb the ladder to the quay, he heard Archie's harsh voice. 'Where the hell d'ye think ye're going?'

'Out of here!'

'Ye've no' done yer job yet! Ye'll no' get a penny if ye walk out.'

Davie ignored the voice, almost running from the dock in his need to get as far away as he could from Archie and from poor broken Johnny, shouldering his way through the group of men still waiting for work by the gates, paying no heed to their questions and the voices that called from behind him. All that Johnny's death meant to them was the chance for one of them to take his place.

Davie went to the tenement in the Vennel, needing to talk to Lessie, to be soothed by her calm presence. But Lessie wasn't there; the flat, as clean as she could make it, was empty. So he went back out into the streets and walked, hands fisted in his pockets, eyes on the road, stalking through Greenock and along the coast road and into the neighbouring town of Port Glasgow without noticing where he was. All he could think of was Johnny – Johnny with his pinched blue face, yearning for enough work to pay for a bed for that night. Johnny alive, determined to cope with a task that was beyond his undernourished strength. Then Johnny crumpled in the hold of a ship, being winched up on a plank of wood, removed hurriedly so that the unloading could continue.

Tears suddenly filled his eyes and he blinked them away, scrubbing his hand over his face and swinging round the nearest corner in case anyone had noticed. Someone who had just stepped from a shop a few feet before him said, 'And what brings you to Port Glasgow, Davie Kirkwood?' and he looked up, dazed and confused, at the lovely

49

woman confronting him, stylish and snug in a dark green jacket and skirt edged with pale brown fur. Red curls could just be glimpsed beneath the brim of a veiled hat decorated with a large bow striped in two shades of green.

'Anna? Is it you?'

She laughed, the clear happy laugh he remembered so well. 'Of course it's me. Oh Davie, it's good to see you!' Then she looked at him more closely. 'What's amiss?'

'Nothin'.'

She had the sense not to ask any more questions. Instead she removed one hand from the huge fur muff she carried and laid it on his arm. 'Davie, come and have tea and see my new wee house. Please,' she insisted as he began to shake his head. 'I'm pining away from boredom and loneliness today, and it's too cold tae stay out of doors. Please, Davie?'

Her violet-blue eyes beseeched him through the veiling that misted her features and made them even more beguiling. Davie hesitated, realised that there was nowhere else for him to go, and nodded. Anna beamed at him and slipped her hand into the crook of his elbow. 'It's not far, we can walk there.'

One or two passersby gave them an inquisitive stare as they went along the street, the tall young man shabby in docker's garb, the woman dressed in fine clothes. But Davie was too sunk in his own misery to wonder what they looked like together, and Anna chattered on about this and that without seeming to expect or need any response from him.

They left the busy street and came to a row of small, neat houses, each with its own little front garden, overlooking the river. Anna opened a gate and said, 'Here we are. I told you that it wasn't far.'

Davie followed her up the flagged path and waited while she rapped on the door knocker. The door opened and she drew him with her into a small square hall where wood and brass shone and the air was fragrant with beeswax. Carpeted stairs led up to the floor above.

'Molly, this is my friend Mr Kirkwood, Mrs Hamilton's brother. We'll have some tea, if you please.' Anna's voice was friendly but firm. She sounded as though she had been used to having a servant all her life.

The elderly woman who had opened the door nodded, looked at Davie without curiosity, and disappeared through a door at the back of the hall. Anna opened another door. 'This is my parlour. Sit down, Davie, while I go and take my hat off.'

The room was comfortable, warmed by a good fire in the hearth. Paintings hung on the blue and white striped walls and ornaments and plants were scattered lavishly throughout the room. The table was covered with a blue chenille cloth and blue velvet curtains at the windows framed the view of the Clyde. At either side of the fireplace stood a solid comfortable chair, and a sofa heaped with cushions was against one wall. A clock ticked softly above it. It was a welcoming room.

Davie hesitated, eyeing the sofa, then opted for one of the chairs, only realising when he sank into its comfortable depths how tired he was. He leaned his head back, closed his eyes, and was almost asleep when Anna came in, followed by the maidservant with a large tray.

'I should have asked, Davie, if you were hungry. We've toast and muffins and cake, but there's beef and bread in the kitchen if you want it.'

He had instinctively jumped to his feet when the women entered. 'No, this'll be fine.'

'Sit down,' Anna commanded as the door closed behind the servant. He did as he was told, watching her as she busied herself with the tray. She had taken her jacket off to reveal a full-sleeved blouse of some warm fawn material with a pleated bodice and green velvet ribbon about the throat and wrists. The skilfully cut blouse and skirt and a shawl casually draped about her shoulders all but hid her pregnancy. Apart from some curls round her forehead, her hair had been drawn back loosely into a chignon at the back of her head, exposing her ears and the pearl drops that swung from the lobes.

'Here you are.' She brought him a cup, and as he took it he became aware of her perfume – roses, as always, but a more subtle fragrance than before. Andrew Warren could afford to buy expensive scent for his woman, Davie thought.

'What are you staring at me like that for?' Anna wanted to know as she offered toast.

'You look – different.'

She laughed, lowering herself carefully into the chair opposite his. 'I'm fatter and heavier. Not as able tae skip up and down stairs as I used tae.' She paused, then said carefully, 'Used to.'

'I didnae mean that. I mean . . .' he floundered, then said, 'You look just right in this place.'

Her smile lit up her face. 'What a lovely thing to say, Davie. So you think I make a fine lady, do you?'

'I always did. Are ye happy?'

'I'm very happy,' said Anna at once, and he knew a twinge of jealousy for the man who had the power and the money to give her such pleasure. He wondered how often they sat like this together, Anna and Andrew Warren, facing each other in comfortable intimacy across the fireplace. 'Lessie's been here more than once. Did she not tell you about my wee house?'

'Oh yes.' He knew that Lessie saw Anna only when summoned. Davie wasn't sure whether his sister's continued reluctance to acknowledge Anna McCauley as a friend stemmed from her disapproval of Anna's circumstances, or from envy. Who wouldn't envy Anna this house? Davie imagined Lessie and Ian living here and wished that he could do as much for them as Andrew Warren had done for Anna.

'I hear that there's a man living in my old flat now.'

'That's right. Old Bob Naismith. He's a quiet soul, and civil enough when he's sober.' Davie hesitated then smiled faintly. 'If ye should meet him on his way tae the public house every Saturday afternoon,

51

he passes the time o' day an' his old mongrel dog gives a wee wag o' the tail. Then after a few hours the two o' them come back along the road, old Naismith staggerin' an' cursin' an' shoutin' at everyone he meets an' the dog snarlin' an' makin' runs at folks' ankles on the end of its string. An' it's no' even had a drop tae drink. The next day,' he went on, warmed by Anna's peals of laughter, 'there they are, civil as ye please, tail waggin' an' a'. Wee Ian cries him Mr Nicesmith on his way tae the pub an' Mr Nastysmith on his way back.'

Anna mopped her eyes with a lacy handkerchief. 'Lessie didnae tell me about that.'

'Lessie wouldnae.' Then all at once, unexpectedly, the memory of Johnny lying crumpled in the hold came into Davie's head and he got to his feet and walked clumsily to the window, unseeing, bumping against a corner of the table and setting the china on the tray jangling softly.

'Davie, what is it?'

'Nothin'.' Then, because he didn't want to let what had happened to Johnny taint this safe, pretty, feminine room and he had to say something he said bleakly, 'I don't want tae go back tae the docks again. I don't want tae work wi' my father. I'll no' dae it!'

Anna let the silence stretch between them for a few moments before she said, 'Davie, if you could do anything in the world, what would you choose?'

'Tae be an engineer,' said Davie, his heart in his voice.

She levered herself to her feet and came to stand by his side. Together they looked out at the cold winter's day. 'How long d'you have to go before you've finished your studying?'

'Six months.'

'Could you not find work in a factory now?'

'Who'd take me on?'

'You'll not know until you try,' said Anna. 'Go out and find the sort of work you want, Davie. It's the only way to get out of the docks.'

'An' what if I fail? I'll have tae go back tae the docks wi' my tail between my legs.'

'At least you'll have tried. And you can keep on trying until you succeed. Do it now, this minute. And mind and come back to let me know how you get on. I'd like to see you again.'

He stared down at her, suddenly realising that she was right. There was no rule that said he couldn't aim for what he wanted.

'Aye,' he said slowly. 'Aye. I will. You're right, Anna. There's nothin' wrong wi' failin'. The fault's in no' tryin'. An' by God, I'm goin' tae have a damned good run at it.'

She smiled at him, a smile that warmed him all through, and said softly, 'That's my Davie.'

And all at once he felt that he could move mountains, if Anna asked him.

7

The man who came into the shop to buy matches was vaguely familiar, though Lessie didn't remember seeing him on the other side of
the counter before. He had friendly hazel eyes, a square face and fair
tumbled hair that teased at the edges of memory until, as she was
handing him his change, it came to her.

'Are you not Murdo Carswell that used to go to school with my
brother Joseph?'

For a moment he stared and she thought that she had made a mistake. Then his face split into a wide grin. 'By God, it's wee Lessie
Kirkwood! What're you doin' in this part o' the town?'

'I live here. And my name's Hamilton now.'

'The pretty ones aye get snapped up before I find them,' said Murdo
Carswell in mock sorrow. 'That's why I'm still unwed myself. Dae I
know yer man?'

'No, he came to Greenock not long before we were wed. He . . .
died a while back.'

'I'm sorry tae hear that, lass.' There was an awkward silence, then
he said, 'An' how's Joseph? I've been in Glasgow these past two years
so I've lost touch wi' him.'

'Och, he's well enough.'

'Still the same rascal he was at school?'

'Still the same,' she agreed. 'D'ye mind the time a crowd of us went
up the braes and Joseph dared you tae have a ride on a big horse in
one of the fields?'

His grin widened into a laugh. 'I'm no' likely tae forget that. I
thought my arse was broken when the bugger took to its heels and I
went flying off.'

'You'd no sense in you at all in those days. You'd take on any daft
dare, and our Joseph knew it. Are you back in Greenock now, or just
visiting?'

'I'm back, like the bad penny. I'm workin' as a joiner at Scott's
shipyard.' Murdo seemed to be prepared to stay and talk, but the shop
was busy and there were customers waiting patiently for attention.
He glanced round at them, shrugged, and picked up his matches. 'I'll
be sure to look in again, now that I know you're workin' here.'

The memory of his final sunny grin stayed with her for the rest of
the afternoon while she served in the shop. Murdo Carswell had been
a solemn boy, much quieter than Joseph and the other lads in the
'gang'. He was the only son of a widow who considered herself to be

53

a cut above everyone else and frowned on street games and packs of lads roaming around together. Murdo, though, had defied her, slipping out after school to be with his friends. In order to be more like the other boys, he had, as Lessie had reminded him, been willing and eager to try anything, no matter how dangerous.

She collected Ian from the back room and made her way home to prepare Davie's evening meal.

Murdo's smile seemed a lot readier now, she thought as she peeled potatoes, her hands red with cold. Going to work in Glasgow, away from his mother, had done him good.

'Davie!' yelled Ian with open delight as heavy boots tramped up the stairs. He toddled to the door and Lessie dropped the potato knife and went after him, scooping him onto her hip and opening the door. When she saw Archie standing there her heart somersaulted crazily and she felt the blood drain from her face.

'Davie?'

To her relief her father said, 'Is he no' here?'

'No. I was just expecting him home.' She backed into the kitchen ahead of him and set Ian down. 'I thought when I saw you that he'd met with an accident. Did he not finish along with you?'

'He did no'. The damned fool walked out and left a ship half unloaded.'

'Why? What happened?'

'Ach, some clumsy creature who wasnae fit for the work managed tae get himself killed. But that was no excuse for Davie tae dae whit he did,' Archie said fiercely. 'I came tae gie him the sharp edge o' my tongue, but since he's no' here I might as well be on my way home. Here.' He dug into his pocket and tossed some coins on the table. 'This is what's owin' tae him. See that he gets it an' tell him tae be at the dock gates good an' early tomorrow. There's anither ship due in.'

'You'll stay an' have something to eat?'

'Better no'. Yer mother'll be expectin' me home.' He had stayed on his feet throughout his short visit. Now he ruffled Ian's hair and turned towards the door. 'I'll see mysel' out. Ye could mebbe visit yer mother some time, lassie. She's no' well.'

'What's wrong with her?'

'How should I ken?' Archie demanded grumpily as he left. 'I'm no' a bloody doctor. Just visit her.'

Davie arrived home an hour later, coming into the house quietly, without his usual cheerfulness. He sat down at the table and stared at the money that still lay there. 'What's this?'

'It's your wages. Da brought it.'

He pushed the money away violently. 'I don't want it!'

'Well I do!' Lessie dumped a pot of steaming potatoes down on the wooden table and scooped the money up. 'We need money to pay the rent and buy the food. You worked for it and you earned it.' Then, catching a glimpse of his face, she said more gently, 'Da told me a man was killed today. Is that what sent you away?'

'He—' Davie started explosively, then stopped, clenching his fists

54

on the table. 'He was someone I used to know. I couldnae stay after – after it happened.'

Lessie put a hand on his shoulder, then withdrew it when he flinched away. 'Da says he'll expect you at the gates tomorrow morning.'

'He'll have a long wait. I'm done wi' the docks.'

'Davie, for God's sake! You've got to go back. You cannae give up your work because of an accident. How're ye supposed to live with no wage comin' in?'

'I've found another place.'

'What? Where is it?'

He lifted his head, grim triumph in his face. 'A wee engineering shop in Port Glasgow owned by an old man called Beattie. Jo—' He stopped suddenly then said, 'I heard he needed someone so I went along tae see him. He's no' got much money an' I've no' got my papers yet, an' the way things are just now the place could close down, but I'll dae my damnedest tae see that that doesnae happen – an' I told him that.'

Lessie sank in a chair opposite him. 'You're on the right road now. Oh, Davie, I'm proud of you – and pleased for you!'

He shot a look at her from beneath lowered lashes, then said swiftly, apologetically, 'It's no' as much as I can get at the docks.'

'But it'll be regular, and that's more than you can say for being a docker.' She leaned forward and put her hand on his. 'We'll manage, the three of us. We'll manage fine.'

'Aye,' he said, then with a glance at the clock he jumped to his feet. 'I'll be late for my evening class.'

'You've not eaten yet.'

'I'll have something when I get back,' he said, snatching up his books and departing without changing out of his working clothes. Alone, Lessie got Ian ready for bed, wondering why, when he should be overjoyed at finding the sort of work he wanted, Davie should be so dour and unsmiling about it.

'It's only a cough,' Barbara Kirkwood said impatiently when her daughter called on her. 'Everyone gets colds at this time of year.'

Lessie, helping Thomasina to dress her doll, and almost crushed against the wooden arm of her chair by the weight of her sister's body leaning cosily against hers, asked mildly, 'D'you have any soothing syrup for it?'

'I'll get some if it doesnae stop soon.' Barbara coughed again and wiped her mouth with a handkerchief. Thomasina imitated the dry pecking sound and giggled behind her outspread fingers. Then she snatched the doll from Lessie and plumped herself down on the floor beside Ian.

'It's the poor Queen you want to be worryin' yersel' about. They say she's very poorly.'

'She doesnae need me tae worry about her. She's got enough doctors an' soothing syrup tae cure the ills o' half the folk in the country.'

55

'Lessie! That's no way tae talk o' your Queen!'

'She didnae hear me, Mam. An' she's had a good long life – everyone has tae die some time. Some earlier than others,' Lessie added sombrely, thinking of Donald.

'You're too young tae ken what it'll mean tae the likes o' me if the old Queen dies. It's the end o' more than just one life. The world'll never be the same again without her.' Barbara coughed again and looked longingly towards the bedroom door. Lessie knew that behind it, in some hidden place, was a whisky bottle.

'Mebbe that won't be a bad thing either, in some ways,' she said, and got another scolding that ended in a further outbreak of coughing.

Within the next week, Greenock, like every other community in the country, was in mourning for Queen Victoria. And yet Lessie, who had had her own private mourning to do some eighteen months earlier, felt the world was beginning to brighten. Although he'd had to work hard in his first week and brought home less than he had from the docks, Davie was happier. He and Mr Beattie, his new employer, got on well together. From the beginning, Mr Beattie encouraged Davie to volunteer ideas and opinions and he was already learning fast now that he was among the machinery he loved. Ian continued to thrive, the whooping cough a dimly remembered nightmare now as he seemed to grow overnight from babyhood to boyhood.

Murdo Carswell soon took to dropping in at the shop and even at the house, his cheerful grin lighting up many a long day. Once or twice, if the weather permitted and Lessie had time, the two of them went walking with Ian trotting ahead or between them, clutching their hands, demanding to be swung off his feet and into the air.

'He fancies you,' Davie said one day when Lessie and Ian returned from a long walk with Murdo.

'Away ye go! He's just looking for a bit of company,' she said swiftly, busying herself with the task of taking off Ian's coat, turning away from Davie, ignoring his dry, 'Oh, aye?'

She enjoyed Murdo's company, but she had put all thoughts of love behind her when she buried her Donald and she wasn't ready yet to think of Murdo as anything but a good friend. Once or twice, when their eyes met over Ian's red head or their hands happened to touch fleetingly, she felt a slight tremor of pleasurable excitement, but each time it was sternly suppressed.

Anyway, it took two to make a romance, and she was quite sure that if a lad like Murdo was looking for more than mere friendship he could easily find it with a pretty unmarried girl unencumbered by a child.

The only cloud on Lessie's horizon as the winter began to drop behind and spring made itself felt, even in the Vennel where there was not a tree to burst into leaf or a patch of soil where a grass blade could flourish, was the money she still owed to Anna McCauley. The rent had to be paid and food had to be bought and now that Davie was earning less, money was even tighter than before. Ian seemed to be continually growing out of his clothes and Lessie scoured the second-hand shops for jerseys and trousers and shoes for him, often buying larger garments that still had some good wear in them, unpicking them, and making them over to fit the little boy.

Edith was good at handing down clothes that Peter had outgrown, but all too often they were impossible. Lessie couldn't bring herself to turn her Ian into a laughing stock by dressing him in the velvet suits that poor Peter had to wear. Guiltily, hoping that Edith would never find out, she took most of the little suits along to the pawnbroker to raise a shilling or two. But even so, she never had enough left over to pay off the debt that continually nagged at her conscience.

In her fine little house with her fine clothes and her maidservant and Andrew Warren visiting her whenever he could, Anna was becoming bored, missing the bustle and variety of life in the Vennel. As she grew fatter and heavier she took to summoning Lessie for afternoon tea once a week and Lessie, ever aware of the twenty shillings she owed, felt that she had no option but to go to Port Glasgow, busy though she was. Once the debt was paid, she told herself each time she caught the horse tram that ran between the two towns, she need never see Anna again. They were people with entirely different outlooks on life, and now that her former neighbour was living in the house Andrew Warren rented for her, their lives had grown even further apart. At the same time she was uncomfortably aware that as far as Anna was concerned they were friends and would always remain so. Lessie felt she was caught in a difficult situation.

In the early spring Murdo brought an invitation to visit his mother's home for Sunday tea. Lessie stared at him, astonished and flustered. 'I couldn't!'

'Why not?'

'I, well, why does she want to see me?'

He laughed. 'Why shouldnae she want to see you? She's heard me talking about you, that's all. You'll come, won't you? Please, Lessie,' he begged, and she nodded, not wanting to disappoint him yet feeling that she had been caught in a trap.

Mrs Carswell lived with her two unmarried children, Murdo and his younger sister, in the top flat of a well-kept tenement in Roxburgh Street. Her late husband had been a bookkeeper in one of the big sugar houses, a thrifty man who had left his widow well provided for. Mrs Carswell considered herself to be superior to most of the Greenock folk, but she greeted Lessie kindly enough, her eyes travelling approvingly over her guest's best clothes, a blue woollen skirt and jacket over a blue and white striped blouse, with a straw hat decorated with a blue ribbon.

The clothes had originally belonged to Edith and Lessie had ironed them carefully for the occasion, using a damp cloth to protect the material from the hot iron. The blouse was fastened at the neck by a garnet and filigree brooch that had belonged to Donald's mother. He had given it to Lessie on their wedding day and she treasured it. 'One day,' he had said as he handed it over, 'I'll be able to buy you a ring and a necklace to match.' Then he had added, grinning down at her, 'Mebbe this time next year.'

The Carswells and their guest had tea at a table by the window – boiled potatoes and thick glistening slices of cold potted meat with a spoonful of peas carefully measured onto each plate. When Lessie praised the spicy meat, Murdo's mother informed her that she had made it herself, and rattled off the exact price of the shinbone and the beef she had used without a pause for thought.

'Murdo tells me you're a widow like myself, Mistress Hamilton,' she went on as she dispensed tea. 'With a wee boy to raise.'

'Ian's almost two years old now.'

'Murdo was five when I lost his father.' Mrs Carswell made it sound as though she had mislaid the man somewhere. 'I'd four wee ones to bring up on my own, but I pride myself on having done well. Two of them are well married, and Katherine here's walking out with a very nice young man who works in the shipyard offices. It was him who got Murdo into the shipyard. I hope your son grows up to be as successful as my four.'

'I'm sure he will,' Lessie said, adding hastily as her hostess's eyebrows rose, 'This meat's lovely, Mrs Carswell.'

Katherine caught her eye and gave her the shadow of a wink.

They finished off with a syrup tart and as they ate it Mrs Carswell reeled off the cost of the syrup as well as the brand of tea she bought specially for visitors. It was a relief when, the meal over and the table cleared, Murdo suggested an outing. 'Can you ride a bicycle?'

'A bicycle? I've not been on one for more years than I care to remember.'

'You can borrow Katherine's.' Murdo glanced at her clothes. 'You'll manage fine in that skirt. Come on.'

The bicycles, old but lovingly maintained, were kept in a shed in the back yard. Wheeling her machine, Lessie followed Murdo nervously through the close and into the street, quite certain that she would have forgotten everything she had ever learned about bicycling. At first, to the open amusement of the women leaning from their windows and the children playing on the pavements, her machine wobbled precariously and once or twice she had to slap a foot hastily onto the ground to prevent herself from toppling over altogether. But by the time they had negotiated the stretch to the corner of the street her sense of balance was returning and she was able to follow Murdo in a fairly straight line.

Mercifully, he didn't expect her to go far. The Carswells lived further inland than she did, and they only had to turn out of Roxburgh Street and follow the rising sweep of Captain Street to reach the water-filtering system on the higher limits of the town, almost in the countryside. Here, at a stretch of rough winter grass, Murdo dismounted and waited until Lessie, breathless, reached him. He laid both bicycles on the grass and he and Lessie leaned against a drystone wall and looked down towards the river.

It was an exceptionally beautiful February day with more than a promise of the spring to come. The air was as clear and fresh as moun-tain water, the sky blue, with only a few fluffy clouds on the horizon and the snow-streaked hills on the other side of the river to remind them that it was still winter. The sun had warmed the stones at their backs and woven a broad rope of shimmering gold across the river to link Greenock with Helensburgh. A steam tug and its tow, a sailing ship on the way upriver to its final destination, vanished from sight when they entered that dazzling golden band, then reappeared, the tug as a black beetle, the lofty sailing ship with its masts and spars turned to black lace against the bright background. Then they broke free of it and became themselves again. Here and there brightly coloured paddle-steamers beat the glassy river into sparkling white foam as they fussed from one quay to another.

For some strange reason Andrew Warren came into Lessie's mind. To her left lay Gourock, where he and his family lived in their big house; before her was Greenock, where the Warren sugar refinery was situated, and to the right lay Port Glasgow, where Anna McCauley now lived in a house rented by Warren. Three neighbouring towns, Lessie thought, spanned by the power and wealth of one man.

'What are you thinking about?' Murdo asked at that moment.

'Nothing at all.' She closed her eyes, feeling the sun's warmth on her lids, and promised herself that one day in the summer she would bring Ian to this place, where he could run about and play in the sun-shine. Then she jumped as a shadow fell over her lids, Murdo's hands cupped her elbows, and his mouth brushed hers gently.

'Murdo Carswell!' She straightened up, pulling away from the wall, staring in shocked outrage at the face only inches from hers. 'What d'you think you're doing?'

'Kissing you. What's amiss with that?' His breath was soft on her cheek.

'You can't do that – you went to school with our Joseph!'

'School,' said Murdo, his mouth twitching in a suppressed smile, 'was a good long while ago.' Then he kissed her again, this time draw-ing her into his arms, holding her close, his mouth lingering on hers.

It was the first time a man had kissed her since Donald's death, the first time since then that anyone had held her, apart from the tight clutch of Ian's little arms and an occasional affectionate swipe from his sticky little mouth. It was good to be held by a man again, and Lessie's arms slid round Murdo's back as the kiss deepened. She could feel his heart and hers pounding, and parted her lips as the tip of his tongue slid gently along them. He broke the kiss just long enough to let his mouth taste the angle of her jaw, one ear, the silkiness of her neck, then returned to find her mouth soft and open and eager for his again.

When they finally drew back from each other Lessie said shakily, 'I must get back. My mother's got Ian an' she's enough to do with-out him under her feet all afternoon.'

One of Murdo's hands brushed back a lock of her hair and tucked it behind her ear. His touch sent a pleasant shiver down her spine.

59

'We'll do this again, Lessie,' he said, and released her, turning and stooping to lift his sister's bicycle while Lessie, dazed, wondered whether he meant the outing or the kiss.

She was still shaky and somewhat weak about the knees when she knocked at her mother's door a short while later. It opened on a waft of whisky breath and peals of amusement from the kitchen, Thomasina's high-pitched laugh threading its way through Ian's deeper bubbling mirth.

'Ye're earlier than I thought ye'd be,' said Barbara. 'Did your visit go all right?'

'It was fine, but I didnae want to leave Ian for too long.'

In the kitchen Thomasina was dancing round Ian, who stood in the middle of the floor dressed in one of her summer frocks, the waist-line almost at his knees, the neck slipping over one of his shoulders. Thomasina's best straw hat was tipped at a drunken angle over one ear and his face was split by a huge delighted grin. When he saw his mother he advanced towards her, skiffing his feet to keep Thomasina's shoes on, and almost tripping over the hem of the frock.

'Bonny wee lassie!' Thomasina screeched, and Ian echoed, 'Bonny!'

'So you are, but a bonnier lad than a lass as far as I'm concerned, ye wee imp.' Lessie swept him up into her arms, lifting him right out of the shoes, and hugged him, then glanced sharply at her mother as she started to cough. 'Have you not got rid of that cough yet?'

'It's goin', it's goin'. It's no' near as bad as it was. My new syrup's helpin' it.' Barbara lifted a dark medicine bottle from a shelf by the sink, found a spoon, and swallowed down several doses of a clear amber liquid. By the time Ian had been restored to his normal self and they were about to go home to the Vennel, Barbara had had another coughing attack and had needed several doses of her syrup. Each time the bottle was uncorked the pungent smell of whisky was noticeable. As she made for the door, Lessie said gently, 'Best not to let Edith see you taking so much of that cough syrup, Mam. She might no' understand.'

Barbara blinked, then gave her daughter a tired smile. 'Ye're a good girl, Lessie,' she said. 'A good girl.'

8

'I'm going to call her Dorothea,' Anna said proudly. 'I found it in a book.'

'It's a lovely name.' Lessie settled the baby more comfortably into the crook of her arm and eased Ian's inquisitive fingers away from the tiny face nestling in the midst of the froth of silk and lace and delicate wool on her lap. 'Just look at her, pet, don't touch. She's too wee to be touched.'

'I sent word for you to come two days ago, Lessie. Did you not get it?'

'Mr McKay's been ill again. I couldnae get away from the shop.'

'I don't suppose Mr McKay was as ill as me.' Anna, rested and beautiful, lying back against a mound of pillows with a shawl about her shoulders, a silken quilt over her legs and her red hair freshly brushed, looked the picture of health and happiness. 'I never knew childbirth could hurt so much, Lessie. I swear I'll never go through that again!'

'It's not as bad as that, and it's easy forgotten. Besides, it's worth it, isn't it, my bonny wee love?' Lessie crooned to the baby, who had opened clear blue eyes. Dorothea yawned and Ian laughed at her then wandered off to explore the room. Lessie watched him carefully. There were so many ornaments in this beautiful bedroom, so many fragile things to tempt inquisitive little fingers.

'Oh, it's worth it now, but never again.' Then Anna's head lifted from the pillow as the door knocker rattled. 'Who's that come to call?'

They heard the servant opening the door then the murmur of a deep voice. Her face lit up.

'It's Andrew! Here, give her to me.' She held out her arms and Lessie went to the bed and carefully handed the little bundle over. With swift hands Anna arranged the baby's shawl, then she lay back against her pillows again. When Andrew Warren tapped on the door and entered, she smiled at him and reached out her free hand. 'Andrew, I didnae think to see you today.'

'I'd business in Port Glasgow.' He took the proferred hand. 'How are you, my dear?'

'Oh, a little stronger than yesterday.'

'I'm glad to hear it. Good day to you, Mrs Hamilton.'

'Mr Warren.' Lessie had returned to her chair, but she couldn't sit down. If she had known that Andrew Warren was going to visit the house that day she would never have come.

'Here's a fine wee Scotsman, with his red hair. What's his name?'

Warren, quite at his ease, smiled down at Ian, who had moved close to his mother's skirt and was staring at the newcomer, one thumb in his mouth.

'Ian.'

'A good Scots name too. And how's our little Dorothea?' To Lessie's astonishment he lifted the baby from Anna's arms and walked over to the window with her, holding her as easily as any woman would.

'She's a wee angel. Scarce a sound out of her.' Anna's voice was smug.

'What d'you think of her, Mrs Hamilton?'

'She's a beautiful baby.'

Andrew's eyes met Anna's over their daughter's head. 'I agree,' he said. 'And she's going to be a beautiful lady one day, like her mother. She's going to have everything her heart desires.'

Lessie, used to men showing no interest in their offspring until the children were old enough to earn money, was dumbfounded by Warren's frank adoration of a child that had not even been born in wedlock. True, Donald had openly delighted in Ian when he was born, but Donald had been special, above other men. She found it hard to believe that a man with Andrew Warren's power and money could care so much for children. But there was no doubt that he did. In fact, he and Anna and the baby were such a complete family, such a happy family, that envy twinged suddenly and unexpectedly, like an aching tooth, in Lessie's heart. As soon as she could she made her excuses, gathered Ian up, and left.

'You'll come back soon to see me?' Anna asked as she was going out of the door. 'I'll be needing your advice now that I've got a bairn of my own to see to.'

'I'll be back when I can.'

Her hand was on the latch of the outer door when Andrew Warren came swiftly down the stairs from the bedroom. 'Mrs Hamilton, I hope that you will continue to visit Anna.' As he stood over her, the little hall seemed even smaller. 'She needs a good friend and it comforts me to know that she has one in you.'

Lessie's heart sank. She had hoped that once the child was born Anna would be too busy, too content, to look for her company any longer. But she couldn't say so, not to this solemn man who adored babies.

'I'll certainly continue to call if Anna wishes it,' she heard herself saying pompously. Miss Peden would have been proud of her.

'Thank you.' He stooped and took Ian's small hand in his. 'Good day, Master Ian. We'll meet again, I'm sure.'

Then he opened the door and ushered them through it with as much courtesy as though they were gentry like himself. She was so bemused that she paid no attention at all to Ian's excited babbling and they were halfway to the tram stop before Lessie discovered the coin clutched tightly in the little boy's fist, where Warren had placed it.

Although he had accepted his new role as the manager of the family refinery because there was no other way, Andrew resented it bitterly. He had always assumed that by the time he was required to return to Greenock from Jamaica to take over the family business he would be the sole owner, with a free hand in the management of the place. But with only one uncle dead and the other determined to become an invalid and at the same time retain his shares and therefore his hold on the refinery, Andrew was in a difficult position. The place needed to be revitalised; the machinery should be modernised or at least improved, but James Warren's attitude to everything that Andrew suggested was one of caution bordering on fear.

'We'll lose every penny we have if you get your way,' the old man grumbled each time his nephew tried to reason with him. 'D'you take me for a fool? I've no intention of losing all my money.'

'But the Continental refiners are seeking to take the sugar monopoly away from the British Isles. You mark my words, Uncle James, if our refinery isn't improved soon, we'll be in danger of falling behind. There are already too many good sugar houses in Greenock being forced to close their doors and dismiss their workers. I don't want it to happen to Warren's as well.'

'This is no time to pour more money into the business. Parliament's just pushed our taxes up to a shilling in the pound, damn their thieving hearts. A fifty per cent increase! At this rate I'll be fortunate if I don't die in the workhouse.'

'We could borrow from the bank. God knows our name's good. We'd have no trouble in raising the capital we need.'

'I'll not go begging to any bank, nor will I be plunged into debt. You hear me, Andrew?' The old man sucked in his lips and scowled. He looked like a large sulky baby and for a moment Warren was tempted to treat him like one, sending him to his bed and making him stay there until he saw sense. But he knew that he had no option but to continue to do the best he could without the free hand that he badly needed.

The workers, too, were unsure of him and slow to give him their trust. He was in the throes of trying to persuade them to set up a scheme whereby they would each pay in a halfpence a week from their wages so that any man forced to take time off work through illness would be entitled to payment for at least part of his time at home, but the whole process was proving to be as sticky and sluggish as the sugar and syrup mixture they fed into the centrifugal machines to be separated. Although workers in some other firms had started their own 'sick clubs', the majority of the Warren employees were too cautious to part with their hard-earned money. Andrew was working patiently on the younger men, explaining the benefits of such a scheme, in the hope that they would see the light and convince the others. He had even offered to contribute management money amounting to half the sum collected from the workers each week, but he didn't dare tell his uncle that.

But now there was something for Andrew to rejoice over, and rejoice he did, in secret, as he walked from his office to the yard where his small carriage was kept. He had a third child now, a beautiful daughter. He relished the prospect of watching Dorothea thrive and grow, untrammelled by nursery staff who thought that fathers were merely there to provide money and should be neither seen nor heard.

The yard was awash with sunlight that softened and warmed the harsh greys and browns and blacks of the cobbles and the stone walls. Two women came from the warehouse, rolling a huge barrel of kieselguhr between them, struggling to keep it moving over the cobblestones. The melted sugar was poured over troughs of kieselguhr, a fine earth almost entirely composed of minute animal skeletons, to cleanse it of impurities before it was crystallised. Although their task was hard, the women were laughing over something, lifting their faces to the sun.

A cart piled high with empty sugar sacks was rattling out of the gate on its way to Boag's factory, which had been set up to wash sugar bags from all the refineries and prepare them for re-use. The old buildings fronting the yard hummed and clanked with the steam-driven machinery that filled them. Studying the buildings while he waited for a stableman to harness his horse to the carriage, Andrew frowned. The plan of the place was wrong; it had been built about a hundred years earlier and a lot of time was wasted in transporting sacks and barrels from one section to another and back again, instead of starting the refining process at one end of the building and completing it at the other.

But the plans he had in mind would take money, a great deal of money. A surge of frustration swept over him as he climbed into the carriage and picked up the reins. He knew the refinery well, knew every stone, every beam, every piece of machinery. Like his father and his uncles, Andrew had begun by working his way through each department. He had toiled in the warehouse, weighing, grading, marking and lifting the great bags of refined sugar; he had served his apprenticeship as a pan floor boy, where the heat generated by the huge vacuum pans was almost intolerable and nobody could bear to wear anything on their feet. He had worked in the char house and as a liquor boy, washing out the big tanks, learning to overcome the queasiness caused by the heavy, sweet, pervasive smell of the sugar. He had spent time in the laboratory, where they tested sugar samples and worked continuously at perfecting the process.

He wondered, as he drove out to Gourock, if Martin would serve such a gruelling apprenticeship before taking over command, then decided with a wry smile that Madeleine would probably fight such an idea tooth and nail.

At nine o'clock that evening James finished reading his newspaper, folded it into a neat rectangle, and announced that he was going to bed. Madeleine had been playing the piano, but when the door closed she rose and came across the room to where her husband sat working at his desk.

'Andrew, I know about your woman.'

The sentence was so blunt, so unexpected, that for a moment he

64

gaped at her. Her lovely face was expressionless, her hands folded demurely before her.

'I won't demean us both by pretending innocence, Madeleine,' he said at last, pushing away the ledger he had been working on and standing up. He felt strangely weak and shaky, as though he had just suffered a mortal blow.

She turned away from him and walked to a sofa, seating herself with that delicate grace that always enchanted him. 'I attend afternoon soirees, I help to raise funds for our soldiers in South Africa. I cannot help hearing gossip. And I have heard that there is a woman, and a house, and a child.'

'Who told you?'

Her shoulders lifted in one of her lovely shrugs. 'That is of no matter. Malicious people sometimes like to carry bad news.'

'It happened—' he started to say, but she held up a hand to stop him.

'I have no desire to know any of the details, Andrew. I only wish you to know that I am aware of the situation.'

'Are you asking me to give her up?'

'Why should I, when I am quite sure that you would only replace her with someone else?'

'You have a cynical idea of men, my dear.'

'I learned from my father. And now I am learning from my husband, am I not?'

Beneath her faint, almost pitying, smile Andrew felt the colour rise to his face.

'I am not a child,' she went on. 'I know that it is apparently not easy for men to be faithful. A man is almost expected to have his paramours.'

'Madeleine—'

'And a woman learns to accept these things. I was taught that by my mama. I do accept, but there are conditions.'

'Conditions?' He could scarcely believe that they were discussing his infidelity in such a matter-of-fact way. He would have expected tears, anger, accusations. He would have welcomed them, welcomed the opportunity to beg her forgiveness, to comfort her and so comfort himself. But that was not what Madeleine sought.

'I am your wife, and I intend to remain so.'

'That's my intention too.'

'My children and I will always come first,' the light voice with its charming accent went on implacably. 'This woman and her child will never come to this house to shame me before my children. My son will inherit his birthright. Any other sons you may have will have no claim to your money or your position.'

Helpless anger had begun to fill Andrew. He was being treated like a badly behaved servant, and he had no way of defending himself, for Madeleine was in the right. 'I would never consider denying your rights as my wife or denying our children their birthright,' he said stiffly.

Madeleine's head bobbed in the slightest nod and the sapphire earrings Andrew had given her only a few months before glittered in the lamplight. 'Then we understand each other. One more thing, Andrew. You will no longer come to my bedchamber. Never again.'

'Madeleine, if I was to give the woman up—'

'Never,' she repeated, and walked away from him, out of the room, her back straight and her small head, piled with the glossy black hair that had never been cut, held high.

The sight of that hair, carefully coiffed and pinned, reminded Andrew of the feel of the soft silky locks in his hands, against his face, his naked body. As the door closed, he strode over to a small table in the corner of the room and fumbled at the whisky decanter, dropping the stopper in his clumsiness. The sound of it bouncing off the inlaid table jangled through him and his hands shook as he measured a generous amount of the liquid into a glass. The stopper had landed intact on the deep carpet and, dazed, he took time to search for it and return it to the decanter before moving to one of the big windows that overlooked the river.

The sun had gone down but a pale pink memory of it remained just above the water. Above that the sky was delicate grey shading into charcoal and the first stars were beginning to glimmer palely. Lights from the boats moved across the water. As Andrew watched, everything blurred and misted and he was horrified to realise that there were tears in his eyes.

Hurriedly, ashamed of them, he scrubbed them away and took a deep swallow from his glass. The whisky burned into his mouth, his throat, his gullet, but brought no comfort. It tasted of his own self-disgust.

He had suggested giving up Anna. Now he turned the thought round, studying it, and realised that he would have done it if that had been what Madeleine wanted. Anna was a joy and a comfort, but she was also an indulgence whereas Madeleine was his wife, now and for as long as they both lived, and he loved her as much as he ever had. He realised this with astonishment, for since the birth of the twins he had come to accept that love was no longer a part of his marriage. He had been wrong; now that he had lost her respect he knew that his feelings for Madeleine had never changed.

He drained the last of the whisky and refilled the glass. If he had only examined his feelings closely a year ago he might have been able, somehow, to win Madeleine back again. Now it was too late; he had lost her through his own foolishness.

The second drink, more comforting than the first, began to wash away the humiliation. He poured a third and returned to the window to watch the last remnants of the sunset fade. He still had Anna. She loved him, depended on him, trusted him. And he had Dorothea. Although he would have relinquished the woman for the promise of his wife's forgiveness, he could never relinquish the child they had made together, his daughter.

He filled his glass for the fourth time.

★★★

Lessie's secret fears came true that summer. Mr McKay's health had become so bad that he and his wife decided to give up the corner shop and move to Rothesay on the Clyde island of Bute, where the old man could rest and enjoy what remained of his life.

'I'm sorry, my dear, for you've been such a help to us over the past year.' Mrs McKay's thin fingers kneaded each other nervously as she broke the news. 'But there's nothing else for it. I'll put in a good word with the new owners for you.'

'Is there someone interested?'

'Not yet.'

'It'll likely be someone with a family to help in the shop,' Lessie said desolately, and went home to fret over this latest blow. There was nowhere near for her to work, and most of the shopkeepers in the town would frown on the thought of Ian tagging with her. The only answer was to find more house-cleaning to do, but there again Ian was the problem. Now that Davie was earning a smaller wage, what little the McKays had paid her, sometimes in goods instead of money, had gained in importance. It meant the difference between managing and going hungry most weeks.

And there was Anna's twenty shillings, briskly receding so far into the distance that Lessie could see no way at all of repaying it. She went about her work that day in a haze of misery, saying nothing about her problems to Miss Peden as she took a cup of tea after scrubbing the stairs. The old lady might offer to lend her money and Lessie felt that she was already burdened with debt. She hoped that she would never again have to owe money to anyone.

She held her tongue when Davie came in at night, full of excitement because Mr Beattie had agreed to an amendment Davie had suggested in one of the machines they were turning out. He had just passed his final night-school examination and was entitled to an increase in wages, but Mr Beattie couldn't afford to pay him more. Rather than try elsewhere, where he might not have the freedom to put forward his own ideas, Davie had decided to stay on for the same money.

'But only if you agree,' he had said to Lessie just two weeks before, when the matter arose. 'It'll be worth it eventually because I'm learning a lot. And if I leave I'll mebbe be out of work for a wee while with no money coming in at all.'

He had looked so hopeful that Lessie had agreed, unaware at that time of the McKays' plans to give up the shop.

That night before going to sleep she ran through her usual prayers in her mind, then added, 'Donald, help me to find a way to look after Ian the way you'd have wanted.' Since her widowhood her prayers had been a mixture of appeals to God and to Donald who, she was certain, would do all he could to put in a good word for her. She sometimes wondered if this was insulting to God, but if so it couldn't be helped. Better to insult God than to ignore her Donald.

She fell asleep at last with the memory of her husband's face, his voice, his touch close in her mind and her heart like a talisman, and wakened in the morning with an idea so startling, so ridiculous, that it could only have been put there by someone else. By Donald, she thought, dazed, scrambling out of bed and knocking on Davie's door to rouse him before getting dressed.

And if it was indeed Donald's answer to her dilemma, she must do all she could to make it work.

9

'Lassie, ye could never dae it!' Mr McKay protested. 'Ye've got enough tae worry aboot wi'oot takin' ower the shop as well.'

'I could, if I gave up the cleaning work. And I'd make enough money to pay you and leave somethin' over tae keep me and Ian, once I got started.' Lessie heard her voice crack and knew that she was almost begging. But she didn't care.

'Even so,' Mrs McKay said gently, her eyes sad, 'there's no sense in us leaving you to look after the shop for us. We need the money we'd get from selling it. My sister in Rothesay's willing tae have us, but we'd have tae pay our way. An' there's the cost o' gettin' over there, an' takin' the bits o' furniture we want tae keep by us.'

Lessie swallowed her disappointment. 'How much are you looking for?'

'Seventy pound, my dear.' Then, at Lessie's gasp of horror, the old man explained in his hoarse, breathless voice, 'The shop an' the wee house are nae' – he paused for breath – 'ours, o' course. They're rented at twelve pound a year. But there's a' the . . . the stock in the shop, an' the goodwill. We bring in seven . . . pound in a good week an' it's . . . customary tae ask ten . . . pound for every pound taken . . . in a week. It's a fair . . . askin' price.'

'D'you need it all at once?'

Mrs McKay glanced at her husband. Years of close companionship made spoken consultation unnecessary for these two; Lessie had often marvelled at the way each knew what the other was thinking, and envied them. It was a gift she and Donald might have shared one day if only he had been spared.

'Fifty pound in oor hands wid jist aboot dae it,' Mr McKay was saying, while his wife nodded agreement. 'An' the rest peyed ower . . . the next year. But there'd be the rent ower an' . . . above that, an' new stock tae . . . tae buy for the shop as ye run . . . oot.'

'It'd be too much for you, Lessie. Best to forget about it,' Mrs McKay urged.

Lessie didn't want to forget about it. The idea fired her with enthusiasm. She took Ian home and gave him a crust dipped in sugar to chew so that she could work out sums on the back of one of Davie's many exercise books. She and Ian and Davie could live in the two rooms behind the shop. As well as being in better condition than her own flat, it would make a small saving in rent. And give her an annual rent of twelve pounds to meet, an inner voice added, and was smartly dismissed. With her own shop she could support Ian and look after him by herself. When he grew older he could be her errand boy and eventually, when she was too old to run the shop by herself, it would be his inheritance. The McKays claimed that the shop could take in six or seven pounds in a good week. To Lessie, that was wealth worth having.

After his first appalled reaction to her scheme, Davie began to catch some of her enthusiasm. They sat together that night after Ian was asleep, adding and subtracting and planning but not getting very far.

'Nae use in askin' Da for the money. Even if he had it he'd no' part wi' it. An' Edith an' Joseph are of no help at all.' Davie dismissed their family in a few words, then went on slowly, 'I could dae more for you if I left Beattie's an' went tae a larger firm that could afford tae pay better wages.'

'You're happy where you are. I'd not hear of you moving.' Lessie tried to tuck up a strand of fair hair that had fallen over her face. 'Besides, I want to do this myself. It was my idea and it should be my worry.'

'There's Miss Peden—'

'I'll not ask her for help.'

Davie sighed. 'You'll have tae, Lessie. She's the only person we know wi' a bit o' money.'

'I'll not be in debt to her!'

'See sense, Lessie.' Davie's voice was suddenly exasperated. 'Ye cannae hope tae take on a shop without borrowing money – everyone in business borrows. Most from the banks, but they'd no' be of any use tae ye. Ye've got tae decide how important this shop is tae ye. If ye want it badly enough, I think Miss Peden'd be the person tae go tae. She'd help ye willingly, an' she'd know ye could be trusted tae pay back the money.'

Lessie started to chew on the end of the lock of hair. 'Mebbe you're right. But I'll only ask her when I can say I've got as much money as I can raise myself.'

'I'll sell my engineering books.'

'You need them.' Davie had slowly managed to put together a library of textbooks. She knew how hard he had worked for each one.

'Not all of them. Not the earlier ones. I'll sell them. Lessie . . .' He hesitated, then said awkwardly, not meeting her eyes, 'There's Donald's good suit still hanging up in the cupboard.'

Two pairs of eyes went to the cupboard door. Behind it was the suit Donald had been married in, and a good winter coat of his that Davie sometimes wore when the weather was bitter. Lessie kept them both well brushed and free of damp. It had always irked her that Donald had been buried in his working suit, but poor people couldn't afford to consign good clothes to the grave and she knew that his spirit would never have forgiven her if she had done so.

'I'll take it tae the pawn tomorrow. And the coat. I'll get them back out before the year's up, for I'll be able tae afford it by then,' she said round a lump in her throat.

'And I'll give you my good suit as well. I can manage without it for a month or two. Until the winter, anyway. Don't take them tae that old twister McConnachie,' Davie warned. 'He always cheats. Go somewhere else.'

'Oh, Davie, ye're a good brother tae me!'

'I should be better. I should be earning what I'm worth now that I've got my papers,' Davie said gruffly. Lessie leaned forward to put her hand on his and the lock of hair, slightly damp at the end now, fell forward again. She began to lift it back, hesitated, studied it, squinting a little, frowning, thinking, planning.

'What in the world have you done to yourself?' Anna McCauley stared, shocked, as her friend took off her hat.

Lessie ran a hand through her short fair hair and shrugged. 'It was nothing but a nuisance. I decided to have it cut off.'

'I don't believe you.' Anna's voice was blunt. 'Did you have nits?'

Lessie felt her face grow scarlet. 'I did not!'

'Tell me, then, if you don't want me to go on thinking it was head lice.'

Lessie began to refuse, then stopped and bit her lip. Anna would pester her until she got the truth.

'Ian, away out and play in the back garden. It's all right,' Anna added over her shoulder as she opened the door for the little boy. 'Dorothea's out there with Molly watching over her. She can see to two as easy as one. I'm fortunate to have Molly,' she went on, closing the door and returning to her chair. 'She thinks the world of Dorothea.'

Today she was wearing a fawn blouse richly embroidered with violet and green threads on the bodice and sleeves. Her pleated skirt was also fawn, and her red hair was caught up at the back with a jet comb. Lessie, watching her seat herself with easy grace, marvelled at how swiftly Anna had settled into the role of a wealthy young woman. It was very difficult, now, to remember that she had once lived in the Vennel.

'Now,' Anna leaned forward, her lovely eyes wide with curiosity, 'tell me what you're up to.'

Once the story had spilled out, she looked disappointed. 'Is that all? I thought you'd had your hair cut off to please a man.'

'As if I'd do that! Donald didn't ever want me to cut my hair, and I wouldn't have if I hadnae needed the money so badly.' Lessie heard her own voice quiver slightly on the last few words. The business had been far harder than she had imagined. Clean though her hair was, the hairdresser had washed it again, then cut it off carefully, exclaiming in pleasure over the long strands, drying to a soft silkiness, assuring her that he would put it to good use. She had taken the proffered money and left the shop feeling as though she had just sold Ian. Every time she looked into the mirror she felt like a murderer.

'You suit it short,' Anna said thoughtfully. 'Stand up and turn round and let me see it. What does Murdo say to it?'

'It's of no concern to me what Murdo Carswell thinks. I keep telling you, Anna, we're just friends.'

'So you say.' Anna eyed her slyly from beneath long lashes. 'How much more d'you need for the shop?'

Lessie bit her lip again. Donald's good suit and coat had been pawned, together with Davie's suit. Davie had sold some of his engineering books to a secondhand dealer and her beloved garnet brooch had also found its way into the pawnbroker's safe. Davie had gone behind her back and told Miss Peden the whole story, and the former schoolteacher had swept down to the Vennel, marched into Lessie's house, and handed her a twenty-pound note.

'It's all I can raise at the moment, my dear, but it's yours,' she had announced.

'I cannae take your money!'

'I know you'll pay me back when you can. Davie's told me how you feel about loans, but I'm not in a hurry, and surely we know each other well enough by now for you to accept my help graciously. You've done a lot for me, my dear,' Miss Peden had said, her voice suddenly losing its usual steel. 'You've given me friendship and company, and I'm only pleased that at last I can give you something in return.'

'How much more?' Anna asked again.

'I still need twenty pounds.'

'Is that all? I can ask Andrew to give it to you.'

'You'll do nothing of the sort!'

'My dear Lessie, he'd never miss it.'

Lessie got to her feet. 'Anna McCauley, if you dare to ask him for money for me, I'll – I'll never come back tae this house. D'you hear me?'

'For goodness sake, money's money. What does it matter who you get it from?'

'It matters tae me.' It was difficult enough to accept help from Davie and Miss Peden, but Lessie was damned if she would take charity from a man who knew her so vaguely that he would probably walk past her in the street without recognising her. 'I mean it, Anna. I'll not come back, not ever.'

'You couldnae turn your back on wee Dorothea, and her just getting to the interesting stage.'

'Yes I could.'

There was a short silence during which their eyes locked, Lessie's hard and determined; then Anna shrugged and pouted. 'Very well. But you're being very foolish. I don't think you want this shop as much as you say you do.'

Oh, I want it, Lessie wanted to say. I want it so badly that the fear of losing it haunts me every minute of my life. But she kept quiet, for Anna would never understand. As she sat down again and accepted a chocolate from the box by Anna's elbow she wondered yet again how she could ever have allowed herself to be drawn into Anna's web. The two of them were as alike as chalk and cheese, though Anna didn't seem to notice.

'It suits your face like that. I never thought a woman would look so beautiful with short hair.' Murdo reached out to touch it and the back of his hand brushed against Lessie's face. They had cycled up to the water filters again; this time the grass beneath their feet was rich and green and scattered liberally with white and purple clover. Lessie, embarrassed by his suddenly intent look, the way his hand lingered on her cheek, stooped to pick some clover, twisting it round in her fingers, staring down at it because otherwise she would have had to look at Murdo.

'I've been thinkin' about the shop an' you wantin' it so much,' his voice said from above her downbent head, 'an' I was wonderin' . . .' He paused, cleared his throat, then said stiffly, 'I could help ye tae take it over.'

'You've got enough with your mother and sister to look after. You can't go lending money to me. Besides, I'd not—'

'I wasnae thinking' o' lendin' it. I've got a bit saved up, an' we could live in the rooms at the back. An' wi' me workin' in the shipyard an' you managin' the shop we could dae well for ourselves.'

'We? Living in the back shop? Together?' Lessie stared up at him, the clover falling forgotten from her fingers. 'Murdo Carswell, what d'you think—'

'I'm talkin' o' marriage, Lessie. You an' me. I'd be a good husband tae Ian an' a good father tae you if – I mean, a good father tae him an' a good husband tae—' He stopped, utterly confused, then said, 'Dammit, Lessie, no need tae laugh at a man jist because he gets tongue-tied. I've never proposed marriage tae a woman afore. Oh dammit!' he said fiercely, his face crimson with embarrassment, and turned away to stare hard at the distant river and the familiar shipyard skeleton of cranes etched against the water.

'I'm not laughing at you, Murdo,' Lessie said, small-voiced, angry with herself for having belittled him. 'I just – you took me by surprise.'

'Ye must've known how I felt. Why else would I hae wanted tae keep seein' ye?'

'I knew you liked me, and I like you. But as for marriage – who wants to take on a widow with a child?'

'I do!' Murdo spun round, caught her in his arms before she could move back. 'I love you, Lessie Hamilton. I've watched ye struggle tae make ends meet an' I've wanted badly tae take the worry of it all away from ye, tae look after ye, an' the bairn as well. But it was too early tae tell ye. I was afraid o' frightin' ye, and losin' ye. Now's the right time – now, when we could take over the shop between us an' my wage could support us while ye find yer feet.'

'What would your mother say?'

'My mother?' he asked in bewilderment.

'We have to think of her.'

'No we don't. My father left her well provided for. She'll manage fine. An' she thinks a good deal o' ye. Lessie, don't turn me down. Ye care for me, don't ye?'

73

She looked up into his hazel eyes, usually carefree and brimming with amusement, but now pleading, afraid of rejection.

'You know I care for you,' she said, and his mouth took hers, preventing her from saying any more. She clung to him, closing her eyes, thinking of Donald. But Donald was dead and she was alive, still young and in need of love and loving and a future. Donald was in the cemetery but Murdo was here, holding her, offering her not only a way to obtain the shop but to know again a way of life that she had thought she had buried in the grave for all time when she buried her husband.

It all fell into place with an ease that told Lessie that it had surely been meant to happen. Mrs Carswell accepted the news that her son and Lessie Hamilton were to marry without making the fuss that Lessie had expected, and within a week or two of hearing about his sister's plans Davie found a room for himself in Port Glasgow, near to the engineering works.

'But there's no need for you to do that,' Lessie protested when he came home and told her. 'You can stay on with us. Murdo, tell him!'

'Of course ye're welcome, Davie,' Murdo said, but to Lessie's mind his voice lacked conviction.

Davie shook his head. 'There's not enough room for us all behind the shop. Anyway, married folk need to be on their own.'

'But Davie—'

He patted her arm reassuringly. 'It's best this way. Besides, I've got plans of my own. I've suggested tae Mr Beattie that he should only pay me enough tae meet my rent and my food. The rest o' my wages are goin' back intae the business. One day there'll be enough o' it tae pay for a junior partnership. Mr Beattie's agreed tae it.'

'God, man, o' course he's agreed!' Murdo said in horror. 'Ye're a fool, takin' less than the money ye're entitled tae! Ye're no' bein' paid what ye're worth as it is.'

'It's settled between him an' me.'

'But the man could cheat ye oot o' your wages an' no' gie ye anythin' in return.'

'Davie,' Lessie said nervously, suddenly aware that Murdo's words made sense, 'wouldn't it be better if—'

'It's all right, Lessie, I trust Mr Beattie an' he trusts me.'

'Ach, gang yer ain way,' Murdo said. 'but ye're a stubborn fool, Davie. Ye'd no' find me workin' for less than I was worth.'

'It'll work out well for me in the end, you'll see,' Davie insisted.

'At least stay with us so that I can make certain that you're eating enough.'

'I told you, I've already taken the room. An' I'll no' have you spendin' a penny o' your money – or your man's – on me.'

His voice was calm, and looking into his clear eyes Lessie knew that there was no turning him. For the first time she realised that her marriage and her venture into shopkeeping closed another door in her life. Never again would she and Davie be as close as they had been.

They were moving apart, emotionally as well as physically, and there was nothing she could do about it.

The MacKays handed over the shop and went off to Rothesay. The wedding date was set and Anna, after she had met and approved of Murdo, insisted on contributing the wedding gown. Lessie was rushed off her feet reorganising the shop and cleaning out the rooms behind it in readiness for the move. To her surprise Edith offered to help with the cleaning.

'Men are no good at it and there's no sense in asking Mam. She'd only have to bring Thomasina and her fingers would be into everything,' she said, brushing down the walls of the kitchen as though attacking a hated enemy. Peter and Ian were playing in a corner with some toy soldiers Peter had brought with him. 'And I don't see that long-nosed mother of Murdo's going down on her knees to scrub floors.'

'His sister Katherine's offered to help at nights, though. I'd not ask Mam anyway. She's still got that cough, for all that it's summer,' Lessie said from the depths of a cupboard, plunging her scrubbing brush into the pail and thinking with pleasure of the stone sink in the tiny back porch. It would be luxury to have her very own sink.

As she emerged from the cupboard, Edith swiped at another spider's web. 'They didn't keep this place very clean, did they?'

'They did their best. Mr McKay was an invalid, and his wife had more than enough to do looking after him and seeing to the shop as well.' Lessie emptied her pailful of dirty water into the sink and wiped her hands on her sacking apron as the street bell clanged. She had refused to close the shop, and spent each day dashing between it and the back rooms.

'I just hope that wee rascals like the one I saw in the shop thon day don't manage to rob you of every penny of profit while you're trying to do two jobs at once,' Edith said dourly when she reappeared.

'Och, don't worry about them. I've shifted the good biscuits to behind the counter and put the broken ones in a box at the street door. They can knock that one down to their hearts' content and buy the contents cheap, but the best biscuits are safe.'

'You've made a wise decision, Lessie,' Edith said unexpectedly. 'He seems like a good man, Murdo Carswell. You've been fortunate, finding two decent men. God knows there are few of them about and most of us,' she gave a loud disparaging sniff, 'fall foul of the wrong kind.'

Lessie pleated her apron between her fingers, idle for once, then said, 'I know Murdo's a good man, but it's not like the first time.'

'I doubt if it ever could be.'

'When I met Donald,' she said, remembering, smiling at the memory, 'when he first smiled at me, it was as though I'd been completely emptied inside then filled to the brim with warm golden sunshine. When I lost him most of the gold poured away but there was enough left to keep me warm, whatever happened. It's still with me. It'll always be with me. With Murdo there's a good feeling, but it's not like sunshine.

75

I suppose that'll never happen to me again. I suppose—'

'You're altogether too fluttery at times, Lessie. Don't let Murdo hear you talking like that or he'll mebbe have second thoughts about—'

'Look, Mama,' said Peter loudly, pointing. 'There's a baby spider playing in your hair.'

Edith screamed and began to scuttle round in circles, flapping her hands frantically in the air. Lessie stifled a giggle and ran to the rescue, all thoughts of Donald and the past swept aside.

Murdo's mother had graciously invited the Kirkwoods to high tea in her house following the marriage ceremony in the Carswells' minister's house. Only Edith, as best maid, and a shipyard friend of Murdo's as best man attended the ceremony. When the bridal party arrived at the house, the wave of relief from her relatives was so strong that Lessie could almost have touched it.

Her mother, with the faintly desperate look in her eyes that indicated that she hadn't had any of her 'medicine' for several hours, perched uncomfortably on the edge of the sofa, one hand gripping Thomasina, who shifted and squirmed restlessly by her side. Joseph and Archie had refused to attend, for they both hated family get-togethers, but Davie was there, handsome in his best suit, which had been brought out of the pawn for the occasion, and so was Aunt Marion, Barbara's sister. The table in the bay window was laden with salad and cold meats, cakes and biscuits, all presided over by a large silver teapot polished until it blazed in the sunlight.

'So there you are,' Mrs Carswell said as though she had been wondering where on earth they had got to. She came over to kiss her son and then her new daughter-in-law with cool lips that fluttered a fraction of an inch from their faces then withdrew. 'You look bonny, Lessie. D'you not think so, Mistress Kirkwood?'

Barbara's tired face lit up with a genuine smile as she looked at her daughter in the rose-coloured gown that was Anna's gift. 'Very bonny.'

'Thanks, Mam.' As her mother made no move towards her, Lessie went to the sofa, bent, and kissed Barbara's cheek. She felt awkward, because the Kirkwoods were not a demonstrative family,, but Mrs Carswell had kissed the bride – or made a pretence of it – and Lessie was determined that her own mother should not be left out.

'Me too, me too,' shrilled Thomasina. Barbara flinched and shushed her, but Lessie laughed and gave her little sister a hug and a smacking kiss. Ian, who had been hanging back, peering round his Uncle Davie's knees at this unexpectedly different mother in her pretty pink dress, lost his shyness and came scuttling to claim his own hug. Lessie picked him up and held him close. Today, at Edith's insistence, he and Peter were both in velvet suits. Beneath the soft material, Ian's wiry little body wriggled and moulded itself against Lessie's as it always did. Still holding him she turned, laughing, and saw Murdo watching them both. She held out a hand and he came to her. My husband, thought Lessie with contentment as their fingers entwined. My man.

He was summoned from her side almost at once to pour out the sherry wine that Mrs Carswell had bought so that the happy couple's health could be drunk. As her son poured, she told the company where she had bought the wine and how much it had cost her. Aunt Marion fluttered and cooed and admired and Mrs Carswell visibly warmed to her, while Barbara's eyes fastened greedily on the pale liquid splashing into elegant glasses, the price of which, Mrs Carswell informed them, she could only estimate since they'd been one of her own wedding gifts. When Barbara received her glass she clutched it, holding herself back with difficulty until the toast was made and she was free to drink. She meant to sip it, but before she could stop herself the glass, which held a pitifully small amount, was empty. Guiltily she glanced at her hostess but Mrs Carswell was too busy talking to Edith to notice and Davie had casually moved so that his body shielded his mother from Mrs Carswell's view.

Lessie watched the little scene, her heart going out to her mother. She wondered again what terrible thing could have happened to make Barbara, the most upright of women, turn to drink as she had. Deep inside her mother there must be a reservoir of unhappiness, hidden away and never shared with anyone, least of all her daughters.

'Thank you, Davie,' she murmured to her brother when he drifted her way, collecting empty glasses. 'Mam needs folk like you to care for her.'

'She cared for us when we were wee and helpless,' he said quietly, then, 'I hope you'll be happy, Lessie. You deserve it.'

'I will be.' The crease between her brows, the crease that had come to stay, deepened. 'You're looking thinner. Are you not eating properly?'

'I'm fine. Don't you start worrying about me.'

'Well, we'd best sit in and eat,' Mrs Carswell shooed them all towards the food, told them where to sit, and urged them to help themselves. Thomasina looked at the food, her eyes like saucers, and reached out greedily. Her mother, ever watchful, caught her hand in mid-stretch.

'Sit by me and be a good lassie, now,' she whispered, tormented with worry in case her beloved youngest child humiliated them all in front of Mrs Carswell and spoiled Lessie's wedding day.

'That's the prettiest dress I've ever seen, Lessie.' Katherine Carswell's eyes rested enviously on the pale pink satin gown, high-necked and trimmed with rose-pink silk net. The skirt, falling at the back in a slight train from a rose-pink bow, rustled slightly as Lessie took her seat. Smiling at her new sister-in-law, Lessie suddenly wished that Anna and Miss Peden, who had given them a handsome china figurine of Rabbie Burns, her favourite poet, could have been there. But as Mrs Carswell had arranged what she called the wedding breakfast, Mrs Carswell was the one who had the right to decide who should attend.

Mrs Carswell senior, Lessie corrected herself, looking down at the new ring on her finger. There were two Mrs Carswells now. It would take time to get used to not being Lessie Hamilton. Her mother-in-law was indulging in her favourite topic, telling everyone what the cold tongue and the cold ham cost, and Lessie wondered if Murdo and Katherine had had to go through this recital every time they sat down at their mother's table. She looked at Murdo, by her side, and he grinned and whispered, 'I'll be glad when this is all over an' we can be alone.'

Barbara took very little food onto her plate, picking at it, her eyes wandering now and again to the sideboard where the half-empty bottle of sherry wine stood. Most of her energy, though, was taken up with making sure that Thomasina behaved herself. Mrs Carswell, Lessie realised with a stab of anger, had ignored the little girl, though she had fussed over Peter and Ian. When they all left the table she drew Thomasina into the circle of her arm and talked to her, letting her sister finger the pretty wedding gown and the tiny pearl earrings that Murdo had given her as a wedding gift.

The party broke up not long after the meal was over, on the pretext that the children were in danger of becoming over-excited and needed to get to their beds. Barbara and Edith and Aunt Marion left together, taking Ian with them. He was going to spend the night with his grandmother. Davie ambled off in the direction of his tiny rented room, and after Mrs Carswell had firmly rejected Lessie's offer of help with the dishes, the bride and groom were free to go to their new home behind the shop in the Vennel.

The shop, which had been closed for the day, was waiting quietly for them in the midsummer evening dusk. Lessie sniffed with pleasure at the mixed smell of meal and tobacco as she went in. She loved the knowledge, each time she stepped into the shop, that it was hers. Hers and Murdo's, but hers to run, because he already had his job at the shipyard.

He locked the door carefully behind them as Lessie moved, sure-footed in the gloom, between sacks and boxes and behind the counter to the door that led to their home. In there, the smell was of paint and carbolic and cleanliness. The best of her furniture and some pieces Murdo had bought shone a friendly welcome at her as her husband struck a match and the gas mantles on the wall came to life with a soft plop.

'Would you like a cup of tea?'

Murdo came to her and took her into his arms. 'You know better than that, Lessie Carswell! I want something a lot better than tea.'

'You mean more of your mother's sherry wine?' she teased him, then squealed as his teeth nipped at her earlobe.

'I mean,' he said, then whispered into her ear, his lips tickling.

'Murdo Carswell!' She pushed him away, fisted her hands on her hips, did her best to look severe, though her whole body was tingling. 'I'll have you know that I'm a respectable married woman!'

'Ach, I'll no' tell anyone if you don't,' said Murdo and swooped, scooping her off her feet and whirling to deposit her on the box bed set into the kitchen alcove. The springs creaked, then creaked again as he joined her.

78

'Confound it, I'll have tae find a way o' stoppin' that noise afore young Ian moves into the next room,' he said, his fingers busy with the buttons down the front of her gown. The bodice was half opened and the soft warm curves of her breasts exposed when she pushed him away and sat up.

'Murdo, let me take my nice gown off properly.'

'Ye're a terrible tease!' He rested back on his elbows, watching as she scrambled from the bed.

'I made my nightgown specially for tonight.'

'It'll not stay on for long.'

She paused on her way into the inner room and threw a smile over her shoulder at him. 'I'd be disappointed in you if it did – a young lad like you.'

His laughter followed her into the smaller room and made her fingers shake with impatience as she took off her gown and her underclothes, poured water from a jug into a basin and washed herself, then slipped into the nightgown that had been left out in readiness that morning. It was made of muslin, and in the spare moments she had managed to squeeze from preparing the living quarters and running the shop, she had embroidered and tucked it and edged the sleeves and neck with a few scraps of lace Edith had given her.

She picked up the long drawers that lay beside it, pursed her mouth, then tossed the drawers down again, thinking wantonly of Murdo's surprise and pleasure when he discovered that she had come to him with only the nightgown on. She brushed her short hair until it crackled then opened the door.

The kitchen was empty, and from the little scullery that housed the sink came the sound of spluttering and splashing. Swiftly Lessie climbed into bed and drew the blankets round her shoulders. Murdo came through a moment later, in a nightshirt and with his fair hair damp at the front. He stooped and kissed her gently and she said, 'I wish I could have had my hair long over the pillow.'

'You're beautiful just the way you are.' He bent over her, carefully unfastening the buttons she had just fastened down the front of her gown. His hand slipped inside and held one breast for a moment, squeezing it gently and rousing her with startling suddenness. Then he turned away swiftly, put out the lights, and came to her.

Lessie had forgotten what it was like to feel a man's solid body dipping the mattress as he got into bed. She had forgotten how wonderful masculine arms felt, reaching through the darkness for her and claiming her. She had forgotten the pleasure of mingled breath on a pillow, the murmuring of private loving words in the darkness. Now, in Murdo's arms, she wondered how she could have borne to be without the intimacies of marriage for so long.

She moved willingly into his embrace, touching him, feeling the deep trembling that shook his body, the blessing of his hands on her skin, drawing the nightdress hem up from knees to thigh, from thigh to hip. She smiled in the darkness when his hand stopped suddenly and he caught his breath then gave a murmur of delight at her

79

unexpected nudity beneath the gown.

Then she raised her hips from the mattress to allow the gown to be drawn up further, gasping at the touch of his fingers and then his lips on her breasts.

The whispering stopped, then the silence of the room was broken by scrambling and creaking as Lessie sat up and drew the nightgown over her head, tossing it carelessly away to land on the floor. It had served its purpose. Murdo writhed and twisted in the bed, too impatient to sit up and take off his own nightshirt properly. She helped him, and at last the cumbersome garment was in her hands and sailing off into the dark.

Then their bodies were touching, lithe and young and impatient. Murdo raised himself above her, his broad muscular body lowering itself on to hers. And at last he was inside her and she was clutching at his hair, clawing his back, crying out in her ecstasy.

At last she was a woman again.

10

Jess Carswell, born on the day the Boer War ended, was as pretty as a blue-eyed rosy-cheeked flower. Her head was covered by a thick mass of dark hair and her soft full mouth and heart-shaped little face captivated everyone except her half-brother Ian who, four months past his third birthday, had little time for babies.

Murdo, who had made his preference for a son clear during Lessie's pregnancy, was spellbound by his daughter from the moment he first saw her. 'We'll have a laddie the next time,' he said, stroking the tiny soft face with his finger. 'In the meantime, this one'll suit me fine.'

Lessie, pale and weak from a long birthing, winced at the thought of having another child and wondered if she and Murdo were going to find themselves at odds over their views on the size of their family. She had always loved Ian, and she already loved this new baby, but she loved her shop as well and she had no intention of giving it up in order to raise a large brood. They had just finished paying off their debt to Miss Peden, and she was impatient already to be up and about again and in the shop. She knew, from the gossip she had heard in the shop, what women could do to prevent unwanted pregnancies. She had heard about vinegar soaked sponges and pessaries made from flour and margarine, and was determined to make certain that there were no more children until she had made a success of the shop. As for Murdo, 'What a man doesnae ken doesnae hurt him,' one of the women advocating home remedies to prevent children had once said in the shop. 'It's us that has tae carry an' bear an' tend tae the bairns, an' the decisions should be oors an' a'.' And Lessie agreed with her.

Anna came to inspect the new baby within a few days of the birth. She swept into the room behind the shop, resplendent in a blue corded silk gown with broad bands of cream lace let into the bodice, a pert little hat trimmed with a large blue bow and a curling feather perched on her red hair, and cast a brief glance into the cradle where Jess slept.

'She's beautiful, but then who would expect otherwise with such parents? You and me,' she said, seating herself in a comfortable chair and drawing off her gloves, 'are fortunate in having handsome men.'

'You think Murdo's handsome?'

'Oh yes, even though I don't think he approves of me.' Then she held up a slender hand as Lessie, blushing, started to speak. 'Don't trouble to deny it, I can see the truth in your eyes. You never were able to hide your thoughts, Lessie. Not that your husband's approval matters. I get on very well without it.'

'Would you like some tea, Anna? If Elma isn't too busy in the shop she'll make it for us.'

'Don't trouble yourself, I can't stay long.' Anna cast a look round the room. 'Is there nobody to see to you?'

'Edith comes in when she can, and my mother too, though I don't like to ask either of them. They've got enough to do. There's Elma, but the shop keeps her busy. I don't know what we'd have done without her. I'll be up and about in a few days anyway.'

'I envy you sometimes, Lessie. You've always got things to see to, things to do. Times I find it hard to fill the hours.'

'You've got Dorothea.'

'The maidservant sees to her. I'd not know how to manage her if Molly wasn't there.' Anna rose and moved restlessly about the room, picking items up, studying them without seeing them, putting them down again. 'I've no friends except you, and I've scarcely seen you since you took over this shop. And now that his uncle's died and he's in sole charge of the refinery, Andrew spends far too much time away from Greenock. Sometimes I think that he only visits to see Dorothea.' Her mouth hardened slightly. 'He worships that child – and spoils her, to my mind. Even when I do see him he can talk of nothing but sugar and the changes he hopes to make in his dull refinery.'

'Davie tells me that Mr Warren has asked him to suggest ways of improving some of the machinery. Was that your idea?'

Anna was by the window now. She peered out into the small back yard where Murdo had planted some vegetables and Lessie had installed a small flower border. 'Your garden looks pretty,' she said vaguely. 'I believe I did mention that your brother was an engineer and might be of help to him.'

'It was kind of you.' Then, as Anna turned back into the room and Lessie saw the shadow in her eyes, the new droop to her mouth, she added, 'Surely you could find some friends to visit and to entertain?'

The lovely mouth lifted to shape itself into a faint ironic smile. 'The sort of people I'd want to know have no intention of mixing socially with a kept woman. As for the rest,' she shrugged dismissively. 'No, I must just look forward to the day when Andrew ends his wandering and settles back in Greenock. If that day ever comes.'

After she left, the room was fragrant with the scent of roses, but Lessie's spirits were low. She lay back against the pillow, wondering why she always felt somehow responsible for Anna's happiness. The woman had everything, and yet in many ways she seemed to have nothing, whereas Lessie's life was full to overflowing. She had two children and a home and a husband to care for now, not to mention worrying over her mother's deteriorating health. If anyone had a claim on what little time Lessie had to spare, it was Barbara, thinner by the week, coughing all the time now, almost dragging herself around the house and out to the shops. Or Miss Peden, still sturdily independent, but looking older and more frail than she had last year.

Then there was the shop. By good fortune a woman who lived nearby had offered her services during Lessie's pregnancy, and proved to be a reliable and hard-working assistant. Without Elma Buchanan the shop would have had to be closed during Lessie's enforced absence. She had worked behind the counter until the first pains gripped her and sent her, gasping and clutching at furniture for support, to her bed. Elma, tall and angular, grim-faced but scrupulously fair and polite enough to those customers who in her opinion deserved it, had sent for the midwife, seen to Ian, and kept the shop going while Lessie was in bed. Murdo attended to the business of buying in stock from the retailers, dealt with the account books, and spent as much time as he could in the shop when he wasn't in the shipyard. The small wages Elma received were a drain on their resources, but it was better to have the shop bringing in a little money than none at all.

'Thinks she's a fine lady these days, that Anna McCauley,' Elma announced now, tramping into the room and rousing Lessie from the light doze she had drifted into. 'But at the end o' the road we a' find that we've no' travelled far from where we started. Will ye tak' a cup o' tea?'

'If you've got time tae make one.'

'Aye, it's quiet enough oot there for the moment.' Elma measured tea into the pot, added water from the kettle simmering on the range, and went into the scullery to refill the kettle. On her way back she peered into the crib.

'Sound asleep, bless her bonny wee face.' The words were gentle, and so were her eyes, but her voice was as usual – flat and matter-of-fact. Watching her setting out cups, Lessie wondered if Elma would have been different if she had known love and a home and children of her own. It was hard to imagine her in a man's arms. Plain and dour, she lived with her sister, her unemployed brother-in-law, and their five children in two tiny rooms. Elma enjoyed working in the shop and never minded how late she worked. 'It's no pleasure tae go back tae that hoose,' she told Lessie once. 'Fightin' frae mornin' tae night ower money an' the bairns – an' ower me, I ken that fine. If I'd somewhere else tae go I'd be oot o' there today. It's no pleasure tae be bidin' whaur ye'r no' wanted.' She drank her tea standing by the door, ready to dart through it if a customer appeared. 'I like the way ye've got the shop arranged. It's better than the way the McKays had it.'

'It's just a question of finding out how things should be done as I go along.' Lessie sipped at the tea, strong, hot, with plenty of milk and sugar in it. 'I'm missing it.'

'It'll be good tae see ye back behind the counter. Everyone says that,' Elma informed her, then the bell above the street door gave a brisk ting, and she set down her cup and stamped out to attend to the customer.

Despite her pretty little face, Jess turned out to be a baby with a will of her own. Unlike Ian she demanded attention, doubling tiny fists and roaring out her anger if she felt that she was being neglected. She liked to linger over feeds and Lessie found herself giving more time to her little daughter than she had planned.

'It's just her way.' Murdo poked a fond finger into the baby's fist, delighting over the way her own tiny fingers curled possessively round it. 'The shop can wait for you. Elma does well enough, though a smile for the customers now and again wouldnae go amiss. An' I can manage.'

'You've enough to do with your own work without having to stand in the shop in the evenings and on Saturday afternoons.'

Murdo shrugged. 'The football season's over so I don't mind givin' up my Saturdays. I'm quite enjoying being a shopkeeper.'

It couldn't be said that Ian was enjoying the changes in their lives, Lessie thought guiltily, remembering the days when it had been just the two of them and she had always had time, between helping in the shop and scrubbing stairs, to spend with her son. He had taken to Murdo from the start and throughout the winter the two of them had gone off to the Saturday football match, Ian riding high on Murdo's shoulder, coming back with his small face glowing from fresh air and excitement. Now, unless Davie dropped in to take him for an outing, he was confined to the pavement outside the shop and the yard at the back. But he was an easygoing little boy and he bore the new limitations stoically, apart from an occasional disgusted glance at the lacy crib when his half-sister started squalling again.

The crib had arrived from Anna's house, together with a bundle of clothes and shawls. 'Now that Dorothea's grown out of them you might as well have the use of them,' she'd said carelessly when she brought them. Lessie had fretted in case Murdo objected, but to her surprise he had been quite pleased.

'It'll save us a deal o' money,' he pointed out. 'An' God knows we need tae save all we can if you intend tae pay the McKays off within the year as you promised.'

Murdo, Lessie had discovered soon after their marriage, had inherited his mother's irritating habit of pricing everything – the food they ate, the clothes they wore, even toys that he himself bought for Ian. But otherwise he was a good man, an attentive, loving husband and a fine father to Ian as well as Jess. And she could never have saved enough to pay off her debt to Miss Peden and to give the McKays the rest of their money without his wages coming in. She could surely put up with one little flaw, she told herself as she laid Jess down in her crib and prodded the potatoes with a fork to see if they were ready.

At the table Murdo was calculating the overall cost of the home-made soup he was eating, smugly taking into consideration the saving made by using ingredients from their own shop. Ian, his audience, had long since lost interest and was busily breaking off lumps of bread and dropping them into his bowl, turning the soup into a satisfying mushy mess.

Jess was a full seven weeks old before Lessie finally got back behind the shop counter one Saturday afternoon. At first Murdo protested, but she waved his arguments aside.

'Ian's fair dying to get out with you again. Take him from under my feet and Elma and me'll manage fine.'

Elma had agreed to stay on full-time until a routine had been estab-
lished. Then she would go back to helping out only when she was
needed. The welcome Lessie received from her regular customers
touched and warmed her.

'My, Mistress Carswell, but it's guid tae see ye back where ye
belong,' the first woman through the door said, adding hastily, with
a look at Elma, 'Though we've been very well seen tae, o' course.'

Elma sniffed, but said nothing.

'Ye're lookin' that well, tae. Hoo's the wee yin?'

'She's fine, Mrs Douglas.' Lessie poured sugar crystals from the
gleaming scoop into a sheet of paper that she had deftly twisted into
a cone, then tucked in the top and handed it over.

'An' I'll hae twa pound o' lentils.'

Ian, waiting for Murdo, was at his favourite game, pushing his small
fist hard into the side of the lentil sack then withdrawing it quickly
and watching the dent he had made disappear just as fast. Gently
Lessie set him aside, taking time to smooth his tousled red hair, and
began to scoop out the lentils. Murdo came from the back room and
Ian claimed him at once and led him out onto the street, chattering
excitedly. Mrs Douglas watched them go, then asked, 'Will yer man
be workin' on in the shop noo that ye're back?'

'Mebbe. Now and again when I'm busy with the wee one.'

'Oh aye?' The woman's voice was suddenly flat. 'I'm a wee bittie
short the day. Will ye pit it in the book for me, dearie?'

'I'll do that.'

Lessie laughed as she and Elma watched the woman waddle from
the shop a few minutes later. 'Some women hate to be served by a
man. I mind myself when I first came to live in the Vennel, always
hoping it would be Mrs McKay at the counter when I came in here.
As if it makes any difference!'

'It does tae some folk.' Elma's voice sounded just as flat as Mrs
Douglas's had been.

Lessie fetched out the big black-covered tick book from its usual
place beneath the counter and opened it to record Mrs Douglas's purchases. Before putting it away she ran her eyes down the row of
shillings and pence, a few written in the assistant's awkward hand,
most entered in Murdo's firm black script. 'Folk round here must've
been celebrating the end of the South African war. They've been buying
more than usual, surely.'

'No' that I've noticed.' Elma turned aside to dust the tops of some
jars of preserves. The tick book, a fixture in every small shop, was
used to record sums due by the many customers who, through unemployment or illness or grindingly low wages, were unable to pay for
goods as they got them. Lessie, well taught by the McKays, dealt with
it carefully, forcing herself to turn away those least deserving, least
likely to honour their debts when a little money came in. Even so,
Murdo had objected to the use of the book at first, seeing it as the
road to ruin.

'Look at this,' his finger had stabbed down one page, 'the same folk comin' in again an' again an' no' payin' a penny. Most of them never will, an' then where'll we be?'

'They have to live, and they have to feed their bairns.'

'Exactly. They have tae feed their bairns and we've tae feed ours. It's no' our responsibility tae put food in their children's bellies. I pay my way, why shouldn't they?'

'Och, they'll pay, you don't have to worry about that. The folk round here might be poor but they're not dishonest. They don't like being in debt. They'll pay!'

And pay they did; sixpence here, a shilling there, striving all the time to clear themselves of debt, but never quite succeeding. Only a few of them had ever let Lessie down and when she forced her natural sympathy down and refused, hating herself, to give these few any more tick, they usually cursed her with automatic fluency then took themselves off to find another shopkeeper who would, for a short while, allow them to buy on credit.

People came and went over the next hour, then a little girl, prim and sedate in her dark smock, her hair scraped back until her eyes were almost pulled up at the corners, arrived to buy a pound of best tea.

'How's your mother, Mary?' Lessie smiled down at the serious little face barely visible above the counter, inwardly promising herself that never would her Jess be robbed of her childhood the way this child had been. Like Thomasina, Mary was a late baby born to a middle-aged mother who was now busily raising her to be a middle-aged child.

'She's fine, Mistress Carswell. An' she says,' said Mary severely, 'that she'd be obliged if ye'd weigh oot the tea afore ye pit it intae the paper poke, no' efter.'

Lessie blinked down at her and was stung into retorting sharply, 'I always do.'

'Aye, but yer man doesnae,' Mary snapped back. 'My mither says she's no' gaun tae pay for the paper too. I've tae be sure tae look.'

Lessie swallowed hard, torn between anger and amusement at the thought of this child, scarcely thirty-six inches high, lecturing her. She poured fine dark tea leaves onto the scale, aware of the little girl's pale eyes watching intently until the pound weight on the other side had swung level.

'Does that suit you?'

'Aye,' said Mary, and when the tea had been packed neatly and the paper 'poke' stowed safely in her pocket, she handed over the money and departed, straightbacked.

'Did you ever hear the like?' Lessie asked Elma and the woman she was serving. Elma said nothing; the customer's eyes slid away from Lessie's and she said evasively, 'Some shopkeepers weigh the paper in with the tea or the sugar an' folk don't feel they're gettin' what they paid for.'

'Mebbe so, but it never happened here while the McKays had the place, and it won't while I'm running it.'

'If ye say so, Mistress Carswell,' said the woman, and scuttled from the shop just as Jess's voice was raised in hunger in the back room.

Lessie's tiredness was offset by her pleasure over the customers' delight at seeing her back in the shop. Perhaps it was because she had been away for too long or perhaps it was the fatigue that blinded her to the true meaning behind the effusive welcome she received from one woman after another. But not until late afternoon when old Cathy Petrie came in did Lessie find out why they were so pleased to welcome her back, and what had been going on in her absence.

'It's this week's saxpence for the tick book,' the old woman said humbly, handing over a coin that was hot from the clutch of her hand.

'Thanks, Cathy.' Lessie opened the book, found the entry, and was about to note down the payment in the 'paid' column when she stopped and looked again at the full entry. The smile faded from her lips.

'Cathy, all that's down in the book for you is a packet of tea and a bag of oatmeal and you've paid two shillings off on them already.'

'Aye, I managed to get some cleanin' work at yin o' the shops, but I couldnae mak' enough tae pay it all off, so Mister Carswell said he'd take saxpence a week till I wis clear. Is there somethin' wrang?' The watery old eyes filled with apprehension.

A cold hand seemed to grip at Lessie's stomach as she looked at the words and figures written in her husband's hand then ran her eyes swiftly over the other entries, her mind adding and subtracting. 'No, there's nothing wrong,' she managed to say calmly despite her growing consternation.

'Here then.' Cathy pushed the sixpence at her. Lessie, aware of Elma's close scrutiny, took the coin and put it into the drawer behind the counter then drew a deep hard line across the entry.

'That's you paid it all off.'

'B-but Mister Carswell said last week that there wis—'

'Mr Carswell made a mistake, Cathy. It's all paid off. Here.' Lessie came round the corner swiftly, snatching items from the shelves and pushing them into the old woman's hands. 'Here's some tobacco for your man's pipe – and a packet of biscuits and a jar of preserves. Elma, hand me that loaf.'

Cathy looked in horror at her burden. 'But Mistress Carswell, I cannae afford—'

'They're gifts. Off you go, Cathy, and God give you both health to enjoy them. Good day to you.' Lessie almost pushed her out and whirled to see Elma disappearing through the house door. 'Elma Buchanan, you get back here this minute!'

'I think I heard the wean,' Elma said, and kept going. Lessie pushed down the snib on the door; before going into the back shop a sudden suspicion caused her to run her fingers beneath the pan suspended on the weighing scales. A greasy lump of bacon fat dropped from the underside of the pan into her palm. She stared down at it, chewing her lip. It was the custom of unscrupulous shopkeepers to stick a lump of fat beneath their scale pans so that customers received short weight.

87

It was a nasty, deceitful trick that Lessie had sworn never to play on the people who frequented her shop.

'What if a customer comes in?' Elma quavered as her employer closed the kitchen door firmly behind them.

'I've locked the street door. Now, what's been going on?' She folded her arms and waited; although she was a good six inches smaller and about two stones lighter than Elma, the other woman retreated across the room as though afraid that she might be attacked. 'Just what have you and my husband been up to while I've been in here?'

'Mistress Carswell! If you're saying that—'

'Don't pretend you don't know what I mean, Elma Buchanan! Every one of these entries in the tick book are for more money than the goods cost.'

'It wis Mister Carswell that wis in charge, no' me. It's him ye should be speirin'.'

'Mr Carswell's not here, but you are, and you're not getting out of this room until you tell me the truth!'

'All I know is that he telt me tae add a penny on here an' a penny on there when I wrote in the book. When folks argued aboot it he said it wis tae make up for the inconvenience o' havin' tae wait for the payment. He said that a' the shopkeepers dae it.'

'Did he tell you to weigh the tea and sugar in the wrappings as well?' Lessie tossed the lump of bacon fat on the table. 'And did you know the scales had been weighted?'

Elma's face went dusky red. 'Mistress Carswell, it's no' my place tae argue we' whit yer man decides,' she said, her voice pleading. 'I need the money I earn here. I have tae dae whit I'm telt, whether it's you or him that does the tellin'.'

Jess stirred and whimpered. All at once Lessie felt very tired. 'All right, Elma, nobody's blaming you. But from now on we go back to the way things were before, d'ye hear me? Go on home now, I'll not be opening the shop again today.'

She had to wait until both children were settled for the night before she spoke to Murdo. He and Ian had come back from an afternoon spent down at the river's edge, watching the boats passing, throwing stones into the water, fishing with string and twigs. They arrived home hungry and happy. Their happiness made things all the worse for Lessie; she was on edge all evening. As soon as she was sure that Ian was asleep in the inner room, she faced her husband, the open tick book in her hands. 'What's been going on?'

He glanced at the figures, all scored out now and with the correct amounts written in beside them, and shrugged. 'Everyone charges a wee bit for givin' credit.'

'The McKays didn't. I don't.'

'An' look what happened to the McKays – livin' out the rest o' their lives on the charity o' relatives. Lessie, we're no' runnin' a shop for the benefit of those who havenae the money tae buy what they need.'

'I told you, they pay when they can. There's very few that don't.'

'An' each time someone doesnae pay, each time someone steals from us – for that's what they're doin' – we're expected tae take the loss an' say nothin'? We're surely entitled tae take a penny or two from the others tae cover the losses.'

'It's not their fault that some folk are dishonest.'

'It's no' mine either. But the money has tae come from somewhere. We've all got tae earn as much as we can, as best we can.'

Lessie stared at her husband, shocked by his refusal to see that he had wronged her customers. 'And what about this business of weighing wrapped goods so that you provide a wee bit less for the same money? And the weight on the bottom of the scale pan?'

'For God's sake, woman, a few grains o' sugar, a few leafs o' tea! Who's tae miss that?'

'We agreed before we got married that the shop was tae be my concern. It was tae be run my way. An' I'm not goin' tae make myself rich by clawin' my way ontae the backs o' poor souls like Cathy Petrie that have less than we have ourselves.'

'But that's how the rich become rich! D'you no' understand that I want tae make enough money tae get us out o' this place. I want tae give you an' the weans a nice house, everythin' that you could wish for.'

A sudden memory of Donald saying laughingly, 'This time next year' swept over her. But Donald wouldn't have cheated folk to make the money he needed.

'I'll not condone dishonesty, Murdo, not for any reason.'

His face suddenly dark with anger, Murdo snatched up his jacket and strode to the door.

'Where are you going at this time of night?'

'Out, before I forget mysel' an' take my hand across yer face for what ye just said tae me,' said Murdo thickly, and disappeared into the dimness of the shop. She heard the bell jangle then jangle again as he slammed the street door shut, rousing both children from their sleep.

He didn't come home until late. Lessie had wept, dried her eyes and gone to bed to lie sleepless, wondering if he was going to come back at all. It was a relief to hear the bell, then Murdo cursing softly as he bumped into something. She lay listening to the sounds of him undressing in the dark, then a waft of cold air brushed her back as he lifted the blankets and the mattress dipped beneath his big body.

He whispered her name and she turned to him at once, eager to make up the worst quarrel they had had. His breath was soured with the taint of whisky, but his mouth was warm and eager on hers, his hands demanding, his body taut and hungry. They made love fiercely, silently, smothering their cries against each other for fear of disturbing the children. Then naked, entwined, they slept.

The next morning Murdo was his usual cheerful self. They dressed the children in their best clothes and visited his mother, then walked to the water filters above the town, Jess gurgling in her pram, Ian galloping ahead on an imaginary horse. They were a happy family once more.

89

Lessie took over the running of the shop again after that and there was no more bacon fat, no more extra pennies added to the tick book, and no more sullen stares from aggrieved customers. Murdo's misdeeds were never again mentioned, and it wasn't until a long time later that Lessie realised that he had never actually admitted that he had done anything wrong.

11

'I drove past your house yesterday,' Anna said casually, her eyes and hands intent on the task in hand. She was carefully wrapping a large multi-coloured velvet ball, a gift to mark little Jess Carswell's first birthday.

'You did what?' Andrew Warren, sprawled in an easy chair by the fireplace, sat upright, almost dislodging Dorothea, who perched on his knee. She gasped then giggled as he caught and held her, believing that he was playing a game with her.

'Anna, you promised me—'

'I promised you that I'd never try to speak to your lady wife or your children. I promised that I'd never go to your door or to your refinery. But surely even the Warrens don't own the road outside their house?'

'Why choose to drive along that particular road?'

'Dorothea and I wanted some fresh air. We went along the waterfront as far as McInroy's Point, then we turned and drove back. Dorothea enjoyed herself. Didn't you, my pet?'

'Yeth, Mama.' Dorothea, busily trying to undress the doll that Andrew had brought back from his recent trip to Liverpool, answered automatically and without interest. Andrew lifted her to the floor and put the doll into her arms.

'Run out into the garden and show dolly the pretty flowers,' he suggested, and the little girl hurried off obediently.

'I saw your son and daughter – your elder daughter,' Anna corrected herself. 'They had been out for a ride too, in their little dog-cart. Such pretty children. The boy will set hearts fluttering one day, just like his father.'

Then, as he said nothing but just sat there, watching her through narrowed eyes, she suddenly pushed the wrapped gift aside and said in a burst of angry words, 'It's us – it's me and Dorothea – that should be with you in your grand house instead of hiding away here!'

'You know that's not possible. We agreed at the beginning—'

'Oh, the beginning!' Anna said stormily. 'I was grateful to you then. I'd have agreed to anything to get out of that rat's nest I lived in. But now I want more, Andrew. I need more!'

'Anna – my dear . . .' He rose and went across to her, but when he tried to draw her into his arms she pulled back.

'I'm not your dear. She is – that woman who lives in your house and bears your name. I've been patient for long enough.' The thoughts

91

that had been building up in her mind since Dorothea's birth over two years earlier broke free. 'I've been patient, Andrew. I've waited, and still she lives in your house.'

'Madeleine is my wife. Martin is my heir.'

'And Dorothea? Is she nothing to you?'

'You know that I adore her.'

'Yes, you do, don't you? Sometimes I think you only come here to see Dorothea.'

'That's untrue. I come to see you both as often as I can.'

'Not often enough!'

'For God's sake, Anna, I'm away from Greenock a lot. I've got a refinery to run, customers to seek. Madeleine and the twins see as little of me as you do.'

'Not quite, surely.' She broke away from beneath his hands, paced the floor, the skirt of her stylish dress making a swishing sound as she made the sharp turn again and again. 'You spend your nights with her – most of them. And she's the one with the right to go about the town with her head held high and folk bowing and scraping to her because she's Mistress Andrew Warren. But not me! I must hide away here, pretend that you mean nothing to me. And what about my child?'

'Dorothea will never want for anything. I told you that the day I found out that you were carrying her.'

She turned, and he thought that she had never been more beautiful than she was now, with her violet eyes burning, her red hair glowing about her perfect face. Motherhood and maturity had improved Anna's looks instead of diminishing them. 'Divorce her, Andrew. Marry me.'

He stared at her in dismay. 'I can't do that.'

'You can. You can do whatever you want. She's got money of her own – a wealthy father, I've heard. And she hates Scotland. Let her go back to her own people, Andrew.' She came to him, put her hands on his arm. The scent of her perfume surrounded him as though the two of them were in a rose garden. 'Then we can be together, you and me and Dorothea.'

He stood motionless, unable to say what she wanted to hear. The light died from her face and she stepped back. 'You care more for her than you do for me.'

'She's my wife, can you not understand that?' Andrew tried again to take her into his arms and was shrugged away. 'Anna, you must see that things have to be left as they are.'

'If she died,' Anna said in a hard, cold voice, her back towards him, 'would you wed me?'

'What's the sense in talking like—'

'Or would I not be good enough for you? Am I just your whore, Andrew?'

'Mind your tongue, woman!

'You've not answered my question,' she said relentlessly, then as he did not reply, 'Go away. Go home to your lady wife and your son and heir.'

'Anna—'

The door slammed behind her and he heard the patter of her feet on the stairs. For a moment he stood undecided, then shrugged. He well knew Anna's tempers, though there never had been a scene such as this one before. She was best left to her own devices. He let himself out of the house and went round to the back garden where Dorothea was sitting on the grass picking golden-hearted daisies and tucking them into the wide blue sash round the new doll's waist.

Andrew watched her for a moment and wished that he could commission a portrait of her just as she was then, in her pretty frilled white dress, her mouth pursed, long lashes brushing pink cheeks, his dark hair, but with Anna's auburn showing in deep red glints, framing her perfect little face. She looked up, suddenly aware that she wasn't alone, and the daisies were forgotten as she scrambled to her feet, beaming, and ran to him. Heedless of what the grass might do to his dove-grey trousers, Andrew dropped to his knees and caught her in his arms.

'Papa's going away now. Be a good girl and look after your mama while I'm gone. Promise?'

Dorothea nodded and he buried his face for a moment in her soft curly hair, kissed her smooth round cheek. This love-child had given him more pleasure in her two years of life than either of the children he had fathered on Madeleine.

Dorothea, tired of being hugged, squirmed free and went back to pick up her doll. 'Pretty dolly.'

'Not as pretty as you. You're the prettiest little girl in the whole world,' said Andrew, and wondered wryly what his employees and his business colleagues would think if they saw how he, a grown man, doted on this little scrap of a thing.

Anna watched from the open window above, half-hidden behind the curtain in case Andrew looked up. Not that he would, she thought bitterly. He was too engrossed in his precious daughter to care about her. She saw him hold the little girl close and was engulfed by a wave of jealousy so strong that it made her gasp.

She turned away from the window, her arms wrapped tightly about her body, suddenly feeling lonelier than she had felt in many years.

'You've done a good job, Kirkwood,' Andrew said with satisfaction. 'It's running as smoothly as it did before.'

Davie acknowledged the praise with a brief nod as he watched the centrifugal machine, one of three on that particular floor of the refinery. Near the ceiling a large hopper received the massecuite – the sugar and syrup mixture – from the vacuum pans on the floor above. The mixture ran into the centrifugal pans that separated the syrup from the crystals. The great machines set up a throbbing in the floor and the walls, and the heavy sweet smell turned Davie's stomach, more used to the smell of machine oil. He wondered how the refinery workers could bear to be in such an atmosphere all day and every day.

'Aye, she seems to be fine now.' A carefully casual tone hid his pride in his work. Centrifugal machines were notorious for causing trouble;

if they weren't charged at the correct speed the baskets started swinging and toppling from their flexible mountings. If the fault wasn't discovered in time and the machine shut down, the basket could slam into the outer monitor case and wreck the entire machine.

The two men, Andrew the taller by a few inches, walked towards the wooden staircase, Davie studying the other machines intently as he passed them, his eyes and ears attuned to the slightest deviation in their rhythm. When they had gained the stairs and started down to the ground floor he said bluntly, 'These machines are old. They'll soon need replacing.'

'I know that.'

'Have you thought of using electric motors?'

'I'd not trust them. My uncles lost money by experimenting with direct-coupled steam when it first came in and they were glad enough to go back to a belt drive. I'm content to stay with it.'

'Electric drive's safer, and more controllable than direct-coupled steam. I've been learning a bit about it, for it's going to be what all modern refineries use from now on.' Davie's voice was crisp and authoritative, as it always was when he spoke of anything connected with his chosen career. Warren eyed him with interest.

'You think so?'

'I know it.'

'They'd cost a deal of money.'

'Aye, but they'd be a saving once they were installed. Belt-driven centrifugals'll always be a problem. You must know as well as I do that you'll never be free of the worry that one or more of them'll come off the mountings and slow the production down.'

'Could you cost the electric motors for me?'

'I could.' They stepped out into the yard and Davie drew in a deep thankful breath. The smell of the sugar was strong out here, too, but diluted by fresh air.

'I'd be interested in seeing what you come up with.'

'It'll take a while, for I've got more work than I can handle, and with Mr Beattie more or less retired I've to see to the paperwork as well as everything else.'

Andrew nodded. 'Would you be willing to look after my present machinery in the meantime, if you're needed?'

Davie's face was still expressionless. 'Aye, I'll do that.'

'I appreciate it.' Andrew held out his hand and for a moment Davie hesitated. Not many men of Warren's wealth and power were quick to shake the hand of ordinary tradesmen and he was taken aback. Then he reached out his own hand, calloused with hard work.

The physical contact between the two men was as brief as Davie could make it. On his first visit to the refinery he had been prepared, almost eager, to hate Andrew Warren. This was the man who possessed Anna McCauley. This was her lover, her protector, the father of her child. The hand Davie had just shaken had caressed Anna's face, her hair, her body as Davie himself longed to do. But he had developed a reluctant respect for Warren, recognising the other's love

94

for his refinery, his determination to keep it going and improve it just as Davie cared for the small engineering shop under his own supervision.

There was guilt in Davie's mind as well, because at least once a month he entered this man's house in Port Glasgow without his knowledge to spend a precious hour in Anna's company. True, they only took tea together and there could never be anything but friendship between them because now Anna was faithful to one man, but to Davie it was enough to be with her. These visits kept him going day after day in the factory; the memory of her smiling at him across the tea table brightened and warmed the dingy room he lodged in. He had many reasons for preferring to dislike her lover. Now he nodded, then swung round and made for the yard gate, stepping out in his need to get away from Warren.

Andrew, watching him go, was impressed by Davie's quick mind and ability. He had made it his business to find out something about the lad before allowing him to deal with the Warren machinery, and had received nothing but good reports. Davie Kirkwood was a fine engineer who had learned his trade through sheer hard work, relying on night school for his paper qualifications. There were some who said that old Beattie's engineering works would have been closed down by now if Davie Kirkwood hadn't happened along. At twenty years of age he was more or less in full charge, working all the hours he could cram into each day and taking little financial reward, choosing instead to plough the profits back into the business to develop it.

There was a lot about the lad to remind Andrew of his sister Lessie, Anna's closest friend and confidante. They shared the same steady gaze, the same way of straight talking. Andrew grinned as he recalled the way the lassie had almost snapped his nose off that first day when he had found her working over the stone sink on the landing of the old hovel in the Vennel, and had asked how much rent she was expected to pay for the privilege of existing there. Anna had told him of Lessie's marriage and the move to rooms behind the little shop. He was glad to hear that her life had improved and glad that Anna had thought to recommend her brother when the refinery was in need of the services of a good engineer.

He wondered, as he walked to the office door, if one day it might be worth his while taking Davie Kirkwood on as an employee. Each time machinery broke down, valuable hours or days were lost, and to Andrew's mind a thriving refinery would be the better for having its own engineer on the premises.

Molly put the tray on a small carved table by Anna's elbow and turned to leave the room.

'Take Dorothea with you.'

The little girl shook her head, tucking her fists behind her back as the woman held out a hand to her. 'Doffy stay here.'

'Go with Molly,' Anna ordered sharply, the beginnings of a headache stirring behind her eyes. It was cold outside, too cold for Dorothea

95

to play in the garden. She had been indoors in her mother's company all day, and her prattle was beginning to wear Anna's patience thin.

'Come and help me to make some biscuits,' the maidservant coaxed, but Dorothea's head swung to the left and right so violently that her black curls bounced across her eyes.

'Doffy stay with Mama!'

Anna, recognising the beginnings of a tantrum, gave in. 'Leave her here, Molly. But you're a naughty girl!' she added as the door shut. 'You'd better behave yourself or you'll be put in your bedroom.'

Dorothea thrust out her bottom lip and scowled, looking so like her father that it was all Anna could do to keep herself from slapping the round baby face. Then she plumped down onto the carpet, almost on Anna's feet, and shook the doll she held. 'Bad girl,' she told it in a fierce whisper. 'Bad bad girl!'

Anna leaned forward and poured tea from the delicate little china teapot. Molly had made it just as she liked it – very weak, so that it could be taken without milk. She added sugar, lifted the cup to her lips, and hurriedly returned it to the saucer. It was freshly made and far too hot to drink. She eased herself back against the cushions and closed her eyes, wondering if the spring weather was ever going to arrive. During the past weeks, all but a prisoner in the little house because of rain and cold winds, her growing frustration with the limitations of her life and her resentment against Andrew for his refusal to divorce his wife had almost driven her mad. Dorothea's continual presence, her resemblance to Andrew, had set up a dislike of the child that had grown until she could scarcely bear her daughter's presence. Although she was not yet three years of age, the little girl already, as Andrew never tired of telling Anna, showed promise of the beautiful woman she would become. And as she grew into that beauty, so Anna would age and lose her own looks. Measured as it was now in the growth of her child, time was passing faster than ever before.

'Biscuit?' Dorothea's voice broke in and the pain behind Anna's eyes seemed to leap.

'No!'

Dorothea chewed at her lip, thought for a moment, her plump little fingers combing through the doll's woollen hair, then looked up again, wreathed in smiles as she remembered the magic word. 'P'ease?'

'Naughty girls don't get biscuits.'

The little upturned face went blank with astonishment. Anna closed her eyes again. It was a petty triumph, but it would suffice. Already Andrew was more captivated by the daughter than by the mother. Each time she looked at the child Anna saw her own decay, her descent into lonely old age. The prospect had started to haunt her.

Almost as though she sensed her mother's fears, Dorothea had become more possessive, more determined to be with Anna. In her more despairing moments, Anna even wondered if the woman lying dormant in the little girl and waiting to blossom forth was already aware, already taking delight in Anna's growing uncertainty and fear. She had never wanted Dorothea, she reminded herself, thinking of her desperate attempts to induce an abortion. It was Andrew who had wanted her, Andrew who loved her more than he loved Anna herself. Her thoughts squirreled round and round and the headache increased.

She was aware that Dorothea had scrambled to her feet, breathing heavily. Anna let her lids flutter open a fraction and saw her daughter gazing up at the table top. One hand released the doll and small fingers began to stalk slowly up the white linen cloth, ready to be snatched back if Anna's eyes opened.

Up, up, the fingers crept, up towards the spot where the saucer stood a little too close to the edge. Steam feathered into the air from the pretty china cup with its border of pink roses and blue forget-me-nots. Anna knew that she should move quickly, pull Dorothea back from danger, but at the same time another Anna, a cold stranger, kept her motionless, watching as the chubby fingers finally reached the top of the table and fumbled around for the plate of biscuits.

'P'ease?' Dorothea said on a breath, anxious not to wake her mother but justifying her actions by using the special word. Anna stayed where she was, watching as her daughter caught the curved edge of the saucer and tipped it over. Watching as the teacup slowly, slowly heeled and the amber tea, still too hot to drink, flowed in a graceful fountain over the edge of the table, missing the spotless white cloth, to spill itself over Dorothea's upturned face.

Lessie, summoned from the shop, arrived to find Anna huddled in a chair in the parlour, her face white, the cheekbones standing out as though she had lost weight overnight.

'She's taken it that bad,' the serving woman murmured when she let Lessie in. 'I had to send for you, Mrs Carswell – she insisted on it. She even made me send a laddie tae the refinery with a note for Mr Warren, though goodness knows what he'll say tae that.'

'I think he'd want to know. How's the baby?'

'Sleeping, poor wee mite. The doctor says her sight's all right, but her bonny wee face'll be scarred.' There were tears in the woman's eyes. 'Such a lovely wee thing, too.'

When the parlour door opened beneath Lessie's touch, Anna's head jerked up; for a moment she pressed back against the cushions, then she left her chair and came to throw her arms about Lessie. 'Oh, Lessie, my poor wee bairn!'

'It's all right. She's going to be fine.' She held Anna, feeling the other woman's body shaking as though in the grip of a violent chill. 'What happened?'

'I'd . . . I'd just poured myself some tea—' Anna broke free, turned away, her hands at her face. 'I'd a bad head so I closed my eyes for a minute. I th-think I fell asleep. Then I heard her screaming—' Her voice broke. She recovered herself and said desperately, 'It wasnae my fault, Lessie. It wasnae!'

'Why should anyone think it was?'

'Andrew loved Dorothea. He'll no' love her if her face is spoiled. He'll think I did it on purpose!'

'Don't be daft, Anna!' Lessie took her by the shoulders, deliberately putting a cold edge into her voice. 'You love Dorothea too, don't you?'

The reprimand brought Anna's head up. She drew in a deep breath and clasped her hands tightly together. 'Of course I do!'

'Then why should Mr Warren think ill of you?' Then Lessie said more gently, releasing Anna, 'Take me up to see her.'

'I cannae go.' Anna drew away, shaking her head. 'I cannae!'

'I'll go myself, then. I want to have a wee look at her. I'll not be long.'

The curtains were drawn and the toy-filled bedroom dim. Dorothea, her favourite doll beside her, lay on her back, one fist thrown above her head. All of the right side of her face, including her right eye, was swathed in white bandaging. Beneath it her black hair escaped to pour over the pillow. Her breathing was slow and even, but now and again it caught in a hiccup and a soft whimper.

As Lessie moved to the bed someone knocked impatiently on the front door and almost at once there were steps on the stairs. The bedroom door opened and Andrew Warren came in, sparing her only one swift glance, stepping at once to the other side of the bed to bend over his daughter.

'Dear God,' he said softly, and put a gentle finger into the cupped hand on the pillow above Dorothea's head.

'Let her sleep. She needs to sleep.'

He nodded, removing the finger and brushing it across the exposed cheek so lightly that it was like a breath. It was a gesture of pure love and tenderness.

'Will she be all right?'

'Of course she will.'

'Thank you,' he said humbly, though whether he was thanking her for her reassurance or accepting it as a solemn pledge she didn't know. Then he looked fully at her for the first time, seemingly surprised to see her there.

'Where's Anna?'

'In the parlour.'

His brows knotted. 'She should be here, with—'

'Mr Warren,' Lessie said firmly, 'Anna's in a terrible state about what's happened. She blames herself, though there's no reason why she should. She needs comforting. You've seen for yourself that the wee one's all right. I think you should go to Anna now.'

For a moment anger flared in his grey eyes, then he turned to the door without a word. Lessie, unsure of what to do, followed him downstairs. In the parlour Anna stood with her back to the window, watching Andrew warily, making no move to go to him as she had run to Lessie. When he reached her, he took her into his arms and at last she let the tension flow from her slender body and sagged against him.

'It wasnae my fault,' she said, as she had said to Lessie.

'I know that, my love.'

From where she stood Lessie could see Anna's face, her eyes wide but seeing nothing. 'Andrew, she'll be scarred,' she said into his shoulder. 'Her wee face – you'll not love her any more.'

'Of course I'll love her,' he said fiercely, his voice muffled. 'D'you think I could ever stop caring for her?'

Anna's eyes closed and two large tears came sparkling from beneath the soft fan of her lashes.

Lessie shifted uncomfortably from one foot to the other. 'I'd best go.'

Anna said nothing but Andrew released her and turned. 'I'd appreciate it if you could stay for a little longer, Mrs Carswell. I must get back to the refinery. I'm sorry, my dear,' he added as Anna gave a whimper of protest and tried to cling to him, 'but I must. I shall come later tonight to see how Dorothea is. Thank you,' he added under his breath to Lessie as he slipped past her.

As soon as the front door had closed behind him, Anna flared into anger. 'How could he? How could he leave me at a time like this?' She raged on, pacing the floor, while Lessie, unsure of what to do for the best, sat waiting for her to work her own way out of her temper. 'It's always the way of it, always! If it's not the refinery he must get back to, it's his children or his precious wife. Why should he always go running back to be with her when it's me he should be married to now?'

'You?' Lessie asked incredulously, 'You think that Mr Warren should marry you?'

'Why not? I'm the mother of his daughter.'

'He already has a wife.'

'Och, she hates Greenock, everyone knows that. She'd be happy to go back to her own people if Andrew would just forget his stupid pride and send her away.'

'For any favour, Anna McCauley, are you never satisfied with what you've got? Money and a fine home and a man who's looked after you just as he said he would, for all that he's got a wife and family of his own. Must you be always girning and wishing for more than you have?'

Anna blinked, her mouth falling open in astonishment. For a moment tears threatened to spill into her eyes, then she blinked them back. 'You've got a caustic tongue, Lessie Carswell!'

'I thank the good Lord for it, then. I'd not manage to keep my customers under control otherwise.' Then Lessie added more gently, regretting her outburst of anger at such a time, 'Don't fret, Anna, just learn to be grateful for what you have.'

'And what do I have? Sometimes I feel that if it wasnae for Dorothea I'd never see Andrew at all.'

'You're being unfair. He cares for you.'

'You think so?' Anna gave a curt little bark of laughter then said with another sudden change of mood, 'Dorothea's fortunate, and so's your Jess. My father never cared about me, from what I remember of him. Did yours?'

Lessie recalled the sound of her father's feet stumbling up the stairs, his flushed face, the smell of drink, the slurred voice and the fear she had known each time he came into the house. He hadn't set foot in her new home; his visits had stopped with her marriage to Murdo, and he was a stranger to her again.

'I must go, Anna. Elma's got the shop and the bairns to see to and I said I'd not be long.'

'Everyone leaves me.' Anna's voice was bleak and her eyes expressionless. 'Nobody stays. You've all got your own lives to live.'

'And you've got yours. Dorothea'll be all right, Anna, and the servant's here. You're not on your own. I'll look in tomorrow.' She hesitated at the door, anxious to get outside but reluctant to leave Anna in that strange mood. 'Will you be all right?'

'I'll have to be, won't I?' Anna retorted in a brittle voice, her head turned away.

As Lessie walked downhill to the tram stop she fretted over what was happening to Anna and what was going to become of her. How long would Andrew Warren tolerate her demands that he put aside his legal wife in Anna's favour? What would happen to her – and to Dorothea – when his patience ran out, as it surely would?

12

To the uninitiated, Port Glasgow, Greenock and Gourock appeared to be one long town, so closely were they linked along the shoreline; but to those who knew better, each community had its own individual stamp. Andrew often walked home from the refinery, as he did one pleasant May evening, his path taking him past the shipyards where some men still worked although the bulk of the workforce had finished for the day. Laughter and the clatter of voices came to his ears from the public houses placed conveniently near to the yards. Leaving the cranes and masts and funnels behind, he detoured to take in the Esplanade, a broad and elegant road where tall houses gazed across their front gardens to where the river widened at the Tail o' the Bank, the edge of a huge stretch of shallows over a sandbank. A cluster of cargo vessels was moored out in the deep water awaiting their turn to unload at one of Greenock's busy harbours.

Once beyond the Esplanade, he entered Gourock, more of a residential area than either Port Glasgow or Greenock. After turning in at the gates of his own house and walking up the drive between great banks of rhododendron bushes, Warren hesitated, hearing the sound of children's voices, then followed the driveway round to the rear of the house where the coachhouse and stables and kitchen-garden lay. Beyond them was a small paddock where a pony had been installed for his children.

Helene was sitting in a canopied swing that had been set up on a patch of grass, singing a nursery song at the top of her voice to a large and beautiful French doll, a recent gift from her mother's parents, which nestled in the crook of her arm. The nursemaid, seated on a wooden kitchen chair nearby, was busy with some mending while Martin, astride the pony, rode up and down the gravel paths brandishing a wooden sword, enacting a cavalry charge. The gardener's lad ambled along behind him, ready to take the animal when its rider grew bored.

Andrew halted at the corner of the house and watched his children. In another month they would reach their seventh birthdays; the babyness had already faded from their faces. They were their mother's children, with Madeleine's rich dark beauty. All too soon Helene would be breaking hearts and Martin being sought after by every society lady with a marriageable daughter in the area. Andrew himself had passed his thirtieth birthday and although he felt no different he realised as he looked at the twins that time was ebbing away and little could be done to halt it.

The nursemaid caught sight of him and jumped to her feet, dropping her mending in her haste to curtsey. The children, alerted by the sudden movement, immediately fell silent and became little adults, Helene slipping from the swing to dip her own curtsey, Martin struggling down from the pony to stand by its head, sword resting on his shoulder as his father advanced.

'Good evening, Papa,' they chorused, eyeing him warily. The days when they ran willingly into his arms were gone. Madeleine had seen to that.

'Good evening Helene, Martin. Are you enjoying yourselves?'

'Yes, thank you, Papa,' they said, still in perfect unison.

Andrew, at a loss for something to say, cleared his throat and glanced up at the sky, where the sun was setting. Unfortunately the nursemaid mistook the movement as a reminder that time was passing. She announced breathlessly, nervously, that it was time to prepare for bed. The children, their faces carefully blank to hide any disappointment they might have felt at having to go indoors, immediately obeyed, Helene hurrying to fetch her doll first. He saw the soft unblemished curve of her cheek as she turned to run back to the maid and his heart twisted within him as he recalled the angry red puckered scar that ran down Dorothea's face from ear to mouth. She had made a good recovery in the three months since her accident and was as much of a delight to him as ever, but each time he saw her scar he was reminded anew of how vulnerable children were. He wanted to call Helene to him, to pick her up and hold her close and safe before it was too late, but the twins had disappeared through the kitchen door, and he was alone.

He couldn't follow them, for it was quite wrong for the master of the house to enter his own kitchen. Instead he walked round to the front door, where Edith, no doubt alerted by the nurserymaid, was waiting, tall and angular and prim-faced.

'Mrs Warren is in the drawing room, sir. Dinner will be served in twenty minutes.'

Madeleine, as slim and as beautiful as the day he had first set eyes on her, was turning the pages of a magazine. She lifted her face for his kiss, presenting him with a smooth cool cheek, then returned to her reading. Andrew half filled a glass from the whisky decanter and sat down opposite her, sipping the drink, watching the way the last shafts of sunlight haloed his wife's hair, the soft regular rise and fall of the lace frills on her bodice as she breathed, the shadow of her lashes on her cheek. Watched, and wanted her with the hopeless yearning that maddened him yet refused to leave him alone.

There were always women willing to lie in his arms – Anna, when he was at home, others when he was away on business. Sometimes he paid for the favours he received, but not often. It was surprising how many well-bred ladies had a streak of the wanton in them, mingled with boredom and a liking for mild sinning. Madeleine had been the first to teach him how passionate some women could be. His blood raced and his body tingled and began to come alive at the memory of that teaching, and he took another mouthful of whisky and forced the memory back. It fought him all the way. Nobody, not even Anna, could slake his thirst for his own wife, the one woman he could not have.

'Dinner will be served soon and I do not like to keep the servants waiting. Should you not prepare?'

He grunted a reply and heaved himself from the chair to make his way up to his own room. As he went, concern over Anna began to niggle at him like a bad tooth. She was unhappy. He was making her unhappy and he didn't know what to do about it. She knew, she had always known, that although he would never desert her or Dorothea, there could be no question of marriage between them.

Washing his hands in the basin of hot water that had been poured out in readiness for him, Andrew sighed and hoped that Anna would have the good sense to see that things must be left as they were. Why did women have to be so complicated?

But he wished, as he made his way downstairs again, that there could have been some way to recognise Dorothea openly as his daughter.

The wind rattled a handful of rain against the windows and in the garden the trees writhed in the grip of a summer storm. It had been a gloomy day and Anna had been glad to draw the curtains early. The gaslight highlighted the gleam of brass and china and glistened on raindrops still caught in Davie's thick hair as he lay back in his chair, eyes closed. She watched him, the restlessness that had gripped her for the past few weeks draining away, leaving her at rest. His presence, the youthful adoration that was still there although he hid it well, always soothed her.

A coal burning in the grate gave a sudden crack and he stirred then opened his eyes and smiled sleepily at her. 'It's a poor visitor that falls asleep.'

'You're tired.'

'Aye, I'm tired. But it's good to feel tired after putting in a hard day at work you enjoy. It's not like the tiredness I felt day after day when I was working on the docks with my father.'

'D'you ever see your family now you're in Port Glasgow?'

'Not Joseph or the old man – I'd not weep if I never saw either of them again. I visit my mother and Thomasina now and then.' His grey eyes darkened. 'My mother's thinner each time I see her, and more tired. Sometimes I see my sister Edith there. And I look in at the shop for a word with Lessie most weeks.'

Lessie. Anna smiled inwardly, for not even clever Lessie, who had tried so hard when they all lived in the Vennel to keep her young brother and Anna apart lest he be corrupted, knew about their friendship. Anna's maidservant was discreet and it amused her to have a secret. Davie's gratitude when she had recommended him to Andrew Warren had warmed her. It pleased her to know that she had had the power to help him.

He yawned and stretched his arms far above his head, fists clenched.

103

She saw his teeth white against the red of his tongue, watched the muscles cording in his sturdy neck. Something that had been lying dormant for a long time stirred deep within her, a subtle primitive thrill that caught and held her as though her body was controlled by a silken thread.

As Davie completed the stretch and sat up, the little mantel clock chimed and he squinted at it in disbelief. 'Is that the time? I must go.'

'Not yet.' Anna leaned over impulsively and laid a hand on his. For a moment the contact, skin upon skin, made the silken cord tighten and tug again, then he snatched his fingers away, reddening.

'I must. It's not seemly for me to be visiting you so late. Your serving woman'll be waiting to get to her bed.'

'Molly's not here. Her brother's sick and she's gone off to take her turn at sitting up with him tonight.'

Davie's flush deepened as he swiftly got to his feet. 'Then I should never have come into the house. You should've told me!'

'I wanted you to come in. I wanted your company. What's amiss, Davie? Don't tell me you're worried about my good name? There's folk in the Vennel that would tell you I lost that many years ago.'

'Don't talk like that! Don't demean yourself!'

She was going to give him a laughing answer, but the look in his eyes as he stared down at her killed the words before they were uttered. For a long moment they gazed at each other and in that moment the silken thread within Anna became a living thing, tightening and coiling and seeming to draw her, step by step, towards him, although her body stayed where it was, in the chair, hands demurely clasped. She knew by the tightening of his jaw muscles that Davie, too, sensed the insistent tugging. Something that had lain unnoticed for too long had flared up between them, and Davie Kirkwood was afraid.

'I must go.'

'Davie—'

'I must!' He plunged into the hall, wrenching his coat from its peg, pushing his arms into it swiftly.

'Don't go,' Anna said from the parlour door. 'Stay. Stay with me.' The words jerked themselves from her throat and he shook his head, pulling away from her when she reached for his arm. The brief contact, the feel of him, even through the layers of cloth between them, sent sudden heat through her body. 'You know you want to stay with me.'

'For Christ's sake, Anna!' He ground the words out as he tore the door open. The storm, glad of entry, surged in, whipping her skirt against her legs, loosening tendrils of her hair, making the gas flames gasp and dance within the fragile protection of their mantles.

'Davie!'

The door closed and he was gone. The coats that had been set swinging where they hung slowly swayed to a standstill, the gaslight recovered itself, a few wet leaves that had been gusted into the hall flapped limply on the floor like fish torn from their watery home. The invisible thread jerked and tightened and hurt. Anna, alone again, held her aching body in crossed arms, turning to press her face against the flock wallpaper, aware of a low keening deep in her throat that she couldn't stop.

The door rattled and the latch, which had only half caught, slipped open. Hands came from the night and caught her and turned her so that her face was now against a wet coat with buttons that mashed into her soft skin.

'I cannae just leave you like this. Oh God, Anna!' said Davie thickly, and kicked the door shut properly at his back, forcing the wind and the rest of the world out. He tried to tighten his grip on her but she resisted, leaning back to fumble at his coat, his jacket, his waistcoat, wanting him now, with no more waiting. There had been more than enough waiting for the two of them.

The fire ran through her, through her insistent fingers, and caught at him. They staggered, locked together, into the parlour, bumping off the door frame, then the corner of a fireside chair. Their fingers tore and groped, forcing buttons through buttonholes, catching the ends of ribbons and pulling bows apart, dragging studs and hooks and eyes open. His coat, her blouse, his waistcoat, her skirt, his shirt, her chemise flew about the room like large snowflakes, landing where they may.

The fireside rug was rough beneath Anna's back, the flames daubed their two naked bodies with red and gold as they rolled together, now away from the firelight into cool shadow, now back to the heat that was nothing compared to the heat within. As their sweat mingled, his skin slid easily over hers; her thighs were damp with her wanting and his salty body taste was on her tongue. His hands and mouth travelled over her, making her arch her back and writhe with pleasure.

When he finally lifted himself above her Anna opened her body to him willingly, drawing him deep into her, wrapping her arms and legs about him to hold him fiercely captive. Instinctive to each other's desires although it was their first coupling, they moved, paused, moved again, finally reaching their climax in perfect unison. Even after that he stayed with her, edging her round gently so that they lay side by side, their faces touching. He kissed her throat, her ears, her eyes and nose and forehead and mouth with kisses that were butterfly-gentle, then drew his head back and smiled at her.

'I love you.'

'I love you, Davie,' Anna said, and knew that although she had said it often in her life, and had thought that she meant it when she first said it to Andrew Warren, she had lied. Only when she said it to this man, who had amused her with his clumsy awkward adoration when he was a mere lad, who had until that night been no more than a friend, did she speak the truth.

'We'll sell it, of course.'

'Sell it? We will not! We'll live in it.'

Murdo looked at his wife with exasperation. 'And what about the shop?'

'It's not that far away. I can walk to it and back here each day. The dear Lord knows I've walked the distance many a time, carrying Ian or pushing him in that broken-down old baby carriage. And if we move here, to Cathcart Street,' said Lessie with growing enthusiasm, her quick mind planning ahead as usual, 'Elma could live in the rooms behind the shop and pay us a wee bit of rent out of her wages. She's desperate to get out of her sister's house, for it's far too small for the family as it is without Elma there as well.'

'But think of the money we could make by selling this place. Not to mention the furniture.'

Lessie moved to the empty range and gathered one of the china 'wally dugs' into her arms, hugging it to her protectively, glaring at her husband across its rounded glossy head. 'I'd not consider selling one stick or one thread of Miss Peden's things. She left all that she had to me, God rest her, and she meant us to live here. I know she did, Murdo.'

Then the room, strange and cold without Miss Peden's vital, dominant presence, suddenly wavered and broke up. A tear fell onto the china dog. 'I just wish I'd known, Murdo. I wish I could've been there at the end to keep her company.'

He crossed the kitchen in two long steps and gathered her, wally dug and all, into his arms. 'She didnae know anythin' about it, hen. Ye know what the doctor said, she just went tae sleep an' didnae waken up.'

'I could have vi-visited her that week. I m-meant to, but what with the shop and M-mam no' being well—'

'Hush now.' He rocked her in his arms, then kissed her forehead. 'You did a lot for her, else why would she leave you her house? Though I still think you should consider sellin',' he added carefully as she sniffed and broke away to scrub at her face with one sleeve.

'D'you not want to move out of the Vennel?'

'Of course I do. An' we will in time. Wi' the money from this place in our pockets—'

Lessie shook her head. 'Miss Peden knew how much I wanted to take Ian out of the Vennel when it was just the two of us. It's why she left me the flat. I'll not go against her wishes, Murdo.' Then she tutted and hurriedly put the china dog down to swoop along the passageway to the door as small boots thudded along the close outside.

'Will you two be quiet? D'you want the folk to think we're a tribe of heathens?'

'There's doos in the yard, Mam!' Ian's nose was red from the cold of a frosty November day, but his eyes shone. 'And the lavvy's just at the back door, not at the other side of puddles the way it is at home!'

'It's a garden, not a yard, and they're pigeons, not doos. They belong to someone who lives up the stairs. You can look at them, but keep out of the way. I don't want anyone complaining about you, d'you hear me? And it's a lavatory, not a lavvy.'

'Piggins,' Jess verified cheerfully, flapping her arms as best she could within the limitations of a long adult scarf covering her fair head then

106

crossing her chest and fastened at the back. 'Lavvy.' She was getting over a cold and Lessie, worried about her persistent cough, insisted on wrapping her up warmly when she took the child out. That was another reason why she was determined to move into Miss Peden's flat; even though the rooms behind the shop were more weathertight than the flat she and Ian had lived in before her marriage, Lessie wanted to get her children out of the Vennel, where an unacceptable proportion of the children died before reaching school age. She didn't want to see that happen to her two.

'Lavvy!' Jess, liking the feel of the word on her tongue, danced around the close repeating it on a higher note each time. It floated on giggles, and Ian joined in the laughter, encouraging her. It was at that moment, to Lessie's horror, that Mrs Kincaid, the old woman who lived on the top floor, the woman who had always made her life a misery when she scrubbed the stairs, rounded the landing above and started down the final flight, pulling on her second glove as she came, her shopping bag over her arm. At the sight of her all Lessie's nervousness flooded back and she snapped, 'Hold your tongues!' so sharply that both children stopped at once and stared up at her, round-eyed. Then, as Mrs Kincaid reached the bottom step, they swivelled to gape at her.

'Good afternoon to you, Mistress Kincaid.'

The old woman said nothing for a moment, looking down her nose at the group by the open door of the flat. Jess, suddenly subdued, moved closer to her mother for protection as the cold eyes ran over her, and Lessie was glad that beneath the protective scarf her daughter was wearing a neat little velvet coat and good boots that had been passed down from Dorothea.

'It's you,' the woman said at last, her voice as forbidding as her look. 'I heard Miss Peden had left you her flat.'

'That's right.'

'I don't know what she was thinking about. I hope your bairns are well behaved. We don't have bairns in this close. We've never wanted bairns in this close.'

Ian, too, had moved to stand against Lessie's legs. She put a protective hand on each child. 'You will have, Mrs Kincaid, and soon. And my bairns are very well behaved.'

'Hmph. Well, there's one blessing, I suppose. The body that's doing the stairs now isnae up to much. At least you'll be handy for that, living here. You can start back at it next week. I'll tell her when she comes tomorrow.'

Lessie gaped at her, feeling the colour flooding into her face. Then Murdo's hand landed on her shoulder, as protective as her own hold on the children.

'My wife'll no' be scrubbin' any stairs for you or anyone else, missus,' he said, his voice courteous but hard. 'She's no need tae skivvy for the likes o' you any more tae earn her food. She's got me now.'

Mrs Kincaid's breath hissed in through her open mouth. She went crimson and seemed to shrivel in on herself. She pushed past them without another word.

107

'Nasty ol' woman,' said Jess, and Ian nodded in agreement.

'If she doesnae watch out I'll – I'll kick her legs,' he said gruffly, then grinned when his stepfather gave a howl of laughter.

'Ian! Murdo, will you stop encouraging the laddie? Come inside, the lot of you.' Lessie scooped them in and shut the door. Ian scurried ahead into the kitchen; when the others arrived he had drawn the net curtain aside and was peering out of the window.

'Ian! Leave that curtain alone!'

'Och, don't keep on at the laddie,' Murdo told her, his voice roughening. She knew that he was disappointed by her refusal to sell the house. Murdo liked to have money. He had opened a bank account and each week he carefully stowed away as much as could be saved from the shop. They lived on the money he earned at the shipyard.

'He'll have to learn how to behave if we're to live here.'

The curtain fell back into place as Ian spun round, wide-eyed. 'Here? Are we goin' tae live here?'

'Wi' neighbours like the evil-eyed old biddy we've just met?' Murdo added quickly.

Lessie, seeing her daughter's eyes on the china dog, picked it up and put it back on the mantelshelf out of harm's way. 'Aye,' she said. 'Aye, we're goin' tae live here.'

13

Most of Miss Peden's ornaments were carefully packed away, out of reach of the children. Murdo's suggestion that they should be sold met with a firm refusal from Lessie.

'D'you think of nothing but money?' she wanted to know, wounded by the very idea of betraying the old woman.

'I've a family to support. I've no time for sentiment. Better the money than all that stuff takin' up room that we need. My mother says—'

'I might have known that she'd come into it. Well, you can tell your mother that I'll decide what happens in my own house.'

'So that's it, is it? Your house, an' me an' my daughter supposed tae thank you for lettin' us live here, I suppose?'

'Och Murdo, you know I didnae mean it like that! I meant that it's ours, not your mother's.'

As the door slammed behind him, she could have bitten her tongue out. Why, she wondered wearily as she scrubbed Ian's neck and got Jess ready to go out, did Murdo have to set such store by money? But she knew why. Anyone brought up by his mother, with her fascination for pricing everything, would be the same. And it was his only fault. Day in and day out Lessie had seen women with bruised faces and split eyes and even broken arms come into the shop, usually on a Monday after their husbands had been drinking at the weekend. She had seen cowed children who flinched at a sudden movement from an adult. She often felt angry with the battered women, convinced that she herself would never allow a man to treat her in such a way. But no doubt some of the victims had thought the same, once. She was fortunate to be married to a good man like Murdo.

She tugged at the woollen tie of Jess's glove as she remembered how he had said, 'Me and my daughter.' It wasn't like Murdo to make a difference between the children. She had hurt him badly this time.

'Ow!' said Jess plaintively, and Lessie suddenly realised that in her preoccupation she was tying the poor child's wrist up like a parcel.

'Sorry, pet.' She loosened the tie and Jess, her eyes reproachful, mutely held up her wrist so that the red line biting into her white skin could be kissed better.

'You've got a bad mammy, so you have. Come on, Ian, we'll never get to Granny's at this rate. I promised Elma I'd be at the shop by eleven, and it's near enough that now.'

They had only been in the flat for two months and Lessie knew a thrill of pleasure as she locked the door when they left. The knocker and bell pull and wooden panels shone from the polishing she had given them that morning. Out at the back the small patch of ground that belonged to them had been dug over by Murdo in readiness for planting potatoes and leeks and onions and kale – all except a little border that was already bright with the daffodils and crocuses that Miss Peden grew every year. Lessie had wondered whether she would feel at home in the house she had only visited before, but there was a good atmosphere about the little flat, a warmth and serenity that welcomed them all.

Now that Elma was contentedly settled into the rooms behind the shop, she was very willing to take over more running of the place. She was a reliable assistant, and Lessie was glad of that, for as her mother's health flagged, she and Edith had taken over a lot of the household duties in their parents' home. And there was Anna, too, often sending for Lessie on some pretext or another. Dorothea had made a good recovery from her accident, though her little face now carried a red puckered scar running diagonally across her right cheek almost to the mouth. In time, the doctor said, it would fade, but it would never disappear. Dorothea was marked for life.

Since the accident Anna had started fretting over her own health, something that had never bothered her before. She had sent for Lessie several times, and each time, mindful of the assurance she had given Andrew Warren, Lessie had gone hurrying off to Port Glasgow to find Anna seeking her opinion on a new dress, or bored and in need of company. Murdo thought that she was a fool to bother with Anna McCauley, but since that day in the Vennel when the two of them had hurriedly dragged Frank Warren from Anna's bed and dressed him and propped him on a chair, their lives had become entangled. It seemed to Lessie, sometimes despairingly as the increasing demands of her own life made visits to Anna's fine house more and more difficult, that they were bound to each other for life.

Now that her financial situation had eased and the shop was paid for, she had tried on more than one occasion to give the twenty shillings back to Anna and each time it had been refused, or returned slyly as gifts for the children. In Lessie's eyes it was a debt still outstanding, a debt that seemed to have no end to it.

Jess trotted along by her side, chattering happily. Ian scuffed behind them, red head down, continually having to be told to hurry up. He was due to start school at the end of the summer, and he was ready for it, bored at having to be with his mother and sister. There were other children in the street and he had got to know them quickly enough, but in Lessie's opinion he was too young to be left on his own while she visited her mother. Once he was at school, she thought with relief, turning to hurry him yet again, she would get so much more done with only Jess to see to.

Thomasina opened the door and was so pleased to see them that she forgot to step back to allow them in to the narrow hall. It took a few minutes for Lessie to get the three of them in and the door shut. Thomasina was fifteen years old now; if she had been born with a whole mind she would have been starting work now, going out with her friends, giggling about the laddies they knew at work or saw in the street. But instead she was an overgrown child, at home with her mother and scarcely ever out now that Barbara wasn't fit to manage the stairs.

Lessie gave her young sister an extra hug in an attempt to make up for all that she had lost, then went on into the kitchen, where Barbara, her face drawn, was washing clothes, supporting herself with one hand clenched over the rim of the sink while the other kneaded and rubbed as best it could.

'Mam, what d'you think you're doing?'

Barbara lifted a tired face, flushed with effort. 'They'll not wash themselves.'

'You know fine that Edith and me see to the washing for you now.'

'It's things that have to be done right away.'

Lessie hung her coat up on the peg behind the door. 'Thomasina, help Jess off with her coat, hen. Then you can all go and play in the bedroom for a wee while.' She went to the sink and looked down at the old torn strips of sheeting, the pink-tinged water. 'Oh Mam, is it Thomasina?'

'It's no' Joseph,' her mother said with grim irony, staring down at the evidence of her youngest daughter's maturity.

'I thought it might not happen to her.'

'Don't be daft, our Lessie, it's her mind that's no' grown. She's got a woman's body, poor lass, though she's been awful late startin',' Barbara acknowledged.

'Does she know what to do?'

'I gave her a bundle o' cloths an' she seems tae be managin'. Poor wee lamb, she thought she'd sat down on a knife an' cut herself. She was that upset. Then I had an awful bother gettin' her tae hold her tongue. She was all for tellin' her father about it.' Edith leaned against the sink and sighed. 'It's just another burden sent tae try us.'

'Sit down over here.' Lessie gently urged her mother to a chair and delved into her bag. 'I've brought you some calves' foot jelly. And an orange.'

'The orange'll do for Thomasina.'

'I brought one for her too.' Lessie fetched a sharp knife and carefully sliced the orange into small pieces which she arranged on a plate. 'There you are – eat it all before the bairns come through and want it.'

'You shouldnae be spendin' your money on such luxuries. Anyway, I'm not hungry,' Barbara protested, but under her daughter's eagle eye she obediently picked up a piece of glistening orange flesh and put it into her mouth. 'It's – it's pleasant,' she conceded.

'It's good for you, too. You can have the jelly tonight, when Thomasina's in her bed. It's all for you, mind.' Lessie turned her attention to the cloths in the sink, rolling up her sleeves, kneading and scrubbing the material between her knuckles to get rid of the stain. They all knew now that Barbara's 'wee cold' was consumption although nobody used the word, as though feeling in some superstitious way that it couldn't hurt if it wasn't named. Pthisis, the doctor called it. It could be cured but rarely was in streets and tenements where folk used to working hard all the days of their lives just to keep body and soul together couldn't afford to avail themselves of good food and fresh air and rest. It was Lessie's hope that if they could just keep Barbara going until the summer they could take her up to the braes behind the town where good clean air and sunshine might just work its magic. She would have to be carried down to the closemouth, then lifted into a hired cab. Murdo and Davie, maybe her father and Joseph if they were there, could carry her in a kitchen chair. Lessie scrubbed and rinsed and tried not to think of the rage her mother would fly into at the thought of being carried downstairs on a wooden chair instead of going down on her own two feet. That was something that would have to be dealt with when the time came. Nevertheless, she was determined to get Barbara onto the braes with fresh healthy air in her lungs one way or another.

She wrung out the cloths with decisive twists of her wrists and hung them over the fireguard so that they would be dry and folded away before her father got back from the docks. 'Is there anything else to wash while I'm at it?'

'It's all done. Edith was in yesterday morning.'

Lessie reached up to the laden wooden pulley suspended by ropes from the ceiling and touched the clothes that hung there. They had been washed more recently than twenty-four hours ago, but she said nothing as she emptied the sink and dried her hands. She knew that her mother hadn't scrubbed the clothes. She wasn't strong enough.

'Imagine,' Edith had said to her a week earlier, scandalised. 'It's not a man's place to wash and iron. And he doesnae know how to do it properly anyway. There was a food stain on Thomasina's skirt and Mam's blouse was all creased. Why can't he mind his own business and leave you and me to see to things the way Mam wants?'

Lessie had said nothing for there was no point in trying to defend her father against Edith, who had no time for him. But it made her want to cry when she pictured him, slowing now with the passing years, standing in the kitchen after his wife and daughter were asleep, washing clothes in the sink, ironing them with irons heated on the range, doing his best to keep things going. She wondered if her mother was grateful, but even her fairly active imagination couldn't picture that.

'It tastes of sunlight,' Barbara said, showing a rare flash of fancy.

'Murdo says oranges grow in a sunny country. The folk who live there can just reach up and pick them off the trees. Imagine being able to do that!'

'I mind once when I was a lassie, walkin' out in the country. There was a stone wall, an' apple trees on the other side. The branches were hangin' over, all heavy wi' the fruit on them. It was bonny.' Barbara stirred restlessly, pushed the half-empty plate from her, and reached into a small drawer in the cupboard by her chair. She brought out the familiar dark medicine bottle and a glass. There were only a few drops left in the bottle when she tipped it up.

'I'll fetch your medicine. I know where it is,' Lessie said, and went into the bedroom. The children were playing with Thomasina on the floor like puppies, in a giggling, squirming heap. Lessie picked her way round the tangle of moving limbs and bodies and fetched the whisky bottle from the depths of the big dark wardrobe where her mother's and sister's clothes hung.

That was another little mystery that Edith hadn't as yet noticed; although Barbara could no longer go to the wine shop to buy her secret bottles of whisky, there was always drink hidden away in the wardrobe. It could only be put there by her father, Lessie was convinced of that.

She carried the whisky back into the kitchen, filled the medicine bottle to the top and corked it, then filled the glass almost to the brim. Barbara, her face shamed, her eyes lowered, took it and drank greedily. Then she said, 'Lessie, you'll see that Thomasina's all right, won't you – when I'm dead and gone?'

The whisky bottle was cold and hard against Lessie's palm. 'For goodness' sake, Mam, you're not going to die!'

'Och, don't be daft, girl,' said Barbara with tired contempt. 'I'm no' a bairn tae be telt fairy stories, an' neither are you.'

On the way home Lessie decided to give Murdo some boiled ham for his tea as a peace offering. Normally almost everything they ate came from her own shop but she was too tired to walk down to the Vennel, so for the first time she went into the shop at the corner of Cathcart Street. The bell tinged as she and the children went in, and Lessie stared round, her eyes wide with admiration. This shop was far superior to her own. Every inch of space had been carefully utilised, the shelves banked from floor to ceiling and filled with tins and jars and biscuits, sweets, pulses, tea, sugar, jams and sauces and pickles. Behind the counter were tiers of small drawers, each labelled with the name of the spice it held. The floor was covered with thick fresh sawdust that added its own aroma to the tang of coffee beans, which were ranked in marked tins, and a wide variety of cheeses and cold meats was ranged along cool marble shelves.

Great hams, ready for slicing when needed, hung by hooks from the ceiling, and on the long wood-panelled marble counter there were two sets of scales, one of them with a slab for butters and cheeses, a handsome bacon-slicing machine, and – the wonder of all wonders – a large imposing cash register of gleaming brass, with levers to pull down, a cash drawer underneath, and a little glass enclosure on top where tickets jumped up when the levers were manipulated to display the amount of each purchase recorded.

Lessie took her place in the queue, Jess's gloved hand held tightly in hers, and gaped around at the treasure cave she found herself in. Behind the counter Mr Mann, the shop's proprietor, his wife, and their male assistant were each swathed in long snowy aprons. Lessie

113

looked, and marvelled, and thought wistfully of the faded wrap-round flowered pinnies she and Ella had to make do with.

'You, woman – out off my shop!'

It took her a moment to realise that Mr Mann had stopped slicing rich pink bacon and was pointing an index finger straight at her. Everyone in the shop turned to stare.

'Wh-what did you say?'

'Out off my shop,' he repeated, the English words heavy and guttural on his foreign tongue. 'I do not haff to serve you!'

'Willi!' His wife, plump and embarrassed, tugged at his arm, but he shook her off.

'I only came in to buy—'

'I know you!' His voice was booming now and Lessie, her face hot, was sure that half Cathcart Street must hear him. She was aware of Ian gaping up at her, of Jess shrinking back against her skirt, as the man's voice roared on at her, 'I know off your shop. You do not come as honest customer, you come as spy! And I tell you, it is not allowed. Out!'

She went, fumbling for the door, dimly hearing the smug ring of the bell as she herded the children outside, away from the stares and the humiliation, almost running along the road to her own close. By the time they got inside their own front door Jess was crying and Lessie herself was close to tears of anger and embarrassment.

'Nasty man!' Jess wept, then stuck out a small foot, showing a dirty sock wrinkled round her instep. 'My shoe,' she wailed, fresh tears coursing down her little face.

'Oh dear God. Ian, go back and look for your sister's shoe. I'm sorry, lambie!' She gathered Jess up, hiding her own hot face in the child's neck. 'Mammy didnae know your shoe came off. Here, I'll take the sock off and wash your wee foot.'

By the time Ian came panting back, the missing shoe in his hand, Jess's tears had been dried, her foot washed and kissed and exclaimed over, and she was sitting by the fire sucking at a sweet. Lessie wished that she herself could have been as easily soothed and pacified. Her heart was still racing. Frantically, she tried to remember who was in the shop, who had heard her being shouted at. She couldn't remember, for it all had the texture of a bad dream now, a nightmare of pale smudges turned towards her, with only Mr Mann's red face and bristling grey moustache vivid in her mind. She hoped Mrs Kincaid hadn't been there to hear him.

'Mam, why did he shout at us?' Ian wanted to know.

'He wasn't shouting at us.'

'Yes he was, he was pointing at you and—'

'Just forget about it, Ian. Not another word to anyone, and not a word to your daddy, d'you hear me?' The last thing she wanted was Murdo storming along to the corner shop and having a row with the grocer.

She seized the teapot and ladled a generous spoonful of tea into it before filling it from the kettle simmering on the range. As the shock

114

eased, she herself was beginning to simmer with delayed anger. What man in his right mind would think that she was spying? Their two shops were quite unlike each other. Lessie knew what her customers wanted and could afford and it would be madness to try to copy the Manns, even if she had the money, which she hadn't. She had gone into the place as a genuine customer, waiting to make her purchase and hand over her money, admiring the way it was all laid out. It was nonsense to say that she had been seeking to steal his ideas.

'Mammy, why is Mr Mann called Mr Mann and Mrs Mann called Mrs Mann instead of Mrs Woman?' Ian wanted to know. Lessie gave the contents of the teapot a quick stir and filled a cup, in too much of a hurry to wait for the leaves to steep properly.

'I don't know.'

'Dad says it's because they're forn. What's forn?'

'Foreign. It means they come from another country.'

'What country?'

'Germany, I think.'

'Why did they come here then?'

'I don't know,' said Lessie, and wished, fervently, that they never had.

'Don't go to Jamaica, Andrew. Stay with me,' Anna said frantically into his jacket. He held her close, touched by her feelings for him.

'I have to go, my dear. If I'm to raise the money I need to modernise the refinery I must sell the sugar plantation. And I want to make sure I get a good price for it.'

'But a whole year!' Her arms tightened about him.

'It might not take the full year. I might be back before then.' He knew, though, that that was unlikely. Madeleine and the children were travelling with him, and Madeleine would certainly insist on staying in Jamaica for as long as possible. 'They're waiting for me at the refinery,' he said, suddenly eager to get the farewells over and done with. He hated farewells.

Anna raised a flushed face, her eyes drowned violets. 'Make love to me, Andrew, one more time before you go.'

'With Molly and Dorothea in the house?'

'We can send them out for a walk. Please, Andrew.'

For a moment he hesitated. He was tired, beset by problems at the refinery and by Madeleine's preparations for the journey, which had turned the house into chaos. It would be pleasant to lie with Anna in the soft bed upstairs, a breeze wafting the scent of flowers through the open window. But time was against him. He lifted her hands to his lips and kissed them. 'My dearest, I've neglected both you and our daughter, but it seems now that the days don't hold enough hours for me. I have to go.' Then, as the tears began to spill onto her cheeks he added, 'I'll try to come back tonight, when Dorothea's asleep.'

Hope flashed into her eyes. 'You promise?'

'I'll – I promise,' said Andrew, and she finally let him go.

Alone again, she paced the floor, chewing at her lower lip. It had

115

been a long time, too long, since Andrew had last taken her to bed. Too long ago for him to be the reason why she felt lethargic and irritable and too ill in the mornings to take even a cup of tea. She had taken all her usual precautions, but it was becoming all too clear to her that the sweet secret times spent with Davie, mainly in her room during the maid's time off, sometimes in his lodgings, once on soft fragrant grass on the braes above the town, had rendered their account, and it must be paid.

At first she had thought it would be simple enough to pass the child off as Andrew's. Davie himself mustn't know, for much as she loved him and hoped to belong only to him one day, Anna had been too badly scarred by poverty to turn her back on the comfort she now knew and return to narrow little streets and old damp rooms. And Davie must be free to carry on with his dream of building up the engineering business. Old Mr Beattie had recently died and, true to his word, had left the engineering shop to the hard-working young partner who had saved it from earlier extinction. But there was a lot to be done if it was to prosper, and Davie could never do that if he was burdened with a family to support. For now, until she could go freely to her love, Andrew must be the father of both her children.

When Dorothea was in bed and asleep and Molly sent out for the evening, Anna waited impatiently in the parlour. She had put on Andrew's favourite of all her dresses and the scent of roses stirred the air every time she moved. Upstairs a lamp burned in the bedroom and the covers of the big bed were turned back invitingly.

The mantel clock ticked away the minutes, then an hour, before the door knocker rattled. She ran to open it, fumbling with the latch in her impatience. The lad outside handed her a letter and loped off without a word.

Slowly, the certain knowledge that Andrew was not coming to her forming ice crystals in her belly, Anna closed the door and returned to the parlour, the letter that spelled the end of her safe, comfortable life clutched in her hand.

'My dear,' Andrew had written, his strong handwriting sprawling over the paper in his haste, 'my wife has made arrangements for this, our last evening in Gourock, without my knowledge. I have no choice but to stay with our guests. I have made certain that you will have no financial problems while I am in Jamaica. Kiss Dorothea for me. I look forward to the day when I can be with you both.'

The paper fluttered to the floor. Anna bit hard on the knuckles of one hand to hold back the screams of rage and fear that suddenly filled her throat. Andrew had failed her; by the time he returned, there would be another child, a child that could not possibly be his. Her mind feverishly ran over dates, adding and subtracting, coming up again and again with the same answer. He was no fool; she had no hope, now, of convincing him that he had made her pregnant before leaving Scotland. She recalled the ease of Dorothea's birth, the midwife's admiring comment, 'Ye can birth bairns as easy as shellin' peas.'

116

She remembered how hard she had tried to abort the little girl, and how her body, strong even in those days of deprivation, had defied every effort and finally delivered a healthy child, unaffected by all Anna had tried to do.

Now she must try again, and this time nobody would save her as Andrew had. She would not involve Davie, whatever happened. She would not destroy his hopes and his future; she loved him too deeply to do that. Nor would she go back to the life she had known before. This time, if nothing else worked, she would have to visit the old woman in the Vennel – or someone very like her.

Lessie was coping with a shop full of customers when the little boy, barefoot and ragged, thrust his way through the crush, leaving a clucking, ruffled trail of women in his wake, and rapped his knuckles on the counter.

'Missus!'

'Wait yer turn,' Elma said sharply, and he turned his hard gaze, old and knowing before his time, on her.

'It's the ither wumman I want tae see.'

'Cheeky wee de'il,' Elma's customer said.

'Needs his backside dichted, so he does,' said someone else.

Ignoring them, the boy ran a flapping-sleeved arm across his damp nose and said to Lessie. 'Ye're wanted in Port Glasgow.'

'Who says so?'

'A lady-wumman. Tell Mistress Carswell she's wanted in Port Glasgow, she says. An' she says ye'd gie me a sixpence for my trouble.'

Lessie went on weighing onions calmly though anger had begun to simmer deep down. This was yet another of Anna's imperious summonses. 'She gave you the sixpence herself.'

He didn't bother to deny it. 'I ran awfu' fast, but. She said I had tae. She said it wis important.'

'Here.' Lessie deserted the onions for a moment, lifted a jar down from a shelf behind the counter, and took out a peppermint ball. It was in the boy's mouth before she realised that it had gone from her outstretched fingers. He turned and eeled his way back out into the street, creating a second avenue of clucks and complaints.

'You shouldnae encourage wee tinks like him,' her customer told her disapprovingly.

Lessie had returned to her work. 'Och, the poor wee soul won't often get a sweetie. And what's one wee sweetie anyway?'

'That's no' whit yer man'd say,' someone grunted. Lessie pretended not to hear the words, or the ripple of agreement that ran through the crowded shop. She knew well enough that her customers didn't like it when Murdo happened to be behind the counter. Since their quarrel shortly after Jess's birth he hadn't tried to impose interest on credit or give short weight, but these women had thin purses and long memories and they didn't trust him any more. More than once Lessie had spotted someone turning away from the door and walking on because Murdo was serving. She handed over the onions, received money, gave change, and turned to the next customer, pushing Anna and her continual demands for attention out of her mind. In the month or so since Andrew Warren had been in Jamaica Anna had got worse.

'Are you not going to Port Glasgow, then?' Elma wanted to know during a lull.

'I am not. It's time Anna McCauley learned that I cannae go running off whenever she sends for me. She's getting to be as bad as a bairn. The times I've gone trailing out there these past few weeks, thinking to find her ill in her bed, mebbe at death's door, and there she was, with some imaginary ailment, just wanting someone to sympathise with her.' Lessie shook her head and felt around the shelf below the counter for a duster. 'She's not got enough to do, that's her trouble. I'll go to Port Glasgow later, when the bairns are in their beds and the shop's shut. For now, I've got work to do.'

By the time she was ready to visit Anna, it was getting dark and Murdo complained about her going out instead of staying in the house to keep him company.

'I'd best go and see what's ailing her this time. If I don't, she'll be in the shop in the morning, getting under my feet. I'll not be long,' she promised, glad enough to get out for a breath of fresh air after spending all her time in the flat and the shop.

At least there was no need to visit Barbara that evening, for Edith was there, Lessie knew. With the entire Warren family away from home Edith had more spare time on her hands than usual and she spent a fair amount of it seeing to their mother, who was more often than not confined to her bed now. Lessie fretted over Barbara's failing strength as she made the short journey by tram to Port Glasgow then started the walk to Anna's house. The planned summer trip to the braes for fresh air hadn't materialised; by then Barbara was noticeably weaker and the very thought of being carried downstairs 'in front of all the neighbours', as she said, as though they would all be standing at their doors watching her go by like a public procession, had agitated her so much that she had coughed up blood. Lessie wished, as she reached the road where Anna lived, that she could have parcelled up some country air the way she parcelled lentils and leeks, and delivered it to her mother.

The house was in darkness. Lessie hesitated at the gate and almost turned away again, then decided that she might as well try the door. There was no reaction to her knock, but when she tried again she caught a thin thread of sound from deep within, like a cat mewling or a child crying. Lessie pressed her ear tightly against the wooden panels and anger flared in her as she heard it again. Surely Anna and the servant hadn't gone out and left the child alone in the dark?

She hurried round to the back of the house, but the kitchen door was firmly locked and there was no light in the window.

Alarmed now, Lessie retraced her steps and was about to go and get help when the gate swung open and Molly came up the path, peering through the darkness at the figure by the door.

'It's yoursel', Mistress Carswell.'

'Where's Anna? Did you go off and leave Dorothea alone in the house?'

'Indeed I did not!' The woman set down the bag she was carrying and fished about in her coat pocket. 'It was my afternoon off. The mistress wasnae plannin' tae go oot, I ken that, for she didnae look too grand when she came home frae the toon this mornin'. I thought she wis comin' down wi' somethin', but she insisted on me takin' my afternoon. She said she'd go to her bed when the bairn was pit doon for the night.'

She finally located the key and unlocked the door. Lessie pushed past her into the house, shouting for Anna, wishing, now, that she had gone to the house earlier. A whimper came from the darkness at the top of the stairs as a match flared and Molly lit the gas mantle in the hall. 'I'll fetch a lamp frae the kitchen.'

Lessie didn't wait for her to come back. She groped her way upstairs, ascending into darkness, following the sound of Dorothea's little voice repeating over and over again, hopelessly, 'Mama, Mama.'

The child was huddled against the closed door of Anna's bedroom, curled into a tight ball. Lessie's hand touched soft cheeks wet with tears, then Dorothea was in her arms, the small body shaking with fear and exhaustion.

Molly, moving swiftly in spite of her bulk, came panting upstairs clutching a lamp in either hand. Their light showed that Dorothea's face was swollen, her eyes puffed with crying. 'Mama,' she wailed, reaching towards the door.

'Take her down to the kitchen, Molly. I'll see what's amiss here.' Lessie managed to take one of the lamps and hand the little girl over without mishap. She waited until she was alone, then opened the door. The room was in darkness.

'Anna?' There was no reply. The air was heavy with a brassy, unpleasant smell, a smell that made Lessie want to back out again, to close the door and let someone else see to things. Instead she advanced until the pool of light she carried illuminated the large bed Andrew Warren had bought for his mistress. At first it looked as though Anna was wearing a dark skirt and resting on top of a dark coverlet, her face half-buried in the pillow, her hands above her head, fingers curled about the brass rails of the bedhead. Then the golden light picked out the dull sheen from the one eye that Lessie could see.

'Anna?' There was no reply, but by that time she hadn't expected one. She reached out and discovered that the skirt and coverlet were not soft, but hardened and stiffened by a great deal of dried blood.

14

'You? Take on Anna McCauley's bairn as well as your own and the shop?' Edith gave a loud sniff. 'You're letting your heart rule your head, Lessie.'

'What else can I do? She's got no one else, poor wee soul. There was a solicitor at the funeral; he'll pay towards her keep, he says, until it's decided what should be done.'

'A solicitor?' Edith's eyes narrowed. 'Is he the bairn's father, d'you think?'

'Of course not! I mean,' said Lessie, suddenly recalling that Edith, who worked for the Warrens, knew nothing of Anna's story, 'I expect he'll be acting for someone else.'

'So the bairn's father must be someone wi' money, then? It's a strange business. Have you no idea who the man might be?'

'Why should I? It's none of my concern.'

'It should be, if you're goin' to take the bairn on.'

Lessie, still in the black clothes she had worn for the funeral, sipped at her tea and tried to change the subject. 'I'm grateful to you for looking after the bairns, Edith. I wish there could have been more to say goodbye to her.'

'Hmmm! She's fortunate tae be buried in a Christian graveyard, let alone having a big send-off.'

'I can't understand it. How could she go to one of those women? It's not as if the bairn wouldnae have had a good home.'

'Mebbe the man wouldnae have wanted this one.'

Lessie, who knew that her sister was quite wrong, held her tongue as Edith helped herself to more sugar and stirred her tea thoughtfully.

'Some folks are strange, and Anna McCauley was aye more strange than most, in my opinion,' Edith pronounced. 'I can still see her the way she was in the Vennel, painted an' dressed up an' never turning a hair at what folk thought of her with all those men coming and going. At least she died respectable, if you can call being a kept woman respectable. I'd have thought Davie would've come back with you for a cup of tea.'

'He had to get back to Port Glasgow.'

'The Lord knows why he bothered to take time off for the funeral.'

'Davie always liked Anna when he lived with me in the Vennel. It was kind of him to accompany me to her funeral.' She didn't know how she would have sustained the long walk to the cemetery and back or the ordeal of the burial itself without Davie's presence. He had said scarcely a word, but he had been there.

'How could anyone as sensible and hard-workin' as our Davie have liked a woman like that?' Edith said sourly.

'It was the liveliness of her that fascinated him. There were few folk like her in the Vennel.' The memory of Anna, vivacious and laughing, a butterfly amid the grey life they had shared, came to Lessie so strongly that she felt the tears brimming into her eyes. 'Oh Edith, I wish I'd gone to her when she sent that message. She must've visited the – whoever it was – by that time. She waited till Molly's afternoon off and she trusted me to go and look after her. And instead I stayed on in the shop while she—'

'You werenae to know. You said yourself she was aye sendin' for you an' there was never anythin' wrong when you got there.'

'But to turn my back on her the one time she really needed some-one – and I never got to pay her the twenty shillings I owed her!'

'For goodness' sake, what would she care about twenty shillings with the money she had? An' I'd be grateful if you'd not cry over my good silk jacket. I loaned it to you on the understandin' that you'd look after it.'

'That wasn't what I meant.' Lessie mopped at her eyes fiercely, fingered the bodice of the jacket and was relieved to find it free of moisture, then took a mouthful of tea. 'I was in her debt. That's another reason why I must see to Dorothea.'

'Sometimes, our Lessie, I wonder about you, I really do!'

Lessie managed a shaky laugh. Edith's complete lack of understanding was better for her at that moment than all the sympathy in the world.

'And what had Murdo to say about another wean to feed and clothe and look after?'

'He'll not have to find the money. I told you, the solicitor's going to pay for her keep until – until something else can be decided.'

'And when'll that be?'

'We'll have to wait and see,' Lessie said, then held up a finger in warning as the door opened and the children came tumbling into the room. Ian was in front as usual, his red hair leading the rest like a pennant, with Jess and Dorothea hand in hand behind him, Jess towing the older girl along possessively. Peter, nine years of age and thin and gangly, came last, standing by the door, cap in hand, until his mother motioned him to a chair by the window. He was at the best school Edith could afford and she was continually boasting about his cleverness. Lessie still felt sorry for him. But at least he had graduated from velvet suits and sailor suits; today he wore a Norfolk jacket and knickerbockers with long black stockings.

She dispensed biscuits, noting how Peter, after a sidelong glance at his mother, passed by the sugary biscuits and chose a plain one, then returned to his chair and perched on the edge, carefully catching crumbs in the palm of his free hand. Ian, on the hearthrug, crunched his way through his biscuit, then wet a finger and used it to snare the fallen crumbs which he then transferred to his mouth. Edith watched, scandalised, almost chewing her lips into mince in her efforts to keep quiet, and Lessie was glad that her sister had come to Cathcart Street to look after the children instead of seeing to them in the spotless, crumb-free house she and Peter shared with Aunt Marion.

Jess, who had taken charge of Dorothea since her arrival, selected a biscuit for her and sat her down in a chair before attending to herself.

'Isn't that a good wee lassie,' Edith said with a sidelong glance at Ian, and Jess smirked. Already, halfway into her third year, she knew how to impress grown-ups.

Ten minutes later Edith put her cup down and announced that she and Peter would have to go. Her son immediately rose and thanked Lessie for the biscuit, then pulled on his cap and opened the kitchen door for his mother.

When she had seen the two of them out, Lessie went back into the kitchen and began to gather up the cups. Out of the corner of her eye she saw Jess slip from her chair and go over to Dorothea, who was clutching the beautiful doll she had brought with her on the night of Anna's death, when Lessie had carried her home. The doll went everywhere with her. Jess laid possessive hands on it, and after only a token resistance Dorothea let it go without protest, the corners of her mouth turning down. Lessie almost told her daughter give it back, then decided to hold her tongue. Dorothea must now learn to live with other children and fend for herself.

Jess was on her way back to her chair when five-year-old Ian quietly intercepted her and relieved her of the doll. He returned it to Dorothea, who took it, beaming gratefully. Then he went back to the hearthrug, impervious to his young sister's murderous glare. It was all Lessie could do to keep herself from giving her son a hug.

In the evening, Davie Kirkwood, still in his working clothes, walked from Port Glasgow back to the Greenock graveyard to stand alone and unseen before the newly filled-in grave. A spray of late-blooming rambler roses, picked by Lessie from the back garden of Anna's little house, lay on the fresh mound, the small, tight many-petalled crimson blossoms and green leaves brilliant against the black earth that hid Anna from his sight. For a long time he stood motionless, listening to the sound of the birds in the trees, the catch of air in his lungs. He well knew the mother plant those roses had come from, remembered Anna only weeks before, in white blouse and green skirt, standing on the lawn, framed by the roses, smiling at him.

Davie stooped and snapped off one of the flowers, heedless of the thorns that plunged into his fingers and drew drops of crimson blood that drained at once into the earth. Carefully he stowed it into his pocket then turned away and walked back to Port Glasgow, to his lodgings. There, he put the flower into a large book to preserve it. Then at last he wept, lying on his bed with the sheet crammed into his mouth so that nobody else in the rooming house could hear him. It was the first time he had cried in his adult life, and it would be the last, for nothing as terrible as the loss of Anna could happen to him again.

He wept until he was drained and empty, then lay motionless, staring unseeingly at the mould-spotted wall inches from his face. The only woman he had ever loved, could ever love, was gone for ever. He couldn't believe that Anna could have died without him knowing it, sensing it. He had seen her just a week before, made love to her, held her and kissed her and laughed with her. They had arranged, when he left, that he would visit her in another ten days' time. Davie would have made it sooner, but Anna had insisted.

'I'll not stand in the way of your work,' she had said, her soft hand cupping his face. He could feel the touch of her fingers now as clearly as he had then; rolling over, he bit fiercely into the grimy sheet to hold back the animal screams of loss and rage that wanted to wrench themselves out of his aching throat.

After a long time he got off the bed and ferreted in the depths of a small cupboard until he found a box. Inside, nestling against a bed of white silk, lay two gold and ruby cuff links. Davie tipped them out into his hand, remembering the day Anna had given them to him, ignoring his protests.

'But when could I ever wear these?'

'When you've made your fortune and we're together you'll wear them.' She had kissed him fiercely. 'And you'll give me a necklace to match them. We'll make a pretty pair, you and me. Keep them, Davie, they're a pledge between us. If I ever break my word to you, you can sell them and use the money. But I never will.'

Davie's head thumped as he stared down at the expensive baubles. She had broken her pledge. She had gone away from him, so far away that he would never, even if he travelled to the other end of the earth, set eyes on her again. He didn't need anything, other than the rose he had taken from her funeral spray, to remind him of what he had lost. Slowly he turned the cuff links over and over, a sense of purpose beginning to seep into the great hollow space the tears had left behind. All that he had left in the world now was his work and his ambitions – and deep resentment against the man who had possessed Anna more completely than he, Davie, had ever possessed her. Andrew Warren had been her protector until the end. He owned her even in death; Lessie had told him that Anna's death was brought about by a miscarriage, and the child that had killed her had been Warren's child, he knew that. She would have told him if it had been his. He wished to God that it had been his. Somehow, he would have managed to look after her, look after them both. She would have been alive today if the child had only been his.

He clenched his fist, heedless of the pain of the cuff links biting into his palm and fingers. The links, bought with Warren's money, would be sold; the money raised would be used to build a few more steps on the ladder. If it took the rest of his life, Davie Kirkwood was going to become as powerful and as wealthy as Andrew Warren. And then they would see which of them was the better man!

***

By the beginning of 1905 it was clear to the whole family that Barbara Kirkwood was dying. A ghost of her former energetic self, she was now bed-bound, racked by an increasingly troublesome cough that more often than not stained her handkerchiefs with red spots and splashes, or tossing in the grip of fever. There was nothing they could do but keep her as comfortable as possible.

Her husband insisted on taking over in the evenings when he was at home, growling that he didn't want the house to be cluttered up with folk when he was in it. He had aged a great deal in the past few months, Lessie thought. The belligerence had gone and his shoulders sagged, weighted down by worry. Barbara answered when he spoke to her, submitted to his ministrations when there was nobody else to tend to her, and steadfastly maintained the barrier that had long since been built up between them.

Thomasina cried when they tried to keep her from her mother, and Barbara seemed to be more at peace if her youngest child was in the room with her. Davie visited frequently, but always when his father was out of the house. He too had aged over the past winter, aged and hardened. The swift, youthful smile had gone and his mouth was stern. Somehow he had found the money to invest in better and more modern machinery; the engineering workshop was prospering and gaining a good name among local businessmen.

Joseph, who disliked sickness, had taken himself off to live with some woman down by the docks. 'And good riddance,' Edith said with feeling when she told Lessie the news.

The sisters sat in the kitchen one cold February day, Lessie with a shopping bag full of mending by her side. The children were growing fast and she was hard put to it to keep them in clothes; now that Ian was at school he came home day after day with torn trousers, scuffed boots, elbows poking through holes in his jerseys, and she seemed to be for ever darning for him. Now she knew the true meaning of the caustic Scottish term referring to someone who had prospered and tried to deny his roots: 'I kenned him when his arse wis hingin' oot his troosers.' Ian hadn't quite reached that stage yet, but only because so far Lessie's needle had managed to keep him respectable.

She smiled at the thought, and was about to explain the smile to Edith when a sudden frightened cry of 'Mam!' from the bedroom sent the work in her hands flying to the floor as she jumped up.

'Dear God,' said Edith as Lessie, her heart in her mouth, ran ahead of her sister to the bedroom.

'Mam!' Thomasina, almost hysterical, was trying to pull away from Barbara's grip on her arm. The sick woman was sitting bolt upright in bed, and as her older daughters appeared together in the doorway, her sunken eyes fixed on them and she said in a strong accusing voice, 'Look at her! D'ye see whit ye've done, Archie? Look at yer new bairn – she's no' right in the head!' Weak as she was, she shook poor Thomasina until the girl's head bobbled on her neck. 'Aye, I can tell even now that she's no' right. An' who's fault is it? Yours, Archie

125

Kirkwood!' The words came out in a spray of saliva, the gaze fixed on Lessie full of such hatred that she felt iced water dripping down the length of her spine. Edith, crammed into the narrow doorway with her, shivered and said placatingly, 'Mam, it's all right now. You're safe—'

'Don't you stand there an' deny it, man. You mind thon night ye beat me so bad I couldnae even drag myself tae the bed. I know ye mind it well enough. Ye let me lie there till the mornin', ye drunken bastard!' The cawing voice had dropped to a hiss that was even more frightening than the shouting. Thomasina, still held prisoner, sagged at the knees and fell half on and half off the bed, whimpering. 'Ye kenned I wis carryin' this bairn but ye beat me a' the same. An' now look at yer daughter. Look at her! God damn ye for all eternity, Archie Kirkwood, an' God forgive ye for what ye've done, for I never will. Never!' said Barbara, then the cough came tearing up from her diseased chest, into her throat and her mouth, choking her, silencing her with strings of red-slashed mucus.

As she released Thomasina and sank back onto the pillow, choking and gasping, the paralysis that had held Lessie drained away. She ran to her mother, lifting her up, supporting her, reaching for the pile of clean rags that was kept by the side of the bed. As she soothed and rocked and mopped at Barbara, she was aware that Edith had lifted Thomasina, who sagged against her, sobbing, 'I've been a bad girl, Edie. I've wet in my drawers but I couldnae help it.'

'I know ye couldnae, hen. Come on, now, let's you and me go through tae the kitchen an' get you nice an' dry an' comfy.' Lessie had never known Edith be so gentle and comforting.

When the paroxysm was over, her mother looked up at her with frightened eyes. 'I was havin' a bad dream, Lessie. I woke mysel' up with my shoutin'. What did I say?'

Lessie tossed the stained rag into the bucket kept by the bed for soiled cloths, dipped a fresh clean cloth in a bowl of cool water, and wiped her mother's face gently. 'You were just dreaming.'

'What did I say?' Then, as Lessie hesitated, Barbara said more insistently. 'D'ye hear me? I'm askin' ye what I said?'

There was no sense in lying. 'It was about Da beating you when you were carrying Thomasina, and how she came tae be the way she is.'

Barbara's gaze was vexed. 'So you know now? You and Edith both?'

'Mam, why did you never tell us the truth of it?'

Her mother's lips firmed into a thin line as she held her face up to be dried. 'A good wife doesnae talk tae folk about her man,' she said when the towel had been lifted away.

Edith, who came in at that moment with a mop to clean the puddle from the floor, asked in disbelief, 'Not even tae her own daughters?'

'No' tae anyone. What goes on between man and wife isnae for anyone else's ears. An' I'd be obliged,' said Barbara with weak dignity, 'if the two o' ye would forget what ye heard an' speak about it tae nob'dy. It's no' your concern.'

'No' our concern? And us havin' tae grow up in this house, wonderin' why ye never looked the road Da was on? If we'd known,' Edith pressed on, swishing the mop across the floor with brisk, self-righteous strokes, 'we'd at least've understood what was wrong between the two o' ye. Nae wonder ye turned from him. Poor wee Thomasina – that was a terrible, wicked thing he did tae her.'

A weak swipe of Barbara's arm caught her elder daughter across the rump. Edith yelped, more with surprise than pain.

'Haud yer tongue!' Barbara hissed through white lips. 'I'll hae no daughter o' mine miscallin' her ain father in my hearin'!'

A final terrifying haemorrhage ended Barbara's life less than a week later. Watching her father standing by the graveside, his big fists clenched on the brim of his black bowler hat, his body wearing his best suit as clumsily as a snail in a crab's shell, Lessie pitied the man. If, as her mother had believed, it was his drunken cruelty that had robbed Thomasina of her right to a normal existence, he had done a terrible thing. But he had surely suffered from it ever since, not only by watching his youngest daughter grow up to become half-woman half-child, but also through his wife's rejection and her drinking. Thinking back to her childhood, to the days when her father had been the drinker and her mother strictly teetotal, she realised that it was Thomasina's birth, and the discovery that she was retarded, that had put a stop to Archie Kirkwood's drinking and at the same time started his wife on the same downward path.

Back at the house, Archie sat uncomfortably on the edge of the chair he had used all his married life and stared into the fire as his two eldest daughters bustled about dispensing tea and sandwiches, cakes and biscuits they had prepared the day before. Thomasina, bewildered and silent, dragged a low stool over to his side and sat down, clutching her rag doll in her arms. Joseph had attended at the graveside but refused to go back to the house. Barbara's sister Marion, crow-like in black, took the other chair where she could coldly eye the brother-in-law she had never approved of. Davie, silent and uncomfortable, stood by the window, drinking tea and refusing food with curt shakes of the head. Murdo sat bolt upright on a hard chair at the table, running a finger now and again round his tight high collar, trying to make conversation and being ignored by everyone but Lessie, who smiled at him gratefully.

As soon as possible she persuaded Peter and Ian to take Dorothea and Jess down to the back yard to play. They went, Peter obediently and Ian unwillingly, his eyes lingering on a plate that still held some cakes. Thomasina shook her head when Lessie suggested that she should go with them, and slipped a hand into the empty calloused palm that lay on Archie's thigh. His fingers jumped slightly at her touch, and for a moment Lessie thought that he was going to reject the girl's hand, but he didn't, though he didn't clasp it either. Shortly afterwards, Aunt Marion announced that it was time for her to go, and both Murdo and Davie immediately declared their intention of accompanying her to the bus stop.

When Archie and his daughters were alone, Edith said briskly, 'Well now, Da, we'll have to decide what's to be done with—'

She stopped short and nodded significantly at Thomasina, who had rested her head against her father's chair and was half asleep. Her free hand was at her mouth, the thumb jammed between her teeth for comfort. The doll had slipped to her lap and Lessie saw, as she took the chair Aunt Marion had vacated, that the bodice of Thomasina's best dress was tight across her young breasts. As her mother had said several months earlier, the girl's mind might be that of a young child, but her body was sixteen years old, and ripening.

'Aunt Marion's too old for the responsibility, and I'm not in the house much, so we can't take her. Anyway, it wouldnae do for Peter to have her living with us. He's growing up.'

'I could take her, Da,' said Lessie, then thinking of Murdo's reaction she added doubtfully, 'though with Dorry living with us just now, and the shop to see to—'

'There's no need for either o' ye to fuss,' Archie said. He had scarcely spoken since Barbara's death and his voice was gravelly, as though it had atrophied at the back of his throat. 'Thomasina'll bide here, where she belongs.'

'That would be the best idea,' Edith agree, openly relieved. 'I'll ask around, there's sure to be a decent woman willing to take on the job. A widow, mebbe.'

'What're ye haverin' on aboot?' her father asked rudely, and she flushed.

'I'm talking about someone to see to the house and to Thomasina when you're not here.'

'There'll be no decent widow comin' intae my hoose,' Archie growled. 'I'll see tae things mysel'.'

The sisters gaped at each other, then at their father. 'What?' said Edith at last, faintly.

'I said I'll see tae the lassie, an' tae mysel' and the hoose an' a'.'

'But how can a man see to a lassie like our Thomasina? She's a – she's not a child. There are things that—' Edith floundered, then said, 'Have you gone clean daft?'

'Don't you speak tae me like that!' Although the words were spoken quietly they contained all Archie Kirkwood's old fire and fury. Lessie flinched and dull red rose swiftly to Edith's cheeks. Thomasina slumbered on, her dark head brushing her father's arm, for all the world, Lessie thought, like a child trustfully squatting between the paws of a lion.

'Da, Edith's right. You can't see to everything here and work at the docks as well. Nobody expects you to,' she protested more diplomatically than Edith had.

'I'm leavin' the docks. I've got enough put by, an' I'll manage. I've thought it a' oot, so the two o' ye can mind yer ain business. It's my responsibility,' said Archie Kirkwood, his hand lying idle and open in his youngest daughter's tight grasp, 'an' I'll see tae it!'

15

'Eeny meeny miny MO,
'Sit the bairnie on the PO,
'When he's DONE, wipe his BUM,
'Eeny meeny miny—
'You're it!' The rhyme, yelled out by half a dozen shrill voices, broke up in a shower of giggles and the tight-huddled group of little girls scattered in all directions up and down the street, some dodging round Andrew Warren's knees like foam round a rock.

One of them, arms pumping furiously, heels kicking up behind her, almost bumped into him. A laughing little face was lifted for a moment as she veered to avoid him. She was dressed like the others in a plain smock and long stockings but his heart gave a sudden double thump as he caught a glimpse of wide violet eyes and a grooved scar marring her plump right cheek. He swung round, about to call her name, but she was gone, scurrying into a close like a fieldmouse into its hole among the grasses. All the little girls were gone, except for one wee creature who toiled past Andrew screaming, 'It's no' fair, so it's no'! I'm aye the one that's het. It's shouldnae be my turn!'

Then she too disappeared and Cathcart Street was empty apart from a knot of smaller children hunkered down on the pavement, intent in some game of their own. They stared up at the tall well-dressed man as he passed, gaped at his brown face, tanned by a sun much stronger than the sun they were used to in Greenock, then went back to their own business as he, in his turn, entered a close.

Anna's friend Lessie was only a name in his memory; he thought that he had forgotten her face, but remembered it as soon as she opened the door. She had put on some weight but she was still slight, and the little worry line between her well-marked brows was familiar.

Her face flushed at the sight of him. 'Mr Warren. I heard you were back. Will you come in?' She opened the door and Andrew walked past her into the house.

'The door at the end there,' she said, then followed him into a kitchen that smelled pleasantly of baking and soup and the scent from a bowl of fragrant pinks standing on a small table by the net-covered window.

'I hope I've not come at a bad time. I went to the shop and the woman there told me where I could find you.'

'Sit down, Mr Warren.' She smoothed her already tidy fair hair with the automatic gesture all women used when they were embarrassed or confused and began to fuss round the large table in the middle

129

of the room, gathering up lists and papers, closing a large ledger, tucking the chair she had been using back under the table. Her hands moved competently, restoring order with every gesture. 'I'm sorry about the mess. I've got the other small shopkeepers to agree to buy in bulk from the wholesalers and this is the day I make up the lists.'

'A sensible idea. Was it your own?'

She ducked her head in a nod. 'It saves us all money, and it works out well, though some of them weren't sure at first, with me being a woman.' A smile crinkled her eyes and banished the worry lines. 'Most of them have changed their minds now, though.' Then, obviously deciding to take the bull by the horns, she perched herself on the chair opposite his, on the other side of the gleaming range, and clasped her hands in her lap. 'You've come about Dorry. Dorothea.'

'I think I saw her out there. She looked happy.'

'She's settled down well. Poor wee lass, it was hard on her, losing her mother like that. There was nobody else to take her in, so I thought—'

'I'm very grateful to you. My solicitor's been looking after things, I believe.'

'Oh yes, he's been generous, but we'd have taken her anyway,' she added hurriedly. 'We didnae do it for the money.'

'Mrs . . .' he hesitated for a moment before recalling the name the solicitor had given him, 'Mrs Carswell, can you tell me what happened to Anna?'

Lessie bit her lip, then said evenly, 'She'd a miscarriage, Mr Warren. That's what everyone was told.' She glanced down at her knotted hands then said in a rush of words, as though wanting to get rid of them quickly. 'But to my mind you deserve to know the truth of it. She must have gone to one of those women that can stop bairns from being born. If I'd known what was in her mind I'd not have let her do it. But—'

'She was carrying a child?' Andrew interrupted, his voice harsh enough to jerk her bowed head up. 'How far on was she?'

'About three months.'

'She must have been more than that!'

When Lessie shook her head he got to his feet, bewildered, his mind reaching back to the previous summer when he had been too busy to visit Anna other than brief calls to see his daughter. He lifted a fold of the curtain, his hand mahogany brown against the snowy net, and stared out at the houses opposite without seeing them or hearing the children's voices; seeing instead the plea in Anna's eyes on that last day, hearing her voice as she begged him to make love to her. Because she was with child to some other man? He knew a sudden surge of anger, then remembered that whatever the truth of the matter, Anna was dead and gone and his main concern now was their child.

'Mr Warren?' Lessie said behind him, her voice uncertain. He turned to her, glad for the moment that with his back to the window his face was in shadow. 'About Dorothea, how old is she now?'

'Four past. She'll be five next March.' Andrew remembered how much he had wanted to acknowledge Dorothea as his own child. The wanting was still there, but for the sake of his wife and all three of his children it was impossible. 'Would you be willing to keep her here, raise her with your own children?'

'Of course. We feel as if she's one of our own as it is.'

'I think it's the best way, at least for the time being. I'll tell my solicitor to increase the payments he makes.'

Colour rose in her cheeks and her chin tilted sharply. 'There's no need. The shop's doing well enough and my husband has a good job at the shipyard.'

'I'd not expect him or you to find the money for an extra child. It's all I can do for her just now.'

The door from the close opened and two voices shaky with laughter squeaked their way along the passage. 'Eeny meeny miny MO, sit the bairnie on the PO—' Then the kitchen door burst open and they surged in, a smaller fair-haired girl followed by Dorothea, pushing and jostling at each other.

'Mammy,' said the little one as they came in, and Dorothea too chimed in, 'Mammy, can we—'

'For any favour,' Lessie shot an embarrassed glance at her visitor, 'will you stop saying that silly rhyme!'

The little girls had already fallen into an abashed silence at the sight of Andrew, staring at him round-eyed, moving automatically to the shelter of Lessie's skirts. She took a small arm in each hand and urged them forward. 'This is Mr Warren. Say good afternoon to him and let him see that you're not the pair of tinks he thinks you are.' Then she said levelly to Andrew, 'This is Dorry – Dorothea – and this is Jess.'

The younger girl rammed a thumb in her mouth and battled her way back into her mother's skirt, but Dorothea came forward, her vivid eyes fixed on Andrew's face, a little puzzled frown tucking her dark brows together. His heart turned over. She was Anna in miniature; although her hair was dark like his, it still held a chestnut sheen, a memory of her mother's glowing russet hair. Andrew achingly wanted her to remember him, but at her age memory was short and he knew that it was best for her to know him only as a visitor. Her life was here now, in this house with the Carswell family. He held out his hand. 'Good afternoon, Dorothea.'

She put her petal-soft fingers in his for a moment, then withdrew them all too soon. 'Good afternoon, Mister Warren,' she said, and the formal title, spoken by the child who had once run to him and hugged him and called him Papa, hurt almost unbearably.

'I must go,' he said abruptly, picking up his hat and stick. 'I've business with your brother, Mrs Carswell. I'm hoping that he'll be willing to help me to modernise the machinery in the refinery.' At the door he paused and asked, 'May I visit from time to time, to see the child?'

'Of course, and don't fret about Dorry. She's well and happy.'

'And in the best hands,' said Andrew, and strode out into the August sunshine before she could see the tears that were threatening.

Murdo grumbled at first over his wife's promise to keep Dorothea indefinitely, but a generous increase in the payments that were delivered regularly silenced him. A few weeks later, returning home from the shipyard to find Andrew Warren in the house, he flushed with embarrassment, keenly aware of the working clothes he wore. Awkward, ill at ease, he sat on an upright chair by the table, since Andrew was comfortably settled in the chair by the fire that was Murdo's by rights, staring at his hands and answering briefly when Warren spoke to him. To his relief their visitor left soon after.

When Lessie came back from seeing him out, Murdo had reclaimed his chair and had the newspaper open.

'I see those suffrage women've been makin' themselves noticed in Parliament again. By God, Lessie, I'm glad ye've got more sense than tae think like them.'

'I do think like them,' she snapped, 'but I've got too much to do to go shouting out at meetings.'

'That's just as well. If I ever hear o' ye makin' a fool o' yersel' like that—'

'It's not only women who can make fools of themselves. You might have been more civil to that man, Murdo.'

'I'll decide who I'll be civil tae in my own house,' he said without looking up, his voice muffled.

She bit back the retort that it wasn't his own house. Murdo hated to be reminded that he lacked complete financial control over his own wife. He had his good points, but all the same, Lessie thought, it was men like him who were making it impossible for women to gain the vote. 'I told you he asked to visit regularly to see Dorothea and I said yes. He's surely got the right to see his own child.'

'I don't see why. She doesnae know who he is. She thinks I'm her father now.'

'Och, Murdo, she's still his daughter. Would you not want to see Jess if you were in his position?'

'I'd no' farm Jess out tae strangers,' Murdo said. 'Anyway, he'll only take the lassie away when he's good an' ready, an' then ye'll break yer heart over it. Ye're storing up trouble for yerself, my girl.'

'He'll not take her. How can he, with a wife an' two children at home?'

'You wait an' see,' Murdo said darkly, and buried himself in his newspaper with a great rustling of pages.

Lessie fetched a knife, ran water into a basin, and began to peel the potatoes. Ever since she had heard from Edith that the Warrens were home – Mrs Warren as beautiful as ever and the twins grown out of all recognition and quite the little lady and gentleman, Edith had gushed – she had been worried in case Dorothea, who had settled into the Carswell household with very little difficulty, was going to be uprooted and sent off to live somewhere else among strangers. She was a happy little girl, undemanding – unlike Jess, who was spoiled by her father

132

– and easy to look after. Lessie had grown to love her and to dread the thought of losing her. It had been a great relief to her when Andrew Warren decided to leave the little girl where she was. Although Murdo complained now and again about being expected to look after other people's brats he had accepted Dorothea and to Lessie's relief he treated her as one of his own.

The thought made her feel guilty about her nagging over his attitude towards Andrew Warren's presence in the flat. Of the three children in Murdo's household, only one was his. It took a special man to care for other men's children. She put the knife aside, dried her hands on her apron, and went over to kiss him.

'For God's sake, woman, what's that for?'

'You're a good man, Murdo Carswell.'

'An' you're gettin' dafter than ever,' he grunted, putting the paper down and brushing her aside so that he could get to the sink. Watching him rolling up his sleeves and grasping the bar of soap, Lessie recalled that a few years earlier he would have seized the excuse to hold her and kiss her and even suggest that they retire to the box bed in the alcove for a wee while before the children came in from their street games. But somewhere along the way, busy with the shop and the shipyard and the house and the children, the magic that had been between them in the early days of their marriage had ebbed away. She supposed that it was only to be expected. It might well have come about between herself and Donald, had he lived longer.

That, she thought as she retrieved the knife from the brown water in the bowl and got on with her work, was what growing older was all about.

Since his wife's death, Archie Kirkwood had taken to visiting his daughter's shop in the Vennel twice a week to buy food. For one thing, it provided a walk for him and Thomasina, and for another he reckoned that he might as well benefit his own flesh and blood with his money than a stranger. But the main reason, the need to see Lessie frequently, was one of the many secrets Archie kept to himself. Edith was uncomfortably like her mother as she had been in the days since Thomasina's birth, grim-mouthed and unforgiving. Lessie, on the other hand, was a reminder of Barbara in the early days when Archie had met and courted her. She too had been slim and fair, kindly, gentle, quick to smile. That was why Archie had started to call on her after Donald Hamilton's death; she would never know, for wild horses wouldn't have dragged the admission from him, how much he had treasured those peaceful hours in the damp room in the Vennel, away from Barbara's continual silent condemnation. He had missed them after her marriage; he had no reason to believe that Murdo Carswell was a bad husband to Lessie, but from the first there had been something about the man that Archie mistrusted and disliked. He didn't feel comfortable with his new son-in-law.

But now that he and Thomasina were on their own, Archie hankered for brief contact with Lessie again, and his visits to the shop provided them. He took comfort in her cheerfulness, her gentleness, the smile that lit up her thin face.

'You know that Ian would be glad to bring the food to you, don't you, Da?' she asked, all unknowing, as she packed the basket neatly in that deft, economical way she had. 'You don't have to come all the way down here every time.'

'Don't want me an' the lass in yer shop, is that it?' Archie barked at her.

Her eyes were hurt when she looked up from her work. 'You know fine that that's not what I mean! You look tired and I just thought it would be easier on you if Ian carried the shopping. He's used to it now that he works for me on Saturdays.'

'I can manage fine.' He fumbled in his pocket and produced some coins. 'An' ye can gie me the right change – I'll no' take charity just because I'm no' at the docks any more. I can afford tae pay my way. An' add on the price o' her sweeties.' He nodded at Thomasina, who had hurried round to the back of the counter as soon as she preceded him into the shop and was carefully measuring some sweets out of a large glass jar into the scales, her tongue poking out between her teeth as she struggled to measure the right amount. She loved to use the scales.

'I can surely give my wee sister a poke of sweeties now an' then,' Lessie protested.

'No' when your man's out o' work an' no' bringing' a pay intae the hoose. Is there no word o' a job for him yet?'

Lessie bit her lip. 'He's sure to get something soon.'

'He should be helpin' you in here while he's idle.'

'He was here earlier. He went after a place he heard about in the Lithgow yard.'

'Oh aye?' said Archie, who had seen his son-in-law idling at a street corner with a group of men not ten minutes earlier. 'I doubt if he'll get it, for the gaffers in Scott's and Lithgow's joiner shops drink together. Any man that falls foul o' one o' them'll no' be taken on by the other.'

'Mebbe Murdo'll be lucky,' Lessie said without much hope.

'He should've kept his tongue atween his teeth an' no' answered the gaffer back. When I was workin' on the docks I'd have nothin' tae dae wi' a man known tae have a temper. They're nothin' but trouble,' Archie said sharply, then turned to Thomasina. 'Come on, you, time we were home.'

'Careful, pet, you're going to have the scales overflowing.' Lessie gently eased the jar from her sister's hands. 'That's right. Now pick up the paper and twist it into a poke the way I showed you.'

Flora, the young girl Lessie had taken on to work in the shop part-time with herself and Elma, sniggered at the sight of a grown woman behaving like a child and was silenced by one look from beneath Archie's lowered brows. Patiently, Lessie helped Thomasina to wrap up the sweets and put them into the shopping bag she carried.

'Will you not come through the back for a cup of tea, Da? You look as though you could do with a bit of a rest before you've to walk back home.'

Archie would dearly have liked to accept, but he had had a bad night and he wasn't feeling well. He was anxious to get home again before the pain that had become a part of his life in the past six months or so came back, so he shook his head and made for the door. Thomasina immediately scurried after him, pushing her hand into his, turning to wave to her sister with the shopping bag, which almost hit another customer in the face.

'Come on!' Archie said, then added placatingly as his youngest daughter's lower lip trembled, 'It's time for Bonny's tea.'

At mention of the budgerigar he had bought for her a year earlier, Thomasina brightened and trotted happily by his side, stopping now and then to fish a sweet out of her bag and pop it into her mouth. She had chosen raspberry balls and frequently, as she sucked and chattered, a ribbon of pink saliva drooled down her chin. Each time, Archie put down his heavy bag and wiped her mouth with a handkerchief kept specially for the purpose. Thomasina's mother had always kept the girl immaculate and since she had gone, it had become Archie's self-imposed task in life to make sure that though her poor head might be in disarray, Thomasina's outer shell was always beyond reproach.

It was a task that had become increasingly harder in the four years and two months since Barbara's death. He knew that Lessie would help if asked, and so would Edith, though in her case he would have to suffer comments about her knowing fine and well that he could never manage and it only being a matter of time before he discovered the obvious for himself. But he had taken the task on for life when Barbara was forced to lay it down, and he would die before he would seek help from anyone. Aye, he thought grimly, he'd die first.

As they drew nearer home, Thomasina skipped ahead. Some people turned to stare at her while others, those who knew the Kirkwoods, either smiled kindly or turned their heads away, pretending that they hadn't seen the 'daftie'. Archie opened his mouth to call her back, but just then the pain he had hoped to beat home swooped down on him, hammering at his chest, and he gasped and put down the bag. He leaned against a wall, perspiration breaking out on his forehead. If he waited for a minute, if he rode the pain, it would go. It always did, though it shamed him to ride it when his instincts told him to fight it, to force it out of his body, out of his life. It had no right to be there, no right at all.

'Da!' Thomasina was back, tugging at his hand, her breath on his face sweet with raspberry. 'Come on, Da, Bonny's hungry!'

'Wait a . . . a minute,' Archie said through stiff lips. She was fretting him, making it difficult for the pain to go. But at last it began to ease as he knew it would, and he was able to pull himself away from the wall and pick up the bag. Not far to go now, he told himself, gearing up weakened muscles for the task of getting home.

He took the stairs to the house carefully while Thomasina, who had

135

raced ahead, hung over the stair rail watching him, impatient to get indoors to feed her pet. Toiling up one step at a time, one hand gripping at the banister, Archie remembered the far-away days when he had scaled these stairs without even noticing them. Old age was a right bugger, he thought as he reached the landing and felt in his jacket pocket for the key.

By the time he got into the kitchen, Thomasina was at the cage, spilling birdseed everywhere in her haste to fill Bonny's dish. The bird chirruped a greeting then watched her, his head cocked. Archie sank into his chair and rested for a while before getting up again to clean up the spilled grain, unpack the bag and put the groceries away, and make a meal for them both. Afterwards Thomasina helped him to wash the dishes and played with her doll while Archie read the paper he had bought.

'That Lloyd George's set the cat among the dogs wi' his new taxes,' he said with dour amusement. 'The rich dinnae mind payin' for new weapons, but the bit aboot payin' for a pension for the old folk sticks in their fat craws. Hell mend them, for I'll never see their precious pensions.'

Thomasina, buttoning her doll's coat the wrong way, paid no heed. Watching her downbent head, Archie was shocked by a wave of love for her, almost as intense as the earlier pain that had gripped at his heart. In the past four years he had come to know Thomasina well, well enough to realise that he could never leave her to fend for herself. He couldn't bear to think of her in the workhouse, or even dependent on her sisters for charity. Edith had pointed out that the girl could perhaps manage to hold down a post as a kitchen maid but Archie would have none of it. His wee lassie would never have to slave morning to night for rich folk that cared nothing for her. Besides, who would protect her? Her mind might be weak but her body was mature and she was prettier than either of her sisters. The thought of a man taking advantage of Thomasina's trusting nature made him want to spew.

He knew that he wouldn't be able to hide the chest pains from his other daughters for much longer. He hadn't bothered going to see a doctor – he hadn't the money to spare, for one thing, and for another he knew well enough what he would be told. He knew, too, that he wouldn't be able to look after Thomasina for much longer.

It was time, Archie decided as he sat there listening to the child-woman crooning to her doll, to do something about it. Time to put his plan into operation. It had been forming in his head for a long time now, since he had first noticed the growing intensity and frequency of the crippling attacks. His heart, damn it to everlasting hell for its weakness, was going to give up on him, but nothing and nobody decided things for Archie Kirkwood. He, and not his heart, would make the final decision.

He had pondered over the rights and wrongs of what he planned to do, thought long and hard about the alternatives, and had made up his mind. And that was all there was to it. He cleared his throat, rustled the newspaper, and turned to another page, strongly aware of the warmth of Thomasina's body against his leg as she sprawled on the floor with her doll.

'Time for bed,' he said gruffly when he had read every single word, even the advertisements. Thomasina got up obediently and went into the bedroom, reappearing half an hour later with her nightgown on and a hairbrush in her hand. She gave it to him then whisked round and sat on the floor again, her back to him. His hard-skinned hands loosened her dark brown hair and he brushed it until it crackled and shone. After that he wet a flannel and washed and dried her face.

'I want juice,' she said, as she did every night.

'Aye, ye'll get yer juice. Dae I ever send ye tae yer bed wi'oot it?' He fetched the bottle of lemonade, half filled a mug, then after only a moment's hesitation he reached into the back of the cupboard, up on the top shelf, and brought out a small brown bottle. Uncorking it, he shook several drops into the drink, then a few more. When he turned round Thomasina took the mug from him and drank its contents down, trusting as always, apparently unaware of any change in the taste. Archie sat and watched, hands fisted tightly on his knees.

'Night night, Da.' She put the glass down, wiped her mouth on her sleeve before he could stop her, and came to kiss him, her lips cold on his stubbled cheek from the drink. He held her for a moment then let her go. When she had padded off to bed he washed her glass and lit his pipe.

An hour passed, then another, before he tapped the pipe out on the range, collecting the dottle from the bowl in one calloused hand and brushing it into the glowing coals that had become the only source of light in the room now that it was almost dark outside. He lit a candle and went into the bedroom; Thomasina lay on her side, the bedclothes up to her waist, her hands clasped about her doll. He bent over her and saw that her eyes weren't quite closed; the whites gleamed through a slight opening. He put a hand on her cheek. It was still warm, but soon it would cool and harden.

Carefully, Archie Kirkwood arranged his daughter's silky hair over the pillow, remembering how he had delighted in doing the same thing with Barbara's long hair when they first married. He went back into the kitchen, tiptoeing, although no amount of noise would rouse Thomasina again. The bird cheeped at him, rustling along its perch. He checked the cage to make sure that there was ample seed and water.

'Mrs Connelly'll be along in time tae see tae ye, never fear, Bonny,' he told the bird. The motherly woman who lived across the landing had fallen into the habit of taking Thomasina into her house once a week to teach her to bake. Archie knew fine that it was just the woman's kindly way of giving him a wee while on his own, but much as he hated charity he had given in. It was good for the lassie to have a woman's company now and then, and Thomasina loved her baking lessons. Wrapped in a big pinny Mrs Connelly kept specially for her, she sprinkled flour and mixed in water and currants, returning home

137

each time bearing an apple pie or a plate of fluffy spicy scones. Archie always pretended to believe that she had made them all by herself.

The front door wasn't locked; Mrs Connelly would be able to get in when there was no answer to her knock in the morning. Archie was sorry to give the woman so much trouble, but he knew that she had a good, sensible head on her shoulders. She wouldn't run off in a squawking panic as some folk might.

He took out the small bottle of whisky he had been saving and uncorked it, then stopped, the bottle tilted over the glass Thomasina had used. He put it down, picked up the lemonade bottle instead, tilted it in its turn, hesitated once more then, suddenly angry with this indecision at a time when he had made the greatest decision of his life, he put the lemonade bottle away, poured out a generous amount of whisky, added a further generous amount of laudanum from the brown bottle, and drank deep. The spirit burned its way down his gullet and into his stomach, leaving in its trail a satisfying glow that he had long denied himself, but never forgotten. He drank again, emptied the glass, put it down by the laudanum bottle, then blew out the candle and settled back in his fireside chair, his eyes on the pale square of the window, and waited for the silence and the peace to claim him.

'The selfish old bastard that he was!' Edith said fiercely on the following afternoon. Her eyes were dry, and blazing with vindictive anger. 'Imagine what poor Mam would have said if she'd known about the polis coming round and all the neighbours gossiping. He might have thought about what this would all do to the rest of us. I don't care one whit about him, but to kill poor wee defenceless Thomasina the way he did—'

'That's enough, Edith!' Lessie's voice was too loud, she knew that. It clanged through her father's kitchen like a cracked, ugly bell. Murdo put a restraining hand on her arm as her sister's head whipped round, her face blotchy with rage.

'You're surely not going to condone what he did? It was murder!'

'He didnae want tae leave Thomasina alone. She'd already lost Mam; he did what he thought had to be done.' Lessie's fingers dug into the high back of the chair – her father's chair. He and Thomasina were gone from the flat, carried downstairs in wooden boxes, past staring, whispering neighbours. Davie, ashen-faced, had gone with them to make arrangements with the undertaker.

'The man was wrong in the head! We should never have let him keep Thomasina. We should have taken her from him. If I'd only known—'

Lessie turned so sharply that she banged against the birdcage. It rocked violently and Bonny clung to his perch as Murdo moved swiftly to steady the stand. She kept going and didn't stop until she was in the bedroom, the door closed behind her.

The window pane was cool and hard against her palms. It was a sunny day and the sky was blue. A knot of women stood below her at a closemouth in the opposite building, arms folded, mouths busy.

Every now and again one of them turned to stare up at the house where Archie Kirkwood had killed himself and his daft daughter. Lessie stared back without seeing their inquisitive eyes, their clacking mouths.

When someone tapped softly on the door she ignored it. It opened, and she turned, steeling herself to face her sister.

'She's gone, stormed out in a temper,' Murdo said, closing the door behind him. 'We should go too. The bairns'll be home from the school soon.'

'You go and see to them,' Lessie told him, walking to the bed, sitting on it, stroking the pillow that still held the dent made by Thomasina's head.

'Lessie, come on. There's no sense in stayin' here.'

'I'll be home in a wee while.'

'D'you want me to stay with you?'

Yes, she wanted him to stay with her. She wanted, in this house of death, to be held and comforted and told that somehow everything was going to be all right. But more than anything, she wanted that comfort to be given freely, without her having to beg for it. So she said, carefully, 'Suit yourself.'

'Aye, well, the bairns'll need to find somebody at home. I'd best go. You'll not be long?'

Lessie shook her head without looking up at him. The door opened and closed and she heard his feet carrying him away from her along the oilcloth in the hall, then the outer door opened and closed and he was gone.

She picked up Thomasina's pillow and folded her arms tightly round it. 'Oh, my poor wee innocent lassie,' she whispered into the cold material that still smelled of Thomasina's hair. 'Oh, Da!'

Then the tears came, and she cried and cried for her sister, who had never been allowed to know what life was about, and for her father and the terrible anguish he had had to suffer alone. And for herself, because Murdo had gone home to see to the children and she had only a pillow for comfort.

16

'He can't have gone! He can't!' Jess's voice was tremulous, her blue eyes glittering with unshed tears. 'My daddy wouldn't go away and leave me!'

'He's left all of us.' Lessie fought to keep her own voice flat and emotionless. Inside she was quivering with shock and outrage and a terrible sense of shame, but she would have died rather than let the three children know that. Waiting for them to come home from school, she had been working hard at forcing her own emotions away so that she could confront her children when the time came, and tell them calmly that Murdo had walked out of their lives.

Jess started to sob. It was Dorothea, the puckered scar standing out against her sudden pallor, who put an arm round her. Ian, silent and ashen-faced until then, stepped forward to face his mother, his voice belligerent. 'It's your fault!'

'Ian!'

'It is. It's your fault. You were too busy with the shop to think about how he felt after he lost his job.' His thirteen-year-old voice was breaking; it see-sawed up and down comically but Lessie didn't feel like laughing. His eyes, Donald's eyes, were hard as they held hers.

'Hold your tongue!'

'You didn't care about how he felt. I know you didn't. He told me. Now he's gone away and it's all your—'

For the first time in his life, Lessie hit her son. She hit him hard, all her anger and grief behind the blow, swinging stiff-armed from the shoulder. He was the same height as she was now and her open palm caught him squarely across the face, rocking him back, jerking his face away from her, turning off the flow of words. He stumbled and fell against the corner of the table, then steadied himself. Sheer shock had stopped Jess's crying; she and Dorothea stared, wide-eyed and appalled, at the red mark burning across Ian's face.

There was a moment's silence in the room before Ian turned and blundered towards the door, tore it open, and went into the hall.

'Ian, come back here!'

The outer door banged and she ran to open it again. 'Ian!'

'He's off down the street as though a band of thieves were after him,' said Andrew Warren mildly from the close. 'If I hadn't given him right of way on the steps I think he'd have carried me along with him.' Then his voice sharpened. 'Is there something amiss? D'you want me to chase after him?'

'No. Best leave him.'

She sagged for a moment against the doorframe and Warren put a hand on her shoulder. 'What is it?'

'You'd best come in before the neighbours hear me, though they'll know soon enough.' She led him into the kitchen where the two girls still stood, clinging to each other, Jess's face streaked with tears.

'Go into your bedroom for a wee while,' Lessie told them, and as they went, Andrew's eyes followed Dorothea with the hunger that Lessie had come to know well. Then as the door closed and they were alone, she said flatly, 'Murdo – my husband – he's left us.'

His face went blank with shock, then he asked, 'D'you have any whisky in the house?'

She nodded towards a cupboard. 'I'd as soon have tea, myself.'

'You can have both.' Andrew waited until she had made tea and poured two cups, then he added a generous dose of whisky to her cup. She sipped, and grimaced.

'It'll do you good. D'you want me to fetch someone – a neighbour, or your sister?'

'My sister?' Lessie gave a short yelp of laughter. 'Oh, Edith's going to gloat over this!' She took another sip and this time the hot strong mixture was comforting. The steam warmed her face and obscured her vision. Then she realised that her eyes were misty with tears. 'I hit Ian,' she said, her voice shaking. 'I've never hit him before.'

'He must have deserved it, then.' Andrew was in the chair opposite, his own teacup in his hand, leaning towards her, elbows on knees. It wasn't until later that she realised that he hadn't helped himself to whisky. 'D'you want to tell me what happened?'

It was a relief to talk about it, and there was no point now in keeping anything secret, so she told him how moody Murdo had become in the long months of unemployment, how he had grown to resent the family's dependence on the money she earned.

'But I offered to find work for him in the refinery and he turned it down.'

'He wanted to stay in the shipyards,' Lessie lied. When she had mentioned Andrew's offer, Murdo had rounded on her.

'It's bad enough living in my wife's house without having her begging for work for me as well,' he had told her savagely, snatching at his jacket and slamming out of the house, as he always did when they had words.

'Mebbe I did give the shop more attention than I gave Murdo,' she said shakily, her fingers turning her teacup round and round and round. 'Mebbe Ian's right—'

'Never mind about Ian, he'll come back in his own good time. Tell me about your husband,' Andrew's calm voice broke in, and she stared down into her cup, half empty now.

'Nothing seemed to be amiss, no more than usual. I'd to go to the warehouse this morning to order this month's provisions for me and the other shopkeepers, and Elma that works in the shop had the toothache so she was at the dentist. Murdo was to keep the shop going till I got back from the warehouse but when I got there it was closed, the door locked.' She bit her lip, remembering. 'There was a letter on the counter. He's gone off to England to get work in the shipyards there. And—' this was the hardest part to tell, 'Flora – the lassie that used to work in the shop, only I had to turn her off after Murdo lost his job because we couldnae afford to pay her – she's gone with him. And the drawer was empty. The takings were gone. He said in the letter that he'd taken the shop money and half the money in the bank because it was his . . . his due.'

She finished the tea and put the cup aside. 'Elma arrived and opened up the shop and I came back here. His clothes were gone. He must've known for a while what he was going to do and waited till the right moment.'

'D'you want to go after him? Try to get him back?'

Her head came up proudly. 'Indeed I do not! But it's hard on the bairns. He aye thought the world of Jess and he's the only father that Ian and Dorry—' She stopped abruptly, and Andrew finished the sentence for her.

'That Ian and Dorothea knew. He's been good to Dorothea, I'll give him that.'

'He's been good to them all. They're going to take it hard, mebbe harder than me, poor wee souls.'

'Well now,' Andrew said crisply, setting down his untasted cup. 'My sympathy won't fill bellies and stock shelves. How d'you stand financially? Is there enough to keep you going?' He got to his feet and stood looking down on her.

'Aye, for the moment. But the shop'll need restocking next month and I doubt if I'll have the money I need for that. We've depended too much on Murdo's wages coming in and it's been hard since he lost his job. There's only enough to pay the shop rent and keep us going in food for a few weeks.'

'You could get credit at the warehouse.'

She shook her head. 'I'll not start that. For one thing I'll lose my discount, and for another it means I'd be in debt to the wholesalers and that's something I've avoided from the first.'

'Would you let me help?'

'No!'

'But after all you've done for Dorothea—'

'You've paid for her keep.'

'I can increase that, at least.'

'I'll not take more. It's not necessary.'

'So you'd as soon starve, and let your children starve along with you, than accept help?'

'It'll not come to that. It's kind of you,' she said gently, determined to retain her hard-won independence but at the same time unwilling to throw his generosity back in his face, 'but I'll not be beholden to anyone. This is my problem, and I'll work it out myself.'

'That leaves a bank loan as your only option.'

She nodded. 'I'll speak to the bank manager tomorrow.'

143

'At least let me go with you and stand as guarantor for you.' Then as she opened her mouth to protest he added swiftly, 'I'll lose nothing, for I know that you'll pay the loan back yourself. My dear woman, you can't expect to go through life without letting friends help you at all.'

She rested her head on the back of her chair, suddenly aware that she was feeling very weary. 'Thank you, Mr Warren, it's generous of you.'

'Not generous enough. I wish you'd let me do more for you,' he said, and left. Walking back to the office he decided that Lessie Carswell was one of the most remarkable women he had ever met. He had watched her cope cheerfully with her family and the shop and the added burden of his illegitimate, motherless daughter, and minutes ago he had watched all the contentment and serenity leach out of her, leaving her wan and tired. Yet always there was that inner core of steel that had sustained her through desperate poverty and the loss of her first husband. It would undoubtedly continue to sustain her through the loss of a second husband and the struggle ahead.

Murdo Carswell, he thought as he turned in at the gates of the refinery, was a fool to walk away from such a woman.

When he returned home that night Ian refused to talk about Murdo. He spent as little time as possible in the house, and when he spoke to Lessie he avoided her eyes. Tall and rangy, his red hair curly and reluctant to submit to a brush, he looked so like Donald – and yet to all intents and purposes he was Murdo's son, she realised with pain. It was as though they had both betrayed Donald, she by marrying Murdo, Ian by accepting him so wholeheartedly as his father.

As she had expected, Edith almost gloated over Murdo's departure and went on at such lengths about men not being trustworthy that it was all Lessie could do not to scream at her to hold her tongue. Peter, as quiet as ever, was working in the counting house at the Warren sugar refinery now and his mother pointed to his success as an example of how well children did without the disrupting influence of a father.

Lessie had to force herself to go to the shop the day after Murdo left. It was hard to face her customers' inquisitive eyes, hard to fend off nosy questions and to pretend she didn't hear the whispers, but it had to be done, and the sooner the better. Flora had lived only a few closes away from the shop and by the time the shop opened the next day everyone in the area knew the girl had run off with Lessie Carswell's man. Few of the folk in the Vennel could afford to buy the local newspaper, but their grapevine was much more efficient than any paper.

Standing behind the counter, Lessie kept her head high, looked her customers straight in the eye, and dared any of them to say a word. Most had the sense to keep quiet, though the whispering from those waiting in the queue and the inquisitive glances through the open door from passersby were hard to bear. Lessie coped with it all until the early afternoon when a woman known throughout the Vennel for her

144

malicious tongue said to other waiting customers in a voice that rose above a discreet whisper, 'I aye kenned he wis a scoundrel ever since he cheated us a' that time she wis birthin' the wean.'

Lessie laid down the ladle she had been using to measure porridge oats into the scale. 'Did you have something to say, Mrs McQueen?'

Everyone turned and gazed at the culprit, who went scarlet and said, 'I was havin' a private conversation.'

'About my man?' Lessie challenged.

'From whit we hear, he's no' yours ony mair.'

'For once, you heard right, Mrs McQueen. He's run off and left me, and taken Flora Paterson with him.' Lessie put her hands flat on the counter to stop their trembling. She knew that her face was red but mercifully her voice was steady. 'And as far as I'm concerned, bad riddance to him. Well, you all know about it now and I'd be grateful if you'd have the decency to do your whispering and sniggering outside my shop and not in front of my face.'

There was a murmur of approval and almost everyone turned to glare at Mrs McQueen.

'You're quite right, hen,' old Cathy Petrie spoke up. 'Men's no worth the bother, that's whit I say.'

'It's a' right saying that at your age, Cathy,' a plump young woman, recently married, called from near the doorway. 'Ye had yer fill o' them afore ye started runnin' them doon.'

'By God an' I wis filled mair often nor I wanted tae be, I'll tell ye that,' Cathy shot back, and in the great roar of bawdy laughter that shook the shop Mrs McQueen slipped out and took her custom elsewhere. Lessie laughed as loudly as anyone else in a bid to keep back the tears, and from then on she had no more trouble with gossiping tongues.

In spite of her brave words and the calm way she dealt with the situation in front of the children, she missed Murdo desperately. Lying alone in the bed she had shared with him she tossed and turned and longed for him, only now realising how seldom they had made love in the past year or more. Preoccupied with the shop and the children and the house, too tired when she finally climbed into bed to think of anything but sleep, she hadn't noticed that he scarcely ever reached out for her in the dark any more.

Now that he had gone and she was alone, her body ached for him and she was tormented by thoughts of him and Flora together, in each other's arms. She meant what she had said to Andrew Warren: she wouldn't seek Murdo out, or beg him to come back. If he wanted to be free of her, there was no point in trying to get him to change his mind. But she kept hoping that he would find out for himself that he had made a mistake. If he came back to her she would welcome him in with open arms. But he never did.

Davie had gone to Glasgow on business and knew nothing of Murdo's disappearance until he got back a week later. He went to the flat at once, and finding it empty, strode down to the shop. It was a quiet time of day and Lessie was free to take him into Elma's kitchen at the back, leaving the other woman to deal with the customers.

'Where is he? I'll go after him. He cannae be allowed to walk out on his responsibilities!'

'He's in England, where he can earn good wages in the shipyards doing the same work he was doing here. Ian got a letter from him the other day.' Lessie sighed. 'I had to go to see his poor mother. At least he's written to her as well. She's humiliated beyond bearing.' No point in telling Davie how the older Mrs Carswell had tried to free herself of her hurt and shame by blaming her daughter-in-law. When a man ran off, it always seemed to be his wife's fault. It was the unfair way of the world.

'And what about you? What about him humiliating you by going off with a lassie that worked in your own shop?'

'Davie, there's no sense in going on about it. Give folk's tongues a week or two and they'll find something else to wag about.' Outside, it was a glorious August day, but inside the room, inside herself, everything was cold. 'Oh Davie, sometimes it's hard being grown-up, isn't it? There's Mam gone, then Da and poor wee Thomasina. And now Murdo, for all that I'll—' To her horror her voice broke. At once Davie was by her side, his arm about her.

'Don't fret, Lessie,' he said gently. 'I'll look after you, all of you.'

She gave a sniff and straightened up, moving away from him. She had cried silently each night when the children were in bed, but had promised herself that there would be no tears in front of anyone. 'Indeed you will not, Davie Kirkwood. You've got your own life to lead.'

'Now that I've got a wee place of my own, you an' the bairns could move in with me. I'm doin' well now. I could support you.'

'I've no doubt that you could, and I'm proud of the way you've turned out, Davie, but I can manage fine. You did your share of supporting me before I got the shop. Anyway, is it no' time you were thinking of getting yourself a wife?'

Davie's jaw twitched. 'I've no intention of gettin' wed.'

'Why not? You're doing well for yourself, you should marry and have a family of your own.'

'Och, don't nag at me, Lessie. I get enough of that from Edith. Anyway, it's you we're talkin' about, no' me. How are you goin' tae manage for money?'

'The bank's giving me a loan.'

'I'll stand guarantee for you,' he said at once.

'There's no need. Mr Warren's already seen to that.'

He stared at her. 'You let Andrew Warren speak for you?'

'He made the offer and I accepted. Why not? I thought you got on well with the man.'

'I've done some work for him,' Davie's words were as hard as pebbles, 'but I don't like my sister bein' beholden tae him.'

'I'm not beholden. I'll pay off the loan and that'll be an end to it.'

'And if you can't pay it off?'

'I'll pay it off!'

They scowled at each other for a moment, then the anger left Lessie.

'Davie, don't let's fall out about this. Don't spoil things between us just because of Andrew Warren.'

For a moment she thought that he was going to disregard her, then he nodded stiffly, making an effort to smile. 'Aye, you're right. But if I'd Murdo Carswell between my two hands right now I'd squeeze the life out o' him for what he's done tae you!'

'That wouldnae be any sort of answer and you know it.' She put her hand on his arm, smiled up at him, 'We'll manage, the bairns and me. We'll manage fine.'

On his next visit Andrew Warren went over the shop books with her, giving advice and helping her to plan ways of saving money.

'You've got a good business head on your shoulders,' he commented. 'You could do well, given time. You could build up your shop, buy another, then another.'

Lessie shook her head, closing the ledger. 'I only started as a shop-keeper because I'd to support myself and Ian. I'll leave the ambitions to you and to my brother Davie.'

'But money's there to be made. Why shouldn't you make it?'

'Some folk have a burning drive in them to make money, Mr Warren. Davie, for one. But most of us just live our own lives and feel quite content to get by on just filling our needs. It would never do for us all to be one thing or another, but I know which crowd I belong to,' Lessie said firmly. 'I'd not want the stramash of chasing after riches.'

Andrew blinked at her in some surprise, but said no more.

It was hard work, caring for the shop and her family on her own; at times Lessie lay awake at night worrying about whether or not she was going to manage to pay the next instalment of the bank loan and stock the shop and pay the rent and keep the children in clothes and food, but each month she found herself getting by, though it meant that Miss Peden's ornaments and the handsome 'wally dugs' and her own precious garnet brooch went back into the pawnshop for long periods. It embarrassed her acutely to have to pawn her benefactor's possessions, but Lessie was fighting for survival and she couldn't afford to be fussy about such matters.

Around her as she worked and worried, the world moved on through 1913 and into 1914. There were stormy scenes over the proposal to grant Home Rule to Ulster. The decision by Asquith's government to scrap the Franchise Bill caused the suffragettes to step up their militant fight for the vote, including hunger strikes by women thrown into prison for their beliefs. The Government retaliated by bringing in the Cat and Mouse Act, giving authorities the power to release hunger strikers then re-arrest them once they had recovered their strength.

To Lessie, serving women who as often as not bore blackened eyes and bruised faces and split lips, dealing with wan children bandy-legged from rickets, these concerns were like vague messages from a far and unknown country compared to the business of stocking and renting her shop.

Captain Robert Scott and his team died in the frozen wastes of

Antarctica without reaching the South Pole and Lessie managed to persuade Ian, the clever member of the family, to stay on at school instead of leaving as soon as he reached his fourteenth birthday, offering to pay him five shillings a week to deliver goods for her in the early mornings and evenings and at weekends as an incentive. How she was to scrape up the money she didn't know, but she was determined to manage it. To her great relief the boy agreed. Ever since Murdo's going, there had been tension between them. Murdo wrote to Ian, who jealously guarded the letters and said nothing about them to Lessie. Jess, too, received an occasional letter; each time her pretty little face flushed with pleasure and she almost drove Lessie out of her mind chattering on about her father's new job, the room he and Flora had rented, their plans and ambitions. But Jess was an indifferent letter writer and rarely got around to answering, and gradually Murdo's letters to her dwindled and stopped. Caught up in the exciting business of growing older, she didn't seem to notice.

Germany's peacetime army grew. The Panama Canal was officially opened, then one day a foreign archduke and his wife were shot dead during a visit to a small distant country and Lessie looked up from weighing out lentils and giving change and balancing her ledgers to discover that everyone had begun to talk about a war.

'It wouldnae come to that, surely?' she asked Andrew Warren on his next visit. He helped her with her books as a matter of course now, and to her great relief he approved of her way of cutting prices on some goods to attract more affluent customers who might otherwise have got their groceries from further afield. It was a scheme that Murdo had strongly opposed.

Andrew looked tired and worried. 'It may well come to it from what I hear. My daughter's school in France has closed down. I would have sent for her in any case, she's safer at home at such a time of unrest.'

'But they're cousins, our King and the German Kaiser. Surely they'd not go to war with each other?'

The corners of Andrew's mouth quirked up in a brief smile. 'They'd not be the first family to fall out.'

'Thank goodness Ian's too young to fight if it comes to it,' said Lessie, and could have bitten her tongue out when she remembered that Martin Warren, now at a good school in Glasgow, was old enough to go into the army. 'Not that there's any chance of it happening,' she added briskly.

'My son's hoping that it will. He's been a member of his school's Officer Training Corps for some time now and he likes the idea of being a warrior. But let's pray that you're right. What's Ian going to do with his life now that you've got him to stay on at the school?'

'He wants to be a chemist, if you please.'

'A chemist?' Warren was taken aback.

'It's something he decided on a few years back. Murdo and his mother encouraged him. They liked the idea of having a professional man in the family.' The ghost of a smile brushed her mouth.

'And what do you think of it?'

Lessie folded her hands in her lap and eased her shoulders against the back of her chair. 'I want him to be happy. And if that's what makes him happy then so be it. That's why I talked him into staying on at school. I'm trying to save towards the day when I might have to find the money to pay college fees.' She laughed, and released one hand from the other to push back a stray wisp of fair hair that had drifted across her face. 'I never in my life thought I'd hear myself saying that!'

'I could help.'

'Indeed you could not. It's not your worry.'

'For God's sake, Lessie, will you never let anyone offer assistance?' She didn't know when he had started using her first name, it had just happened, not long after Murdo's desertion. 'If the lad wants to go to university it'll take money. I've got enough of that to see to my own family and help yours as well. D'you not think you've earned it, the way you've looked after Dorothea?'

She felt her face stiffen. 'You pay for Dorry's keep as it is. And I'll not take charity.'

'You're the most infuriating, stubborn woman I've ever met!'

'It's the only way to be, for the likes of me,' said Lessie, and refused to discuss the matter any further.

To his mother's fury Martin Warren left school and joined the army as soon as Britain declared war against Germany. 'It won't last,' he pointed out to Madeleine when he came home to break the news and announce that he was about to leave for England to train as an officer. 'I want to do something interesting before I go to university then settle down in the refinery. If I don't go now it'll be over and I'll have missed it.'

Men who had been in the Reservists disappeared from Greenock's streets; not only men – delivery vans and horses were commandeered and fuming merchants who had led the way into the twentieth century with smart new motorised vans had to resort to delivering their goods by bicycle and cart one again. The carts themselves, and those trams still pulled by horses, moved at a sedate pace, drawn as they were by old animals too near the end of their useful working lives to interest the War Department.

Only a matter of weeks after war fever had swept the country came the reality. Scores were killed and hundreds wounded when the British Expeditionary Forces were defeated at Mons; then the cream of the Russian army was defeated on the East Prussian border. An appeal was launched for another half million volunteers and all at once it began to look as though the war against Germany might not be over by the end of the year after all.

17

Lessie wearily turned the corner into Cathcart Street after a busy day in the shop, the basket of provisions dragging at her arm, then lifted her head at the sound of tinkling glass. Across the road from where she stood the Manns' handsome corner shop was a mess, with every window out, glass all over the pavement, the display shelves just inside the windows empty and hanging drunkenly from broken supports. A few men were loitering about, watching Mr and Mrs Mann sweeping broken glass from the pavement. Children stood staring and groups of women hovered at each closemouth, arms folded and heads together in eager talk. Nobody was helping the grocer and his wife.

'What happened?'

The woman Lessie asked, a neighbour from the next close, shrugged her shoulders. 'A crowd came doon frae the town an' went for their shop.'

'Why?'

''Cause they're Germans, that's why,' the woman said in surprise. 'We're at war wi' their sort.'

'Not with the Manns!'

'He's got the same name as the Kaiser. They're a' foreigners. Ye cannae trust foreigners these days,' was the uncompromising answer. Disgusted with the woman's attitude, Lessie marched home, deposited her heavy basket on the kitchen table, and tied an apron round her waist. Then she seized a broom and a shovel and went out again, exhaustion forgotten as she made for the corner.

Mr Mann eyed her warily as she approached, scattering children before her. He had a bruise on his forehead and blood was drying and crusting at the corner of his mouth. 'Vat do you vant?'

'I've come to help.'

He drew himself up proudly. 'Ve do not need help from you.'

'Vilhelm!' His wife, her eyes puffed with crying, tugged at his sleeve.

'You do so need help,' Lessie told him roundly, and started to wield her brush. For a terrible moment she thought that the grocer was going to grab her by the collar and send her packing in front of every-one, just as he had done when she first moved into the street, but after a moment's indecision he turned away and got on with his own work.

Ian and Dorothea arrived and were set to work when they came to see what their mother was up to. An hour later the pavement was clear, the glass safely stowed away in boxes in the small back yard, the windows boarded up.

'Did they spoil much of your stock?' Lessie asked, and the grocer's swollen mouth grimaced.

'Zey took everything. Vy do zey do zat to us? Ve haff been here for many years. Ve do not'ing to harm zem.'

'I can send stuff up tomorrow morning from my own wee shop, and I'll get in touch with the other shopkeepers and ask them to spare what they can. It'll not be much, but it'll help you to stay in business until you can get more supplies in from the warehouses.' The Manns had refused to become part of the group that Lessie bought stock for.

'I vill not take charity.'

'For any favour!' she said, disgusted. 'It's not charity, it's help. We're not all mindless fools, some of us want to help.'

'Vy do zey do zis to us?' he asked again. 'Ve are not German, ve are Sviss.'

'I'm sorry,' Lessie said, and knew that the words were empty, useless, in the face of the hatred and cruelty that had suddenly been unleashed on this middle-aged couple who only sought to earn a living far from their own home.

With borrowed provisions from her shop and from others, the corner grocery opened its doors on the following day. The windows were replaced but a week later they were smashed and the shop vandalised again. This time the Manns had had enough. They left the shop boarded up and vanished from Cathcart Street. Some said that they had been taken away by the military to be put into a camp for aliens. Some said that they had stolen out of Greenock in the dead of night and gone off to Germany, taking with them military secrets.

'How could a grocer and his wife find out military secrets, let alone go off to Germany whenever the notion took them?' Lessie asked, exasperated. 'Anyway, they come from Switzerland, not Germany. He told me that himself.'

The man she was talking to looked at her as though she were simple in the head. 'They're a' foreigners,' he said.

'He's shamed me, Lessie. Shamed me in front of the whole town! What have I ever done to deserve this?'

Edith gulped her tea, set the cup back in its saucer with almost enough force to smash it, and groped in her bag for a handkerchief to press to the end of her reddened nose. 'Why?' she asked piteously, her voice muffled by the handkerchief. 'What's got into the laddie?'

'There's nothing wrong with not wanting to kill folk, Edith.'

'That's what Peter says. But he's not even religious!' Edith's voice broke. 'He says he doesnae even believe in God so he's not got that excuse to fall back on. And there's me workin' for the Warrens an' Master Martin off to France soon to fight the Germans while my son stays safe at home. D'you think he's soft in the head and I've never noticed before?'

'Edith Fisher, he's a decent, honest young man who's decided to stand by his own principles and chosen a hard road to walk. You should be thinking about him, not yourself!'

Edith shot to her feet, tears forgotten, glaring at her sister. 'If he is wrong in the head it's you he gets it from,' she snapped. 'You were aye strange, you and Davie both. I've no doubt he'll not be going off to France either. I'm mortified, so I am!' And she flounced out, tussling in the doorway with Jess, who was just coming in.

'What's up with her?'

'Don't call your Aunt Edith "her". She's upset because Peter won't volunteer to fight in France.'

Jess helped herself to a biscuit. At twelve years of age she was already ripening into maturity and beauty. 'He's in for a rough time, then, and it'll serve him right.'

'Jess!'

The girl shrugged and took a second biscuit. 'I'm only telling the truth. Folk don't like young men who shirk their duty to their country. If everyone was like Peter, the Germans'd get everything their own way.' Her blue eyes brightened and she changed the subject. 'Can I go to the La Scala tonight, Mam? There's a really good film on.'

'I'll see. Leave those biscuits alone, will you! And go and see if the washing's dry. If it is, bring it in from the line,' Lessie ordered, and frowned as her daughter sauntered from the room, her heart-shaped little face bulging with the biscuit she had just crammed into her mouth. Jess was shallow and self-centred, altogether too interested in posing before a mirror and reading women's magazines and sitting in picture houses. Lessie worried more about her than about Ian and Dorry. Ian was practical and sensible, although the old warmth between them had never quite recovered from the boy's accusations after Murdo's desertion. As for Dorothea, she was quiet and biddable, and Andrew had already decided that she should become a schoolteacher.

But Jess – Lessie sighed as she gathered up the teacups and put the biscuits back into their tin. Jess was no scholar. She loved spending money, but as yet there was no indication as to how she was going to earn it when the time came.

A training camp was set up in Wood Street and the Greenock folk became used to the sight of the soldiers swaggering about the streets in their clumsy and often ill-fitting khaki uniforms. Men in ordinary civilian clothes without the armband that showed that they had volunteered and were waiting their turn to go became objects of suspicion, sneered at and on occasion treated roughly.

When he came home on leave before going off to France, Lieutenant Martin Warren was welcomed like a hero. His mother held parties so that she could show him off, and when he toured the refinery to make his farewells, darkly handsome in his uniform, the women employees, regardless of age, gaped in unashamed admiration.

'Not away yet?' Martin asked, pausing by Peter Fisher's desk in the counting house.

'No, Mr Martin.' Peter got to his feet and resisted the temptation

153

to say 'sir'. He had to work hard all the time to overcome the upbringing his mother had given him.

The deep brown eyes beneath the peaked hat were sympathetic. 'Not fit enough?'

Peter swallowed. 'I don't believe in killing.'

Martin Warren blinked, long dark lashes briefly sweeping cheeks that still bore the bloom of naive youth. His eyes hardened, but his voice remained level when he said, 'Sometimes it has to be done, old chap. And someone has to do it.' Then he turned on his heel and left, presenting a broad, upright, khaki-covered back.

Peter was used by now to seeing people's backs. He was used to being ignored in shops while men in uniform or bearing armbands were attended to before him. He was used to sudden silences when he entered public houses or departments in the refinery or even the house he had grown up in. Aunt Marion was as upset as his mother at his decision, and the two of them only spoke to him when they had to. Even the food they dumped down before him tasted different, as though it had been prepared by someone who didn't care. He had always been a loner but he had never known until now what it was like to be an outcast.

Despite the fact that his own son had gone to fight the enemy, Andrew Warren was kind enough to Peter. He continued to employ him and to talk to him when the occasion arose as though everything was as it had been before and there was no war. And there was one other ally, an ally Peter had been unaware of until he happened to meet her in the street one evening.

His first impulse on coming across his mother's sister was to mutter a greeting and hurry by, but Lessie caught hold of his sleeve and he had to stop.

'Peter, I've not seen you for many a long month.' Her hazel eyes crinkled into a smile and he twisted his stiff mouth up at the corners in polite response. Peter was unused to smiling and a complete stranger to laughter.

'Hello, Aunt Lessie. How are you?'

'Och, I'm fine. Getting older, like all the rest of us. Are you off to night school?'

'No, just out for a bit of a walk.'

'I'm on my way home from the shop. Come with me, Peter. It's a long time since we had a visit from you.'

He stared down at her, astonished, then began to shake his head. 'I'd best—'

'Come on.' She took a firm grip of his arm and began to walk. Short of struggling free he had no option but to accompany her. 'I'm getting a crick in my neck looking up at you, and it'd be more comfortable if we were both in chairs. Here, you can carry my shopping bag for me.'

She chattered all the way back to Cathcart Street, apparently oblivious of the pointed stares passersby directed at Peter, the audible remarks from a group of women who were standing outside their closes, arms folded, enjoying the last warmth of the October evening. From the river a boat's siren sounded and a sharp-eyed seagull on a chimney stack high above the road answered it with a harsh scream.

Ian was out delivering goods to shop customers and Jess had gone to the cinema with her best friend, but Dorothea was at home, curled up in an armchair in the kitchen. She got up when Lessie ushered Peter in and put down her book, smiling at him.

'Make a cup of tea, pet,' Lessie told her, taking her coat off. 'And we'll have toast. You'd like some toast, wouldn't you, Peter? You'll find a pot of strawberry jam in that bag you've got. Take your coat off, man, and sit down in that chair, it's the most comfortable. Give him the toasting fork, Dorry, he can see to the bread for us.'

There was a warmth and cheerfulness about the little kitchen that Peter had never found in the house he had been raised in. It began to seep into his bones as he watched Dorothea and Lessie bustle about. He caught the girl's eye, and she smiled shyly at him. She had none of Jess's vitality, but her violet eyes and the auburn sheen in her dark curly hair gave her a quiet beauty. As she stooped to put a plate of bread slices near to his hand he caught sight of the puckered scar that bisected her right cheek. He vaguely recalled his mother saying something to her aunt about that scar and the pity of it, spoiling the girl's chances of marriage. Peter disagreed; Dorothea was too pretty to be marred by a mere scar.

They drank strong scalding tea and ate hot toast and strawberry jam and Peter felt the wound inside, continually aggravated by the results of his decision not to be part of the war, heal a little. He told them something of his job at the refinery and listened to Dorothea talking about school and Lessie's description of the day she had just spent at the shop, and was glad that he had met his aunt. Now and then, as she talked or listened, one hand went up to push back the strands of soft fair hair that kept falling across her face. The sparkle in her hazel eyes and the smile that came readily to her lips made him suspect that his Aunt Lessie would never really look old. Not like his mother, with her mouth narrowing by the year and her dark hair liberally streaked with grey.

When she had finished her tea, Dorothea went off to do homework in the room she shared with Jess. Stacking dishes in the sink, Lessie said quietly to her nephew, 'Are they hard on you, son?'

He didn't have to ask what she meant. 'Mr Warren's very understanding, but the rest of them – and my mother and Great-Aunt Marion – don't even try to grasp what I'm saying. Is it so hard, Aunt Lessie? Is it difficult to believe that some folk just cannae bring themselves to kill other folk?' His hands tightened round the cup he was holding. 'They think I'm scared. They think I'm a coward.' His voice broke on the last word and he swallowed hard. 'I'm not scared about what might happen to me. We all have to die sometime.'

'I know you're not frightened for yourself. You never were, not even as a wee laddie. You aye faced the world and I admired you for it.'

He gaped at her in amazement. 'I wish I'd known that.'

'That's why I'm telling you now. Your mother was too hard on you, Peter. She never meant to be, it was her way of bringing you up properly.'

'She's ashamed of me. And so's Great-Aunt Marion. I'm going to move out, Aunt Lessie. I'll find myself a room to rent somewhere.'

'I wish we'd space for you here, son, but with the girls growing up . . .'

He shook his head. 'It's kind of you but I'd not come here even if you had the room. I'd not want to bring shame on you or get you into trouble with your neighbours.'

'Don't you worry your head about that, I can handle the neighbours!'

He laughed. 'I think you can. But I need to be on my own.'

'You'll come here when you're in need of company?'

He nodded, looking down at the hands clasped between his knees. Then he said suddenly, 'I'll tell you what scares me. I get nightmares about it sometimes. It's not so much killing lads like myself, though that's bad enough. It's what would happen if I didn't manage to do it properly. What if I hurt someone sore and he was left to die slowly, in agony? I cannae get the picture of it out of my mind, and I – I c-couldnae—'

To his horror he felt the tears spill down his cheeks, dripping onto his hands. He tucked his head low so that she couldn't see his face and felt her hands on his shoulders. Then she was on the arm of the chair, turning his face into her body, holding him. She smelled of scented soap and her breast was soft. Peter Fisher pressed his cheek into it and sobbed, deep wrenching sobs that had been waiting for too long for release.

'I'm s-sorry—'

'Sshh,' said Lessie, holding him tightly, rocking him. 'No need to be sorry, laddie. You have a good cry. God knows you've earned it.'

Dorothea had never heard a man crying before. In the small bedroom through the wall she listened, the exercise book she had been writing in forgotten; listened, and felt her heart break with pity for the man who wept so despairingly in the next room.

As time passed, the ordinary people of Britain became familiar with foreign names that had been unknown to them before. The Dardanelles. Gallipolli. Ypres. The liner *Lusitania* was sunk by German torpedoes and the appeals for fresh volunteers continued. In the first two months of the war the required minimum height for a man applying to become a soldier had dropped from five feet eight inches to five feet five inches. A month later it dropped by another two inches, resulting in a great surge in recruitment among men from the poorer areas of Greenock, men who were wiry enough but hadn't grown tall because of poor nutrition in their youth. Some of them volunteered in Greenock's own battalion, the 3rd (Highland) Howitzer Brigade of the Royal Field Artillery, and in the Greenock Naval Company.

The townsfolk grew used to the skirl of the pipes as lines of men marched from the training camp to Fort Matilda Station where they entrained on the first leg of their journey to the trenches in France. Peter, who had found himself a room in the Vennel, grew more and more morose, seeing nothing of his mother and sometimes staying away from Lessie's house for months at a time.

As the men left, the women moved in to keep offices and factories and transport going. There were fewer bruised faces among Lessie's customers and a new air of confidence straightened many a woman's shoulders once she became her family's breadwinner. Those with small children found child-minders among elderly relatives and neighbours and went into munitions or offices or manned the tramcars and buses. They earned good money, though the price of tea and some other goods began to rise, taking with them the cost of living. A lot of domestic servants, too, went into factories for better money, but Edith Fisher stayed loyal to the Warrens.

'It's not seemly for women to do men's work,' she said sternly, and when Jess asked with studied, wide-eyed innocence how the country was to be run in wartime without the help of its women, she snapped back, 'That's for the Government to decide, miss. That's what they're there for.'

'But the Government's decided that w—' Jess began before a warning glare from her mother made her subside.

Andrew Warren, who had lost a fair number of his male workforce, offered Ian a job in the sugar refinery laboratories with the refinery paying for evening chemistry classes at the Technical School. Ian, who had become restless at school, accepted at once and settled in happily.

In August 1915 Dorothea came home just before the new school term started and announced, pink-cheeked and defiant, that she had found herself a job in a small cotton mill in Port Glasgow. Lessie stared at her, dismayed. This was not what Andrew had planned for his daughter.

'But Dorry, we – I wanted you to stay on and become a teacher. You know that!'

'Ian's the brainy one of the family. I'm not nearly clever enough to teach. And since you won't let me work in the shop with you I decided that I'd find something for myself.'

Lessie thought of what Andrew's reaction would be and said in a voice that was not to be defied, 'You can go right back to Rattray's, young lady, and tell them you've changed your mind and you're staying on at the school!'

Dorothea, normally a biddable girl, glared back at her foster mother, her mouth mutinous. 'I'll not do it, Mam. I'm too old for school. I want to earn my own money instead of costing you.'

When Lessie broke the news to Andrew on his next visit he reacted just as she had thought he would. 'You shouldn't have allowed it. You should have ordered her to give up the job and stay on at school!'

'I tried, but she'd have none of it. In any case, I'm not so sure that we've got the right to dictate to young people when it comes to their own lives. We don't own them, we can't force them to do as we want. If you're so set on your daughter being a schoolteacher, you try to tell her what to do!'

'I should have taken her to live with me in Gourock and be damned to what Madeleine thought. I've a good mind to do it now.'

'You'll not get my consent to it, and surely I've got a right to have my say. Dorry's just at the age where she needs to know where she belongs. When the time comes for her to know the truth she'll need to be told properly and given time to come round to the idea, not just snatched out of my life and into yours because you disapprove of what she's doing with herself.'

They glared at each other for a moment, then his face relaxed into a reluctant grin that was startlingly youthful in spite of the touch of silver over each temple. 'I might have known she'd have plans of her own. For a moment there I forgot that she's Anna's daughter too. Very well, let her be – for the moment.'

'There's one good thing; now that she's earning there'll be no need for you to go on paying her keep.'

The smile disappeared. 'Don't talk nonsense, Lessie Carswell,' he said stiffly. 'As long as she's under your roof I'll support her. I've no intention of stopping.'

A flutter went through the young ladies of the town when Captain Martin Warren came home on leave early in 1916. In the past year he had matured into a handsome, confident man who wore his uniform with accomplished ease. Both his parents were taken aback when he announced that he was thinking of making the army his career.

'I know that you were counting on me joining you in the refinery, Father,' he said as he and his parents waited for their guests to arrive for an evening soiree Madeleine had arranged solely to show off her soldier son, 'but the life I've led since this war began has broadened my horizons. I enjoy being in the army. When this lot's over and done with I could apply for a posting anywhere in the world.'

Madeleine, as lovely as ever despite the silver streaks scattered through her thick hair, put a hand on his arm. 'But my darling, Helene and I have worked our poor fingers to the bone knitting and sewing and holding bazaars, your father has lost half his workforce and now that the Government's controlling the buying of sugar he has to work hard to make sure that the refinery gets all it needs. We've scarcely enough servants left to keep the house going. Surely we've all done enough for this war without losing you altogether to a military life!'

'D'you know what I saw this morning in the town?' Martin asked, straight-faced, 'A woman, delivering coal. Carrying a bag of coal into a close on her back.'

Madeleine went white to the lips and drew herself to her full height. 'No doubt she was too ignorant to know how to knit or sew or run bazaars. Or are you making mock of us, implying that your sister and your mother should be doing more, descending to working-class level?'

'Of course not. I'm quite certain that you do more than your fair

158

share as it is. And you know I'd never mock my little maman.' Martin reverted to the old French name that he and Helene had dropped as they grew into adulthood. Madeleine's eyes softened and she reached both hands out to him.

'Change your mind, my darling. Come back to us when this terrible business is over.'

Martin threw an imploring look at his father. Andrew, standing by the drawing-room window watching the sun go down over the river, put his own disappointment aside and said gently, recalling Lessie Carswell's comments about Dorothea's decision to work in the mills, 'My dear, Martin's a man now. He must make his own decisions.'

Madeleine pouted, an expression that had delighted Andrew in their youth, but one that looked decidedly out of place now that she was into middle age. 'I might have known better than to ask you to intervene. You never have cared overmuch about what happens to your children,' she said icily, and swept from the room with a rustle of skirts.

Left alone, father and son looked at each other wryly. 'Sorry, Father.' Martin gave a Gallic shrug of the shoulders. 'I made a mess of that. I should have told you both separately. I might have known she'd be upset.'

Andrew looked at his son and felt a sudden surge of love for him. He bitterly regretted the way he had allowed Madeleine to put a wedge between himself and his children as they grew into adolescence and adulthood. If he hadn't been so immersed in developing the refinery he might have recognised the danger in time and moved to avert it. But now it was too late, and all he could do for his son was to support him – and pray to God that Martin lived through the war and had a future, no matter what he might choose to do with it.

'Is it very bad?' he asked, and the young man shrugged again.

'Oh, you know – like the curate's egg, I suppose. Good in parts.' He grinned, then sobered for a moment. 'The bad parts can be hellish, though. The noise, and losing people one's grown to know and care about. But it's got to be done. We've been lucky with the gas in my area, no problems from it so far. And I like the comradeship, the sense of belonging. I'm sorry about walking away from the refinery, though, I know it'll make things difficult for you.'

'Don't worry about that. You can never be happy if you're not doing what you want. In any case,' Andrew added wryly, 'I still consider myself to be a young man and I intend to live for a good many years yet. You may well have finished with the army by the time your turn comes to inherit the refinery.'

A motor car came chugging up the driveway and came to a halt at the door. The horn tootled unmusically and Helene, slim and elegant and beautiful, burst from the front door and threw herself into the arms of the young man who climbed down from the driving seat. By happy chance her current boyfriend, a naval officer, was on leave at the same time as Martin.

'They look pleased with each other,' her twin said as the couple, arms entwined, moved out of sight towards the front porch.

'They are. I think that this might be the right man for your sister. Bob would make a good husband.'

'He will as far as Mother's concerned. His family's got plenty of money. Which reminds me – I suppose she's got someone lined up for me this evening? Pretty, I hope?'

'Pretty face, elegant background, beautiful bankbook,' Andrew said, and as they laughed together he wished without much hope that Madeleine might spare him some time with Martin this leave.

In June 1916 the Military Service Act came into force and Peter Fisher was summoned to face a service tribunal to explain why he wasn't yet serving in the army. He stood before Andrew Warren's desk, pale-faced but determined, and asked for time off to attend the tribunal. 'If I don't attend they'll come for me, and that'd upset the running of the refinery, sir.'

Andrew sat back in his chair, studying the young man thoughtfully. He had learned from Lessie that his counting house clerk was his parlourmaid's son, though nobody, including Edith, Madeleine and Peter, was aware of his knowledge. 'Do you intend to go into the army?'

'No, sir.'

'They can offer you a non-combatant role as a clerk or a stretcher bearer.'

'I don't believe in the whole business, Mr Warren.'

'Do you belong to the No-Conscriptions Fellowship or some such organisation that might give you backing?'

'I've got my own beliefs. I don't need to join any organisation.'

'I see.' Andrew paused, then asked quietly, 'You know what'll probably happen to you, Fisher?'

'Yes, I know. If you wish,' said Peter levelly, 'I'll hand in my notice now and get out of your way.'

'I've no intention of accepting it.' Andrew rocked his chair back on its hind legs, chewing at his lower lip. 'I could transfer you to another department and claim that you're necessary to the refinery.'

A flush rose to the pale face on the other side of the desk, almost obscuring a large yellowing bruise on one side of the tense jaw. 'It's kind of you, Mr Warren, but I've no intention of hiding. I'd prefer to stand by my beliefs.'

'I see. What happened to your face?'

'I walked into a lamppost.'

'It's easily done.' Andrew's voice was dry. 'Tell me, did you turn the other cheek?'

Peter's eyes widened with surprise as he looked down at his employer, then a faint smile twitched at his mouth. 'I don't believe in that, sir. I gave the lamppost as good as I got.'

'I'm glad to hear it. Tell the chief clerk that you've got my permission to take the day off. On second thoughts,' Andrew said as Peter turned towards the door, 'leave it to me. I'll tell him myself.' He wasn't a fool, he knew well enough that the only time the other men in the refinery spoke to Peter Fisher was to ridicule and revile him. He knew, from Lessie, how the young man had been turned out from one squalid lodging house after another. No doubt he had run into quite a few 'lampposts' as well. Better that the day off came as an order from the refinery owner himself.

Davie Kirkwood, now thirty-three years of age, was also called before a tribunal, but since the Government had taken control of engineering in the interests of the war effort, and Davie had seen the way the wind was blowing in good time and had turned his interests to serving the shipyards, he proved easily that his continued presence in Port Glasgow was far more important than his presence in the French trenches.

For Davie, the war had come just at the right time. When rumours of war were flying around the country and being discounted by most people, he had carefully started to build up his small company with money borrowed from the banks. Now, with Government backing, he had managed to buy another small engineering shop and had combined it with his own. He had also contracted enough business to keep both his shops going for three years and the loans were being paid back.

To his sister Lessie's annoyance he had not yet married, though with a third of the men of marriageable age away from home there were plenty of bonny women to choose from. For Davie there had only been one woman, and now that she lay in the cemetery, out of his reach but never out of his heart and his thoughts, all his ambition was concentrated on becoming as wealthy and as powerful as the man who had, to Davie's mind, owned her.

It was for Anna that Davie schemed and worked and saved, only for Anna. Jeers and threats and the white feathers the older women handed out to healthy young men not yet in uniform were of no importance to Davie Kirkwood; he accepted the feathers with a bow then let them fall from his fingers and walked on, leaving the donor feeling that she, and not he, had been mocked.

In the first months of the war, as soon as the drive for recruits began to take hold, Joseph Kirkwood had vanished from the town. His sisters and brother had no knowledge of where he was, and whether or not he had been called up or managed to escape being put into uniform.

'But you can be certain,' Edith said darkly when his name was mentioned, 'that our Joseph wouldnae risk his precious skin for anyone. If you ask me, we've all seen the last of him – and good riddance to bad rubbish!'

As he expected, Peter wasn't as fortunate as his Uncle Davie when it was his turn to go before the tribunal. They contemptuously dismissed as unfounded and unpatriotic his refusal to fight and in due course the letter ordering him to report to barracks in Glasgow arrived. When he ignored it, two grim-faced police officers arrived at

161

his lodgings early one morning and bundled him off to the police station. There, he was handed over the military police, taken to Glasgow, and locked in a tiny empty guard room when he refused to put on the uniform that was handed to him.

He lay in the night-dark on the cement floor, tightly curled up to keep out the worst of the cold, his body aching from the rough handling he had received, and tried to sleep. There was worse to come, he knew that well enough even without the graphic warnings the guards had given him.

He hadn't had time to say goodbye to his mother, or to Lessie. Not that his mother would have wanted to see him, for they had become estranged months earlier when he steadfastly refused to change his mind.

But he regretted not being given time to see his Aunt Lessie once more.

18

It began to seem, as 1916 gave way to 1917, as though the war had always been there and always would be there. In France thousands were dying. Death was indifferent to age and nationality, and it seemed to Lessie as she worked on in the shop and looked after her house and her family that the old men who planned and manipulated the war and stayed at home while the younger generation marched out to do their bidding were just as indifferent.

'Mebbe they should give women more than the vote,' she said once to Jess as the two of them dragged a sack of grain across the shop floor to rest against the counter. 'Mebbe they should let them have a turn at running a few countries. Women know more than men about the value of one single life. They'd no' stand by and see thousands cut down in their prime. They'd find some way to stop it.'

The bag was where they wanted it. Jess, panting with effort, straightened up and stared at her mother. 'You've changed your tune. You werenae even interested in the suffragettes, and now listen to you!'

'I was never unsympathetic to them, just busy with my own problems. But a terrible war like this one makes everyone think harder about what's important.'

'Hmmph,' Jess said, and went to put the kettle on for a cup of tea. She had been at odds with her mother ever since leaving school three months earlier, when Lessie had decreed that she should come and work in the shop.

'Elma's rheumatism's got a lot worse and now that Ian's at the refinery I need someone fit and strong to help me.'

'Why me? You wouldn't let Dorry work in the shop, and now she's enjoying herself in Rattray's Mill and I'm miserable here. It's not fair!' Jess had whined, but Lessie had been adamant. Jess, spoiled from the beginning by a father who had then gone waltzing off and left her, never thought of anyone but herself. She immersed herself in women's magazines, lingering over the photographs of models. She turned her aptitude for sewing to making her clothes as fashionable as possible, brushed her long fair hair one hundred times every night, went to bed with her pretty face layered with cream that left grease stains on the pillows, and walked about the house with books balanced on her head in an effort to acquire a stately grace. Lessie had finally decided that it was time her daughter learned that growing up carried responsibilities with it.

Jess had had no option but to do as she was told, but she let her annoyance show in no uncertain way. It sometimes seemed to Lessie that Dorry, Anna's daughter, was a more loving child to her than either of her own. She blamed herself, when her spirits were low, for marrying Murdo and giving Ian a father to replace the one he had never known. Without Murdo around she could have kept Donald alive for Ian. They might have retained the closeness that had been so precious to her during his first few years and had never returned after Murdo left.

But if she hadn't married Murdo, beautiful, enchanting, maddening, selfish Jess wouldn't have been born. Sometimes Lessie thought that that might not have been a bad thing. Her daughter came through from the back shop to hand her a cup of steaming hot tea. 'I gave Elma's face a wipe with the flannel and sorted her pillows and gave her her tea,' she said and Lessie felt guilty at wishing Murdo, and therefore Jess, out of her past.

Some of the men who had set off from the Vennel with hearts high at the beginning of the war were back home again, manoeuvring themselves on crutches because one leg was missing or maimed beyond repair, or with an empty sleeve pinned across their chests. Some were blinded or deafened, some so badly scarred that they were almost unrecognisable, some had their lungs permanently damaged by mustard gas. Their womenfolk – wives, mothers, sisters – took on the task of caring for them as well as earning and seeing to the house and the children.

Some men would never come back; day after day the telegrams arrived: Missing in Action, Killed in Action, Died of Wounds.

One customer came wandering, dazed, into the shop, telegram in hand, disbelieving, needing to share her disbelief with other women rather than with her wide-eyed, wondering children. 'It's like the pawn,' she said bitterly after displaying the briefly worded form. 'They take your man and they give you a ticket for him.' Her face, often marked by a heavy fist in the past, was ashen and desolate as she stared down at the telegram. 'But ye cannae redeem him, no matter what ye're willin' tae pay. Ye can never redeem him.'

Tears began to slide slowly down her face and the other women stood gawping at her, huddled in their shawls. One reached out a hand then drew it back, as though touching the widow might infect her and put her own husband, still alive as far as she knew, into danger. Lessie went round the counter and put an arm about the weeping woman, drawing her to a chair, her own eyes moist.

Peter occupied Lessie's thoughts a lot and she worried about him as though he were one of her own. Once the army discovered that it could do nothing to change his mind, he had been handed back to the civilian authorities, taken to court in Glasgow, and was serving a prison sentence. She received the occasional scrawled note from him, written on prison paper and containing the minimum amount of news. She only knew where he was, not how he felt, what it was like, how he was being treated. She could only guess the answer to these questions, and her guesses frightened and chilled her. She wrote every week, filling her letters with love and caring and support, and sent parcels of food and warm clothing from time to time, but they were never mentioned in his notes and she had a suspicion that they were never given to him. All the same, she kept sending them, just in case.

She said nothing to Edith, who never let Peter's name pass her lips. It was as though Edith had never had a son. Andrew Warren had tried to find out more, but conscientious objectors had no friends, and the authorities remained tight-lipped and unwilling to help in any way.

'It'll probably be worse for him than it would be in France,' Lessie said wretchedly when Andrew reported his failure.

'That's the idea. They want to make life so hard that the men'll decide to opt for army life instead.'

'It's not fair.' Without realising it Lessie resorted to Jess's habitual complaint. 'He's such a gentle laddie. All he's doing is protesting against having to hurt other boys like himself.'

A tear rolled down one cheek and Andrew Warren took an involuntary step towards her, his arms reaching out. Then they dropped to his sides as Lessie scrubbed at her face and stiffened her back and said, 'Well now, this isn't going to balance the books, is it? Andrew,' she had started calling him by his Christian name in private, after a great deal of coaxing on his part, 'I was looking at this ledger last night, and there seems to be more money free this month than usual.'

'That's because you're doing more business. Even with prices going up, the women who use your shop are earning more money now that they're doing men's work and getting decent wages for it. Then there's Ian and Dorothea bringing something in, and you've been shrewd in the way you've handled the shop.'

'That's thanks to you and your advice.'

'Nonsense, I just listened to your ideas and gave you the bit of encouragement you needed to put them into practice. Now it's all starting to show results.'

The cleft between her brows deepened in a way that he had long since begun to find endearing. 'It seems wrong to be making more money than I need at a time like this.'

'Your brother wouldn't agree with you from what I've heard,' he said without thinking, and was rewarded with a cool glare.

'My brother works very hard. Besides, he's dealing with companies. I'm dealing with folk.'

'Lessie, when this war's over – and one day it will be – the men'll come back to claim the jobs the women are keeping open for them. The women'll go back to being dependent on their husbands again and there might not be so much money then for shopkeepers such as you. Make the most of it while you can, my dear. Invest it, make it work for you.'

'How can money work?'

'You lend it to various companies for their own use, and in return they undertake to pay you interest, an annual percentage of the sum you've invested. The capital – the amount you first loaned to them –

is still yours, and the money's earning more money for you instead of lying in a bank.'

Her mouth had dropped open. 'I've never heard the like!'

Andrew hid a smile and said solemnly, 'Most wealthy people live by investing their money and collecting the interest.'

'You think I should do that?'

'If I were you I'd invest a small sum, see how things go.'

'Could I invest it in your refinery?'

He was taken aback. 'You could, but I'd not advise it.'

'Why? Is it not doing well?'

This time he allowed the smile to spread across his face. This was indeed the most interesting woman he had ever come across. 'It's doing fine, but it would be a worry to me if your hard-earned money was in my charge. I'd as soon you talked to your bank manager. He could advise you.'

'If I do, can I ask your opinion on whatever he says?'

'Indeed you can,' Andrew assured her, and she nodded, satisfied, and turned her attention back to the ledger.

In January 1917 Ian celebrated his eighteenth birthday and within two weeks he was on his way to France as a member of the Medical Corps. For the past two years he had taken night classes in First Aid as well as his chemistry classes in preparation for the day when he would join the army.

Tall and broad in his khaki uniform, his red hair glowing like a beacon in the cold February morning, he hugged Lessie on the station platform and said, 'Don't worry, Mother, I'll soon be back. This time next year it'll all be over.'

The old familiar phrase brought the tears she had been fighting back into her eyes. 'Oh, Ian!'

'I'll be fine. I'm only going to be an orderly, they won't be pushing me into the trenches with a gun. They've got more sense than to do that, I'd probably shoot my own mates by accident.' He turned to his sister. 'If you get to America before I come home, Jess, give my love to Mary Pickford.'

Jess had never forgiven him for catching her in front of the mirror one day, acting out one of the famous film star's more dramatic scenes in a film that had recently been shown in Greenock. She sniffed disdainfully and eyed a young couple who were locked in each other's arms a few yards away. Scenes like that were being enacted all over the station platform – men in uniform, tearful women. It was romantic, Jess thought, and wished that she had a soldier in uniform to bid farewell to. Not Ian – someone who looked more like Douglas Fairbanks.

'Ian!' There was a flurry further down the platform and a hand clutching a hat waved high in the air. People stepped hurriedly out of the way and some were nudged aside as Dorothea came flying along, her coat flapping open, her dark hair escaping from the bun at the back of her head. She reached them and stopped, fanning herself with

166

her hat. Her eyes were bright and her face rosy with her run through the cold air. At first glance the scar down her cheek looked like a thin ruffled strip of pink ribbon that had come loose from her hair and drifted across her pretty face as she ran. 'I thought I was going to be too late!'

'Dorry, just look at you!' Scandalised, Lessie began to tidy the girl up. 'You didn't run through the town like that, did you? What would people think? And why aren't you at work?'

Dorothea pushed the busy hands away, her violet eyes fixed on Ian. 'I asked for time off. I couldn't let you go without saying goodbye.'

'You said goodbye to him this morning,' Jess pointed out. She was beginning to shift from one foot to the other and eye the clock. She had seen an advertisement in the *Telegraph* the night before; a smart assistant was wanted in a well-known dress shop in Gourock, the ability to sew an advantage, must be willing to learn. She was impatient to get her mother on her own, to convince her that she, Jess, would be much better employed in a dress shop than working in the little corner shop in the Vennel.

'It's not the same as saying goodbye properly at the station.'

'You're covered in cotton fluff,' Ian pointed out with amusement. Dorothea looked down at herself and laughed.

'I didn't stop to brush it off. I'll be much tidier when you come home, I promise.' Then, as the order came to board the train, she threw her arms about the young soldier and kissed him on the cheek. 'I'll write to you. Take care, come home to us.'

He held her briefly, then turned to his young sister and, finally, to his mother. 'Don't worry, I'll be fine,' he whispered, and for a moment he was the old Ian, Donald's son, Lessie's precious firstborn. Then the warmth of him left her embrace and he was gone, just another arm in the forest of khaki-covered arms reaching out to wave as the train slowly moved off.

Rattray's cotton mill was small and stuffy. It smelled of oil and it was so noisy that the workers could only communicate with the people who sat back to back to them by leaning backwards so that their shoulder-blades touched and bellowing. Wisps of cotton continually eddied in the air like tiny flower petals, landing wherever they pleased – on hair, eyelashes, and clothes. When Dorothea changed out of her working clothes in the evenings she had to carry them out to the back yard and shake them vigorously; when she brushed her long dark hair in the bedroom they shared, Jess complained about the fluff that was teased from its strands.

She worked in the winding shop, winding spun cotton onto bobbins which then went off to loom shops all over the country to be woven into cloth. It was monotonous work requiring continual attention: all too often one of the three threads being combined on the one spindle broke and the ends had to be cut with the knife each winder carried, then blended back onto the spindle. But Dorothea liked the mill. She liked the independence it gave her, the knowledge that she was earning her own keep. Although she was as much a part of the Carswell family as Ian or Jess, there had always been a part of her that knew that she stood alone, without her own parents to care for her. Her father, Lessie had told her, was unknown, her mother a friend and former neighbour of Lessie's. Sometimes, on the rare occasions when Dorothea caught the scent of roses, she fleetingly recalled pictures of another life, a small garden, a beautiful red-haired woman in pretty clothes that rustled. But she wasn't a romantic like Jess and she didn't speculate on her real parents very often, preferring to live in the present.

The mill was mainly staffed by women on war work, together with some men too old or frail for war service and a few lads who were too young to go into uniform. Many of the women were already known to her as customers in Lessie's shop. Two of the men who worked in the place had been invalided out of France: Johnny Morning, who supervised the winding shop, had only one foot now, and stumped about the place on crutches, and Robbie McKinlay, who tended to the machinery, looked ten years older than his thirty years because he had been one of the first of the British Tommies to be gassed in the trenches. His sentences were jerky and breathless and he was often off sick, but he had been a good worker before the war and Mr Rattray had, as promised, made sure that he would have a job to come back to.

Seeing the two men every day made Dorothea fear for Ian, but she kept her thoughts from Lessie, who had enough to worry her, and from Ian himself, writing him long amusing letters about her work in the mill, any gossip she happened to hear around the town, the film she and her friend Aileen had gone to the previous night, and Aileen herself, with her frizzy brown hair and bold brown eyes, her sturdy body and quick mind.

When Johnny Morning decreed that the women in the winding shop could only have three minutes away from their looms to answer the call of nature, it was Aileen who brought angry colour to his face by suggesting with a sweet smile that he could cut the time limit to two minutes by providing buckets, to be hung on the ends of the machines.

'Then we'd no have tae move far from our seats at all,' she said, and Johnny stumped out, followed by gales of female mirth.

On the following day, his three-minute rule, written out and signed by his own fist, was firmly pinned to the privy door. Aileen coaxed a pencil stub from someone and wrote beneath his signature, 'A man's ambition's very poor, to put his name on the shithouse door.' The notice disappeared within the hour, and after that a lad was stationed halfway up the stairs with Johnny's pocket watch in his hand, to time the women as they climbed past him to the privy, each with her own comment to make into his ear so that his face was permanently crimson.

'Och, that Johnny Morning wis a sour-faced bugger afore ever he lost his foot,' Aileen said blithely when Dorothea voiced sympathy for the overseer. 'My ma used tae work here an' she could tell ye a tale or two aboot him. I see nae sense in feelin' sorry for him now. When's he ever sorry for us?' Then she added with a toss of her head, sending a cloud of cotton into the air, 'You're too nice, Dorry. Ye'll never make yer way in this world bein' sorry for every bugger you meet.'

'I've got used to the sound of the machinery all the time. At the beginning it was so deafening that I never thought I would.' Lying on his bunk, Orderly Ian Carswell of the Medical Corps stopped reading his foster sister's letter and wondered if he himself would ever get used to the noise he lived with now, the muffled but continual pounding of the guns, the crack and boom of explosions, the bark of orders, and, worst of all, the continual sound of suffering. He was at one of the advance dressing stations where the men were brought in for emergency treatment before being sent up the line to the casualty clearing stations and base hospitals – or to their graves. By this time he should have grown accustomed to the moaning and the cursing and the screaming, but he hadn't. Every time he went on duty he had to pause for a second outside the tent flaps and brace himself to enter.

Today the noise of the guns and the bombs was louder, without as much as a few minutes' blessed silence. For the third time the Allies were doggedly fighting for control of Ypres and the ambulances were almost nose to tail on the tracks between trenches and hospital tents, lining up to disgorge their quota of stretchers then turning at once, wheels slipping and splashing in the khaki-coloured watery mire, to head back towards the trenches for another load of wounded, dead and dying.

Someone shook his shoulder roughly and yelled in his ear that he was wanted back in the wards because there was another surge of incoming wounded. Ian came to himself with a jerk of fright and realised that he had fallen asleep reading Dorothea's letter. Running outside, slipping and slithering through the mud, he stuffed the letter into his breast pocket. At least the rain had stopped, though the sky overhead was grey and menacing. But the mud was still there. It was always there, Ian thought irritably, splashing through it. On more than one occasion, men left outside the overcrowded wards, their stretchers placed on the duckboards that were supposed to provide a firm path over the mud but rarely did, had sunk into it and drowned, too weak to save themselves.

'Orderly!' someone called as soon as Ian appeared in the big marquee tent that did little to prevent the rain, when it came, from dripping through the canvas onto the wounded. He made his way between beds, past stretchers laid on the ground because there was nowhere else to put the wounded, to the doctor who had beckoned him with a hand that looked as though it had gone rusty with other men's blood.

The canvas walls vibrated to the sound of explosions. The ward was crammed with surgeons, nurses, orderlies like himself, walking wounded stoically waiting their turn. Others writhed and cried out on stretchers and beds, or lay, already treated and drugged against pain, white-bandaged and silent, eyes closed in merciful oblivion or

169

open and staring in confusion and bewilderment at the bedlam that surrounded them. The strong disinfectant the nurses doused the wards with was mingled now with the stench of blood and putrefaction and vomit.

'Hold him,' the doctor said tersely, his own face drawn and ashen with exhaustion. Ian obediently put his weight on the shoulders of a fair-haired lad who was struggling against the hands that tried to help him, hoarsely shouting. He looked too young to be out of school, let alone fighting for his country. His uniform tunic was a ragged mess, some of it ground into the large bloody hole in his chest.

'It's all right, you'll be all right,' Ian told him, lying through his teeth, and the boy glared up at him and struggled harder to get away from the restraining hands and the pain and the sudden mess that had been made of his body and his world. A nurse appeared, hypodermic in hand, and in a moment or two the boy relaxed, his blue eyes closing, and Ian was free to answer another call for help.

Hurrying from one bed to another, his fingers brushed against his tunic pocket and felt the outline of the letter, folded again and again into a small square so that there was no danger of it falling out and being lost. Dorry's letters always bore a faint floral scent. He appreciated the letters he received from Lessie and Jess, but he had begun to look forward especially to hearing from Dorry, who never missed a week and who always seemed to manage to enclose a slice of Greenock, a breath of real life and sanity, between the pages. Sometimes he thought that without her letters he wouldn't be able to cope with the life he led now. 'Tell me about everything,' she wrote each time, but he never could. Instead, he wrote about the better moments, the friendships, the learning, the satisfaction of seeing critically wounded men bandaged up after emergency treatment or surgery, well enough to go on down the line and, hopefully, survive. It would be wrong to let any of his womenfolk know what the war was really like. It would be wrong to expose Dorry, with her shy smile and her gentleness, to the appalling cruelties of life, the terrible things that men filled with hate or fear or a determination to survive no matter what happened to others could do to fellow human beings.

'Orderly!'

With difficulty Ian made his way to the door, to where a doctor and nurse were kneeling beside a stretcher that had just been brought in. The nurse, scissors in hand, was trying to cut the sleeve of the patient's jacket.

'Nearly stood on the poor bloke's face,' the stretcher bearer was saying, looming over the trio. 'If he hadn't let out a groan I'd have missed seeing him. God knows how long he'd been lying in that shell hole. It's a wonder he didn't drown. I don't know how he managed to keep his head out of the water.'

'Let me.' Ian dropped to his knees beside the nurse and took the scissors. The man was an officer; his uniform jacket, sopping wet and thick with clay, was of good cloth and difficult to cut. Specially made for him, Ian thought as he worked, carefully sawing at the material without cutting into the skin beneath. Not like those poor Tommies who had to take whatever uniform they got, whether it was too tight or too loose, too long or too short. He had got into the habit of avoiding looking into faces; it helped to think of the dead and dying men as units rather than people who had been snatched by war from the business of living. But this time his eyes rested briefly on the face above the jacket he was mutilating. The officer's skin was grey with shock and loss of blood and it was easy to understand how the stretcher bearers had almost missed him in the mud. Black hair still dripping dirty water had been pushed back by someone from a face that looked very old, the skin tight against sharp protruding bones, the mouth a thin line, holding back its pain and its secrets.

The doctor's hand was on his patient's wrist, feeling for a pulse. 'He's still with us.'

Ian eased open the sleeve and the shirt beneath it. The wounded officer's arm was icy cold to the touch and slashed with a deep long cut from elbow to wrist. It had stopped bleeding and the lips of the wound were purple and puffy, the bone glinting dully from deep within. Ian moved aside and watched as the doctor's hand deftly travelled over the horrific wound.

'Sword slash. We might manage to save him. Find a bed for him, will you?'

'Over there,' Ian said tersely, and the wounded man moaned as the stretcher was lifted. As they eased him onto the narrow cot, the label pinned to the man's shoulder flipped over and Ian stared at the hastily scribbled words, then at the face.

The last time he had seen this man had been in Greenock, when Martin Warren, now quite unrecognisable as the handsome, confident young man he had been that day, had toured his father's sugar refinery to say goodbye to the workers.

19

Lessie's heart sank as she came in from the pleasant August evening and found Edith in the kitchen with Dorothea, her long, normally solemn face a mixture of expressions. Clearly she had important news; Lessie already knew what it was, and was grateful when Dorothea cut in ahead of her aunt, insisting that Lessie sit down and have something to eat.

'I'll have something later, pet. For now I'd love a good hot cup of tea.' Lessie kicked off her shoes and sank into her usual fireside chair with a sigh of relief.

'Why d'you have to stay open so late these nights?' her sister wanted to know.

'Because most of the women have work to go to during the day. The evening's the only time they've got free to do their shopping.'

'It's too much for you. You're not getting any younger.'

'It's kind of you to remind me,' Lessie said caustically. Not that she needed reminding on that particular evening. Her feet and legs ached, her head ached, and she felt as old as Methuselah.

'And you should have more help in the shop anyway. You've never replaced Jess yet. If she were my daughter,' Edith nagged on, 'I'd not have agreed to her going to work in that fancy dress shop. Not when your need's greater.'

'It's easier to do without her than to put up with her sulks when she's crossed. And with Ian away in France, I'm as well working than sitting at home worrying about him.' Lessie sipped at the hot tea and felt stronger, able to face her sister and ask, 'What brings you to Greenock, Edith?'

'You'll not have heard that Mr Martin—'

'We know about it,' said Dorothea, then flushed, catching Lessie's warning look just too late. The anticipation drained from Edith's face.

'Who told you?'

'Someone in the mill,' Dorothea said swiftly. 'And I ran to the shop in my dinner hour to tell Mam.' In actual fact Andrew Warren himself had told them, arriving at the flat early that morning, hollow-eyed with lack of sleep but restless with the need to talk to someone – to Lessie, Dorothea realised, and had quickly removed herself and Jess out of the house, off to work, leaving the two older people alone.

'I might've known word would travel fast. I came here as soon as I could.'

'That poor laddie – and his poor family,' Lessie said. 'How are they?'

'Mrs Warren's taken it very badly, and so's Miss Helene. We had to fetch the doctor for the mistress and she's in her bed, with nobody allowed to visit her. Mr Warren – well, nobody ever knows what's going on in his head. He keeps things to himself. Mind you, it must have been hard on him, trying to comfort the mistress and her screaming at him that he didn't care about what had happened to poor Mr Martin. She'd have nothing to do with him, so he just turned about first thing this morning and took himself out of the house and off to the refinery as if it was an ordinary day. Out of her mind, she was. We're wondering in the kitchen if she'll ever be right again.'

Dorothea had taken Lessie's cup and refilled it. Lessie bent her head over it, the steam warm on her cheeks. Andrew hadn't said a word to her about his wife that morning. He had just told her, calmly and without emotion, about his only son's death, and then the minute the door had closed behind the two girls, he had given a great shudder and been unable to stop shaking. She had taken him into her arms the way she had held the customer who had brought in the telegram announcing her husband's death in the trenches, and had held him until the trembling eased. Then she had made some tea, with whisky in it for Andrew, and sat on in her kitchen, long past the time she should have been in the shop, letting him talk about Martin as a baby, a toddler, a schoolboy.

'I'll have to go or I'll no' get the last tram back to Gourock,' Edith was saying. 'That's with waiting for you for so long, Lessie. Oh, before I go, our Peter's signed on in the army at last.'

'What?'

'I thought that'd surprise you.' Her sister's voice was smug. 'I got a letter from him this morning. He's finally seen the error of his ways. I knew he would.'

'Is that what he said?'

Edith gave a small shrug of the shoulders, rising to her feet and looking about for her bag. 'He says he couldnae stand up against them any more, whatever that means. The main thing is that he's done it. I don't know how I could have faced the Warrens today if I hadnae had that letter. I'd have been too ashamed. Which reminds me.' She paused at the door. 'D'you ever see our Davie?'

'Now and again. Not often.'

'There's another one that's got out of going to fight.'

'He's doing important work for the shipyards, Edith.'

'Aye, and making a fortune at the same time, from what I hear.' Edith sniffed, then said, 'While young lads like poor Mr Martin and your Ian – and my Peter too,' she added smugly, 'are fighting and dying for their country.'

'Don't talk about dying, Aunt Edith,' Dorothea said sharply, and Edith's eyebrows rose.

'You mind your manners, miss. Working in that mill's not good for her, Lessie. She's become impertinent since she went there. Anyway, I'm right in what I'm saying. Davie should think black burning shame of himself, but I don't suppose he will. Nor Joseph – I'm sure he's managed to keep out of the fighting too, wherever he is.'

'She's got a wicked tongue at times,' Dorothea said when Edith had gone.

'Dorry! That's no way to speak of your elders.'

'Being elder doesn't mean she's better. Why do Mr Warren's visits have to be such a secret?' Dorothea wanted to know.

'They're not a secret. It's just that it's his business who he calls on, not anyone else's. If he wants to tell Edith, it's up to him, not us. I think I'll away to my bed, Dorry.'

'Not until you've had something to eat,' the girl said firmly, starting to set the table.

'I'm not hungry.'

'That's because you're past hunger. It's not much, some potted meat and cold boiled potatoes. It'll not take a minute to fry them up for you. And I'll make fresh tea.' Dorothea touched a spill to the fire and used the flame to light the gas mantles. Part of Greenock was lit by electricity now, but not Cathcart Street. 'What d'you think Peter's up to, joining the army after all he said about it?'

Lessie remembered the few scribbled notes she had received from her nephew. 'I think it's as he said to his mother. He just hadn't the strength to stand up to them any longer, poor laddie.' She sighed, then got up and looked into the mirror hanging on the wall between the two china wally dugs she still thought of as Miss Peden's. The little frown between her hazel eyes had deepened and other lines had begun to spread out from the corners of her eyes and her mouth. She put a hand up to her hair, which was still fair, then noticed that the skin on the back of the hand was beginning to lose its elasticity. It took a moment's mental arithmetic to recall that she was thirty-seven years old now. Time wouldn't stay still for anyone, and in Lessie's case it had flown by unnoticed while she struggled for survival.

'D'you think I'm beginning to look old, Dorry?'

The girl left the frying pan and came to stand beside her, their heads almost touching. Lessie felt herself age as she compared her own face with Dorothea's fresh bloom. The younger woman had some of her mother's beauty; tonight the soft gas light teased auburn glints from her rich dark hair and when she smiled, the sparkle in her large violet eyes brought Anna to life again.

'Never! Mind you, you could do with a bit of colour in your face, and mebbe a nice modern hairdo.'

'Away you go, I've not got the time for that sort of nonsense!'

They were laughing as the door opened and Jess came in from a late evening at the shop where she had been taking part in a special fashion display to raise funds for the war effort. Smartly dressed, her pretty nose wrinkling appreciatively at the aroma of fried potatoes sizzling in the pan, she demanded some as well.

While Dorothea sliced another potato for her, Jess sat at the table chattering about the compliments she had received while modelling the gowns. To Jess the war, like anything else outside her own life, was a minor matter.

175

Ian and Dorothea climbed on, leaving the town behind, stopping once they had gained the hill fields to rest for a moment. Below them the River Clyde, dotted with vessels of all sizes, was folded and tucked between hills and fingers of land that thrust inquisitively into its waters. Gourock's grey stone skirts spilled down the hill and spread comfortably along the shoreline, with shipyard cranes outlined against the water here and there. They could hear the sound of the town's church bells calling through the clear autumn air, summoning worshippers to morning service.

They sat for a companionably silent five minutes before Ian stood and held out his hand. Dorothea sighed, but took it and let him hoist her to her feet. She turned her back on the river and followed him on up the hill. In another half-hour they were over its crest and on the downward walk to Loch Thom, the nineteenth-century reservoir that provided all the water needed by Greenock's residents and had, in the previous century, supplied power for its many mills and factories before electricity took over the running of the machinery. The loch, a flooded valley, lay in a great stretch of moorland cupped by the hills that fed it with burn water and rainwater. On its banks they found themselves a sheltered cranny surrounded by broom bushes that had now shed their golden blossoms. Dorothea spread out her jacket to sit on and Ian dropped onto the grass and opened the bag he had carried, dispensing sandwiches and lemonade.

'It's good to see so much green,' he said appreciatively, looking around at the springy grass, the trees and bushes, the clumps of reeds that fringed the loch like long eyelashes. 'It's like another world. You don't know how much you have until you leave it behind.'

He had said very little about France since coming home, and Lessie and Dorothea, aware that his leave was all too short, hadn't asked questions. Jess hadn't been interested enough to ask.

He slept when they'd finished eating, and Dorothea sat by him, her long legs tucked comfortably beneath her, watching the movement of the water and enjoying the peace of the place, so different from the noise and rattle of the mill. The loch, ruffled with tiny wavelets whipped up by the wind, looked like a stretch of dove-grey silk that some giant hand had carelessly tossed down among the hills. A bird called and was answered by another. The breeze rustled through the nearby bushes.

Ian woke suddenly, startled from sleep by the muffled thump of the guns, the noise of the wounded and dying. He stared around, bewildered at finding himself on the grassy lochside in the sunshine, with no noise but the birds and the soft lapping of small waves among the reeds. With a sigh of relief he unlocked tense muscles and lay back, waiting for his racing heart to slow down, watching Dorothea as she worked on a daisy chain, her head bent over the small white and gold flowers. She turned to smile down at him, then went back to her work. She had loosened her hair and the sunlight had become entangled in it, outlining her head in a halo of glittering bronze.

Ian put his arms behind his head and watched her, drinking in her graceful serenity. In three days' time he would be on his way back; every moment of this leave was precious, something to be stowed carefully away in his head and used as a charm, later, against the horrors he would once again have to face.

He had gone to the refinery on his second day in Greenock to see his former workmates and to tell Andrew Warren about his son's final moments. The man had listened impassively, his eyes hooded, then said, 'Thank you, Ian. I'm pleased to know that at the end he was with someone who knew him.'

'There was no pain, sir. No suffering.'

Andrew firmed his lips and nodded, clearly unable to trust his voice for a moment. Ian was sorry for him. From what he had heard, Mrs Warren had voluntarily become an invalid since her son's death. He wondered if his own mother would go the same way if anything happened to him, then decided that she would be more likely to bury herself in even more work. He hoped to God that she would never be put in that position. He admitted freely to himself, if to nobody else, that he was afraid of dying. He had seen enough to know how hard dying could be for young men wrenched from life before their proper time. He wanted to live, to savour the days and the years, to grow old and acquire wisdom and knowledge, to have something to look back on. He wanted this moment, with just himself and Dorry and the blue sky and the water, to go on for ever. He wanted . . . With a shock that almost took his breath away, he realised that he wanted Dorry with a wanting that had crept up on him, letter by letter, during his time away from her.

'We should be thinking of getting back,' she said at that moment, regret in her voice. She put the daisy chain she had made about her wrist; it was too long and it swung gently as she began to repack the bag. Ian, dazed with his discovery, sat up and stopped her with a hand on her arm. 'Dorry.'

'What?' She glanced at him and her eyes widened in startled confusion as they met the look in his. Soft rose stained her cheeks and she knelt up, pulling away from beneath his hand. 'I told Mam that we'd be back by—'

'Dorry.' He too got to his knees, both hands on her shoulders now, his voice insistent. 'Look at me.'

She started to say something, then fell silent. Her eyes lifted to his and his heart began to speed up again. A man could drown sweetly in that deep pool of violet light, Ian thought, stunned by poetic notions he had never entertained before.

He reached out, cupped the soft hair at the back of her neck, and kissed her. He only had time to register that her mouth was soft and warm and sweet before she pulled back so sharply that she almost overbalanced and he had to tighten his grip to steady her.

'Ian!' She tried to twist away from him, but he held her firmly. 'You can't!'

'I can – we can. Listen to me, Dorry,' he said hurriedly as she shook her head in denial, lashing his cheek with her soft flying hair. 'You're

177

not my sister. We were raised together, but we're not brother and sister!' Words that had been forming themselves in the back of his mind during the past terrifying, threatening months, longings that had somehow been woven into him, tumbled out half-formed, unplanned. 'D'you understand me? I never thought of it until I was away, till I was in France and your letters began to mean so much to me. I didn't think of you not being my sister until then. But you're not, Dorry, you're no relation to me. We're free, both of us, to choose. And I choose you.'

She stopped struggling, looked at him, her eyes moving over his face as though she were seeing him for the first time. His hands dropped from her shoulders to her fingers. He lifted them to his lips then slipped the daisy chain from her wrist and gently arranged it on her dark sun-kissed head. 'I choose you,' he said again and stooped towards her. This time she responded, and her hands and her face and her sweet soft mouth, opening beneath his, tasted of the same floral scent that had wafted from her letters.

'Pneumonia. That's what it says on the death certificate, but the truth of the matter is that she died of a broken heart.' Flakes of January snow still clung to Andrew Warren's coat as he stood in the middle of Lessie's kitchen. A week earlier he had buried his wife; in the past six months, Lessie thought, he had aged a great deal, though his shoulders were still broad, his back still straight. The striking tan he had brought back to Greenock all those years ago had long gone, but even so there was still a hint of more exotic places about the planes of his face and the clarity of his eyes, as though the hot sun and lush foliage of Jamaica were still in his blood.

His hands fumbled with the brim of the hat he had just taken off. 'She was never truly happy after I brought her here, Lessie. She never settled. Perhaps I should have stayed out there, found other work and let the refinery be sold. Or put it into a manager's hands as she wanted, and gone back. But I felt that it was my duty to stay here. I put my family and its traditions first. I let her down.'

'You did what you had to.'

'It's hard to lose a child,' he said without seeming to hear her. 'It doesn't seem right to go on living when your own flesh and blood – your own creation – has gone before you. I knew how Madeleine felt after we lost Martin, though she'd not believe me when I tried to tell her that.' His grey eyes travelled the room without seeing anything. 'God, Lessie, they're all vanishing. Only yesterday I was a young man with my life in front of me, and now they're gone – my uncles, Madeleine, Anna, Martin. All I've got is Helene. And Dorothea, but I lost her too, when her mother died. I wish now that I'd had the courage to take Dorothea into my own house when she was younger.'

Lessie knew a moment's unease. Dorry was a human being, not a figurine to be pushed into the space left by Martin Warren's death. 'You'd only have made your wife more unhappy if you'd done that. Best leave things as they are, Andrew.'

178

'I suppose so. But there are times when I . . .' He sighed, then said, 'But it's wrong of me to speak to you like that. You've lost folk too, and here I am expecting you to listen to me and put up with my girning.'

'You're not girning. Men are too harsh on themselves. Everyone needs to speak their hearts instead of their minds now and again.'

'You never do.'

She thought of Donald and her parents and laughing, trusting Thomasina – and of Murdo, not dead but lost to her. 'Not to you, mebbe, but others have to put up with my complaints.'

'And you've heard enough of mine,' Andrew said, suddenly brisk, making an effort to push his troubles aside. 'Have you heard from young Ian lately?'

'He was fine last week when he wrote to me. He's hoping that mebbe this year'll be the one that sees the end of the war.'

'Who would have believed at the beginning that it would last so long or take such a toll? We were so conceited, weren't we? So – British. So sure that no foreigner could vanquish us. Well, we've got more than we'd bargained for.'

When he had gone, Lessie walked down to the shop, her mind on Ian – and on Dorothea, who had a new bounce in her step and a new sparkle in her eye these days. Nothing had been said, but Lessie had a shrewd idea that her son and Anna's daughter had come to an understanding during Ian's last leave. She wondered, uneasily, how Andrew would react if his daughter fell in love with one of his employees, then decided to leave the worry of it aside until it happened. If it did, she had a feeling that both Ian and Dorothea would be capable of facing the consequences of their actions.

Six months after his wife's death Andrew Warren took Lessie's breath away by inviting her to be his partner at a business dinner to be held in the Town Hall.

'What? You're havering,' she told him bluntly, and he roared with laughter.

'You don't believe in mincing your words, do you, Lessie Carswell? I mean it. Will you accompany me to the dinner?'

'Certainly not! The very idea of it! You the owner of one of the town's largest refineries and me with my wee shop in the Vennel. We'd be the laughing stock of the place.'

'I'd like to see the man or woman that would dare to laugh at either of us. Lessie, I'm serious. It's in aid of war savings and I'll be expected to attend. I'd like you to be with me.'

'It's only been half a year since your wife died.'

'Even so, I'll be looked for. The world's changed, my dear, there are no such luxuries as an official year of mourning now. God only knows the world would be in mourning for evermore if there were, these days.'

'Why don't you take your daughter?'

'Helene would be bored, and she'd show it and embarrass me. Besides, if I must go I'd as soon enjoy myself by going with someone of my own choosing. Lessie,' he said in exasperation, 'have you not done much more for me than I could ever do for you? Let me pay off some of my debt by taking you to the dinner.'

When they heard about it, Jess and Dorothea, far from agreeing with Lessie that the whole thing was preposterous, astonished her by taking Andrew Warren's side.

'The ladies have started coming into the shop for their gowns already. Mam, just think of it,' Jess said, her lovely little face flushed with excitement, 'the richest folk in the area – all the businessmen and their wives. And you in the middle of it all! You can tell us about it afterwards – wait till I tell them at the shop that my mother's going to be there.'

'That's just it, all those rich folk and me. I'd stick out like a sore thumb!'

'Not if we helped you with your hair, and your clothes,' Dorothea said, and Jess chimed in with, 'Go on, Mam, you can't say no. When will you ever get a chance to go to something like this again?'

'Never, I hope,' Lessie told her daughter, but she could hear the surrender in her own voice, and judging from the gleeful looks they exchanged, so could the girls.

The interior of the shop Jess worked in was like a luxurious house and Lessie was hard put to it not to feel awed as she stepped through the glass doors and onto the thick carpet. There were comfortable chairs and sofas, mirrors, soft lights, and racks to the left and right of her held beautiful gowns in all colours and materials. It was like walking into a rainbow, she thought bemused, as Jess swept towards her, pink-cheeked with excitement, slender and elegant and older than her fifteen years in a black dress with snowy white lace at the neck and wrists, her fair hair pinned stylishly on top of her small head. Seeing her daughter in a different setting for the first time, Lessie felt her breath catch. It was no wonder that Jess's employers used her to model their gowns.

'Ma – Mother,' Jessie corrected herself smoothly, 'this is Miss Forsyth. She's going to help you to choose a gown for the dinner.'

The tall, grey-haired woman who came to Jess's side was so imposingly regal that it was difficult not to hold out a hand to her. 'Whatever you do, Mam,' Jess had said that morning before hurrying off to work, 'don't say how d'ye do and shake hands with anyone. You're a client, and clients don't do that.'

Miss Forsyth was already casting a practised eye over her. 'You're right, Miss Carswell, I think the deep blue would be just the thing for your mother. This way, madam.'

Lessie was ushered into a cubicle, stripped to her best underclothes, and dressed in the deep blue gown. Then Miss Forsyth turned her towards a mirror and stepped back. 'What do you think, madam?'

Lessie looked, and looked again. The face was familiar, so was the fair hair drawn back in a bun, but the dress was so breathtaking that for a moment she couldn't speak. It was made of deep blue silk embroidered with tiny silver flowers. The bodice ran from shoulder to waist in a V shape with an inset of pale blue chiffon studded with tiny pearls. The skirt was slightly hobbled, falling from the high waist to the knees in two tiers then gathered at the centre to fall to a slight split at ankle length.

'The skirt needs taking up just a little,' said Miss Forsyth, dropping to her knees with the ease of an ardent churchgoer, as though worshipping the hem of the dress with pins, each one darting into the right place with skilled speed. 'But otherwise it seems to be a perfect fit.'

She put in the final pin and rose to her feet, a faint smile brushing her pale mouth. 'You wear clothes very well, madam. There are gloves to go with the gown and we can provide a chiffon boa and silver shoes to match the embroidery.'

'It's – it's beautiful!'

Miss Forsyth swept the curtain back and Jess, who had been hovering outside impatiently, stood stock still, her mouth falling open. 'Oh, Mam,' she whispered after a moment, completely forgetting her role as a cool assistant, 'you look lovely!'

The smile touched Miss Forsyth's mouth again for just a second before she said briskly, 'The shoes, Miss Carswell, and the gloves and boa, if you please.'

When Lessie was dressed to their satisfaction, both women walked round her as though she was a statue, murmuring their approval, Jess in control of herself once more.

'The hair,' Miss Forsyth said, 'and the face . . .'

'My sister and I will see to that,' Jess assured her as Lessie twisted round to see the back view in the mirror. The back of the bodice was like the front, though it was highlighted at the waist by a rosette in pale blue chiffon and the skirt tiers were shaped in two points which complemented the line of the gown. When the inspection was finally over, she took the dress off carefully, reverently, and got into her own clothes while Jess bore the blue gown off to the back regions where someone waited to take up the hem and make it perfect.

'As to the cost,' Miss Forsyth said in a discreet murmur.

'How much?' Lessie asked bluntly, on more familiar ground now.

The woman named a sum that almost rocked her back on her heels, then said, 'As you are related to a member of our staff and this is a special occasion, we can deduct a small percentage. And it could be paid in weekly instalments of, shall we say—'

'I'll pay the full amount, thank you, and I'll pay it all when the gown's ready for me,' Lessie said firmly, and was gratified to see surprise and chagrin in the woman's eyes.

'Nobody's going to patronise me,' she told herself grimly as she went back into the street and headed for the nearest tram stop. 'If I must do this, I'll do it the right way.'

Thanks to Andrew Warren and his sound financial advice over the years, she was in a position to buy her own gown and pay the same price as the richest lady in the finest house in Gourock. Donald, she thought as she boarded the tram, would have been pleased.

20

When Andrew came to collect Lessie on the night of the town hall dinner, he stood motionless in the middle of the kitchen, elegant in his formal evening suit, his eyes travelling slowly over the woman who waited for him. Lessie felt colour rise to her face as she saw the admiration in his gaze. Jess and Dorothea exchanged a look and smiled.

'You look like royalty,' he said at last.

'I feel like Cinderella with two fairy godmothers,' Lessie told him with a shaky attempt at sarcasm. She was quite shocked herself by her new appearance. Her hair, normally drawn back into a loose bun at the nape of her neck, had been softly curled round her face at the front and piled high in a chignon on the crown. Her lips had been reddened, her cheeks softly dusted with rouge, and a single-strand pearl necklace, unexpectedly loaned by the formidable Miss Forsyth, clasped her long slim neck. The girls had even shaped and buffed her nails and made her cream her hands every night and sleep with them in gloves for a week.

'You look very beautiful,' Andrew told her after he had helped her into the back of his chauffeur-driven car.

'I feel very nervous.'

'No need to be. I'll look after you.' He covered her gloved hands with one of his. At that moment the car stopped, and Lessie said with a giggle, 'We're here. I told you I could have walked – we're only a matter of yards away from the house!'

'Tonight,' Andrew promised her, 'you're doing everything in style.'

The town hall was already thronged with people. They had to wait in line until their names were called and they were welcomed by the Provost and his wife. Long lines of tables awaited them in the main hall, the linen covers crisply white, splashed with colour from the vases of flowers placed at regular intervals down their length. Silver gleamed, glassware sparkled and threw back colour at the chandeliers overhead.

As they were shown to their table, Lessie was uncomfortably aware that heads were turning, people murmuring to each other. She knew that they were wondering who Andrew Warren was escorting.

As though he was reading her mind, the elbow she was holding squeezed her hand against his side briefly, reassuringly. 'Remember that they all wondered about Cinderella too,' he murmured. 'And she turned out to be a princess.'

She laughed, then lifted her head high and looked back at the starers, feeling secure in Andrew's company.

The food was delicious, but afterwards she scarcely remembered any details, much to Jess's and Dorothea's annoyance. Wine helped to ease her nervousness, though when the waiter came round again with the bottle she put her hand over her glass as she had seen someone else do. One glassful was quite enough for a woman who was unused to drink.

After the meal, there were speeches and announcements of donations to the appeal for money for the war effort. Andrew's name was read out, followed by an impressive amount. People in the vicinity smiled their approval at him, and at Lessie. Then another name and amount caught her attention.

'That's our Davie the man's talking about!' she hissed to Andrew.

'It is indeed. He's probably here tonight.'

'Davie? Here?'

'He's become quite a well-known businessman in the town. Didn't you know?'

As they rose later to move into another large room where musicians waited she caught sight of her brother at the other side of the hall. He saw them and nodded to them.

'I'd no idea he had become well known,' Lessie marvelled. 'He never says much about himself when he visits me.'

'Oh, he's done well. He's got a good head on his shoulders. He was the man who first suggested new centrifugal machinery for the refinery, and eventually installed it. I've got cause to be grateful.'

Davie came to talk to Lessie when she was sitting on her own later in the evening. Watching him crossing the floor towards her, as smart as Andrew in his evening garb, but having to work hard at looking as elegant, she felt the old affection sweep over her. She hadn't seen Joseph for years, and might indeed have passed him in the street these days without recognition if he returned to the town, but Davie still had a special place in her heart.

'You're mixing with the posh folk tonight, my lad,' she said as he reached her.

He shrugged. 'It's one of the things I must do now that I've got my own business. It means nothing.'

'And what about the lady you're with? Don't tell me she means nothing.'

Davie glanced over his shoulder to where his dark-haired partner was dancing with an older man. 'I've told you before, our Lessie, none of your match-making.' The old grin broke up the normally solemn lines of his broad face for a moment. 'She's the daughter of one of my best customers – that's him dancing with her now. A man needs a partner when he goes to these soirees, that's all.' Then he said with an undertone of steel in his voice, 'You're a fine one to talk. I was surprised to see who you were partnering. I didnae realise you were so friendly, the two of you.'

'Mr Warren keeps in touch for Dorry's sake. He asked me to partner him since it's only six months since he lost his wife.'

'Is that all there is to it?'

'It is. But that,' said Lessie with spirit, 'is my own business.'

He grinned again. 'Still the same sharp-tongued Lessie, underneath. But on the surface you're beautiful enough to be more than a match for any of the fine ladies here. I wish I'd thought to ask you to be my partner.'

'Kirkwood,' Andrew loomed over them, holding out his hand to Davie, 'good to see you again.'

The smile vanished from Davie's face as he got to his feet, putting his hand forward. 'Warren.'

'Will you and your partner not join us?'

'Thank you, but we're with a party of folk. I'd best be getting back to them. Lessie,' said Davie with a curt nod, and left them, weaving his way in and out of the dancers with ease.

If Andrew noticed Davie's sudden coolness he didn't remark on it. But Lessie puzzled over it for the rest of the evening.

'I'm so close to home that I might as well get into this car and out again through the other door,' she protested later as the diners spilled out through the town hall doors into the summer night.

'We'll do the thing properly,' Andrew said firmly, handing her into the back of the car. 'And thank you,' he added as they moved off. 'You turned a duty into a pleasure.'

'I enjoyed it, once I got over the nervousness. When I think back to the days when I cleaned stairs for a living, who'd ever have thought then that I could go to a dinner like that?'

'You worked for your money, like all the other people there. You deserve tonight as much as they do – more than most. Look at me, for instance. I was born into my livelihood. You had to find yours wherever you could.'

The car stopped and he detained her with a hand on her arm until the chauffeur got out and opened the door for her. In the dark close, Lessie fumbled for her key in the tiny bag she carried, then Andrew's hand came down and claimed it.

'I've enjoyed this evening, Lessie. You should come to Gourock to see the house some time, perhaps meet Helene.'

'No, Andrew.'

'Why not?'

'You know why not.' She had often been alone with him in her kitchen, but never before had she been as aware of him as she was in this dark corridor with nobody there to see the two of them. 'We're from different lives, you and me. And you'd best be going back to your car. The driver'll be wondering what you're up to.'

He laughed, then leaned towards her, the faint smell of hair cream and good tobacco wafting round her. For a moment she tensed, certain that he was going to kiss her, then she heard her key in the lock and the faint creak of the door being edged open. 'Good night, my dear,' said Andrew. 'Thank you for a very pleasant evening.'

In the kitchen, where a light had been left burning for her, Lessie realised with embarrassment and annoyance that she was trembling. She was far too old for such silliness, she told herself briskly, taking off the chiffon boa and putting it over the back of a chair. And yet the faint dizziness she was experiencing woke happy recollections of past loving and courtship. She caught sight of herself in the mirror over the mantel and saw that she was smiling, flushed, almost pretty with her hair curled softly about her rosy face. Then the smile faded as she saw an army-issue envelope propped against the mirror, unopened, her name scrawled on the front.

For a moment she thought that it was from Ian, then she saw Peter's name and an unfamiliar unit scribbled on the back. She ripped it open hurriedly and saw that it held only a few lines, written as though in haste, or when the writer was under strain.

'Dear Aunt Lessie, I'm sorry not to have written to you earlier. I was too shamed. They won, Aunt Lessie. I couldn't let them do to me what they had done to others I saw. So I'm in France and I have a gun and I'm no better than they are after all. My mother is pleased. I'm sorry. Peter.'

All the young man's agony and shame reached out to Lessie from the few words. The dance forgotten, she dug in a drawer for the notepad and pen she used to write Ian's letters and sat down at the table, ignoring the clock that ticked the night hours away. Her letter was brief, for there was no point in overwhelming the lad with the love she badly wanted to give him. And she had the sense to realise that too affectionate a letter might well break down the wall he must have been forced to build round himself, brick by painful brick, in order to cope with the sheer burden of living. She tried to convey as much love and sympathy in her words as she could while at the same time keeping the letter cheerful and matter-of-fact; more than an hour later, with several sheets of paper discarded and burned in the last ashes of the dying fire, she completed her difficult task and rose stiffly to wash her face vigorously with soap and water, cleaning away every vestige of the make-up the girls had put on hours before. Then she went into Ian's room, which she was using in his absence, took off the fine gown and stowed it away carefully in the wardrobe. After that she took the hidden pins from her hair and brushed it hard until it fell down her back, then braided it. She was ashamed of the way she had dressed like a lady and gone out and eaten good food and enjoyed herself while young men like Peter – and Ian – were risking their lives so far from home and from those who loved them.

Jess and Dorothea were disappointed when they came into the kitchen the following morning and found the usual Lessie, her hair swept back into a bun, making the porridge.

'You could have kept the curls for several days,' Jess pouted, 'then I could have done your hair for you again. You looked lovely.'

'Did you not see the way Mr Warren looked at you when he came into the room?' Dorothea chimed in.

'Like Douglas Fairbanks in a film I saw last week,' Jess said dreamily, and was quelled by a look from her mother.

'He thought you were lovely too, I know he did. Did you have a good time?'

'I had a grand time, thank you, Dorry.' Lessie ladled porridge into their plates and fetched the milk jug from its place on the shelf, removing the beaded muslin cover that protected its contents. 'But this is a new day and the dance is over.'

'Mam, why don't you let me do your hair again?' Jess coaxed, stirring milk into her porridge. 'You've got nice hair – you should look after it.'

'I do look after it. It's washed regularly, and brushed every day. As to the rest,' said Lessie evenly, pouring boiling water into the teapot, talking to Andrew Warren and the small rebellious spark deep within herself as much as to the two young girls who sat at the table, 'we're all as God meant us to be, and He meant me to be a shopkeeper. I'm an ordinary woman and I see no sense in trying to change.'

In October Dorothea and her friend Aileen were moved to the mill's weighing room. It was quieter there, with no need to shout or lip-read. The loading bay was situated directly beneath them and a large square hole in the middle of the floor gave access to the hoist which brought the bales of cotton up to be weighed. Each bale was numbered and its weight recorded in a large ledger, and once its contents had been spun into yarn, they, and the waste from the bale, came back to be weighed again and checked against the original weight.

The repartee of the young lads who handled the bales and rode up and down on the hoist with them kept Aileen entertained all day. Dorothea's thoughts were with Ian for most of the time. He was still alive, still unhurt, and from all that was being said, the war was as good as over. She slept with his letters under her pillow now and re-read them whenever she got the opportunity. It was a wonder that Jess hadn't noticed her dreaming over them, but Jess was doing more and more modelling and trying to persuade her mother to allow her to take a job in one of the big Glasgow shops; she was too preoccupied with her own dreams to notice what was going on under her pretty little nose.

Soon, Dorothea thought as she entered figures in the book, for she was the neater writer of the two and the task fell to her, soon Ian would be home. Perhaps he would propose to her properly and they would get married and—

'Cheeky bugger you are, Aileen Lennox,' one of the lads shouted as his laughing face disappeared below floor level on his way down in the hoist.

'My mam doesnae breed buggers!' Aileen retorted swiftly, getting the last word in as usual. The door banged open and the winding shop overseer put his head in and glared at her, catching the final sentence.

'Dorry Carswell, Mr Spiers wants to see you in his office. Now!'

The two girls stared at each other. 'Ooh, Dorry, what've you done?'

'I don't know. D'you think I've been entering the figures wrong?' Dorothea felt as though a cold hand was clutching at her stomach.

She wasn't like Aileen, carefree and able to cock a snook at authority.

'It's almost clocking-off time. Want me to wait for you?'

'No, it's all right.' If she was in for a scolding or, even worse, dismissal, the last thing Dorothea wanted was sympathy.

She tapped on the door of the manager's office on the ground floor and Mr Spiers himself opened it, stepping aside to let her in.

'Miss – er – Carswell, Mr Warren would like a word with you. I'll – er –' He scurried out, closing the door carefully behind him. Dorothea stared at the tall figure by the window. He could only be the bearer of bad news.

'Mam,' she said, her mouth suddenly dry. Then, even more fearfully, 'Ian?'

'There's nothing wrong,' Andrew said quickly, coming forward, his hands outstretched. 'Nothing at all, my dear. In fact, I hope that it's the opposite. Sit down, Dorothea.'

He guided her into a chair then leaned back against Mr Spiers' desk, clearing his throat before he said, 'Dorothea, there's something I must tell you. I've been giving it a lot of thought lately and it's my belief, now, that you should have known it a while ago . . .'

It wasn't like Dorry to be late. Normally she was home by this time, setting the table, peeling potatoes, chattering on about her day at the mill, willing to listen to anything Lessie had to say about the shop. Jess, complaining at having to do the potatoes, fretting about ruining her hands, was a poor substitute.

Just as Lessie was about to go out to the closemouth to see if Dorry was in sight, a car door closed in the street outside and Jess, dripping dirty water, abandoned the basin of potatoes and flew to the window.

'It's Mr Warren come to call – and he's brought our Dorry home in his car!' Her voice sharpened with envy. 'Trust her to get all the luck!'

'Mr Warren? At this hour? Jess, put the basin out of sight, dry your hands.' Lessie ran to the mirror to tidy her hair. The close door opened and suddenly Dorothea was in the kitchen, her eyes hard, the old scar standing out against the pallor of her face.

'Dorry, pet, what's happened? Has there been an accident?'

Dorothea stepped back, away from Lessie's reaching arms. 'Is it true?' she said in a hard voice Lessie had never heard from her before. It shook with shock and anger. 'Why didn't you tell me about – about who my real father was?'

Andrew came into the kitchen behind her, his eyes wary but defiant. 'I thought it was time she knew, Lessie. I want everyone to know the truth.'

Lessie, the blood draining from her heart, took a step or two towards Dorothea, her arms outstretched, but the girl moved back again, shaking her dark head vehemently, dislodging drifts of cotton that had been caught in the curls.

'You should have told me!'

'Dorry, I – we decided that it was for the best that we wait until you were older. Didn't we?' Lessie angrily challenged Andrew, who had the grace to colour and glance away for a second. In the background Jess, forgotten, gaped in astonishment at the drama being played out in front of her disbelieving eyes.

'I thought it was time Dorothea knew everything. She's not a child any more and I want her to come and live with me, to be openly recognised as my daughter. I've waited for too long,' Andrew said, his voice slightly unsteady.

'And you think I haven't waited for a long time to know the truth?' Dorothea suddenly blazed at him. 'All those years you visited, and I never knew that I was your daughter! All those years, wondering. And neither of the two of you bothered to tell me!'

Andrews eyes were anguished. 'I wanted to, but I couldn't, not while my wife was alive. I know I've left it late, but I've never stopped wanting to acknowledge you. Let me make it up to you now, Dorothea!'

'Dorry, you must do as you think best. You'll always have a home here, if that's what you want.'

The hurt and bewilderment in the girl's eyes made Lessie feel as though a knife had been plunged into her own heart. 'Oh, I'll go with him, since he's my own flesh and blood. Whatever you say, I've no rights to this house any more, have I?'

'Dorry!'

'I'll just collect some of my things,' Dorothea said, and turned on her heel.

'Jess, go and help your – go and help her.'

Still gaping, Jess did as she was told and Lessie, heedless now of the mess the kitchen was in and the fact that she hadn't washed her face or brushed her hair since coming home from the shop, rounded on Andrew Warren, so angry that she could have lifted her fist and struck him. 'How could you? How could you do such a thing to the lassie? We discussed this, did we not? We agreed that—'

He flinched, but stood firm. 'I'm lonely, Lessie.'

'To hell with your loneliness! We agreed that when she was told it would be done gently. Surely I've earned the right to be considered as well!'

'Would you have given your consent to her being told now? I doubt it. I've lost Martin, I've as good as lost Helene now that she's engaged to be married – not that I ever had her as a daughter,' said Andrew bitterly. 'I need to have someone of my own to care for.'

'So that's it, is it? You're claiming Dorry, turning her life upside down, just to satisfy your own need? You could have bought yourself a dog!'

His face went scarlet, and suddenly he was as angry as she was. 'For God's sake, she's my daughter!'

'And mine too, as good as!' They were quarrelling in fierce whispers so as not to be overheard by the girls. 'I've raised her from babyhood. How d'you think I feel, losing her like this?'

'You're not losing her. She'll visit you, and so will I, just as I always have. Lessie, try to see things my way.'

189

'How can I?' she began hotly, then stopped as the bedroom door opened. When Dorothea, carrying a small bag, came into the room, Lessie was stirring fiercely at a pot of broth on the stove and Andrew stood gazing out of the window. He turned and smiled at the girl, his mouth stiff, his eyes bright. 'All ready? Come along, my dear.'

At the door Lessie put her arms round Dorothea and kissed her on the cheek. 'This is still your home, love. Come here whenever you want to,' she whispered, but the girl stood stiff and unresponsive in her embrace then turned without a word and followed her father.

Lessie and Jess stood at the closemouth watching as the chauffeur opened the car door and Warren stowed his newly claimed daughter into the back seat as though she were made of delicate porcelain. Children playing on the pavement and women leaning out of their windows and gossiping at the closemouths stared as the door closed on the two of them and the gleaming car moved smoothly away from the pavement.

Dorothea glanced back once, her white expressionless face blurred behind the glass. Then the car turned a corner and was gone, taking a piece of Lessie's heart with it.

'Why her?' Jess wanted to know as they went back into the house. 'It was just like a film, but why should it be her and not me? Dorry always has all the luck. No wonder she was your favourite. I might have known she'd be the rich one and not me, oh no, I'm just—'

'Hold your tongue if you don't want a good skelp across the ear,' said Lessie, and her daughter subsided with a gasp of astonishment and outrage.

'And get on with the potatoes,' Lessie went on as they went into the kitchen. 'We still have to eat.' She lifted the lid of a pot, stirred its contents without knowing what she was doing.

'I suppose there's one thing,' Jess said after a moment, chopping vicious lumps off the potatoes, reducing them to half their original size. 'I'll get the bedroom to myself.'

21

As though to warn people not to be too optimistic about the future now that the tide of war seemed to be turning, one of the most virulent forms of influenza ever known swept the country like a scythe through grass. It took the oldest and the youngest and the weakest. It took Elma, who had worked valiantly for Lessie for so many years.

Lessie wept for her friend as she followed the coffin to the cemetery, then returned home and dried her tears and got on with the business of running the shop and fumigating the two rooms beyond to clear them of the influenza virus. She turned them into storerooms and took on a woman widowed in the war, one of her staunchest customers.

In November the town, like every other town and village in Britain, erupted into colour and noise, its streets thronged with people who, forsaking their Scottish reticence for once, hugged and kissed complete strangers in celebration of the end of the Great War.

Ian was safe, Peter was safe, and for Lessie and Edith, at any rate, there would be young men to welcome home, eventually. But Lessie's joy was dulled by the other loss she had just suffered, for to her Dorothea was as much her child as Ian and Jess. The girl had come back twice to the house in Cathcart Street since her move to the Warren house, elegant in her new clothes, her hair fashionably coiffed by Helene Warren's hairdresser. She had changed inside as well as outside; in a few weeks she had built up a wall between herself and Lessie and remained firmly behind it, no matter how hard Lessie tried to regain their former affection. She had collected the rest of her belongings and tucked the two letters waiting for her from Ian carefully into her pocket.

'Have you any word of when Ian's coming home?'

'Not yet. It'll be a while before they're all back where they belong. Will I tell him, when I next write?'

Dorothea shook her head and the feather on her wide-brimmed hat moved languidly. 'I'll tell him,' she said, and went back to the big house in Gourock, leaving behind only a trace of expensive scent.

Jess fumed with helpless envy over her former sister's new clothes. She wasted no time in removing every trace of Dorothea from the small bedroom they had shared for so long and renewed her demands to be allowed to move to Glasgow where she could get a better job with more chance of modelling.

'Miss Forsyth's willing to give me a good reference and a letter to a friend who's supervisor of one of the largest dress stores,' she nagged. 'I'm sixteen and a half, it's time I started to travel. Anyway, it's terrible here with folk knowing about Dorry. They come into the shop and stare at me and whisper to each other. And they snigger!'

The news of Dorothea's parentage and her entry into the Warren household had indeed been a talking point in the town, but only for a short while, as Lessie crisply pointed out to her daughter. It had quickly been superseded by the armistice, which was of far greater importance. She knew well enough that she would soon lose Jess too, for there was little she could do to keep the girl at home now that she was old enough to make her own decisions. But she managed to persuade her to stay until Ian came back. She couldn't bear the thought of being alone in the house. All at once it seemed as though her life had gone out of control and taken a turn onto a road that she followed against her will.

Andrew still called every week, ostensibly to report on Dorothea's progress. He brought small gifts with him – a box of sweets, hothouse grapes from a business colleague's glasshouse, a tiny bunch of delicate snowdrops early in January, the first that had appeared in his garden. Every time he came, Lessie was aware of his eyes on her, guilty, hopeful of forgiveness. She soon realised that there was no point in letting her anger over his thoughtlessness cause a permanent rift between them. They had been friends for too long, they owed each other debts of gratitude. They were linked, too, by Dorothea, just as they had been linked by Anna. The gifts of fruit reminded her poignantly of the days when her father and Davie brought stolen oranges from the docks for wee Ian; they also reminded her that folk needed folk, and there was no sense in turning her back on a friendship that had in many ways come to mean a great deal to her.

'Dorothea's fine,' he assured her over and over again. 'Naturally it'll take a while to get used to a different way of life, but she's fine. And I can offer her so much – more than I was ever able to offer Anna.' His eyes softened, looking beyond her to the window, and she knew that he, too, was recalling days long past. 'She's like her mother in so many ways, Lessie. I'm reminded of Anna every time she looks at me.'

Lessie said nothing, but wondered if he realised that nobody could fully take the place of someone else. Nobody, particularly Anna's daughter, could be expected to follow the path planned, step by step, for her.

'I know you miss her, but surely it's my turn now,' he said just then, confirming her thoughts.

'It's nobody's turn, Andrew, can you not understand that? The lassie's a living, breathing human being, not a doll!' Then the snowdrops, fragile and beautiful in the little vase she had found for them, caught her eye and she softened her voice. 'I know how you feel, you've stood back from her for a long time and denied yourself. I don't blame you for wanting her. But she must be free to live her own life.'

'She will be. I know that you miss her, but you'll soon have your son home.' There was faint bitterness in his voice and she knew he was thinking of his own boy.

'I'm not sure whether Ian'll settle back to his old life, and at his age I'd not expect to have him with me for much longer. Mebbe I need a new interest in life. The woman I took on in poor Elma's place is worth her weight in gold. I'm scarcely needed in the shop now.'

'It's time you had a rest and a chance to think of yourself for once. We're none of us getting any younger, Lessie, and you don't need to work as hard as you used to, surely?'

'I'm not a horse ready to be put out to graze!' she protested hotly, and he laughed. But his words rankled, and when he had gone she turned them over in her mind, finding them condescending and typically masculine. It was true that the need to work wasn't as sharp as it had been. Jess was earning, Ian would find his old job in the refinery waiting for him when he came home, Dorry had gone. Thanks largely to Andrew's advice over the years, Lessie had managed to put by some money.

She went back to the ledgers laid out on the kitchen table, running her finger down columns of figures, turning pages, checking figures. Since Dorry had left, since the end of the war that had kept them all living on a knife-edge for four long years, she was restless and there was a need to take her life in hand. The shop in the Vennel was ticking along very nicely, thanks to Doreen's efficiency and to the assistance of a girl who had been taken on two months earlier and had proved to be well worth her wages. Since the end of the war, there had been a new affluence among her customers. They bought luxury foods now, items like tinned salmon and cream biscuits, and the takings had risen impressively.

The germ of an idea began to tickle at the back of Lessie's mind. She put the ledgers away, brought them out, glanced over them again, then with a sudden surge of purpose she put on her hat and coat and left the house. There were folk to see, plans to pursue. There was a new idea to be followed up.

Two days later, the groundwork laid, she took a five-minute walk from the shop in the Vennel to a single-end apartment buried in a warren of narrow streets. Here, she had been told, the Manns, who had once run the gleaming, successful corner shop in Cathcart Street, lived, still in Greenock although their shop had remained boarded up and padlocked during the war years.

The stairs were dingy, the building smelled of boiled cabbage, and the door Lessie knocked on was badly in need of a coat of paint. After a long pause, steps came dragging and shuffling to the door and it opened a crack.

'Vat you vant?'

'Mrs Mann? It's Lessie Carswell, from Cathcart Street. Can I come in and talk to you and your husband?'

There was a long pause. The woman, breathing heavily, seemed to be unsure of what to do, then a mumble was faintly heard and slowly, reluctantly, the door opened just wide enough for Lessie to slip in through the gap.

The single room smelled as though it were the source of the building's entire cabbage stench. It was cold and dank and dim, most of the dull January afternoon light kept out. At first Lessie thought that the one narrow window was curtained. After a great deal of panting and shuffling a match was lit and shakily applied to a stub of candle and she saw that the window was covered with pieces torn from cardboard boxes, nailed haphazardly over the gap where the glass had been. Rags were stuffed between the pieces of board in a vain attempt to keep the wind out.

She looked round in dawning horror at the black, mouldy patches on the walls, the empty grate, the bottle and the lumps of bread and cheese on the rickety table, the single shabby blanket on the alcove bed.

'Vat do you vant with us?' A hoarse voice, thick with phlegm, brought her attention to Mr Mann, huddled in a chair by the fireplace. At first she didn't recognise him, for he had shrunk to about half his original size and was almost hidden from view deep within the shabby coat that he wore. He was no longer the big handsome man in the snowy apron who had shouted at her in front of her neighbours and ordered her from his shop. But his eyes were the same, dark orbs glittering defiance at her from under an incongruous red woollen hat that had been dragged over his head and right down to his thick grey eyebrows. His wife, small and stooped, was also huddled into a coat, and on her head she wore an old felt hat, stripped of its former flowers or feathers, over greasy grey hair that escaped in wisps here and there. She had moved to behind Mr Mann's chair, her hands tightly gripping its back. Lessie didn't know whether the woman was sheltering behind her husband or poised to defend him.

'Mr Mann, d'you remember me?'

'The voman vith the shop. The voman,' he said reluctantly, as though the words were being dragged from him, 'who offered help ven the mob took our living from us.'

'Yes.' There was one other chair, an ordinary kitchen chair, in the room. Lessie moved to it and sat down, so that she and Mr Mann were on the same eye level. The chair shook and rocked under her weight, and she dug her feet into the sticky floor to balance herself. 'I believe you still own the shop. Are you not thinking of opening it again now that – now that it's all over?'

'Vat vith, lady?' There was no mistaking the sarcasm in his voice. 'Ze money ve no longer earn? Ze rent ve had to go on paying? Ze health your damned town took from us?'

'I'm surprised you stayed on in Greenock after what was done to you.'

'Ve had nowhere else to go. Our children,' a knotted hand in an old fingerless woollen glove emerged from the folds of the coat and gestured clumsily, 'zey also had persecution because zeir blood is not British. How could ve go to zem?'

'Are they still in Britain?'

He nodded, a tired dipping of the head. 'Still here. Vere else vould zey be? Zey sink of zis country as zeir home.'

Lessie felt the chill of the place seeping into her bones. The smell of age and illness and stale cooking and despair was beginning to grip at her throat. 'Mr Mann, I've been to the factor who owns the building where your shop is. He's willing to transfer the rent to me. I want to open it up again. Would you sell me whatever's still in the shop, and the goodwill?'

Mrs Mann jerked suddenly, and was still again as a rusty mirthless laugh rumbled in her husband's chest. 'Goodvill? You zink zere is any goodvill left, voman?'

'You'll get it for next to nothing,' the bank manager had said in his brisk unemotional way earlier that day, folding his hands on the desk before him. 'What's left inside will be in a terrible condition. You'll have to put a deal of money into it. Offer them the lowest amount possible, Mrs Carswell. It's my belief they'll snatch at it. They're not in any position to bargain.'

Lessie's mind raced, adding and subtracting, considering the amount the bank was prepared to lend, the weekly income from the shop she already had, the amount she would doubtless have to spend on the new shop. When she finally spoke she named a sum which would probably give the bank manager apoplexy and would cut her own financial margin uncomfortably close. But it was a sum that would allow the Manns, once a respectable and respected couple in Greenock, the chance to travel to wherever their family were picking themselves up, repairing the damage done by the war. A chance for them to pay their own way, to hold their heads high again, if they were willing to make the effort.

Mrs Mann's outline jerked again and she put a hand on her husband's shoulder. The old man ignored her. 'Vat? Vat you say? You're mad, you know zat, voman?' he said at last. 'You sink ze ruins of our shop could be worth so much?'

'It's what I'm willing to pay.' Lessie got to her feet. 'I can come back tomorrow for your answer if you want to think it over.'

'No.' His voice stopped her as she reached for the door handle. 'Ve take it.'

'Good.' She went back to him, held out her hand. At first she thought that he was going to ignore it, then it was taken in a chilly clasp that was all skin and bone. Even the wool of the glove he wore was dank against her skin and it was all she could do not to wipe her fingers against her skirt when he released them.

'I'm sorry,' she said at the open door. Sorry that two people who had worked so hard had come to this, sorry that a decent couple who had only wanted to make Scotland their home had been humiliated and defeated in a way far more cruel than the day Mr Mann had ordered her out of his shop.

'Ve are not Germans,' his voice said bleakly out of the gloom. 'Ve are Sviss. Not bad people. Never bad people.'

The following day Lessie turned the key in the padlock and walked into the remains of the Manns' shop, followed by a local joiner who had been invited to name a price for the work that needed doing.

'God, woman, ye've a big heart takin' this on,' the man said, pressing in behind her, looking at the desolation that had once been a smart little shop. He crunched through the debris on the floor towards the windows, taking a claw-headed hammer from his belt as he went, and began to wrench at the planks of wood that had been nailed over the broken windows. They gave easily and daylight flooded the interior, showing the full extent of the chaos wrought by the mob, and by the years that had elapsed since. Something scuttered into a corner and Lessie gave a yelp of fright, then stamped hard on an empty patch of floor to discourage any other little creatures that might have taken up residence.

The marble counter was still there, the wooden panels on the sides dull but intact. So were the spice drawers she remembered, and the two lots of scales, one with a porcelain platform for weighing cheese and butter. And behind the counter, to her great delight, she found the handsome cash register, lying on its side, the empty drawer open, but as far as she could see undamaged. A good cleaning should see it as right as rain. As more of the planks came off the windows and more of the shop was revealed, she stood in the middle of the devastation, looking round at the empty shelves, the hooks waiting for pink and white hams to hang from them, seeing the shop once more as it had been and could be again.

I'll buy a white apron, she thought. I'll hire a young man home from the war and in need of a job. I'll buy two white aprons—

'Ye've a big heart,' the joiner said again.

'Can the place be put right?'

He ran a hand over the marble counter then down a panel like a groom examining a horse. 'Aye, but it'll take a wee while, and it'll cost you.'

'Could you do it? I'll pay you as you go along.'

He shrugged then nodded. Lessie beamed at him through the dust motes that had been stirred up by their presence. The restlessness had gone and in its place was determination.

'Can you start tomorrow?' she said.

Only her pride kept Dorothea from admitting that she was wretchedly unhappy in the handsome Warren house in Gourock. Everything that had given her life shape had gone – her work at the mill, the security of being one of the Carswell family, her sense of belonging. In their place were only loneliness and bewilderment. She felt like a kitten that had been taken from its mother, put into a pet shop, then bought and taken to its new owner's home. There wasn't even the comfort of having butter spread on her paws to be licked off, she thought drearily in those first terrible early days.

Andrew Warren, the man who had suddenly turned out to be her father, had been kindness itself, and she was aware of his eagerness

196

to make her happy, make her feel at home in this large, beautiful house he and his daughter Helene inhabited. But he was away all day and every day in the refinery and beautiful dark-eyed Helene, as shocked and confused as Dorothea herself at the sudden change in circumstances, made no secret of her resentment and rage.

'You're not my sister,' she told Dorothea coldly on the first day they found themselves alone together. 'I have never had a sister and I have no wish to have one forced on me now.'

Dorothea had glared back, refusing to let the other girl see how intimidated she felt. 'I already have a sister. Her name's Jess and I don't need you any more than you need me. If it was left to me I'd not have set foot in this house!'

But it had not been left to her or to Helene, and Andrew, when he realised that there was a coolness between his two daughters, had ordered Helene to make the newcomer welcome. The command, given in front of Dorothea, had only made matters worse. Helene did as she was bid, taking Dorothea to her hairdresser and to the dress shops she herself frequented, telling the people who worked there to see to it that her half-sister – said in a cool, contemptuous little voice – was suitably attended to and provided with the correct clothes. And she took Dorothea to afternoon tea parties, introducing her in the same glacial tones.

Dorothea, unable to refuse to go out because it would have gone against her father's wishes, trailed along miserably, keenly aware of the inquisitive looks cast on her everywhere she went, the whispers and the stifled amusement. Andrew Warren was too important to be denied, and so his new daughter was included in every invitation extended to Helene.

Aileen, with her quick wit and warmth, had vanished from Dorothea's life; a few days after moving to the Warren house she had gone along to the mill at clocking-off time to see her friend, who had come out of the gate arm in arm with two of the other women, talking and laughing. The trio had stopped short at sight of Dorothea in a stylish new jacket and hat that had been bought that very day. After a pause, Aileen had detached herself from the others and sent them on their way while she herself stood waiting for Dorothea, running her eyes up and down the new jacket and skirt.

'What're you doin' here?'

'I thought I'd walk along with you.'

Aileen snorted, dislodging some flecks of cotton from her shabby coat. 'Walk wi' me? Ye're surely too high and mighty for that now!'

'I didn't want it to happen,' Dorothea burst out in an agony of helpless fury. 'I didn't want to stop working in the mill!'

'More fool you, then. If it was me, ye'd no' find me within a mile o' this bugger o' a place. Don't embarrass me – go an' spend yer money,' said Aileen, shrugging off the hand Dorothea put on her arm and moving off. 'Ye don't belong here any more, Dorry, an' there's nothin' more tae be said.'

She had gone back to Cathcart Street a few times, but the people who lived there looked at her the way Aileen had, as though she were a posh lady going slumming. Jess, for all Dorothea's brave words to Helene, had been no comfort at all. Her lovely heart-shaped little face hard with jealousy, she had passed barbed remarks that had finally driven Dorothea out. Mam – Aunt Lessie – Mrs Carswell – poor Dorothea had no idea now of how to address the woman who had raised her since babyhood - had checked Jess sharply, with little success, and had looked as wretched as Dorothea felt. Even so, they had no way of comforting each other. Dorothea had been betrayed and they both knew it.

On the first day in the Warren household she had been pathetically grateful to see a familiar, though unloved and unloveable, face when she wandered into the drawing room. Edith Fisher, in cap and apron, was dusting the room, so intent on her work that she jumped when Dorothea, in a rush of pleasure, said, 'Oh, Aunt Edith, I'm so pleased to see you!'

The plain face beneath the unbecoming cap was suddenly suffused with blood. 'Dor— Miss Dorothea. Can I help you, miss?'

'Aunt Edith—'

'My name is Edith, miss.'

'But—'

'Aunt Edith?' a light amused voice asked from the door and the two women whirled to see Helene Warren standing there, elegant in a walking dress, drawing gloves over her slender hands. 'You may go, Edith. You can continue your work in here later, when the room is free.'

'Yes, Miss Helene,' Edith said with all the dignity she could muster, and fled, the duster clenched in her hand.

'Aunt Edith?' Helene said again, putting emphasis on the first word.

'She's my – my foster mother's sister.'

'Dear me, what a confusion the house is in. What other little revelations do you have for us, Dorothea? Is the cook perhaps the sister you boasted about? And the chauffeur your cousin?'

Dorothea, her face flaming, pushed past her tormentor and fled to her room, followed up the stairs by silvery laughter. From them on she and Edith avoided each other, Edith because her pride had been wounded, Dorothea because she loathed having to treat the woman she had known as an aunt for so many years like a menial.

At night she cried herself to sleep in the lovely bedroom she now had all to herself, lonely in the soft bed, used to Jess fighting to take the lion's share of mattress and blankets.

The only thing that kept her going was the thought of Ian's return to Greenock. She wrote to him every week as before, longing to pour out her unhappiness but drawing back from it because she had no way of knowing what sort of miserable life he himself might be leading and she didn't want to burden him with her own unhappiness. Instead she wrote cheerful letters, telling him only the facts – that Andrew Warren, her real father, had taken her to live in his house. She didn't refer to her own feelings in the matter. When they were together again, when she was safe in his arms, she would pour out the truth, tell him how unhappy she had been. And he would, she hoped, tell her that there was nothing to worry about any more, that he was going to look after her and make her happy and provide a proper home for them both to share.

He, too, made little reference to the new situation. His letters became few and far between, and not as long as they had been, but she put that down to the ending of the war and the preparations his unit were making to return home with the last of the wounded.

It was February 1919 before he got back, and Dorothea, reluctant to go to Cathcart Street where she no longer belonged, waited impatiently for him to come to her. But day followed day and lengthened into one week, then two, and there was no sign of him, no word.

22

At last, in an agony of worry and need, Dorothea was forced to go to Cathcart Street in search of Ian. The house was empty but she found Lessie in the corner shop supervising the replacing of shelves that had been torn from the walls. The place had been swept clean and the rubbish removed; new glass windows were in place, the smell of fresh paint hung in the air and Lessie looked happy, her hands full of lists and plans.

Everyone was happy, Dorothea thought, hesitating in the open doorway, happy because the war was over. Helene was expecting her new fiancé home soon and even Andrew's pain at losing Martin had been eased by Dorothea herself. Perhaps now that Ian was home it was her turn to be happy.

'Dorry.' Lessie had turned and noticed her. The old warmth showed in her face and her voice and Dorothea smiled nervously in answer.

'It's looking grand.'

'I'm hoping to open it for business in two weeks' time.'

'How's Ian?'

Lessie's smile faltered. 'Oh, he's fine. Back at his old job in the refinery.'

Dorothea nodded casually, as though she already knew that. As soon as she could, she left the shop and walked back along Cathcart Street, towards the refinery. She reached it a few minutes before the noon whistle was due to blow, releasing the workers for an hour. An icy wind was gusting along the street, tossing old pieces of newspaper against her smart new shoes and slender ankles. She stepped into a shop doorway, glad of the fur-trimmed coat she wore.

The whistle shrilled and almost at once men and women began to emerge from the refinery gates, some alone, others in twos and threes, some silent, others laughing and talking. It reminded Dorothea of the mill and reinforced her sense of loneliness.

Her eyes took in each figure emerging from the gates, and brightened when, at last, Ian appeared, alone and striding out, his collar turned up against the wind. He was hatless and his red hair glowed against the grey refinery wall. She stepped out onto the pavement and waited for him, her heart beginning to beat faster. He walked with his head down and didn't notice her until she said his name, then his head jerked up and he stopped in his tracks.

For a brief moment he was the Ian she had always known, the Ian she had fallen in love with that sunny afternoon on the banks of Loch

Thom. Then his blue eyes cooled and his face was wiped of expression.

'Miss Warren,' he said politely, as though greeting an acquaintance.

'What d'you mean, "Miss Warren"? It's Dorry you're talking to, you daft lummock!' She laughed and tried to tuck her hand into the crook of his elbow, but he stepped back, his face wary.

'It's my employer's daughter I'm talking to. You shouldnae be here,' he said, and tried to walk past her. She barred his way, blood stinging her cheeks.

'Ian, you surely don't think that me living in Gourock's going to make any difference to us?'

'It makes all the difference! D'you not see that?'

'But you said – you said, that day at Loch Thom—' Dorothea felt as though the only solid piece of ground left beneath her feet had started crumbling away.

'We have to forget about Loch Thom. Sometimes,' Ian told her, his voice hard, 'the past should be left where it is. Goodbye, Dorry.' And with that last bitter use of her old name he walked away and left her alone on the footpath, weeping, not caring who saw the tears staining her cheeks. He didn't turn his head, but walked faster, swinging round the corner and out of sight.

As the last sight of him disappeared, she swung round and began to walk just as fast in the opposite direction, grief taking refuge in an anger that soon stopped the tears. Never ever again would she let anyone humiliate her as he had just done. Never again would she let anyone get close enough to touch her heart then break it. How dare he, she raged, how dare he talk to her like that?

A car passed then drew up. As she came level with it, the uniformed driver jumped out and opened the rear door and her father called to her from the warm interior. She sniffed, hoping that her tears had left no marks, and got in beside him. The door clicked shut and the car slid off again.

'What were you doing here?'

'Just walking.'

'My dear child, it's a cold day for that. You look as though you're frozen through.' He gave her a sidelong glance then said, 'I hope you remember that we're going out to a social evening at the Latimers' tonight?'

'No, I hadn't forgotten,' Dorothea said indifferently. The Latimers were old friends of Andrew's, with three sons in their early twenties. One of them was still in the army, but the other two were back home.

'You'll enjoy it. Time you got to know some young people,' Andrew said, patting her hand. Dorothea gave him a wan smile then stared out of the window. The car was gliding through Gourock now; it passed a shop window where two mannequins posed stiffly, one dressed in black, the other in deep red. They flashed across Dorothea's vision then were gone, leaving behind the memory of sleek, smart clothes, a memory that lingered through luncheon and gradually solidified in her mind into a decision. Since she was no longer Dorry from Cathcart Street, and since she could never, she felt, become the Dorothea that Andrew Warren wanted her to be, why should she not take on a new personality, one that couldn't be hurt by others, one that belonged to her alone? The more she thought of it, the more she realised that taking her future into her own hands was her only chance of survival.

That afternoon Dorothea went into the town and had most of her long hair cut off and the rest shaped so that it cupped her neatly shaped head in a cluster of dark bronzed curls. Then she crossed the road to the dress shop she had noticed earlier from the car. For a moment, as the doors closed behind her, shutting her into a warm, perfumed world, she faltered as her eyes fell on Jess, almost unrecognisably chic in black. She had forgotten that her foster sister worked here. She pulled herself together and started across the carpeted floor, a smile pinned defiantly to her mouth, but Jess, after one appalled glance, had disappeared from view into a back room, leaving the other assistant to deal with Dorothea.

'Can I help you, madam?'

Dorothea reminded herself of the new personality, lifted her chin and said coolly, pitching her voice loud enough to be heard in the back shop, 'I'm looking for a dress to wear tonight at a dinner party. You can send the account to Mr Andrew Warren.'

Two women looking through a rack of clothes turned and stared at her, then at each other, moving with one accord to the other side of the rack so that they could peer and whisper unnoticed. The sales assistant flushed, cast a quick glance at the doorway Jess had melted into, then recovered her professional smile and led the way to a rack in one corner. Dorothea flicked through them and thought of how much she would have revelled in owning any one of them a few short months earlier, when she had been plain Dorry Carswell. She rejected them and turned, her eye caught by a flash of colour. 'Let me see that one.'

It was brought to her and spread out over a chair for her inspection, a lace and chiffon gown in violet, low-waisted and sleeveless, with silver embroidery across the straight neckline and tiny silver balls edging the ankle-length hem.

For a moment Dorothea, remembering Jess's tales of modelling clothes for some of her customers, was tempted to ask that the gown be modelled for her. But even the new Dorothea couldn't be so cruel. Instead she tried it on herself and found that her first impression had been right – the violet of the gown matched her eyes exactly. Ian would have loved her in that dress. But Ian wasn't going to get the chance to love her, not any more. There were other men in the world, Dorothea thought desolately, then defiantly. Her father was wealthy; she could have her pick of men, men who could offer her far more than Ian Hamilton.

'It's beautiful, madam. It could have been made for your colouring.'

'I'll take it. Have it delivered to the house at once,' Dorothea said carelessly and went on to pick out silk stockings and underwear to go with it. Then she dashed her signature across the order form the girl proferred. There was no need to give an address, everyone knew where Mr Andrew Warren lived.

She returned home an hour later to find the dress waiting in her room. She stripped off her afternoon clothes, ran a deep bath, scented it with a handful of salts, then lay in the comfortingly hot water, eyes closed, making plans until the water began to cool and she had to climb out and wrap herself in a huge soft towel that waited close at hand.

She had a pleasing body, she decided later as she posed before her full-length mirror. Slim without being bony, her pink-nippled breasts and her hips rounded and firm, her legs long. Freed of its usual burden of curly hair, her neck was a slender column with her neat-featured face and newly sculpted head poised proudly above it.

She slipped into the satin underwear she had just bought, cream with violet ribbons and lace at breast and knee, then put her dressing-gown on and sat down before the dressing-table mirror, opening the parcels she had brought back with her.

She had never tried using eyebrow liner and rouge and powder and lip paint before, but she had watched Jess experiment with it many times. Now she tried to remember what the girl had done, leaning forward to stare into the mirror, raising her eyebrows, opening her eyes wide, frowning and pouting and smiling as Jess did, trying to find out which feature was her best and which needed artificial aids to beauty.

It was as well that she had decided to give the rest of the afternoon over to the business of making up her face, she thought an hour and a half later, surrounded by the items she had bought, a pot of cream half gouged out, the towel she had used to wipe off the first disastrous attempts lying like a discarded rainbow on the carpet. But at least she had learned by her mistakes. Jess wasn't there to help her and Helene certainly would never have done so. Helene, under duress, had politely told her to make use of her own ladies' maid, inherited from her mother, whenever she wished, but that was out of the question. And she wouldn't dream of summoning her aunt, although it was part of a parlourmaid's duties to assist any ladies of the house who might have need of her. Apart from a natural reluctance to ask for Edith's help, Dorothea couldn't picture her being able to do any better than she herself had. She studied her face, noting the faults that still had to be rectified, applied more cream, wiped her face with a corner of the towel, then started again.

As she worked she heard the front door open and Andrew Warren's deep voice rumble faintly in the hall below. Some time later the door to his room opened and shut, then Helene's arrogant voice called out to her maid and the pipes gurgled discreetly as her bath was run. Helene wouldn't dream of seeing to her own bathwater.

As the hands of the delicate little clock on her bedside table indicated that it was almost time for the Warrens to leave the house, Dorothea stood again in front of her full-length mirror, well pleased with what she saw there. The dress was simple enough to show her figure to advantage, her breasts just lifting the material demurely and the bobbles at the hem flattering her slim ankles. Her shoulders were smooth and creamy, almost matching the pearls about her neck and those swinging from her earlobes. Like the dress, the soft pink lip paint on her mouth and the rouge she had dusted on her cheekbones only emphasised the brilliance of her eyes beneath brows that had been brushed into shape with oil.

Dorothea gave herself a mirthless smile and watched the painted lips in the mirror curve up. The new Dorothea, she thought, then frowned. Dorothea was the name her parents had given to her, Dorry was the name Lessie had bestowed on her. Neither name fitted this new personality.

'Thea,' she said softly, and smiled again, with faint pleasure. Thea was just right for the elegant beauty before her.

There was a tap at the door and Edith came into the room. 'Mr Warren and Miss Helene are—' she began, then stopped, her mouth hanging open.

Thea Warren swung away from the mirror and picked up her evening bag and wrap from the bed, aware as she did so of the scent of violets, the new eau de cologne she had bought, wafting around her. 'I'm ready. See to that, will you?' she instructed coolly, indicating the mess on the dressing-table, the towel on the floor. Dorry would never have had the nerve, but Thea had. Thea could do anything.

Edith, still gaping, stepped aside to let her pass and she went to the stairs, her nerve almost failing her at the last moment as she saw her father and half-sister waiting down in the hall, Helene pacing with impatient little jerky steps. For a moment Dorry surfaced, gripping the banister tightly, yearning to run down the stairs and out of the house and all the way to Greenock to the safety of Lessie's love and Ian's arms. But she had no claim on Lessie now, and Ian had rejected her, she reminded herself, forcing Dorry away, bringing Thea again to the fore, loosening her grip on the polished wooden rail finger by finger.

She took a deep breath and began to descend slowly, one step at a time, concentrating on keeping her back straight and her head high, a faint smile on her lips. The Warrens, disbelieving, watched her come down the last few steps, Helene's dark eyes wide with astonishment, Andrew stiffening as though his first reaction was anger, then forcing himself to relax as his younger daughter came towards him across the hall, her eyes defiant.

'You look – very striking, my dear,' he said, then moved to open the door. 'Shall we go?'

Lessie's new shop opened in March 1919 and thrived from the first day. She spent a great deal of time in it herself, and took on two assistants, a young man newly returned from the war, a former shop assistant with some experience of the grocery trade, and a girl fresh from school. With pride, Lessie dressed the two of them, and herself, in long white aprons that were changed and washed every second day. A lad who lived in the next close took on the job of messenger boy.

'You'll not listen to reason, will you, woman?' Andrew asked with wry amusement when he visited the shop after it had opened. 'I said you should take more time to yourself, not take on extra work.'

She stroked her hands over the cool marble counter. 'Don't fret, I'm not setting out to challenge Thomas Lipton. This'll do me. But who wants to sit back just when the war's finally over and folk are picking up their lives again? It occurred to me when I cast my vote for the very first time a few months back that this is a time for moving forward, not sitting back.'

He nodded and turned towards the door, opening it then pausing so that a woman burdened with a large basket and two small children could enter. Lessie walked round the counter and followed him, nodding a welcome to the harassed customer. On the pavement Andrew stood back and looked up at the wooden panel above the door which bore her name in bold white letters.

'You should have the shop's likeness taken, with you and your employees posing outside.'

'I'll think about it.'

'Lessie, are you certain you can manage? If you ever find yourself in need of a loan—'

'I'll go to my bank, not to my friends,' she finished the sentence sharply, then relented. 'If there's one belief me and my brother Davie share, it's that we shouldnae walk before we can crawl. Don't fret, Andrew, I'm fine. And I'm grateful to you for giving Ian time off to go to England.'

He brushed her thanks off with a quick movement of the hand. 'The boy's fond of his father, it's natural that he'd want to see him.'

'His stepfather,' Lessie corrected him swiftly, adding, 'though the only father the lad knew, I suppose.'

'From what Ian said, Carswell hasn't got long. D'you still miss him, Lessie?'

She considered for a moment. 'To tell the truth, I feel now as if Murdo died when he left us. It was hard at first, but now I've no feeling left for him, apart from the natural pity I'd have for anyone in his place. And life moves on, never backwards.'

'Lessie, does Dorothea ever visit you?'

She thought of the last time she had seen Dorothea, the day when Ian had returned for his midday meal with a face dark as thunder and remained in a foul mood for the best part of a week. She had a fair idea that the two young people had met each other and that the result had been heartbreak for them both.

'Not for a while.'

'She's never at home, never still for a moment. It's as though she's decided to pack an entire lifetime into every moment. She's – she's changed, Lessie.'

'What can you expect? You whisk her away from the house she was

206

raised in without giving her time to get used to the idea of being your daughter, then you expect her to stay just as she was. She'll be fine once she's worked things out in her own mind.'

But she wished she had more faith in her own words as she watched him walk off in the direction of the refinery.

She had a second visitor that day, but she was so busy that at first she didn't notice him waiting in the background. Rob, her senior assistant, went over to deal with him and came back to murmur, 'There's someone wants a word with you.'

She looked up and saw the man for the first time, thin, wearing a suit that looked as though it had been made for someone else, light brown hair just a little longer than the fashion of the day dictated showing beneath a cap. At first she wasn't sure of his identity, then as he turned and his grey eyes met hers, she knew that it was Peter, home at last.

'See to my customer for me, Rob. I'm just going along to the house,' she said, her hands flying to the strings of her apron. 'I'll not be long.'

She went round the counter and put a hand on Peter's sleeve, noticing how he flinched slightly beneath her touch, just as he had done as a child. 'It's good to see you! Come along to the house and have a cup of tea.'

In the kitchen he sat in the fireside chair she indicated and looked around as she busied herself with kettle and teapot.

'This place is much the same.' It was the first time he had spoken; his voice sounded rusty, as though it wasn't used very often.

'It's much the way it was when Miss Peden used to own it. I loved it then and I didn't see the sense of changing it when it became mine.' She turned to face him, her hands clasped before her. 'How are you, Peter?'

'I'm . . .' he gave the appearance of seeking for words, 'I'm still in one piece and that's more than can be said for most.'

'I know. You'll have heard about young Martin Warren?'

'He's just one of thousands – millions. Dead, maimed – it makes a man shamed tae still be alive. My mother seems tae think I'm a hero, just because I'm still alive.'

She made the tea and put a cup into his hands. He stared down at it.

'Are you going back to the refinery?'

His head, shaggy now that the cap was off, swung slowly from side to side.

'So you're looking for work?'

'My mother's looking for work for me. I don't see the sense of it.'

'We've all got to support ourselves,' Lessie said, letting a sharp note enter her voice.

It worked. He lifted his gaze from the cup and asked simply, 'Why?'

'In order to live.'

'Aunt Lessie, they gave me a gun. I kept it by me all the time. I carried it, I slept with it, I damned near stirred my tea with it. They taught me how tae love it more than I've loved a human being in my whole life.' Tears glistened in the depths of his eyes. 'I didnae just carry it and love it, though, I used it. I pulled the trigger and I don't know if I killed or maimed, but I'm sure I must have. I did my bit. And now you all think I should just go on as if everything in the world's back together again.'

'Peter—'

'My mother wanted me tae go back tae the refinery, tae take orders, do as I was told.' He jerked suddenly in his chair and hot tea spilled over his hand. He didn't seem to notice it. 'I've done what I was told. I've taken orders. I let them put the gun intae my hand because I hadnae the courage tae fight them. It was easier tae fight Germans, lads I didnae know and couldnae see most of the time. That's why war's so easy, did ye know that? Because the further away ye are from the enemy, the more stripes ye've got, the easier it is tae kill. Or better still, tae get other folk tae dae yer killin' for ye. It gets tae be like a game.' Again the jerk; this time the cup tilted and fell to its side in the saucer, emptying itself over his hand and his clothes. Lessie started to move towards him then stopped, riveted by the agony in the grey eyes lifted to hers.

'D'ye see what I mean, Aunt Lessie?' Peter demanded. 'D'ye see why I cannae take any more orders? The folk that give them are the folk that end up givin' out guns an' turnin' ordinary nobodies like me intae machines that pull the triggers an' think nothin' of it. I cannae let them dae it tae me any more!'

'I see, Peter. I see.'

'Then I wish tae Christ ye'd explain it tae my mother an' make her understand!' For the first time he noticed the spilled tea, righting the cup and putting it on the table, brushing spots of liquid from his clothes, apparently impervious to the scalding he must have got from the hot tea. 'I'm sorry.'

'Don't worry about it.' Lessie picked up a towel and moved to rub off some of the worst stains, but he got up and backed away, towards the door.

'I'd best go. She'll be wondering. She always wonders if she gets home an' I'm no' there. Deserted. Absent without leave. They shot the deserters, did ye know that? Oh, more than a few of the poor souls that died in the war had their own side's bullets in them.' He blundered out and Lessie was alone, left with the eerie feeling that Peter had been killed on the battlefield, and the man who had just left was only a caricature, an empty husk of the lad who had, so long ago, sworn that he would never hurt a fellow human being at the behest of his country's leaders.

23

Ian stayed away for a week and came home grim-faced with the news that Murdo Carswell was dead. He said no more and Lessie asked him nothing, but she heard from Jess that Murdo had been living alone; Flora, the young woman for whom he had deserted his family, had long vanished. Jess's former affection for Murdo had also vanished, and she scarcely reacted to the news of his death.

'He didn't care enough about me to stay, so why should I care about him?' she said with chilling logic.

A month after he got back, Ian came to Lessie and told her that he wanted to leave Greenock.

'I want to study medicine, Mam.'

'Go for doctoring?'

'It's something I've been thinking about ever since I was in Europe. My chemistry studies and my war experience'll help. I talked it over with Father during his last days and he thought I should go ahead.'

'But how will we manage it? It'll cost a deal of money.'

'I'll go to Glasgow, try to enrol in the university. I've got my school certificates and my chemistry certificate from the night school; they'll count for something, and so will my time in the army, no doubt. I'll find somewhere cheap to stay and get work that'll fit in with my studies. There'll probably be a job of some sort in one of the hospitals, and there are some scholarships for students in need of them. Father left me some money – not much, but it'll help, and there's the money paid to me while I was in the army. I put most of it by and kept it safe.'

'What about Dorry?'

Ian's fair skin flushed scarlet. 'What's she got to do with it?'

'I thought that the two of you – when you came home on leave that last time—'

'You thought wrong.' He got to his feet. 'She's a rich man's daughter now, he'll be looking for her to marry money.'

'Dorry's got a mind of her own.'

'And so have I.' Ian tossed the words over his shoulder as he left the room. 'I'm not a social climber. I'll not court any woman who's considered to be above me!'

His bedroom door slammed and Lessie wisely gave him some time to get over his anger before she took a small notebook from the drawer where she kept her account books and tapped on the bedroom door, opening it only when she heard his muffled permission.

He was sitting on the bed, a chemistry textbook in his hand, an exercise book covered with strange symbols and squiggles on his knee.

'Here.' She handed him the little book and he leafed through it then looked up at her incomprehendingly.

'What is it?'

'The money I got from the War Office while you were away.'

Ian pushed the book back at her. 'That was for you, to make up for missing my wages.'

She kept her hands by her side, refusing to take the book back. 'I didnae need it. I managed fine, as you can see for yourself. I thought at the time that it would mebbe do for you and – and your lassie when you decided to settle down. Now it seems it's to be put to a different use.'

'I could manage without it.'

'I've no doubt you could, being my son. But it's yours, and if doctoring's what you want to do, you'll need all the money you can get.'

'Mam,' he said as she reached the door. The little notebook thumped to the floor and the exercise book pages flapped as he got up and came to give her a clumsy, embarrassed hug.

'Thanks, Mam, I'll not forget this.'

For a moment she held him; for a moment he was her laddie again. Then his embarrassment reached and infected her and she pushed him away. 'Och, for any favour just take it and stop your havering,' she said gruffly, and left him.

When Ian left Greenock in August, Jess, who had achieved her ambition and found a job modelling and selling clothes in a large Glasgow dress shop, went with him. All at once Lessie was alone and grateful for the new shop, which filled her days and her evenings as well, since she was still working between the other shopkeepers and the wholesalers, and a great deal of paperwork and mental arithmetic was required to keep everything going.

In September Davie Kirkwood set Greenock on its heels by announcing his engagement to the daughter of one of the town's shipyard owners, the young woman Lessie had seen him with at the dinner in the town hall.

'I knew it,' she crowed when he came to the house to tell her. 'I knew she was the right one for you!'

'Ach, women always say that. Although the gentry cannae say the same thing – it's set the cat among the pigeons, a man like me marryin' intae their ranks,' Davie said with a certain grim satisfaction.

'She's a fortunate lassie, getting a hard-working man like you. And I'm glad you're going to have someone to care for.'

'God, woman, don't go getting sentimental about it!'

'Are you happy?'

'Happy? I'm pleased about it, if that's what you mean,' said Davie evasively. 'Come April I'm going to walk down the aisle of St George's North Church with the daughter of one of the town's most successful men on my arm.'

'I wish Mam had been alive to see it!'

'And I wish,' his voice was grim, 'that the old man was alive to see it. After all he thought of me, this would surely stick in his gullet!'

Ishbel Wilson, twenty years old and sixteen years younger than Davie, was a pretty young woman with glossy black hair and large, deep blue, expressive eyes. When Davie brought her to the house in Cathcart Street to meet his sisters, she looked round Lessie's kitchen with fascinated interest. It was clear that she had never been in such a small house before. Edith, who had been invited along to meet her future sister-in-law, simpered and twitched and all but curtseyed when the girl complimented Lessie on her 'quaint' home.

'You should see the place where Lessie and me used to live,' Davie told her, but Edith added hurriedly, as Ishbel opened her mouth to ask questions, 'Don't bring up the past, Davie, the future's what we should be talking about. Where are you planning to live when you're wed?'

'David's bought a house in Newton Street,' said Ishbel lightly.

'Newton Street?' Edith squawked, and Lessie felt her mouth dropping open. Newton Street was on the hill behind the town, a spacious tree-lined avenue with large houses set in their own gardens to either side. Newton Street was for affluent folk. She caught Davie's eyes and saw the glint of humour in them. He was enjoying his sisters' reaction, Lessie realised, and pulled herself together.

'It'll be big, then,' she said calmly. 'It'll take a deal of looking after.'

'My mother's training some servants for me. And we'll need gardeners, of course. But we'll manage.'

'Oh aye,' said Davie. 'We'll manage.'

Lessie was relieved when the visit ended; Ishbel seemed to enjoy herself, but Davie was strangely remote, and Edith's almost servile attitude turned Lessie's stomach. When Ishbel left, she turned at the door to flash a smile of farewell, and just for a moment Lessie was reminded of Anna McCauley. Ishbel's long-lashed eyes were deep blue rather than violet blue, but there was something about them, something about the quick way she turned her head over her shoulder, that had belonged to Anna as well.

'Well, who'd have ever thought of it? Our Davie marrying intae the gentry an' living in Newton Street!' Edith exclaimed as soon as Lessie went back into the kitchen. 'He must be doing well for himself. Mind you, she's the only child in the family, so the man that marries her'll stand tae inherit a deal of money one of those days. Imagine it being our Davie!'

Lessie let her prattle on. It seemed clear to her that the girl doted on Davie, but there was still that air of reserve about him, a certain distant courtesy in the way he talked to his fiancée that made Lessie wonder if Ishbel had indeed managed to break through to his heart, or if the engagement had come about simply because Davie felt that it was time he had a wife, someone to give him entry into local society.

'It'll be a big society wedding,' Edith was saying at that moment,

211

unwittingly fanning Lessie's uneasiness. 'We'll need tae get ourselves dressed up, you and me.' Then she added, casting a disparaging glance round the kitchen, 'I told you we should all have met in Aunt Marion's house in Gourock, did I not?'

'It was Davie's idea to bring her here. Anyway, what's wrong with this place?'

'The likes of Ishbel Wilson's not used tae sitting in the kitchen with the range and the sink right in front of her eyes. At least they're out of sight in the scullery in Aunt Marion's house. And she's got a gas stove and not an old range like you.'

'There's nothing wrong with this flat. If she's marrying our Davie she'll have to get to know us as we are.'

'She said this place was quaint. That means—'

'I'm not bothered about what it means,' Lessie cut in, suddenly exasperated with her sister. It did not matter to Edith whether or not Davie was marrying for love. All she cared about was the look of a thing, not the meaning behind it. Whereas to Lessie, he was still the warm-hearted youth who had handed her his wages from the docks and taken very little back for himself, the youth who had come home exhausted and yet forced himself out to night school to slake his burning thirst for knowledge and betterment.

She wanted him to be happy, but for some reason she couldn't understand, he had built such a barricade about himself in those early years of struggle that she had no way of knowing if he was truly content. Even though he could now afford to buy a house in Newton Street and marry into the gentry, she worried about him.

Ian and Jess came to Greenock for their uncle's wedding, Jess so elegant in a fur-edged velvet coat and flower-pot style hat trimmed with satin ribbon that Lessie scarcely recognised her when she walked into the shop. Staff and customers alike gaped as Jess elegantly moved round the counter to give her mother a kiss on the cheek, clearly enjoying the stir she was creating. Even her speech had changed; now she shaped her words with great care, cultivating a deeper tone than usual.

'I can only stay until the morning after the wedding,' she told Lessie when they were in the house. 'There's a dress showing that afternoon and I promised to be back for it.' Then the reserve broke. 'Look, Mam.' She delved into her bag and produced a handful of glossy photographs which she scattered across the table. A dozen or more Jesses stared up at Lessie, some pouting under the broad brims of elegant hats, some smiling above soft fur, some wide-eyed, one with a flower nestling against her cheek.

'Are they all you?'

'Of course they are.' Jess giggled, just as she used to do. 'I'm photogenic. I'm hoping to get my picture into a fashion magazine soon. Oh, Mam, I'm having a lovely time, it's all just what I wanted!'

'I hope you're not posing for the wrong sort of photographs, my lady.'

'What d'you mean?' Jess asked demurely.

'You know very well what I mean. Some of these models in pictures I've seen need to have their bottoms smacked.'

'Oh, Mam, whatever sort of pictures do you look at then?' Jess giggled again. 'I'm a fashion model, I pose to show off clothes and nothing else. Not that I've not been asked,' she added pertly, scooping up the pictures.

Murdo, Lessie thought with an unexpected moment's sadness for his death, would have been delighted with his beautiful, successful daughter. Especially with the money she seemed to be earning.

Ian, who arrived later that day, was altogether too thin for Lessie's liking. When she said so, he brushed her off with an impatient, 'Don't fuss, Mam, I'm fine!'

He had managed to get a small scholarship and a job as a night porter at Glasgow Royal Infirmary, and with the additional help of the money he and Lessie had saved during his war service he was just managing to make ends meet. He had a room in a tenement building not far from the infirmary, and had found his first year as a medical student hard but exhilarating. His blue eyes glowed when he talked about his studies and his work in the infirmary. Jess wrinkled up her pretty nose and opened one of the fashion magazines she had brought with her, but Lessie sat late into the night listening for as long as he was willing to talk. For a few hours, at least, she felt that she had been allowed to peep into the strange new world her son had chosen to live in, and his enthusiasm made her certain that he had made the right choice after all.

In spite of his assurance that he got enough to eat, she noticed that he wolfed down everything she put before him, and she was glad that she had thought to lay in plenty of food. He would have a good breakfast the next morning, she decided – porridge, sausage and fried potatoes and two eggs.

He ate it all, while Jess nibbled at some toast and sipped a cup of weak tea. Then to Lessie's relief he announced that he was off to get his hair cut before the wedding. She hadn't wanted to antagonise him by pointing out, when he arrived home, that it was too long.

He returned, red hair smartly styled, in good time to get into his best suit. It was looser on him that it had been before he went to Glasgow, Lessie thought, but again managed to hold her tongue. It was difficult, but she was learning.

She had bought a slim green dress for the wedding, with a satin-trimmed overtunic. Her brimmed hat, made to sit at a jaunty angle on her head, was a paler green with a dark green feather. Jess nodded approval when she saw it. 'A good choice, Mam. You've got the proper slender figure to show it off.'

Jess wore a cinnamon velvet cape edged with dark silky fur over a brown silky dress patterned with cinnamon rosettes. The skirt was draped and a snug-fitting cap in cinnamon with a tiny brown brim made the most of her fair hair and blue eyes. The colours would have looked dowdy on most women, but on Jess they were just right, enhancing her beauty as green leaves enhanced a perfect rose.

213

Davie had insisted on sending a chauffeur-driven car for them, and for Edith, who arrived as they reached the church door.

'Oh no, would you look at her?' Jess murmured as her aunt approached on Peter's arm. 'Can she never forget that she's a parlourmaid?' Edith had on a new outfit, a coat and skirt in her usual black, with a white blouse. Her son towered over her, and Lessie realised for the first time that Edith seemed to have shrunk into herself. She was getting older – they all were, Lessie thought with a pang as she smiled at the newcomers. A powerful smell of mothballs surrounded Peter, who was wearing a black suit that was too small for him. Lessie was quite sure that it had been borrowed from some neighbour; clothes and household items travelled continually between folk with little money to spare, and as often as not a single decent hat served for all the women in one street, decorating this head or that at funerals, weddings, christenings and any other special occasion that might arise.

They were ushered to a pew near the front of the crowded church, which was filled with flowers. On the way down the aisle, Lessie noticed Andrew sitting with his two daughters. Her heart sank. She hadn't realised that the Warrens would be there. Ian didn't seem to notice them. When Davie appeared with his best man, his eyes sought out his relatives and he gave them a stiff nod before taking up his place before the altar. He looked sternly handsome in his morning suit.

The minister arrived, the organ started playing, and everyone rose as the bride floated down the aisle on her father's arm in a cloud of white silk and lace and orange blossom, attended by two flower girls before her, two pages to hold the long, heavily embroidered train falling from her shoulders, and six bridesmaids.

To Lessie the service seemed to go on for ever, but at last Ishbel and Davie, man and wife, moved to the vestry to sign the register. They emerged arm in arm, Ishbel glowing and Davie handsomely solemn, to lead their guests from the church.

As they filed out into the April sunshine Lessie, holding Ian's arm, felt him stiffen suddenly as a slender figure with a halo of dark red hair beneath the wide brim of her hat moved out of a pew and up the aisle in front of them. Looking up at her son she saw that his face was expressionless, his eyes hooded.

The reception was held in the bride's family home, where a huge marquee had been set up in the garden for the guests. It was a lovely day, and Edith's eyes bulged with disapproval when Jess carelessly tossed aside her cape to reveal the draped top of her dress with its short sleeves and low back. Three strings of pearls clasped her throat and more pearls dangled from her small ears on silver chains.

Jess was just as disapproving of her aunt. 'You'd think she was here to serve the folk, not as a guest,' she murmured to her mother as Edith moved, crow-like, through the crowd. 'Could you not have taken her in hand, Mam, and made her buy something decent to wear?'

'Your aunt's a grown woman, she can wear what she wants.'

'And as for Peter, did you ever see anything that looked as helpless and hopeless as he does? Someone ought to—'

'That's enough, Jess.' Lessie's voice was suddenly chilly. 'Peter's a fine lad who never seems to get a decent word from anyone.'

Her daughter pouted, shrugged, and said no more.

There were so many people present that it was easy enough for Ian and Dorothea to avoid each other. Watching, wondering, loving them both and worrying about them, Lessie saw how time and again their paths seemed to be converging, and how time and again they both managed to veer away without apparently noticing the other. Dorothea came to talk to her when Ian was well out of the way. The girl's face was subtly made up to disguise the faint scar on her cheek, expensive scent wafted round her, but it seemed to Lessie that her expressive violet-blue eyes, so like her mother, were shadowed and carried hurt in their depths. Her mouth, however, was fixed in a bright permanent smile.

'Are you enjoying yourself?'

'It's all very nice. How are you, Dorry?'

One shoulder was elegantly lifted. 'I'm very well. I call myself Thea now, didn't you know that?'

'I heard. But to me you'll always be Dorry.'

For a moment she thought that she had broken through the carefully built up defences; then Dorothea blinked hard and the smile painted itself back into place. 'Excuse me,' she said, 'I've just seen someone I want to talk to,' and she eeled gracefully through the crowd, presenting a slender, beautifully clad back to Lessie, who wanted, all at once, to run after her foster daughter and catch her by the hand and take her home to Cathcart Street.

'Dorry's looking well,' she said brightly to Andrew when they met.

'She prefers to be called—'

'I know about that. And I said, Dorry's looking well.'

A broad grin lit up his face. 'You never change, Lessie. She's fine, but trying to get to know her's like trying to guddle trout. Did you ever do that?'

'I was always too clumsy. But Davie was good at it.' She remembered kneeling on a grassy bank with Donald in their courting days, watching Davie stretched full-length a little further down, his shirt off, one arm in a running burn almost up to the shoulder, a rapt inward-looking expression on his face as his hand, out of sight below the surface, gently tickled at the belly of a plump trout drowsing in the shadow of the bank. She remembered the way he suddenly tightened his grasp and rolled over on the grass, whisking his arm high above his head so that the trout flashed in his fingers like a rainbow in captivity. She remembered squealing as she and Donald were showered with water, the quick way Davie dispatched the fish by banging its head against a stone. She even, for a brief moment, remembered the taste of it when Donald and Davie had cooked it over a fire made of twigs. Then she came back to the present, the crowded garden, and Andrew Warren.

'And it seems he's still got the knack,' she finished briskly. 'He's guddled himself a bonny fish today.'

This time Andrew laughed so hard that several people turned and stared. One of them, Lessie noticed, was his daughter Helène, her lovely face disturbed by a frown as she saw her father with someone of no account.

Lessie bit her lip, and would have turned away if Andrew hadn't taken her arm. 'Come and look at the garden,' he said. 'I'm tired of all these folk. You'll have heard that I'm making a lot of changes at the refinery?' he went on as they walked. 'I've always wanted to modernise it, bring in new machinery and change some of the departments round so that the refining process moves sensibly from one area to another without the sugar having to be carted back and forth. It's a big job and it's taking all the money I've got. I'm going to have to sell some shares, but it's still going to be worth it.'

'You're looking tired. You surely don't have to be there all the time?'

'No sense in leaving things to other folk who might make the wrong decisions.' He steered her down a gravel path to where a small bench had been placed in a wind-free corner. They sat down and stayed there in a companionable silence for some time while behind them, nearer the house, the people who had been summoned to celebrate Davie Kirkwood's marriage and his entry into local society sipped champagne and chattered. The sun was warm; Andrew leaned back and closed his eyes, while Lessie watched some early butterflies flit through the banks of daffodils and hyacinths that still bloomed in brilliant splendour.

After a while she turned and looked at her companion. His dark hair was well streaked with silver and there were new lines between his eyes and at the corners of his mouth, but he was still a handsome man; if anything, maturity had enhanced his looks. But now that his face was at rest, his tiredness was more obvious, she thought compassionately, suddenly realising that he had become as much a part of her life as her own children. He was dear to her, this man who had fathered her foster daughter.

At that moment Andrew's hand moved, searching for hers, finding it, covering it. 'You're so filled with energy, Lessie,' he murmured without opening his eyes. 'And yet you're such a peaceful woman to be with at times.'

She said nothing, and they sat on for a while, her hand in his, under the April sky.

24

Shortly after Davie and his bride left for Italy on their honeymoon the influenza which was still haunting the country claimed Aunt Marion, Barbara Kirkwood's sister. Edith, who took over her tenement flat, was quick to suggest that she and Lessie should consider setting up house together.

'It would save money for us both and it would mean company for you,' she said as they washed dishes together in the tidy little Gourock flat after the funeral. The boiled ham meal that was obligatory at Scottish funerals was over, the few mourners had departed, and only the clearing up was left to do.

'I'd not get much company with you at the Warren house most of the time and me at one shop or the other,' Lessie pointed out, drying a gilt-edged cup rich with blue flowers and green leaves.

'It's still better to be in a house where there's more than just yourself,' Edith argued. 'A lived-in house.'

Lessie said nothing, carefully setting the cup down on the wooden coal bunker that, topped with oilcloth, acted as an extra work surface. In Cathcart Street her coal bunker was outside the back door, but Aunt Marion's flat – Edith's flat, now – boasted a tiny separate kitchen known as a scullery which housed the gas cooker, sink and bunker. It meant that when the coalman called, sheets of newspaper had to be laid down all the way from the door of the flat so that he wouldn't leave black marks on the linoleum, and every surface and item in the scullery had to be wiped free of coal dust after his visits. But even so a scullery was considered by the tenement dwellers who made up most of Scotland's population to be a step up the social scale.

This house had never been what Lessie would call lived-in. It had a chilly, forbidding air about it. She pitied Peter, who had had to do his growing up in such sterile surroundings.

'It suits me to be in Cathcart Street. I'd be too far away from both the shops here.'

'I was thinking about that. If you gave them up you'd have enough money to live on, would you not? We could mebbe do up the living room here, get rid of some of Auntie's old furniture so that you could bring some of yours.'

Lessie gave her sister a sidelong glance. Edith never gave without receiving more back, and it had suddenly become plain that she was more interested in renovating the house than in offering Lessie a new home.

'I've no intention of giving up the shops. They're both doing well and I mean to see that they do better.'

'All you're interested in these days is making money.'

'All I'm interested in,' Lessie countered sharply, placing the last blue-flowered saucer atop the pile of clean saucers, 'is keeping a home for my children to come back to whenever they want, and paying my way. I know there's a pension for old folk now and no doubt I'll be very grateful for it one day, but I've got a good few years to go yet and I still have to earn my living.'

No point in telling Edith her guilty secret, the first exciting dabbles into the stock market that Andrew had told her about so many years ago. Lessie had discovered that her love of figures and order was to her advantage, and she had started investing a percentage of the little money she saved each year instead of putting it all into the bank as before.

Edith dried her hands and started to put the china away, her fingers gentle as she came to the blue-flowered set. 'Aunt Marion always kept her things nice. I'll make another cup of tea.' As she filled the kettle she said over her shoulder, 'I'd not depend on your two to come back if I was you. Children today are ungrateful, with no thought to what their parents have suffered for them.'

'I don't see why you should be so harsh on Ian and Jess.'

Edith sniffed and put two cups and saucers – not the pretty ones, Lessie noticed – onto a tray. 'You'll find some milk in a jug in the larder. Let me tell you, Lessie, none of today's young folk can be trusted. Look at that Dorry of yours – Miss Thea, she calls herself now, if you please. Gone completely wild, that one. She should think black burning shame of herself, so she should, after the way you brought her up. Out till all hours, painting her face, showing her legs, and making eyes at every young man that comes into the house.'

Lessie fought to keep sudden anger under control. 'From what I hear, that's the way all the rich young folk behave nowadays. Is she that much different from Mr Warren's other daughter?'

Edith sniffed again and tucked a crocheted cosy over the teapot. 'We'll have our tea in comfort through in the room. I'll grant you that Miss Helene does some of those things,' she went on once they were settled on either side of the fire and she was pouring the tea. 'But she's gentry. Dorry's not.'

'She is now. The poor lassie probably thinks that if she doesnae behave like the rest of them she'll be laughed at for being different.'

Edith put the teapot down then folded back her skirt to let the fire's heat get as close as possible to her wool-covered knobbly knees. 'There's a difference between behaving like the rest of them and going a lot further than the rest of them.'

'Och, Edith! Dorry's a good girl, she'll settle down in her own time.'

'You're forgetting whose daughter she is.'

'Mr Warren's. We all know that now.'

'She's that Anna McCauley's daughter too, that's what I'm getting at. And if you ask me she's taken after her mother. I mind well enough

218

the way that one used tae carry on with all sorts of men. Blood will out, and bad blood won't be denied.'

'That's enough, Edith. Dorry's a good girl and I'll not hear her miscalled!'

Edith shot her sister a glance from beneath lowered lashes then said sulkily, 'No need tae fly into a temper. You'll find out soon enough how it is with young folk. You're too trusting, Lessie, you always were. Too quick tae see the best in folk.' Then, after a long silence broken only by the ticking of the clock, she burst out, 'Lessie, I'm that worried about Peter!'

'What's amiss with him?' Peter had attended his great-aunt's funeral but had left with the other mourners, sliding out of the door before Lessie had a chance to talk to him.

'What's amiss?' she repeated as Edith said nothing but stared down into her tea. When her sister finally looked up, Lessie was shocked to see tears in her eyes.

'The polis were at the door last night asking about him.'

'What?'

'A big constable with a moustache.' Edith's cup rattled faintly in its saucer as she put it down. 'Wanted tae know where Peter was the night before. He went away when I said the laddie had been here, at home.'

'And was he?'

'Of course he was! I'd no' tell lies tae the polis, not for Peter or anyone else!'

'So he hadnae done anything wrong.'

'Not that time, but they know him, Lessie,' Edith wailed, a tear escaping to trickle down her cheek. 'The constable said tae tell him they were keeping an eye on him. Thank God Aunt Marion was safe in her coffin in her room and not sitting here tae see the shame he was bringing down on us!'

Lessie leaned over and touched her sister's hand. It was dry and rough.

'It's just like the old days when the polis came looking for Da – and Joseph too. He'll go just the same way as our Joseph,' Edith wailed. 'Named in the police court reports in the *Telegraph* for all tae see, having tae pay fines and go tae the jail. I'll not be able tae show my face in the street! And what'll the Warrens say?' She withdrew her hand from beneath Lessie's and fished in her pocket for a handkerchief. After scrubbing at her eyes and blowing her nose she went on more calmly, 'After all I've done for him! He could have gone back intae the office at the refinery when he came home, but would he? Oh no, not Master Peter! He's been in one job after another and he's lost them all. He'll not keep his mouth shut or his hands tae himself. My Peter that looked so nice in his wee velvet suits and was clever at the school and never said a bad word tae anyone. He's working on the docks now, did you know that? A common labourer just like Da was.'

'Edith, he'd a hard time during the war.'

'So did other folk and they've not disgraced their mothers.'

219

'Peter had it harder than most. He's unsettled, that's all. Give the laddie time.'

'Give him enough rope and he'll hang himself, more like,' retorted Edith, stuffing the handkerchief back into her pocket, snatching up the teapot and dashing more tea into her cup. She hurled a spoonful of sugar in after it and stirred the brew so viciously that it was as well she hadn't used the delicate china. 'It's what I was telling you before – he's just ungrateful. They're all ungrateful! Nothing'll ever be the same again. They're going tae ruin this country, the young ones!'

To mark their first wedding anniversary, Davie and Ishbel Kirkwood held a dance at their grand house. Davie himself came to the shop to hand Lessie two white envelopes.

'Mebbe you'd see that Ian and Jess get these. I'd just as soon not have bothered, but Ishbel wants to have some folk of her own age about. She's even booked one of those terrible American-style jazz bands.'

'You can't blame her for wanting that sort of party, she's young yet.'

'I suppose so. I'd have been just as happy having you up for the evening. I feel comfortable with you.'

'I was there just the other week. You must let your wife have her own way sometimes.'

'It seems to me,' said Davie dourly, 'that she gets her own way most of the time. Her father spoiled her and she expects me to do the same.'

Lessie eyed him thoughtfully, then changed the subject. 'Jess is in London just now, she's working for a big modelling agency there. But I'll try to get Ian to come down for your party. It's time he had a bit of pleasure. He works far too hard in my opinion.'

'A man cannae work too hard. It's what we were born for.'

'You sounded just like Da then,' Lessie said without thinking.

Davie scowled and said sharply, 'I'm nothing like him!' then turned on his heel and left without another word. She watched him go, the usual little frown tucking itself between her fair brows.

Ian, looking tired and strained but refusing to be fussed over, came to Greenock to attend the party, and with him came Jess, in a coat of corded blue velvet with a huge fur collar and a tiny hat perched on top of her fair head. She brought more photographs, taken this time during modelling sessions in London, and chattered on incessantly about the wonderful time she had had in the city and how she just couldn't wait to go back there. Her lovely long hair had been shingled – 'Everyone's doing it, Mother' – and Ian was amused to hear that Douglas Fairbanks had been supplanted in her affections by a young actor named Rudolf Valentino.

'I've heard about him. A gigolo, a smarmy ladies' man.'

'He is not!' Jess flashed. 'I went to see him in *The Four Horsemen of the Apocalypse*, and he's the most handsome man in the world, and the best actor. You're just jealous!'

'I would be if he could remove an appendix without having to open the patient up first,' retorted Ian, and ducked as his sister threw a cushion at him.

'For goodness' sake, you two, when are you going to grow up?' scolded Lessie, secretly revelling in the all-too-brief pleasure of having them both under her roof again.

Her eyes popped when her daughter came into the kitchen on the night of the dance. 'Jess Carswell, you're surely not going into company looking like that!'

Jess glided over to the mirror and peered into it, running the tip of one finger round the outline of her glossy red lips. 'Why not?'

'You're scarcely decent!'

'Oh, Mother! Ian, what do you think?' Jess appealed to her brother as he came in tying his tie. He watched as she revolved slowly in front of him, a bird of paradise in a crimson silk short-sleeved dress that hugged her slender figure and fell in skilful folds from hips to mid-calf. Jess's shoes were crimson and black and a crimson band about her head sported a curling black feather.

'You look all right to me,' he said at last, without much interest, and Lessie knew that she had lost the battle.

The lights were blazing in the Kirkwood house, the open windows letting out strains of jazz music when Ian and Jess stepped from their hired car. Jess's feet began to tap on the gravel at once and she hurried up the stairs ahead of her brother, eager to join the party. He handed over their invitations and his coat and followed her more slowly across the foyer and into the large drawing room at the front of the house.

The sliding doors between drawing and dining rooms had been folded back; a wooden dais had been set up against one wall to hold the band, who were playing enthusiastically. The carpets had been rolled back and the furniture pushed against the walls, and the middle of the floor was already filled with dancers.

Ishbel and Davie were standing by the door to greet their guests; Ian had a brief word with his uncle and the pretty girl who was now his aunt although only a few months older than he was, then he joined his sister.

'Looks like a good evening,' Jess said, then with a change of tone, 'Isn't that Dorry?'

Ian spun round and for a moment the blood stopped in his veins. Dorothea was at the other side of the room, dancing with a tall fair-haired man, laughing up into his face, one slim hand on his shoulder. She was dressed in violet, a lacy dress that seemed to drift about her body. Like Jess's, it was short-sleeved and short-skirted. As her partner swung her round, Ian saw that the bodice was cut low in the back to show her smooth white skin. Below a broad cream satin sash that hugged her hips, the dress fell in floating panels of various shades of lilac, violet and purple to a jagged hem. On her short bronze hair, feathers in the same shades as the skirt nodded in a cream band.

'What a wonderful dress,' Jess said enviously. 'It must have been made specially for her. I never would have thought that Dorry could be so stylish. Come on, let's talk to her.'

'You can if you want to.'

'You're not still sulking about her going to live with the Warrens, are you?'

'It makes no difference to me.'

'Then why are you behaving like a spoiled kid?' Jess wanted to know. 'If I'd had the chance I'd have gone like a shot. And I doubt if you'd have missed me the way you seem to miss her.' Then she shrugged. 'Please yourself, I'm going to talk to her.'

Left on his own, Ian made his way to the bar that ran down one corner of the room and helped himself to a glass of punch. He drank it slowly, his eyes roaming round the room, returning again and again to Dorothea, who was talking animatedly to Jess now that the dance was over. Jess indicated him; Dorothea glanced across and waved, a casual, disinterested wave. Then she turned back to Jess, her face vivid and happy. Ian drained his glass, and went to find a partner for the next dance.

The evening drifted along on a cloud of laughter and music. Balloons were released from the ceiling and greeted with cries of delight that turned to shrill squeals when some of the men started popping them with lighted cigarettes. The sky outside darkened and the first stars appeared. Ian danced with one girl after another, took someone in to supper, danced again. Occasionally he and his partner of the moment danced past Dorothea, who never seemed to notice him, but was always clasping her partner about the neck, laughing and chattering and enjoying herself. She had no shortage of escorts, Ian noticed. All at once he wanted to get out of the house, away from the revellers, the music, the sight of Dorothea being happy with other men.

Jess and he had scarcely exchanged two words all evening. She, too, had had no problem finding partners. When Dorothea disappeared into the hallway hand in hand with the fair-haired man Ian had seen her with earlier, he decided that he had had enough. He sought out his sister and drew her away from the group she was with. 'Let's go home.'

'Why? I'm having a wonderful time and it's still early.'

'I'm fed up with the whole business.'

'Off you go, then. I'm staying here,' she said, and swung back to her friends.

He shrugged. Jess was old enough to look after herself. In the foyer it was cooler, and a little quieter. Several couples could be glimpsed in shadowy corners, in each other's arms, and there were bursts of stifled laughter now and then from the stairs where several groups perched. Ian was looking about for a servant who could find his coat for him when he noticed Dorothea's escort striding alone from the door leading to the conservatory, his handsome face flushed and scowling. He brushed past Ian and disappeared back into the drawing room.

Ian hesitated, glanced at the front door, then at the conservatory.

She was probably fine, he told himself. If he went to make sure of that she would only laugh at him. He would just be giving her the chance to hurt him as he had, of necessity, hurt her when she accosted him outside the refinery gates over a year ago. But he knew that she had had several drinks, and obviously her partner had tried to take advantage of that. Perhaps he should make sure that she was safe before going home.

He bit his lip, then walked across the hall and reached out towards the door handle.

The conservatory was large and humid. Water dripped softly somewhere, but apart from that the place was pleasantly quiet and Dorothea inhaled the lush spicy smell of green growth, her arms wrapped about her body, trying to still the trembling deep within. She shouldn't have hit Jack so hard. He had been an amusing escort for some time now, but no doubt he would never speak to her again. On the other hand, she told herself, close to tears, he had had no right, no right at all to assume that—

She swallowed hard but the lump in her throat wouldn't go away. She felt dizzy and wished that she hadn't had so much to drink. Drinking was a smart thing to do, but she had never really cared for it. She took a good long look at herself and wondered if, after all, Jack had been so wrong in assuming that she would do whatever he wanted. She had led him on just as she had led other young men on. Usually she was able to back away before she got herself into danger, and usually the men were gentlemanly enough to leave it at that. But Jack, too, had had a lot to drink tonight, and he was quite a bit older than she was. No doubt he knew more about women than most of the immature youths she went out with. No doubt he was unused to a woman saying no.

She felt sick. She wanted to go home. She turned round, staring through the dim light at the green jungle about her, unsure, for the moment, where the door was. She located it and had taken a step towards it when the greenery at her back rustled and she spun round, eyes wide, suddenly aware that she wasn't alone.

25

Davie Kirkwood hated jazz. He hated having his house invaded by crowds of shrill-voiced, empty-headed strangers. He would have been happy to stay away, to spend the evening in the factory office going over the books, but Ishbel had insisted on his being there, playing the host. It was all right for Ishbel, she enjoyed this sort of nonsense; as soon as he could manage it, Davie had retreated to the peace of the conservatory with a glass and a bottle of good brandy, which was now almost empty. He was aware that he drank quite a lot these days, but he could hold his liquor and he needed something to make life bearable.

By the time he had returned home from his honeymoon, Davie had become bored with his young wife. He had courted her because he felt that it was time for him to marry, to have a wife by his side as he advanced into society. Ishbel herself had been the key to that society, to respectability. People who wouldn't have looked at Davie before had to accept him now because of his wife. And his father-in-law's wealth had been another reason for marriage to Ishbel. The success of his business, largely thanks to the war, wasn't enough for Davie Kirkwood. He still had a lot of ambition and he still had a score to settle. Ishbel and her family's money would help him in that direction too. He might be invited nowadays to the same events as Andrew Warren, he might be Warren's equal in business, but even so resentment still smouldered deep within and he wasn't done with the man yet.

Thinking of Warren made him think of Anna. Not that there was a day that passed without thoughts and memories of her. Marriage hadn't eased the pain of her loss; at first there had been something about Ishbel – her liveliness, perhaps – that had seemed to Davie to have faint echoes of Anna McCauley, but no more. His wife had none of Anna's vitality or her courage, and certainly none of her passion. Davie had found that out within hours of their society wedding. He poured more brandy into his glass and drank it down.

Dimly, he heard the sound of the door leading to the house opening and closing, then there were whispers and a distant giggle, followed by a scuffling sound and the sharp echo of someone clapping their hands together – or a slap. He neither knew nor cared which, he only realised that some of his wife's confounded guests had found his hiding place, and he stayed still, hoping that he wouldn't be discovered and required to make genteel conversation. When the door opened and closed again and the place fell silent, he assumed he was alone again. With relief he settled back in his wicker chair, shook the bottle to find out how much remained, and was about to pour more brandy into the glass when he heard a light step and his nose caught the sudden scent of roses, the perfume Anna had always worn.

Quietly, not daring to hope, he put the bottle down and got to his feet, parting the branches before his face. In the shaft of moonlight that lit up the path before him he saw a young woman, her back to him. Alerted by the sound he made, she turned; the movement, the bronze gleam from her hair, and the glimpse he had of wide eyes set in a face shaped just like Anna's set Davie's heart racing. Part of his mind told him that what he saw was a drink-induced mirage, but all the same he reached out and found his fingers touching warm flesh, catching an arm, pulling the girl closer. It was Anna – her height, her build, her face looking up at him, lips parted and eyes huge and dark in the moonlight. But he knew the true colour of those eyes. They were violet-blue.

'Oh God,' said Davie hoarsely, dragging her into his arms, rejoicing at the feel of her, the warmth of her, the sweetness of her held close to his heart after all the empty years. 'Oh, Anna!'

Ian didn't stop to find out the identity of the man struggling with Dorothea. All he knew was that someone was holding her, kissing her, and that far from kissing him back she was fighting to free herself, whimpering like a child in the grip of a fearsome nightmare. He charged towards them, snatched at the man, tore him away from Dorothea, spun him round and hit him with all his might without giving him time to defend himself. In the instant before his fist connected and the other man crashed back into the greenery to the accompaniment of rending branches and agitatedly whipping leaves, he saw that it was his Uncle Davie. But it was too late to stop the blow and he didn't want to stop it anyway. At that moment he would have struck down the Archangel Gabriel if he had found him in the same situation.

Without giving the older man a second look he whirled, stooped, and plucked Dorothea from the ground where she had fallen when Davie had been wrenched away from her. 'Are you all right?'

She clung to him, sobbing his name over and over again. Her feathered band had disappeared and her short, soft hair lay against his cheek. Ian half carried her to a bench and, detaching her grasping fingers, sat her down. He plunged into the shrubbery and located his uncle, lying on his back, with the strong smell of brandy about him. Running skilled fingers over Davie's head and face, Ian satisfied himself that though unconscious and with a growing knot on his jaw, Davie was in no danger and owed his slumber more to drink than to the blow. Then he gathered Dorothea up from the bench and hustled her out of the conservatory and across the large foyer. A serving-man materialised in front of them, his face carefully expressionless as he took in the dishevelled young couple, the girl in tears, the man tousled and angry. 'Can I be of assistance, sir?'

'Just get out of my way,' Ian told him, and managed to open the front door. With one arm about her waist he got Dorothea down the steps and halfway down the drive before she wrenched herself free and staggered to the bushes, where she sank to her knees and vomited. He followed her and held her head, then helped her to her feet and wiped her mouth with his handkerchief.

'You'll feel better now. Come on.'

'Where – where are we going?'

'I'm taking you home.'

The night chill had gone some way to sobering her. She pulled away from him. 'I want to go back to the party!'

'Why? Because you were having a good time?'

The sarcasm in his voice did more than anything else to clear the last of the drink-induced confusion from her head. 'You've got no right to—'

'Someone has to. You're not fit to look after yourself.'

'How dare you!'

'Don't be a fool, Dorry,' Ian said wearily, and started on down the drive.

She hesitated, then ran after him. 'Go back to the house and ask them to telephone for a car.'

'I've just knocked out my uncle. I'll have to go back there tomorrow and have it out with him once he's sobered up, but not before. We can walk.'

'All the way to Gourock?'

'It'll do you good, Dorry.'

They had gained the gate now. Ian started out along the road, walking fast. She had to run to catch up with him. 'My name is Thea!'

'Your name is Dorry.'

'That was before.'

'Before what?' Ian wanted to know, stepping out, not looking at Dorry struggling to keep up with him.

'Before I knew about – before you turned your back on me.'

'I'd no choice.'

'You had a choice! You didn't have to turn away from me, leave me alone the way you did!' Then she said, her voice shaky, 'I'm cold.'

He stopped so suddenly that she almost bumped into him, and pulled his jacket off. He put it round her and fastened the buttons, his face remote, his brows drawn together, before moving on.

'You've been behaving like a fool, Dorry. D'you know that?'

'What does that matter to you?'

'It matters!'

'Why didn't you tell me that it mattered when I needed to know?'

'Because – for God's sake, Dorry,' said Ian in anguish, 'can't you understand anything? Can't you see that it could never have worked out once you became a rich man's daughter?'

'I can't understand how anyone can just walk away from the person he's supposed to love. Perhaps I have been behaving like a f-fool, but what else was there for me to do? I'd n-nobody after you left

227

me, Ian. Mam wasn't my mam any more, Jess and Helene both loathed me, even Aunt Edith w-wouldn't have anything to do with me.' The tears had begun to flow again; her body shook with them and she stumbled on the pavement, unable to see where she was going. 'It's all been terrible. I've n-never been so alone in my whole l-life!'

He stopped, and again she walked into him. Ian looked down at her, at the downbent head, the slim shoulders shaking beneath his jacket. 'Oh, Dorry,' he said helplessly, shaken by such a wave of love and longing that it could no longer be denied. She lifted her face to his and he saw that it was wet with tears and almost misshapen, in the moon's light, with the grotesque effect of smeared make-up.

She gave an almighty sniff, then said with as much dignity as she could muster, 'My name's n-not Dorry. Not any m-more. It's Th-ea.'

'Not to me, Dorry.'

'Th-thea!'

'Dorothea,' he said, taking out his handkerchief again and carefully, tenderly, wiping her face. 'Dorothea. My darling Dorothea.'

He ran a finger gently down the line of her scar, then drew her into the shadow of a gatepost and into the shelter of his arms, and kissed her wet eyelashes, her nose, her lips, again and again and again.

Dorothea refused pointblank to stay in Greenock when Ian went back to Glasgow, even though her father had given his consent to their engagement.

'I'm not going to be separated from him again,' she told Andrew mulishly, and he finally had to give in. She also refused to accept more than a token amount in financial support.

'I have to get used to earning my own living again, Father,' she insisted, and finally Andrew obtained a post for her in the offices of a Glasgow sugar refiner he knew.

'She's obstinate,' he complained to Lessie.

'So was her mother.'

'Not like that. If you ask me, Lessie Carswell, she's learned it from you. I don't see why she had to go to lodgings in Glasgow when she could have been living in comfort here. We're not that far from the city, she could have seen as much of Ian as she wanted to without having to move away from Gourock.'

'They're young and they're in love. Let them enjoy their lives for as long as they can.'

'You talk,' said Andrew, 'as though being in love is a privilege that only belongs to young folk.'

'Mebbe it is. When we get older we're too busy just trying to survive to think of such things.'

'Oh Lessie, Lessie,' said Andrew, studying her with a disquieting light in his eyes. 'What am I going to do with you? There are times when I know that you've still got a lot to learn yourself.'

***

It seemed to the Greenock folk that Davie Kirkwood had a midas touch. Aided by financial support from his wife's family, he began to expand even further after his marriage, buying up small engineering shops and extending his business interests to take in other small companies such as Rattrey's spinning mill, where Dorothea had once worked. A year after the party which had ended with Davie being found unconscious in his own conservatory, an empty bottle by his side and a tender blue lump on his jaw, he prepared to make the largest killing of his career.

Lessie first heard of it when Andrew came charging into the shop in the Vennel, his face dark with anger.

Her mouth went dry at the sight of him and she abandoned her customer without so much as an apology. 'Ian? Dorry?'

'They're fine.' His voice was clipped, cold. 'I must talk to you.'

All the women waiting to be served, and the assistant behind the counter, were gawping at him now. Lessie pulled her pinny off, asked Doreen if she could manage on her own for a while, then snatched her coat from its peg behind the inner door and hurried from the shop, hearing the buzz of inquisitive talk break out at her back as she went. Andrew was pacing the narrow footpath outside. As soon as she emerged, he took hold of her arm and started to walk, not up into the town as she had expected, but down towards the river, splashing through the puddles that were always to be found in the Vennel no matter how warm and sunny the day might be.

'I've got a shop full of customers back there – not that you noticed,' Lessie said breathlessly as they barrelled along.

'Did you know what that damned brother of yours was up to?'

'Davie?' He could scarcely mean Joseph, who had never returned to Greenock after disappearing at the beginning of the war, nor contacted his brother or his sisters. 'What's Davie done?'

'I've just had a visit from my lawyer,' Andrew said grimly. 'It seems that your brother's out to take the refinery away from me.'

She stopped short, staring up at him. 'You're not serious!'

'Do I look as though I'm joking? For God's sake, Lessie, what's the man playing at? Are you certain he said nothing to you?'

They were down at the docks now. Across from where they stood a ship was being unloaded, only its upper decks and grimy funnels visible above dock level. A line of lorries waited where once there had been horses and carts.

'Nothing. But how—'

'At your brother's wedding I told you that I'd had to sell shares to raise the capital needed to modernise the refinery. I retained forty-eight per cent and the other shares were parcelled out to ensure that no one person could buy more than a safe amount. It seems that Davie bought some under various names and since then he's been calling on shareholders, buying up their shares. Now he holds thirty-seven per cent.'

'Not as many as you hold.'

'Not yet. But fifteen per cent of the shares are unaccounted for. If he gets his hands on them, he has the controlling interest. He can take over and force me out, if he's a mind to.'

'And if you get your hands on them you're safe?'

'Assuming I can find the holder or holders before he does. Assuming that I can top his offer.' He hesitated, gnawing at his lower lip, staring at the far shore of the river without seeing it, then said, 'Almost all my money's tied up in the refinery, Lessie. Helene's wedding cost a great deal and I've no doubt that with his father-in-law's wealth behind him your brother will be in a position to offer more than I can at the moment. I'm done for, Lessie.'

'Mr Wilson might not agree to giving Davie the money to buy you out.'

Andrew gave a short grim laugh. 'Old Wilson won't hesitate to back him, for all that he's known my family all his life. To him, business is business and the Warren refinery's worth having, especially after all the work I've put into modernising it over the past few years. But why my refinery? Why should he be so hellbent on putting me out of business and doing it in such an underhand way?'

'Because I'm a businessman and the Warren refinery's worth the having,' Davie said coolly when Lessie asked him the same question. 'I've put in a fair amount of work on the place over the years and I know its value.'

The two of them were in the study of his house, Davie behind a massive desk, Lessie opposite. The air was rich with the scent of his cigar.

'Davie, the Warrens began that refinery well over a hundred years ago. It means more to Andrew than a collection of buildings and machinery. More to him than it could ever mean to you.' She knew that she was begging, and hated herself for it. But she desperately wanted to prove to herself that the old Davie was still there, still reachable behind all the trappings of wealth and power. 'It's his whole life.'

'And making money's my life.'

'Och, you don't need to make any more. You've got as much as any one person could ever want.'

Good living had begun to make its mark on Davie. He was putting on weight, there was a florid tinge to his face now, and his mouth had hardened. 'You might have forgotten what it was like to be poor, Lessie, but I haven't. I'll never have enough money.'

'I've forgotten nothing, including how good you were to me and Ian after Donald died and how hard you worked for us. But you don't need the refinery.'

He eyed her coldly across his desk. 'If you've come to ask me to give up my plans, you've had a wasted journey. Why should you worry about Andrew Warren anyway? Save your pity for folks that need it.'

'Folks like you? Why d'you dislike the man so much, Davie? What has he ever done to you? He gave you work when you needed it badly, he's always been fair to you.'

Davie's colour deepened and he ground out his cigar in an ashtray. 'You'd not understand.'

The question was out before she even knew that it was in her mind. 'Has it got anything to do with Anna McCauley?'

Taken off guard, he gaped at her for a brief moment before recovering himself. 'Why should it?'

'You'd a soft spot for Anna all those years ago when she lived on the same landing as us in the Vennel. But it was Andrew Warren who won her.'

'Aye, because he had money.' Her brother's voice was suddenly grating and bitter. 'And you wonder why I'll never have enough? If I'd had it then—'

'What difference would it have made? You were just a laddie. Anna never took you seriously.'

'You think not?' said Davie, and all at once the missing piece fell into place in the puzzle that had been Anna McCauley.

'Davie, were you the man she was seeing before she died?'

'Who told you there was another man?'

'Nobody. Nobody needed to.' Then she said quietly, 'Anna bled to death after aborting the child she was carrying.'

'You mean that she'd tried to get rid of it?' When she nodded, he said explosively, 'You see? Warren's child, and she didnae want it because it was his. He killed her as surely as if he had put his hands round her throat!'

'Not Andrew's child, Davie. It couldnae have been his. He was certain of that when he came home from Jamaica and heard about it. I believed him then, and I still do. That's how I knew there had been someone else.'

He lunged forward as though he was going to throw himself across the desk at her, his face draining of colour then as swiftly flushing again until it was brick-red. 'Mine? But she didnae . . . I knew nothing—'

'You were struggling to keep the engineering works going, Davie.' It was all clear in Lessie's head now. All she had needed to know was the identity of the child's father. Once she had that, she knew why Anna had had to have an abortion. 'You'd nothing to offer her at that time except the sort of life Andrew Warren had rescued her from. She couldnae face that again, and she couldnae face him with someone else's bairn in her arms when he came home from Jamaica.'

Davie's mouth twisted as if he had just bitten into something unbearably sour. 'When I'd enough money I was going to take her away from him. And his bairn, too; I'd have taken the bairn willingly, for her sake.' Now that his secret was a secret no longer, the words spilled out. His hands, linked on the blotter, were shaking. He looked at them, then up at Lessie. 'It was his bairn she was carryin', no' mine! His, an' it killed her!'

'You're wrong, Davie. You've nursed your hatred all these years and you were wrong. You cannae blame him.'

'Anna!' The word was torn from Davie's throat and his eyes flooded

231

with sudden tears; he got up so violently that his chair fell over, and lurched to the window. Lessie rose and went to put her hand on his arm.

'Davie, it all happened a long time ago. No sense in raking up the past. No sense in hating Andrew now for something that wasnae his fault.'

His arm jerked back from beneath her hand as he swung round on her, his wet eyes blazing. 'You think anything's changed? She was mine, and he held her because he had money and I hadnae!'

'The only thing that held Anna was her own fear of going back to the sort of poverty she'd known in the Vennel. You'll drive yourself insane if you go on letting bitterness fester in your head, Davie.'

'Mind your own business!' He had his emotions under control again. 'You can beg all you like, beg on your knees if you want to, but I'll not change my mind. I'm going to have that refinery. I'm going to let Andrew Warren know what it feels like to lose the most important thing in his life!'

'You still need the other fifteen per cent.'

He walked past her and picked up the fallen chair, his movements sharp and vicious. 'I'll get it. I can offer more than he can, once I find the holder.'

'Davie, let the matter end here and now. For my sake if not for Anna's.'

'What's Warren to you?'

'A good friend. Dorry's father.'

His lower lip stuck out, reminding her strongly of their own father in one of his tempers. 'You'll be able to tell him you've done your best for him. I hope he's grateful. But it's not enough.'

'It will be.' Then she took a deep breath and said, 'That fifteen per cent you're looking for – I hold it.'

For a moment he gaped at her foolishly, then found his voice. 'You?'

'I bought the shares in my broker's name when Andrew was modernising the refinery.'

'Does he know?'

'Not yet.'

Davie's hands were white-knuckled on the back of the chair, the light of the hunter in his narrowed eyes. 'I'll give you double what they're worth on the market just now. I'll give you whatever you want for them.'

'They're not for sale.'

He released the chair and caught at her arms, his fingers digging in. 'Damn it, Lessie, you're my sister! You said yourself that I'd done a lot for you and Ian when you'd nothing, and nobody to lean on. It's your duty to sell to me!'

It was her turn to pull free. 'I'll not help you to seek revenge on a man who's done you no wrong.'

'You'd turn from your own flesh and blood for the sake of someone who probably thought you werenae even good enough to clean his boots in the old days?'

232

'The old days are gone,' she flashed at him. 'It's now we're talking about!'

'You can never escape from the past. Lessie, I'll give you whatever you want for those shares.'

'I'm not like you, Davie. I only need enough, not everything in the world.'

'I'm your flesh and blood,' he said again.

'Sometimes,' said Lessie, suddenly bone-weary, turning towards the door, 'flesh and blood doesn't count for much.'

'You and Ian would've starved if it hadnae been for me.'

'I'd rather have starved than seen what you've turned into.'

'Lessie!'

She didn't answer, didn't turn round. There was a sudden clatter as he swept everything off his desk with a violent movement of his arm. 'You bitch!' she heard him say as she opened the door and stepped out into the foyer without looking back.

26

Glasgow was never silent, even on a Sunday afternoon when the shops and markets and factories and offices were shut. The single room Ian Hamilton rented near the Royal Infirmary was right at the top of an old tenement building but even on a Sunday he could still hear cars rumbling down the narrow cobblestoned street below where horses used to pull carts. Trams groaned and rocked their way along the nearby main road, children shrilled at their games, and women leaning comfortably on cushions propped on windowsills or standing at the closemouths called to each other and erupted now and again into peals of laughter.

He stretched, yawned, and said reluctantly against Dorothea's silkily smooth back, 'It's time I was getting up. Time to go to work.'

'If you must.' She turned and smiled at him. Her hair was tousled and she was beautiful.

He bent his head and kissed the soft slope of each breast lingeringly. 'And you'll have to get up too. Time you were back where you belong.'

'This,' said Dorothea, reaching out to stroke her hands seductively down his naked body, 'is where I belong.' Then she squealed as he threw the blankets back and let cold air into the cosy little nest they had made for themselves. 'Ian! It's freezing!'

'Get up, woman.' He crawled over her and stood upright on the faded linoleum, reaching for his clothes, feeling his skin tauten in the chill air. 'You'll have to get back to Mrs Prissy before she starts wondering if you've been kidnapped.'

'It's Mrs Plessey, and I wish I didn't have to go back there.' Dorothea crawled reluctantly from the bed. 'Why can't we get married now and live here together?'

'Because I won't marry until I can support my wife,' he told her for the umpteenth time, forcing himself to avert his eyes from the hills and valleys of her nude body. He didn't have time to take her back to bed, much as he wanted to. 'And I'll not have you living in a hovel like this.'

'You're being daft. With what I earn we could manage. We could find somewhere a wee bit—'

'I want us to do more than manage. I saw what happened to my mother and stepfather because of the need to bring in more money.'

Dorothea, a stocking dangling from one hand, came up behind him and put her free arm about his waist. Her cheek was soft and warm against his back, through the material of his shirt. 'That'll never happen to us.'

'I won't let it happen to us. Not much more than another year and I'll be through. Then we're going to have the best marriage there ever was.'

She sighed, released him, and shook the kettle to make sure there was water in it before putting it onto the tiny gas stove and lighting the ring. 'Why did I have to fall in love with a stubborn man?'

'Because I'm irresistible,' said Ian, shrugging on his jacket and attacking his red hair with a brush. Between them they tidied the bed then gulped down some hot strong tea before leaving the room and clattering hand in hand down flight after flight of the stone stairs, and running along the dark close. The group of women clustered at its mouth split to allow them through then reformed at their back, nodding and whispering to each other.

'They're talking about us.'

Ian put his arm about her. 'That lot talk about everyone.'

'D'you think they know what we've been doing?' Dorothea asked with a giggle.

'Probably. But I hope to God your father doesn't.'

Her heels pattered briskly on the paving stones by his side. 'I don't care. I know what I want, and I want you.'

They paused at the corner, where their paths separated. 'I do love you, Dorothea,' Ian said through a sudden lump in his throat. 'When I think how close I came to losing you—'

'Hush!' She touched the corner of his mouth with the tip of one finger, a touch as light as a butterfly's wing, yet erotic enough to send a tingle of pleasure and wanting through his body.

'Tomorrow night? I'm off duty.'

She made a face. 'I've got a class.' To fill in her evenings, when Ian was more often than not working or studying, Dorothea was taking classes in shorthand and typewriting and bookkeeping at night school to help her in her job. She enjoyed her work at the sugar refinery; when she visited Greenock she always made a point of going to the family refinery, asking question after question, getting to know the business inside out.

'I'll get some studying in then and meet you outside afterwards. We'll buy a fish supper between us.'

'Good.' They looked at each other one last time, then reluctantly split up, Dorothea heading for the boarding house for young ladies that Andrew Warren had insisted she stayed in, Ian striding off to Glasgow Royal Infirmary where he worked as a night porter.

The rain had stopped and although the sky and water were still dull on that March day, the sky had managed to lighten from slate-grey to dove-grey. A shaft of sunlight pierced the clouds to form a shimmering circle, a large golden sovereign far out in the Clyde. Beyond it the soft blue hills on the other side, folded and tucked neatly, guarded the hidden entrances to Loch Long and the Holy Loch. A

236

filmy scarf of mist tossed carelessly down by some giant hand was caught between two of the hills, giving them a silvery lustre.

Lessie studied it, entranced, and Andrew Warren had to say her name twice before she turned away from the window, smiling at him. 'It's beautiful. You're fortunate to have such a splendid view.'

'I spend many an hour at the windows myself. But for now, come and pour the tea.'

She moved to the low solid table conveniently set beside a comfortable couch and poured milk into delicately fluted china cups. On the opposite side of the fireplace where a cheerful blaze crackled, Warren watched her. 'It's good to see you here at last,' he said.

'It feels strange.' Getting out of the car he had sent for her, standing on the gravel sweep before the front door, she had almost panicked, almost turned and run down the drive and out into the road. It was fortunate that Andrew himself had opened the door at that moment to rescue her from such a ridiculous flight.

'You should have been in this house long ago,' he said firmly, leaning forward to accept his cup from her hand.

'I remember walking past it with Donald and Ian, and Donald saying that this time next year we'd have a place just like it.' She smiled at the memory. 'It was his favourite saying – this time next year. It kept me going many a time after I lost him, thinking that this time next year things might be better, might be worth waiting for. But neither of us ever dreamed that one day I'd actually be inside the house, sitting here and pouring tea like a lady.'

'And looking as though you belong here,' he said quietly. Glancing up, she caught the look in his eyes and felt foolish colour rise to her cheeks.

'I'd certainly not be here if Edith was still working for you.' Lessie thought of the way Edith would have reacted if she had come into this room in her maid's uniform and seen her sister sitting like a lady of leisure, and felt the corners of her mouth turn up in a broad smile.

'It's thanks to her that I've finally got you to cross the threshold, so I should be grateful. Even though it irks me not to be able to call in at Cathcart Street when the mood takes me.'

'I'd no option but to take her in, Andrew. She's my own sister, and I could scarcely leave her on her own after that heart attack. I don't have the time to run back and forth to Gourock to keep an eye on her.'

'It can't be easy for you.'

'She's not a bad patient,' Lessie said swiftly, but Andrew was right; there was little pleasure to be found in her home now that Edith was lying in regal state in the box bed in the kitchen, demanding attention and finding fault.

'You should have let me pay for a nurse companion to see to her in her own home.'

'You've done enough, settling a regular pension on her. Most employers don't bother, no matter how long folk've worked for them.'

'I didn't do it for her as much as for you. And before you fly up like

237

a turkey cock at me, I'll never be able to make it up to you for the way you saved the refinery.'

'Och, that didn't cost me anything.'

'It cost you the good money Kirkwood would have paid you for those shares. Far more than I did. And then there was having to decide between us – between your own brother and me.'

A cloud drifted over Lessie. She had heard nothing from Davie since their quarrel and didn't expect to. She knew that she had lost him for ever now. Somewhere along the hard road he had created for himself, Davie had become an unforgiving man. She sipped at her tea then said, 'I couldn't go along with what he was going to do. It wasn't fair.'

'I just thank God that you went behind my back and bought those shares. Thanks to you I hold over fifty per cent now and I'll keep them. I've learned my lesson.'

Lessie finished her tea and put down the cup. 'I must go.'

'Not yet.'

'Edith'll be wondering where I am. I've got a meal to prepare.'

She got up a little stiffly, thinking wryly that her age was beginning to tell. But when Andrew stood up to take her hands in his, his tall body unfolded itself effortlessly. 'Come and have a look round the house before you leave. I thought women always wanted to see round houses,' he added in surprise when she shook her head.

'It wouldn't be right, me poking about the place.'

'My dear woman, Helene's safely tucked away in her husband's house down in Dumfries, and I can assure you that Madeleine's ghost isn't stalking the place.'

'Even so, it wouldn't be right.'

Warren shrugged and sighed. 'I still haven't got the measure of you,' he said resignedly, then to her surprise he stooped and brushed his lips along the line of her cheekbone. 'But thank you for being you, Lessie.'

In the car on the way home Lessie lifted a gloved hand and pressed her fingertips lightly against the place his lips had touched, half pleased and half afraid. Pleased because over the years, and particularly since they had been alone, their grown children scattered, Andrew had become very dear to her. Afraid because the look she sometimes glimpsed in his eyes made her wonder if he read more into their friendship that there could ever be. Men hated being alone, they took it harder than women, but the common sense that had kept her going throughout the ups and downs of her life told her that there could never be anything more for either of them. The very idea was a nonsense and she put it firmly from her mind as she stepped from the car. She thanked the uniformed chauffeur and rounded the corner to walk down Cathcart Street. She couldn't take the chance of letting the car deliver her right to her own close. Lessie knew her sister well enough to realise that Edith would be shocked and humiliated by a friendship between her sister and her former employer. Edith's snobbishness reached into every aspect of her existence.

'Where have you been?' she wanted to know as soon as Lessie stepped into the kitchen. She lay in the box bed in the alcove as Lessie had left her, with not an added crease in the pillow or the coverlet. She must have lain like that, motionless, all afternoon. 'I've been choked for want of a cup of tea. I thought you'd have been back before this.'

'I was just visiting.' Lessie hurried to where the kettle simmered on the coal range, not stopping to take off her coat. The doctor had said that Edith could get up and do things for herself, providing she rested often, but Edith, who felt that she had spent more than enough time caring for others, had opted for total invalidism and the luxury of someone tending to her for a change. Peter had left Greenock by the time his mother suffered her heart attack, and so far Lessie had been unable to trace him. Edith seemed indifferent to her son's disappearance. 'He'll turn up again like a bad penny,' she said peevishly when he was mentioned. 'He was never any good. If you ask me he inherited more from Joseph than from me.'

'When are you ever going to get rid of that monster and put in a gas cooker?' she wanted to know now, scowling at the gleaming range.

'I'm quite happy with things as they are.'

'It's old-fashioned, and it takes far too much cleaning. Who were you visiting?'

'Just an old friend,' said Lessie.

Just before Ian began his final year as a medical student, Dorothea got her way, and the two of them came down to Greenock for their wedding. As Andrew escorted his daughter down the aisle, radiant in ivory satin and lace, her face glowing beneath a circlet of orange blossom, Lessie let tears of joy run unashamedly down her face, much to Edith's annoyance. Her sister, who had consented to rise from her sickbed to attend the ceremony and was wearing the same black skirt and coat and white blouse she had bought for Davie's marriage, nudged her painfully in the ribs with a bony elbow. 'Stop shaming me in front of all the folk,' she hissed.

'I'll cry at my son's wedding if I want,' Lessie hissed back, and smiled through her tears at Andrew as he stepped away from the altar, his task done.

'I've got a name of my own at last,' Dorothea confided to her new mother-in-law at the reception in the Warren house. 'First it was McCauley, because that was my mother's name, then Carswell when I lived with you, then Warren, but none of them belonged to me. Now I'm Dorothea Hamilton, and it fits me fine.'

'I hope that being Mrs Hamilton brings as much happiness to you as it did to me, and for a great deal longer,' Lessie said, and Dorothea suddenly threw her arms about her and hugged her.

'Oh Mam,' she used the old title unselfconsciously, 'I'm so happy!'

Davie and Ishbel attended the wedding, but Ishbel was on her own at the reception. Davie nodded formally to Lessie when the guests left the church, but didn't speak to her. Although she felt that she had done the right thing in helping Andrew to keep the refinery, she missed her younger brother, and mourned him too, for to her he was dead and a stranger inhabited his body and used his name. They had each selected a certain road in life, she thought sadly, and their roads no longer ran side by side.

'Davie's got to get back to the factory,' Ishbel apologised on his behalf at the reception. 'He's so wrapped up in work just now.'

Lessie put a hand on her arm. 'I know he's busy. Don't worry about it.' In the four years of her marriage, Ishbel's eyes had lost their sparkle, her mouth had taken a downward turn at the corners. Lessie felt sorry for her, realising that her life couldn't be easy, and was relieved when Jess, who had come up from London where she now worked, took charge of her young aunt and brought a smile to her face. Jess was beautiful in a low-waisted vivid orange dress with a dramatic orange-embroidered black panel down the front from neck to hem and deep black cuffs to the sleeves. Several long strands of pearls were looped about her slim neck and her narrow shoes were orange with black heels. Heads turned wherever she went; she was featured frequently in fashion magazines now, and in great demand in the fashion world.

It was hard to believe that she had once been an ordinary little girl, playing in the Greenock streets with the other children. Lessie felt, each time Jess visited, as though she were holding an exotic butterfly in her hand – brilliant, fragile, settling for only a moment and impatient to be off again. She was proud of Jess, and she loved her, but she had lost the girl almost as completely as she had lost Davie. Their former closeness had long since faded. She felt that of the two girls, Dorothea was truly her daughter. For years now, Jess had had no need of a mother.

Ian and Dorothea settled in a neat little house in Glasgow, Andrew's wedding present to them. Although Ian was still a student they managed to scrape by on his scholarship and the money Dorothea had saved from her job. To Dorothea's fury Ian refused point-blank to allow her to go back to work, even for the final year of his studies. 'I'll support my own wife,' he insisted. 'You got your way about marrying before my finals, and I'll have my way about this.'

'I'm used to working,' Dorothea told Lessie mutinously during a trip to Greenock. 'I liked working in the refinery. They'd have kept me on and I'd only just become the manager's secretary. We could fairly do with the money, too, though he's almost proud of being poor and getting by. I don't know why he's so stubborn.'

'Some men hate the thought of their wives having to go out to work. It makes them feel inferior.' Even as she said the words, Lessie wondered if Ian was testing his young wife, making her prove to his satisfaction that she could manage without the Warren money.

'And it makes women feel inferior to be dependent on a man. Mam, I've got the housework done in a morning, and I'm not the sort to spend all my days embroidering or visiting.' Then Dorothea added guiltily, 'You'll not let him know what I've been saying, will you? I don't want to hurt his feelings. I love him and I'm so happy with him.

240

I don't mind doing without things and having to be careful with the housekeeping money, really I don't. I just wish I'd more to do with my time, that's all.'

Two months later she and Ian arrived together in Greenock, eyes shining, to announce that Dorothea was pregnant.

'That'll keep her busy,' Lessie said with relief to her sister when she returned with the news from the Warren house where the young couple were staying for a few days.

'Fetch me that calendar,' Edith ordered, and Lessie obediently brought the calendar from where it hung on a nail.

She watched her sister mumble through it, brows furrowed, and said dryly, 'Nine months, Edith. They were wed in August and the bairn's due early in June, Dorry says. They'll not shame me – or you.'

'Hmmm.' Edith relinquished her grasp on the calendar. 'It's gey quick, all the same. They'd have been better to wait for a wee while. At least until he'd finished his studying.'

'Love and bairns don't go by the calendar,' Lessie told her sister solemnly, and Edith scowled at her. 'They'll manage, and it's good to see them so happy together, making plans. It minds me of when Donald and me were waiting for Ian to be born. They say that the time passes slowly, but I never noticed it myself. With Jess I was busy with the new shop, and with Ian every day of the nine months just seemed to fly past. Happiness'll do that for Dorry and Ian too. D'you not mind it yourself, Edith, when you were carrying Peter?'

'I mind the heartburn and the backache and the discomfort. And I mind being left on my lone wi' a bairn tae raise.'

'Were you ever happy, Edith?'

Her sister's mouth pursed like a prune. 'I did my duty by Peter and by my employers and by Mam. I've nothing to reproach myself with. Life's not for enjoying – not for the likes of us, anyway. It's a hard business an' I'll not be sorry when the time comes tae lay down my burden.'

'Och, Edith, don't be so depressing! You've got years ahead of you yet.'

Edith shook her grey head. 'Life must go before life comes.'

'That's an old wife's tale!'

'There's truth in it, you mark my words, our Lessie. There's a new life to come now and before it does a life has to go. It'll be mine,' said Edith, almost smugly.

'You'll live to hold Ian's bairn in your arms, I'll make sure of that, if only to prove to you what nonsense you're talking,' Lessie said firmly. 'I'll make a nice cup of tea before I go along to see how they're managing in the shop.'

Edith Fisher's iron will held to the end. Despite Lessie's determination to prove that there was no truth in old wives' tales, she came home from the shop in the Vennel four months later to find her sister lying dead in the box bed, her hair in two iron-grey plaits on her shoulders, her hands clasped across her stomach.

241

For a few minutes she sat by the bed, looking at the sallow face on the pillow, certain that the half-closed lids would suddenly fly open and Edith's complaining voice would ask what had kept her, and if there was such a thing as a cup of tea going. But the silence deepened and she knew that she was alone, and that Edith, like Mam and Da and Thomasina and Donald, had finished with this life. She got to her feet, patted her sister's clasped hands, and went out to seek help.

Edith was laid in the cemetery close to the other family graves. Standing by the grave, Ian and Dorothea on either side of her, Lessie looked up as the minister's voice droned on and saw Andrew, who had taken time from the refinery to attend the funeral. As their eyes met he smiled faintly; she nodded in return then let her gaze travel on, round the small semi-circle of mourners, to where Davie stood alone, hat in hand, staring sombrely down at his sister's coffin. She wondered if he was remembering the old days when they had all been children.

There was movement beside her as Ian stepped forward to take one of the ropes, his young face solemn above his dark clothes, his hair a flaming beacon in the graveyard. Davie came forward too, and the undertaker's men held the other ropes as Edith Fisher was lowered to her final rest. They sang 'The Lord's My Shepherd', and as Ian's strong bass voice and Dorothea's clear alto soared above the others the words, 'In His house for evermore my dwelling place shall be,' Lessie had a sudden picture of Edith, not resting in that heavenly mansion, but working her way grimly from room to room armed with a tin of polish and a cloth. For a terrifying moment she thought that she was going to giggle, right there at the graveside, and shame Edith for eternity, then scalding tears came instead, and at last she wept for her sister, not only for her death, but for the grey days of her life, and for all the pleasure Edith had somehow missed in raising her son.

Where Peter was on that day when his mother was being buried, Lessie had no idea. Nobody had been able to trace him and Edith had died without a final sight of him. Jess, too, was missing; she had an important modelling assignment in London and was unable to get away in time for the funeral.

The psalm ended and Lessie stooped, lifted a handful of earth from the pile by the grave, and scattered it over the coffin. Then, the tears drying on her cheeks, she turned away.

Davie hurried off without speaking to anyone. He looked straight ahead as he was driven off by his chauffeur.

'I thought Ishbel would have been here too.' Dorothea clutched Ian's arm as she negotiated the pebbly drive; she was in excellent health but the growing baby had made her top-heavy and clumsy on uneven surfaces.

'She's in France on holiday with her mother,' Andrew told her. 'She's more often away from her home than in it.' He shot a sidelong glance at Lessie then said, 'There's talk that the marriage's foundering.'

'I thought you'd more to do than listen to idle gossip,' Lessie said sharply, and stalked ahead of the others towards the entrance. Her

242

Davie might be as dead to her now as Edith but she'd not allow folk to miscall him. She had never told a soul, and never would, about his love for Dorothea's mother, a lost love that had soured and warped his whole life; since discovering the truth of it herself she had come to understand more about her brother and to pity him with all her heart. But her understanding had come too late; Davie had mourned Anna on his own for many years, and didn't need or want anyone to share his secret. The very fact that Lessie knew of it had probably been enough in itself to make him turn away from her.

Just before she reached the drive leading down to the street she glanced to one side and saw the little stone that marked Anna's grassy grave halfway along a row. Every year, on the anniversary of Anna's death, Lessie laid flowers on the grave – twenty shillings' worth of flowers. She always would, for as long as she herself lived.

27

Morag Anna Hamilton was born at the end of May 1924, a few weeks before her father graduated as a doctor. She was a sturdy baby with her father's red hair tempered to a rich auburn by her mother's dark colouring, but with her mother's and grandmother's unmistakable violet-blue eyes. Holding her, looking down into those beautiful large eyes, Lessie felt her heart jolt, as though she had taken a step back in time.

She and Andrew had travelled up to Glasgow together to see the baby; on the train back to Greenock that evening it was Andrew who put their shared thoughts into words.

'She's the image of Anna.'

'What?' Lessie, who had been watching the countryside flash by and remembering with pleasure the utter happiness in the little house she had just left, took a moment to return to the present.

'Wee Morag.' Andrew, opposite her in the swaying compartment, folded his hands over his silver-topped cane and rested his chin on them. 'She's the image of Anna. It's as if she's come back to us.'

'It's strange how the mixture of Ian's red hair and Dorry's dark hair's just caught the colour Anna's was. And she has her eyes, there's no getting away from it.'

He grinned across the compartment at her, a boyish grin with mischief in it. 'D'you realise that Morag links us together for all time? We're grandparents now, with a shared grandchild.'

'I suppose we are,' she agreed with amusement. 'Being a grandmother doesnae make me feel any older.'

'You look younger than ever, to me.'

'It seems just last week that I went to Port Glasgow to see Dorothea for the first time. D'you miss Anna still, Andrew?'

His eyes softened, seeing beyond the carriage walls, looking into the past. 'I wish to God she'd not died so young, or died the way she did. Anna deserved better. But if I was to be honest – and I always have to be honest with you, Lessie – I'd have to say that I don't think that what was between her and me would have lasted.'

For a moment she wondered if he knew something of Davie's involvement with Anna, then he went on, 'It was a physical affair as far as I was concerned, and I think my money was more of an attraction to her than I was. Oh, I liked her dash and daring and her love of life, and I admired her courage. But if it hadn't been for Dorothea, I doubt if I'd ever have set Anna up in her own house. If it hadn't been for Dorothea I might even have stopped seeing Anna by the time she died.' He paused, then gave a rueful laugh and admitted, 'I loved my wife more than I ever loved Anna. But I didn't realise it until it was too late. I'll always regret that. Always.'

'It's good to have loved, though. To have it to look back on, and remember.'

'It's good to be in love at any age. And better to have love now than in the past.'

'You're an old romantic, Andrew Warren!'

He laughed as the train whistled shrilly and rocked round a corner. 'And you, Lessie Carswell, are altogether too practical for your own good – or mine.'

Two weeks later they were back in Glasgow for Ian's graduation. Sitting in the lofty university hall, Andrew unselfconsciously reached out to take Dorothea's hand in his left and Lessie's in his right as Ian, solemn in his robes, stepped forward to accept the scroll that entitled him to call himself Dr Hamilton from that moment on. Just as unselfconsciously, Lessie let the tears run down her cheeks. Edith would have been furious if she had seen them, but Edith wasn't there.

Ian started working as a junior doctor in the infirmary where he had worked as a porter, able at last to support his wife and his little daughter without recourse to Dorothea's savings or the occasional financial gift from her father.

In May 1926 Britain was hit by a general strike. It was bitter but soon over for most of the strikers, though the miners stayed out and the subsequent drop in coal supplies forced local factory owners to close down and lay men off. To Lessie it was a strong reminder of the hardship she herself had gone through after Donald's death. She opened up a 'tick book' in the Cathcart Street shop and extended the list of debtors in the Vennel shop.

'They'll pay when they can, and if we don't give credit to our customers they'll try elsewhere – and stay elsewhere when things improve,' she told her staff, and taught them to distinguish between fly-by-night customers who would never honour their debts and those who could be trusted to pay off their accounts when they could. Mindful of the way Murdo had once treated customers who owed money, she kept a close watch on the financial dealings of both shops and made sure that nobody was charged interest on their debts.

Poverty held Greenock in its choking grip. Soup kitchens were set up, but despite their own misery the local people were generous to the miners' bands that marched through the town, hungry and suffering men dependent on their own class for aid in a country ruthlessly prepared to starve them and their families into submission. Rallies and meetings were held throughout the country and at one such rally in Well Park there was a riot when the police moved in to arrest two men speaking in the park without official permission. One man was taken but the other fled with the help of sympathisers before he could be arrested.

'The word going round is that the missing man's called Peter Fisher,' Andrew told Lessie, his brow furrowed.

Her heart gave a double thump. 'Edith's lad? Here, in Greenock?'

'So I've heard. I didn't see him myself but I'm told that he gave a fine stirring speech before the constables got there. You've had no word from him?'

She shook her head. 'I hope I will, though. Surely he'll come to me.'

'He's a wanted man, Lessie.'

'D'you think I'd give my own nephew away? Anyway, I've no doubt that he was speaking in support of the poor miners and their families, and I've no quarrel with that. I hope he comes to me,' she said again.

'Probably not. He'll not want to get you into trouble.'

Andrew was right. Although she waited anxiously for several days and woke in the night at the slightest noise, always hoping for a gentle tap on the door, the sound of fugitive footsteps in the close, Peter didn't turn up.

Towards the end of the year, relief to able-bodied unemployed men was scaled down and Lessie's tick books began to fill up rapidly.

'How would the Members of Parliament like it if they were expected to feed and clothe and house their families on one pound and fifteen shillings a week?' she raged helplessly. 'It must cost them more than that to keep their wives in hats!'

'You're beginning to sound like one of those communists,' a customer told her, grinning.

Lessie shot back, 'If the communists believe in keeping folks' bellies full and giving them the right to work, then good luck to them!'

The coal strike finally came to an end in November 1926, and only then because the miners were so weakened by the hardships of their long and arduous strike that they had no option but to accept reduced wages and longer hours. The mills and factories went back into production and Greenock began to try to get back to normal.

Shortly after Morag's third birthday Dorothea suffered a miscarriage and was ill for several weeks. Lessie hurried up to Glasgow and looked after the family until Dorothea was on her feet again. Then, at her suggestion, Dorothea and Morag travelled back to Greenock with her for a holiday. Ian was left behind in Glasgow.

'I can't just take time off whenever it suits me,' he said.

'You look tired,' Lessie argued. 'You could do with some sea air yourself.'

'I'm fine, but I'd like Dorothea to have a good rest. She needs it. She took the baby's loss badly, poor lass. Look after her for me, Mam, I can look after myself,' he insisted.

It had been agreed that Dorothea and Morag, now an energetic red-headed bundle, should stay in the Warren house. Lessie took time off from the shops and as Dorothea's strength returned, the two women went for long walks along the river road, Morag trotting ahead of them. They sat talking for hours in the Warren house or in Cathcart Street and Andrew took them on a day-long river trip on the Clyde paddle steamer *Juno*, to the beautiful Kyles of Bute.

Although Lessie had lived all her life within sight and smell of the Clyde, this was her first trip on the river, and she was as excited as Morag, clambering down the companionways to see the great engines pounding as they forced the paddles through the water, hurrying up and up to the top deck where she stood by the rail, one hand holding her hat on her head, the other clutching Morag's small fist, watching as the steamer was manoeuvred skilfully alongside a pier, or gazing back at the foaming white wake unravelling itself behind them like the long lacy train on a magnificent gown.

Andrew watched her with amusement. 'You're like a child yourself, Lessie. You never lose your sense of wonder at new things.'

'Life's too short as it is,' she retorted. 'I'd lose a lot of pleasure if I started taking things for granted.'

Jess arrived on an unexpected visit, smoking cigarettes that she fitted into long elaborate holders and talking enthusiastically in a voice that had taken on a slight English drawl about Greta Garbo and Mae West and P.G. Wodehouse, who had apparently written funny books that were 'all the rage, darling', about a butler named Jeeves. It was hard for Lessie to believe that she had given birth to this elegant, worldly woman and raised her in the rooms behind the shop in the Vennel. Jess had recently flown to Paris on a modelling assignment and hoped to return soon. Paris, she said, was invigorating and absolutely the only place to be.

'I can't understand why you're not married by now,' Lessie said one evening, marvelling over the way her vividly beautiful daughter seemed to light up the kitchen simply by being in it. Jess shrugged elegantly.

'I've no intention of marrying. I'm an independent woman. I'm enjoying life far too much to devote it to one man.'

'You'll change your tune when the right man comes along.'

Jess fitted another cigarette into her holder. 'That's a sweet thought, Mother, but it's for the likes of Dorry, not for me. One day when I'm too old to model any more perhaps I will marry – but he'll have to be rich and able to support me in luxury in my old age.'

She brought with her a portable phonograph and a box of records, and the small flat was filled every day with seductive male voices singing, 'Ain't She Sweet', 'Ol' Man River', and 'I Can't Give You Anything But Love, Baby'.

Lessie tolerated the records, and secretly grew to like 'Ol' Man River', but she refused point-blank to allow Jess to buy her a wireless.

'Why not, Mother? It'd be company for you now that you're living on your own.'

'I'm not in the house all that much, and when I am I appreciate the peace and quiet,' Lessie said firmly. 'I couldnae be bothered with all the fuss of a box talking and singing at me.'

'You don't have to switch it on if you don't want to.'

'Then what's the sense in having it at all?' Lessie asked triumphantly, and Jess glared and blew smoke from both nostrils, for all the world like a small angry bull.

When Jess hired a small Austin open tourer and insisted on taking her mother, sister-in-law and niece for a 'spin', Dorothea and Morag accepted eagerly, clambering into the little car without hesitation, but Lessie hung back.

'You mean you can drive this thing by yourself?'

'Of course, Mother,' Jess told her impatiently. 'I drive all over London. There's nothing to it. Climb in and let's go.'

Cautiously Lessie got into the small high seat at the back with Morag clutched tightly to her side. Jess, in a bronze silk jersey suit with a tight-fitting cap of the same material and colour pulled over her shingled head, released the brake and moved off with a triumphant throaty bray from the horn that brought all the Cathcart Street residents to their windows and Lessie's staff and customers to the door of the corner shop. As they proceeded along the street Lessie, holding tightly to Morag's skirt with one hand and the side of the car with the other, thanked the Lord that old Mrs Kincaid who had lived on the top floor had long since died. She could just imagine the woman's harsh disapproving stare and her comments that she had always known that the Carswells were the wrong sort of residents for the street. To her surprise Jess turned out to be a confident and accomplished driver, and before the drive along the coast to Largs and back was over, Lessie had relaxed and was enjoying herself.

Two days later she arrived back from the corner shop to find the short hallway filled with rounded energetically waggling bottoms and slender backward-kicking legs. Jess and Dorothea had their hands flat against the wall at shoulder level, elbows bent, and their feet in the middle of the passageway. Jess was singing breathlessly and the two of them were twisting their feet and kicking their legs back from the knees. Morag, jiggling about between them with a doll dangling from one hand, was screaming with excitement.

'Da – da-da – kick – da-da – da-da,' Jess panted as Lessie walked in. 'What on earth?'

The gymnasts peered at her over their shoulders, then slumped against the wall, giggling. 'It's the Charleston,' Dorothea managed at last. 'It's a dance.'

'Lord's sake!'

'It's all the rage, Mother,' Jess chimed in. 'I'll show you. Out of the way, Morag.' She held her hands in the air and launched into an intricate sequence of kicks, wiggles, and foot twisting, her red-tipped fingers fluttering as though playing an invisible piano that was suspended from the ceiling.

'It's great,' Dorothea enthused.

'It's daft!'

'Not with the proper music. Come on, Mother, try it.'

'I will not!'

'Yes you will. Come on.' Dorothea seized her hands and planted them on the wall. 'Now put your feet back here so that you're bending forward. Now twist your left foot as if you're – er – squashing a cockroach.'

249

'And while you're doing that, kick to the side with your other foot,' Jess instructed. They took up their positions on either side of her. 'Ready? Da – da-da – and twist-kick, twist-kick, that's it, Mother, you've got the rhythm – da – da-da.'

Twisting, kicking, waggling her bottom, Lessie wondered again what Mrs Kincaid would have made of it all. Then she decided that she didn't really care. She was having a good time, Dorothea was getting better, and that was all that mattered.

Jess went back to London but Dorothea stayed on. Ian came down whenever he could, which wasn't as often as Lessie would have liked. As her health improved, Dorothea began to spend time with her father at the refinery, leaving Morag in Lessie's care. The little girl adored her gran's shops and was content to sit for hours, if Lessie was busy, with a bowl of barley and some twists of paper and a tiny ladle and scales that Andrew had bought for her, playing at shops in the corner while the customers came and went.

'There always seems to be more to do in Greenock,' Dorothea said one night when she had gone to Cathcart Street on her own to visit Lessie. She sat on the rug before the range, looking fit and relaxed.

'I thought it would be the other way round.'

'In Glasgow there's the house, and Morag, and going to the shops, and seeing a few friends. Here there's the river and the boats – and the refinery. I've enjoyed helping Father in the office.' Dorothea hesitated and looked down at her hands, twisting her wedding ring on her finger. 'I enjoyed working before we got married. I was good at it. Sugar refining's interesting.'

'You must have inherited the Warren mind.'

Dorothea smiled fleetingly then looked back at her hands. 'I've been on at Ian to let me go back to work but he'll not hear of it.'

'He probably thinks you've got enough to do.'

'He's wrong, then. There's not going to be any more children, Mam; they told us that when I lost my baby. And with Morag starting school fairly soon I'm going to find time heavy on my hands. I'm not like Helene, I can't fill my time with charity work and afternoon teas and sewing parties. I want to do something, to have a life of my own. I wish Ian could understand. But he thinks—' She stopped abruptly, then said, 'He thinks that's what destroyed your marriage – you working all the time, especially once his stepfather was out of work. Some men just don't take kindly to being supported by their wives.'

Lessie remembered Ian's accusations when Murdo left them and felt a return of the pain she'd known then. 'But lassie, I had to work. There was no sense in letting you all starve in order to save Murdo's pride.'

'I know,' Dorothea said, staring down at the rug so that Lessie could only see the top of her dark bronze head. 'I know.'

'I'm going to miss her,' Andrew said as they stood on the platform

250

watching the train carry Dorothea, Ian and Morag back to Glasgow.

'We both will.'

'She's got a damned good head on her shoulders, has Dorothea. I'm proud of her, and glad I didn't lose touch with her when she was growing up.'

Together they turned and walked from the station, back to their everyday lives.

28

In a faraway American thoroughfare called Wall Street, ruined businessmen, if stories were to be believed, were raining down the sheer slopes of high buildings like the tears down the faces of the thousands who had lost all their savings in the financial slump. The crash was so tremendous that it echoed across Britain and unemployment soared, but thanks to Andrew's advice and her own shrewd instincts, Lessie managed to salvage most of the money she had had invested. But things were nonetheless changing in Lessie's world.

The Vennel had existed in Greenock for over two hundred years, and was part of the original town. By 1931, tenements that had been built to hold a fraction of the numbers who now burrowed into them like mice were rightly and finally deemed to be grossly overcrowded and in a poor state, with inadequate facilities for the men, women and children who lived there. A Housing Enquiry was held and Greenock Corporation was granted a Compulsory Purchase Order that spelled the end for the Vennel.

The building that housed Lessie's shop was bought out and the shop forced to close. As it happened, one of the girls who worked in the Cathcart Street shop had just left, so Lessie found room there for the two women who had worked in the Vennel.

'It's not a problem for me, not now,' she told Andrew as they sat in her kitchen one evening. 'It's sad, losing the wee shop and the rooms behind it. They were the saving of me years ago. But the folk that live in the buildings'll be found better accommodation now, and the job of bringing the place to the ground and building new'll give work to a good number of poor souls who've been idle for too long.'

'Will you look out for another shop?'

Lessie considered, then shook her head. 'No. Mebbe it's time to take your advice and have more time to myself.'

He stared at her and his brows knotted together over grey eyes that were as clear and direct as they had been when she first met him. 'Woman, you've never taken sensible advice in your entire life. Why should you start now?' Then he said gruffly, taking his pipe from his mouth and contemplating the glowing bowl, 'I think you need another interest.'

'Jess has taught me to dance the Charleston and Amelia Earheart's already flown the Atlantic. What's left for me to do?'

Andrew didn't laugh. Instead he laid his pipe down carefully, got up, took a turn about the room, then said, 'You could marry me.'

'What?'

'You could take me in hand. And don't tell me I'm daft,' he added swiftly as she opened her mouth to speak. 'If I am it's only because I've waited all this while to ask you.'

'Andrew, it could never work!'

'Why not?'

Lessie floundered, and realised that her heart was skipping along at a ridiculous pace and her face was probably the colour of a tomato. She groped for words. 'You're one of the Warrens, and I'm—'

'You're a local businesswoman, a woman who's looked up to far more in this town than you realise. You're self-made, Lessie; you started with nothing but determination and you've worked damned hard for what you've got. You raised three children – one of them mine – and did it on your own for most of the time,' said Andrew almost angrily. 'The Greenock folk have got more sense, most of them, than to judge people by what they were born into. They appreciate good hard work. I doubt if I could have done half what you have, given your beginnings. So that takes care of whether or not you're good enough. Anyway, to hell with what they might think. It's me that should be worrying about my own worth—'

'You've got nothing to worry about!' she said hotly.

'—but I'm not even going to think of that, because I know what I want – and you're what I want, Lessie,' he finished, running out of steam at last.

'But I'm fifty-two years old!'

'And I'm sixty-two years old. You don't believe all that nonsense about love only belonging to the young folk, do you? Let them think that if they want, but they don't have the experience or the wit to know what love really is.' His voice softened. 'It's being old enough to know your own mind. It's watching someone mature and grow into her own special beauty in spite of what life throws at her. It's wanting to warm my hands at the glow she gives off and be with her and take care of her for all the days left to me.'

Tears came suddenly to Lessie's eyes and Andrew misted, wavered, and broke up. 'You should have been a poet,' she began to say mockingly, but her voice, too, wavered and disintegrated. She felt his touch on her, felt him drawing her to her feet, moving his hands to cup her face.

'My dearest, dearest Lessie, don't cry,' he whispered, and kissed her. His mouth was soft and warm at first, his grey moustache harsh on her face. Then his lips firmed, parted, and her own mouth opened beneath his in response as his arms moved to hold her.

She had thought that passion was long gone from her life, even before Murdo left her. It was an emotion that surely belonged to the heady days of courtship and early marriage, something that couldn't last. But now she discovered that it had only been lying dormant, and despite the half-century she had already spent in the world it was as clear and strong and wonderful as it had ever been. Nobody could have found it except Andrew Warren, she thought as she clung to him

254

in the clock-ticking peace of her little kitchen, returning kiss for kiss, tasting his skin on her tongue, letting her fingers know the texture of his thick hair and the strong solid breadth of his back beneath the tweed jacket he wore.

When they finally drew apart they were both breathless. Lessie reached up and touched his cheek, smoothing away the dampness left by her own tears. His eyes were blazing with triumph as he smiled down at her.

'Now try to tell me you don't love me, Lessie Carswell.'

'I hate a man who always thinks he's right,' she said, her voice still shaky, and he laughed.

'I promise you, my love, that from now on we'll take turns in being right.'

'What's Helene going to say?' Lessie asked later, when they were seated on opposite sides of the range again. She had made fresh tea and the hot strong brew brought the taste of normality back to a life that had suddenly taken on the feeling of a fairytale.

'I'm not bothered about what Helene says. She's comfortably settled in her own home in Dumfries and I'm old enough to do as I please. I think Ian and Dorothea will approve. And Morag. Especially Morag. Now she'll have her gran and her grandpa together under the one roof. If you've got any more reservations, my love,' he added, eyes creasing with laughter, 'just tell yourself that we're doing the right thing by Morag.' Then he leaned forward and caught her hand in his. 'Let's go to Glasgow tomorrow and tell them – they should be the first to know.'

'Not yet, Andrew. Give me time to – to get used to the idea.' What she really wanted was time to relish her new happiness, to hold it close and marvel over it in secret before it became the property of other people.

'I'm off to London on Saturday. It's supposed to be a week-long business but I could get it over in five days, I'm sure. We could go to Glasgow together on the following Saturday to tell them.' Then his hand tightened on hers. 'Come to London with me, Lessie.'

'I couldn't just up and leave the shop.'

'Yes you could. When did you last have a holiday? When did you ever have a holiday?'

Lessie, taken aback, had to admit that she had never in her life taken time away from her duties and from Greenock.

'Then come to London. We'll see the sights together and when I'm at meetings you can go shopping for your trousseau. We'll choose a ring, too.'

'Andrew, don't rush me along at such a rate! Anyway, your trip's all been planned. I might not get a room in your hotel and I'd be frighted to stay in a big city like that on my own.'

'I always book a double room,' Andrew said diffidently, not meeting her eyes. 'I find single rooms claustrophobic.'

'You mean we'd share a – a—'

255

'A bed, Lessie. That's what you're trying to get your tongue round. Why shouldn't we book in as husband and wife? Nobody in the hotel would know the difference.'

'I'd know the difference!'

He came to kneel by her chair, taking the cup from her hands and putting it gently to one side. 'I love you, Lessie. I've loved you for years. I don't want to be apart from you any more.' Then he added with mock seriousness, 'If you're scared that I'll change my mind about marrying you after I've had my way with you—'

'Don't be d—' She bit down on the word, then said, 'It wouldn't seem right. Not in a hotel, with the folk there thinking we were wed and our own kin knowing nothing about it.'

He sighed and got to his feet with a slight cracking of joints. 'Very well, but as soon as I get back we're going to Glasgow to tell Ian and Dorothea, even if I have to drag you away from your bacon-slicer in front of all your customers and cause a scandal in the town. Then we'll buy a ring and we'll have a party in my house, and that's when we'll tell the rest of the world.'

She nodded, almost in tears again, loving him all the more for his understanding. 'I'll buy a fine dress for the party while you're away.'

'And a wedding dress. I want you to buy your wedding dress soon, Lessie. That way I'll know that you're really going to be mine.'

'I'll go to Glasgow for it.'

'Buy the best and have the bills sent to me.'

'I'll do nothing of the sort,' she said at once. 'I can afford to buy my own clothes.'

He grinned and gave in. 'If you must, but just remember that once my ring's on your finger, it'll be my right – and my pleasure – to pay for them. Don't take money with you, my darling, this damned country's thrown so many honest hard-working men out of employment and into hopelessness that some of them can scarcely be blamed for taking any opportunity they can find to lay their hands on some money.'

'I've got my own chequebook. You can't run two shops and buy in supplies for other grocers without the use of a chequebook these days.'

'Another thing, you can be thinking of our honeymoon while I'm away. Anywhere you want, Lessie. What about a cruise?' he said enthusiastically. 'France and Spain, the African coast, Jamaica. Oh, Lessie, I'd love to see Jamaica again, with you by my side!'

When he had gone, with one last reluctant kiss, Lessie felt as though she had been caught up in a whirlwind, tumbled about for hours, then dropped back into her kitchen. Dazed, she peered into the mirror and saw the same well-remembered face peering back at her. Her fair hair glittered silver here and there, but it was still soft and in good condition. Her face had rounded out a little and the worry lines that had reigned between her eyes for as long as she could remember had been joined by fine lines stretching along her forehead and radiating from the corners of her eyes and mouth. She had never been one to try to fight against the passing years, using paint and powder as allies. But her skin was still quite good, and her eyes, tonight, were wide and luminous, her mouth softened by Andrew's kisses.

The thought of these kisses, of his arms about her, the look in his eyes as he said goodnight to her, made her feel as though she had shed thirty years. She remembered talking to Edith while they were getting the rooms behind the shop in the Vennel ready for habitation, describing her love for Donald as something that had filled her up with warm liquid gold. Tonight the gold was back, glowing through every fibre of her.

She was so fortunate, Lessie thought as she began to wash the teacups they had used, to have found such love twice in one lifetime.

The next day she was certain that the customers in the shop and the staff working with her behind the counter must be able to tell at a glance what had happened. Dorothea and Jess would certainly have known, so it was a good thing that neither of them were in Greenock. But apart from being told once or twice how well she looked, nothing else was said and she was able to nurse her secret in peace.

Andrew called in briefly on the evening before his London trip. He came in the door shaking his head, a vexed frown between his brows.

'All the years I've walked along this street and into this close and knocked at this door and never given a thought to who might see me and what they might think. But tonight I found myself skulking along and nearly looking over my shoulder because of what's happened between us.'

'I know.' Lessie giggled. 'We're a pair of silly old fools.'

'It's a great feeling, isn't it?' He took a small box from his pocket. 'This is for you – until we get a ring.'

Inside the box a delicate little brooch in the shape of a gold leaf with tiny diamonds along the stem lay on white velvet.

'Oh Andrew, it's beautiful!' Then she said nervously as she lifted it from its box, 'They're not real diamonds, are they?'

'Only very small ones.'

'It must have cost a fortune! I can't wear it!'

'Of course you can. You must. I told you, it's a stand-in engagement ring.' Strong though his fingers were, they were also deft and gentle enough to pin the brooch onto the jumper she was wearing. As his hand brushed against the curve of her breast it hesitated briefly, and Lessie felt weak with longing for him. She wished, then, that she had agreed to go to London with him. But it was best to leave things as they were.

Andrew secured the brooch and stood back. 'There. I chose an autumn leaf because we've found each other in September, and I suppose some folk might say this is the autumn of our lives. Although I fully intend us to celebrate our golden wedding together when the time comes.' His lips were hard and warm on hers, his arms strong about her. 'Look after yourself for me, Lessie,' he whispered before releasing her. 'The next five days are going to be the longest of my life.'

★★★

257

Lessie had only been to Glasgow a few times in her life, once with Donald, once or twice with Edith or Jess or Dorothea. She had never visited the city on her own and it took three days for her to muster up enough courage. With Andrew's brooch pinned on the lapel of her coat to give her added confidence, she left Greenock early one morning by train and emerged into Glasgow's busy streets just as the shops began to open, clutching her handbag firmly, her mind buzzing with all that she had to do before returning home.

First, she went to the nearest hairdresser's, where she firmly resisted the suggestion that she should have her hair shingled. Instead, it was washed and trimmed then softly drawn back into a chignon at the nape of her neck, with a fringe over her forehead. The style, softer than her usual bun at the back of the head, flattered the shape of her face.

'You have lovely hair, madam,' the hairdresser said, and Lessie, suddenly reminded of the day she had sold her hair to raise money for her first shop, was glad that she had insisted on retaining its length.

Feeling a little bolder now that the first step had been accomplished, she walked back onto the street, fingering Andrew's autumn-leaf brooch, then plunged into the first large store she came to.

It took her three hours to complete her task. She bought a green crepe georgette dress gently draped about the hips and falling in a flared skirt to mid-calf length, with a plain neck and bodice and short sleeves. That, she thought, eyeing it in the full-length mirror, would do for the party that was to be held in Andrew's house. The colour suited her hazel eyes and she allowed herself a smug moment to note that the elegant lines of the gown emphasised a figure that was still slim despite her advancing years. With the dress came a long coat in the same colour, snug-fitting in the bodice and waist and flaring slightly at the hem. It was fastened with a large ornate button at the side.

For her marriage she selected a cream wool crepe suit with a fashionably short low-necked jacket embroidered on the pockets and cuffs with bronze stitching. A plain bronze-coloured silk blouse completed the outfit.

By the time she had selected shoes and handbags to match both outfits, as well as cream gloves and a brown cloche hat with a scalloped brim and a side knot of bronze flowers for the wedding suit, she had run up a bill that would have kept the entire family well fed for a month in the days when she was struggling to raise three children. She brushed her fingertips against the leaf brooch then took out her chequebook and filled a cheque in with hands that, for a wonder, didn't tremble and betray her uncertainty as she had expected.

Back on the street again, leaving her purchases behind to be delivered, she drew in a long breath and felt some of the day's tensions draining away. She had managed everything, and now she was free to go home. But first, she thought, she would celebrate her success with a cup of tea.

The tearoom was quite busy when she entered, but she found a table for two in a corner and sank gratefully onto a chair.

'A lunch menu, madam? We're still serving lunch.'

Lessie hadn't realised that it was early afternoon. Several of the people at nearby tables were enjoying a full meal, but although she hadn't had any food since leaving Greenock she was too excited to feel hungry. She ordered a pot of tea and a scone, then sat back and looked round the room, thinking idly of her purchases, hoping that Andrew would approve, eager to see his reaction to the wedding outfit.

Then all thoughts of clothes were swept from her mind as a family party in the middle of the room rose from their table and she had a clear view to the far corner where a man sat hunched over a cup of tea, his head almost sunk onto his chest. He was turned away from her, but even so there was something familiar about the thin body in the long shabby coat, the light brown hair, in need of cutting, the almost gaunt line of the jaw. Lessie got up and forged her way across the room, bumping into an empty chair in her haste to get to him.

'Peter?'

Peter Fisher's head jerked up. For a moment his grey-blue eyes stared blankly, then slow recognition dawned.

'Aunt Lessie?' he said disbelievingly.

'Oh, Peter, it's so good to see you!' She pulled out the other chair and sat down; her knees had suddenly become so weak that she didn't think they were going to support her much longer. She reached across the table, past the half-empty cup, and put a hand on his. His skin was calloused and his nails were bitten down to the quick.

'What are you doing in Glasgow?'

'Just – doing some shopping. Where have you been? I heard you'd been speaking in Greenock. Why didn't you come to see me?' She blinked hard to keep back tears, knowing that that was the last thing he would want to see.

He bit his lip and stared down at the table. 'If you know I was there you'll know that the polis were after me. I could scarcely lead them to your door.'

'I'd not have minded. I'd—'

'Your tea, madam.' The harassed waitress loomed over them, her reproachful eyes telling Lessie that her feet hurt and she had more to do than chase around the tearoom looking for folk who should have the sense to stay put and not move to other tables.

'I'll have it here. And bring another cup – no, wait,' Lessie said swiftly, 'I think I will have lunch after all. I'm starving all at once. You'll join me, Peter? Two plates of bacon and egg and sausages and tomatoes,' she rattled on, not giving him the chance to refuse. 'And we'll have some chips with it, and a plate of hot toast and a plate of scones as well.' Then when the girl had moved away, she said gently, 'Peter, son, did you know that your mother had died?'

'I heard,' he said gruffly. 'When I was in Greenock.'

'It was her heart. She stayed with me for the last months. It was a peaceful ending when it came. I tried to find you, but nobody knew where you were.'

'I was in Newcastle – or Manchester. I cannae mind now.'

'So you've been travelling around a lot?'

He nodded and told her something of the life he had been living, finding work where he could, living rough when there was no money.

'There are plenty of us doing that these days,' he said bitterly. 'Men that fought all through the war for their country, praised for their valour then thrown on the scrapheap when they werenae needed any longer.'

Their meal came and while he ate hungrily Lessie, who had no appetite at all, cut her food up neatly and made a pretence of enjoying it. When Peter's plate had been emptied and wiped clean with a piece of toast, she pushed her own plate over to him, saying briskly when he hesitated, 'Eat it up when your auntie tells you to. You're still a growing laddie.'

He grinned, showing teeth that had gone bad with neglect, and started to eat. Lessie ordered another pot of tea and a plate of cakes and went on listening. Peter had become involved in politics and had, she gathered from a few disjointed words, spent time in prison for his beliefs.

'Oh, Peter! And to think that all this time there's been money waiting in the bank for you.'

He blinked at her in disbelief. 'For me?'

'Your mother was thrifty; she had a bit put by. And Aunt Marion's house was bought, not rented. I sold it and the money's been lying in the bank, waiting for you.'

'I don't want it.'

'Don't be silly, man!'

Peter chewed on his lower lip then said, 'I don't feel that I've a right to her money. I let her down.'

Rage flooded through Lessie. 'For God's sake,' she said, loud enough to turn a few heads at the nearby tables. She lowered her voice, leaning across the table towards him. 'If anyone let anyone down it was Edith, not you. I know she was my own sister and we shouldnae speak ill of the dead, but what chance did you ever get? Having to go to school in velvet suits, never getting a proper childhood, not being understood when the war started and you had the courage to stand up for what you believed in.'

'I lost that courage, though.'

'And no wonder, with what you must have had to suffer. You didn't shirk doing what you had to do once you went into uniform. If our Edith had had any sense she'd have thanked God every day for blessing her with a son like you. And you think you're not entitled to her money? If you ask me, it's little enough compensation for what you've been through.'

During her tirade he had at last lifted his head and looked straight at her. His eyes had started to glisten and he blinked hard to clear them. When Lessie stopped, there was a silence, then he said gruffly, 'I wish I'd been your son.'

'So do I, Peter. I always wished it and I always will.'

'Even so, I don't want the money.'

'And I don't want the responsibility of it. You can give it away or make a fire with it or spend it on sweeties for all I care,' she said, getting a faint smile from him. 'It'll be yours to do with as you want. D'you know where the nearest Bank of Scotland is?'

'Aye, but I'm no' a customer of theirs,' he said wryly.

'That doesnae matter.' She got to her feet, nodding to the waitress to bring the bill. 'Take me there. I'll sort it all out.'

Within an hour she had seen the manager, made him telephone to her bank in Greenock to confirm that she was a respectable customer and not a madwoman, written the largest cheque she had ever signed, and opened an account for Peter, who stood silently by her side throughout.

'I don't think I'll be staying in Glasgow,' he said when they emerged into the street again. 'And it's not a good idea for me to have a bank account. Folk can be traced through bank accounts.'

'You'll have to give it three days, then you can take the lot out in cash and close the account,' Lessie told him briskly. 'I've hinted to the manager that that's what you'll be doing. After that, what you do with the money's your own business, and now my conscience is clear.' She held out her hand. 'I hope I'll see you again, Peter. You know you'll always find a welcome in my house.'

To her surprise he ignored her hand and bent to kiss her cheek. For a brief moment his fingers were painfully tight on her shoulders. 'Goodbye, Auntie Lessie,' he said, his voice hoarse. 'God bless you.' Then he turned and was gone, slipping into the passing crowd as though he had trained himself to vanish from sight swiftly.

On the train home she sat in a corner seat, staring out of the window, seeing nothing but Peter's thin face, the way he had attacked the food she had bought for him. He hadn't once asked about his cousins or anyone else from Greenock. She had said nothing to him about the family, guessing that part of his defence against a world that had treated him too harshly was the rejection of people who had once mattered to him. She knew that she would never see him again, probably never find out what happened to him, unless he did something that got his name into the papers. She hoped, for his sake, that that wouldn't happen. She hoped, too, that he would never find out that Aunt Marion's house had been rented, not bought as she had told him.

As the train rocked along on its way home she wondered what would have become of Peter if the war had never happened. He would still be working in the refinery, maybe married by now, with a nice wee home of his own and some children. He would have made a good father, would Peter. The war, she thought, had a lot to answer for. There were more casualties of battle than those who carried the physical scars for all to see.

'A terrible shock to his family,' the man beside her said, raising his voice slightly as the train rattled over some points. He and his companion, who sat opposite, were dressed in sober office clothes; they had entered the carriage together and opened their respective newspapers at once, conveying pieces of news back and forth to each other.

'You never know when your time's coming,' the other man agreed. 'Is there a family?'

'A daughter – two daughters, I believe. His only boy died in the war.'

'I wonder what'll become of the refinery?'

'He's done a great deal for it, I've heard. A good healthy business in spite of the current—'

The word 'refinery' had stabbed into Lessie's brain like an icicle, scattering all thoughts of Peter. 'Excuse me,' she interrupted, and almost snatched at the newspaper only a few inches away. She saw the headline almost at once. 'Greenock Refiner Dies'. And underneath it in stark black letters was the report of how Greenock businessman Andrew Warren had become ill at a meeting and been taken to St Thomas's Hospital. He was dead on arrival. It was believed, the newspaper informed Lessie impersonally, that Mr Warren had suffered a severe stroke. His family had lived in Greenock for . . .

The words started to slide together then dance around the page. There was a buzzing in her ears as though her head was filled with bees. She looked up and saw that the two men and the elderly couple who had been dozing in the far corner were all staring at her with varying expressions of astonishment and disapproval.

'I'm sorry.' She returned the paper, crumpled from her tight grasp, to its rightful owner and said lamely to the staring eyes, 'I'm – I was acquainted with the Warrens.' Then she turned away from their murmured sympathies and stared out of the window again, this time listing all that she saw carefully in her mind in an attempt not to break down in front of her travelling companions. A group of houses, cows in a field, a horse pulling a cart along a lane, a farmhouse, a river.

When she left the station, the *Greenock Telegraph* news boards by the entrance had 'Death of Local Refiner' scrawled over them. Lessie turned away and walked aimlessly, travelling up one street and down another until after a long time she found herself on one of the quays by the river's edge. Men were unloading a ship further along, but where she stood it was quiet, with only gulls for company. Grey water, echoing the gathering clouds in the sky, lapped against stone steps several feet below her.

Andrew had promised her a golden wedding anniversary and then he had gone away, and now she was so frighteningly alone that her whole body shook with the terror of it. He had gone, leaving her with only a small autumn-gold leaf to mark their September promises to each other, only the memory of a few – too few – kisses and caresses and some wonderful, half-formed plans that had died with him.

No, she corrected herself sharply. He had left her with far more than that. She had the memories of over half a lifetime of friendship and comfort and support. He had given her more than any other human being, even Donald, had ever given her. If it was true that people lived on as long as others remembered them, then Andrew would continue to exist for many years, and many more years after that, for as long as anybody remembered Lessie herself. He was a part of her, a part that death could never touch.

The thought comforted her briefly. She tried to hold tightly to it but it was whipped away in a sudden storm of remembering the way he had kissed her and held her. He had asked her to go to London with him to share his bed there, and she, like a fool, had declined. Now she would never know what it was like to lie in his arms, to belong to him. Stupidly, blindly, she had denied that special loving to them both. Because of her stupidity Andrew had died alone and now she must live alone, without him.

She stood on the quay for a long time, until early night came, bringing the rain with it, until the wavelets below were freckled with rain and the ground round her feet was dark with it and her face was wet with it. Or tears. Or both.

29

A pile of boxes was delivered on the following morning, boxes bright with the Glasgow store's emblem. Lessie, her hair brushed out and restored to its usual bun at the back of her head, pushed them deep into the recesses of the huge walnut wardrobe that had belonged to Miss Peden. She would never wear the clothes and the hat and the shoes now, never look at them again.

Dorothea and Ian arrived, bringing Morag with them, less than an hour after the delivery man had gone whistling out of the close. Ian's face was sombre, Dorothea's ashen. She started to cry as soon as she saw her mother-in-law, and Ian deftly scooped Morag up and carried her out. 'Come on and look at the pigeons,' Lessie heard him saying as the door closed on Morag's wondering little face, looking back at her mother over Ian's shoulder. 'When I was a wee boy I liked looking at the pigeons. We called them doos . . .'

'It must be just as hard for you, Mam,' Dorothea sniffed when her tears began to subside. 'I only knew him as my father for a few years. You knew him for such a long time.'

'Aye. I'll miss him,' Lessie said quietly. In the long wakeful hours of the night she had decided that there was no point in telling anyone about the plans she and Andrew had made together. What was over was over.

In the church, which was filled to overflowing for the funeral service, she watched dry-eyed as Andrew was carried past her in his coffin. She had done her weeping on the day she heard the news and in the terrible never-ending night that had followed. In the cemetery she looked among the crowd of mourners for Davie but didn't see him. Ishbel had left him two years earlier but he still lived in the big house in Newton Street, alone except for the servants. Ishbel had left the district; Lessie had heard that she had gone off with another man, a man less buried in his work and more able to give her the loving she needed, and that her father had signed a considerable slice of his wealth over to Davie as the purchase price of a discreet divorce, to prevent him from causing a scandal and dragging Ishbel's name through the local mud. Lessie wasn't entirely surprised by her brother's absence, for she was quite sure that he had never been able to bring himself to stop hating Andrew for having been Anna's lover.

The greatest test of her strength came when she had to go into the Warren house and sit in the drawing room that reminded her so strongly of Andrew's warm, vital presence. The drawing room, she thought, looking around, that she might have entered as mistress, if the fates had been kinder. She shook her head when a black-gowned housemaid offered tiny delicate sandwiches, but although she disliked drink, she took a glass of sherry wine from a proffered tray. Holding it gave her something to do with her hands, and she felt that she needed the comfort of alcohol on that day of all days.

Helene, elegantly stylish in black, acted hostess, ordering the servants around with the impersonal confidence of one who has been conscious of her own superiority all her life. Apart from a cool little nod of recognition she ignored Lessie, who wished, for one impish moment, that Helene had known how close they had come to being stepmother and stepdaughter. The young woman would have hated that.

Lessie lifted her glass, studied its pale golden contents, said in her mind, 'To you, my dearest,' and drank the wine down.

Dorothea and Ian had to stay on to hear the reading of the will, but Lessie left as soon as she possibly could, using Morag as her excuse for hurrying back to Cathcart Street. As she stepped onto the gravel drive outside, she let her breath out in a long shaky sigh of relief. The ordeal was over and now she would be free to mourn in peace and privacy.

She fetched Morag from a neighbour's house and spent the rest of the afternoon playing with her. The little girl's cheerful grin and incessant chatter was an antidote to the strains and tensions of the past week, and for the first time since Andrew's death Lessie found herself laughing again. She gave Morag her tea, bathed her and dressed her in her little nightgown, then tucked her into the box bed. Morag loved it, and always insisted on sleeping there when she was in Cathcart Street. Lessie always shared it with her, for it was high and there was a danger of the little girl rolling out of it in the middle of the night. She read her way through half a storybook before Morag's eyelids finally lost the fight and closed. She drew the curtains across the alcove to shade the child from the light and started tidying up the kitchen.

She knew as soon as Ian and Dorothea came in that something had happened. Ian's mouth was grim, while his wife, looking pale and distressed, fidgeted with her bag, her gloves, the cup of tea that Lessie put into her hands.

Andrew, it seemed, had left a few bequests to members of his household staff; and everything else – the house, the money, the refinery – he left to his daughters.

Lessie felt dismay run her through like a sword. How would Ian react to his wife being wealthy in her own right? It made sense for Andrew to leave everything to his own flesh and blood but when the will was written and signed he had had every intention of living for a very long time. Had he died an old man, Ian and Dorothea, mellowed by middle-age and many years together, would have been more able to cope with her inheritance. But it had all happened too soon – too soon for her son and daughter-in-law as well as for herself and Andrew.

266

Looking at Dorothea's strained face, Lessie saw that her thoughts ran along the same lines as her own.

'So now Dorothea and Helene have to decide whether to sell the refinery as well as the house, or whether to try to find a trustworthy manager to run it for them,' Ian was saying, his voice taut with reaction. 'It's going to take months to sort out. A sale would make sense, but this might not be a good time to sell a business, with the country in a depression. Dorothea, if you ask me—'

'Not now, Ian.' Her voice, too, was tense. 'I need time to think about what's best.'

His brows tucked together. 'Helene didn't have any trouble in making up her mind. She wants to sell, lock, stock and barrel. You're surely not thinking of keeping the house on, are you? Apart from the fact that my work's in Glasgow and I don't want to move from the Royal, I couldn't afford the upkeep of a house that size. And I'm certainly not going to live on my wife's charity.'

Dorothea, who hadn't touched her tea, put the cup aside and got to her feet. 'It's been a long day. I think I'll go to bed. Was Morag all right?'

'She's been as good as gold.'

Dorothea peered between the curtains drawn round the box bed then went out of the room without another word. Scowling, Ian followed her. In bed later, with the heat from Morag's curled-up body reaching across the mattress towards her, Lessie could hear her son's voice murmuring through the wall, with an occasional brief word from Dorothea. She wished that Ian would leave the girl alone to think things through instead of trying to force her into a swift plan of action.

They left for Glasgow in the morning, Dorothea still quiet, Ian still moody, and Morag as bright as a button. Lessie stripped the beds and put the sheets in to soak, then went along to the shop, stepping into its aroma of sawdust and coffee and cheeses with relief. Being back in her usual routine was like putting soothing salve on a burn.

Dorothea and Ian were rarely far from her mind for the next few weeks. She felt a niggling anxiety about them, and kept telling herself that it was none of her business and they were sensible enough and loving enough to come to some agreement over her daughter-in-law's new-found wealth.

But when Dorothea arrived unexpectedly at the house one evening, alone and with an air of nervous defiance about her, Lessie's heart sank.

'Where's Ian – and the bairn?' She tried to keep her voice light as she led her daughter-in-law into the kitchen. 'Did you come down on your own?'

'Morag's in Gourock and Ian's in Glasgow.' Dorothea sat down on the edge of a chair and said in a rush of words, 'Mam, leave the kettle. I don't want tea. I – I've decided to take over the refinery and run it myself.'

267

'What?' It was Lessie's turn to sit down, abruptly. 'But how can you?'

'I've thought hard about it and I believe I can do it. I learned a lot about sugar refining when I worked in Glasgow, and when I was staying here after the – after I lost the baby.' Dorothea's hands twisted and turned in her lap, her gold wedding ring catching the light. 'I've read books about it too. My father reorganised the refinery so well that it can be run more easily now. I'll do things the way he did them, and that'll keep me on the right lines.'

'And what about Ian?'

Dorothea's hands were like trapped butterflies now. Lessie longed to reach out and still them, cover them with her own and calm them. 'He's staying in Glasgow. That's where his work is.'

'Oh, Dorry!'

'I know it's not the best way to run a marriage, but I can't go on sitting in the house day after day, watching my life go by and never doing anything with it. It's got worse since Morag started school. And Ian refuses to let me go back to work. I have to find out if I'm any good at making sense of the refinery and my own life, Mam. Helene's agreed to rent me her half of the house for the moment – the money my father left me will cover that. And she's agreed to give me six months with the refinery. A meeting of the other shareholders has been called, but I think I can persuade them to let me go ahead. If I can make a success of it in the next six months I'll buy Helene out and buy her share of the house. I've put Morag into a school down here for the time being.'

'You've done that already?'

Dorothea coloured and the scar on her cheek showed as a faint white line. 'I've been down here for over a week. I wanted to find out if things would work before I told you, and I wanted to find out if I could be apart from Ian.'

'And you've discovered that you can.'

Dorothea's flush deepened. 'He's not tried to persuade me to go back to Glasgow. He'll come down to see us when he can and I'll take Morag to Glasgow often to visit him.'

'Is there not some other way the two of you can work this out together?'

'If there is, we can't think of it. It would be just as bad if I went along with Helene and sold the refinery. You know that, don't you? I'd be rich and that would make Ian unhappy anyway. This way when he sees me working to keep it going, and managing to care for Morag as well, he'll mebbe accept things and come down to work in one of the hospitals here so that we can be together again.' Then she said in a rush of words, 'Mam, I know it's difficult for you, being Ian's mother and my foster mother. But I need you to help me. It's all very well having a housekeeper but I can't concentrate on the refinery without knowing that Morag's all right. I need to know that she's got you as well as me.'

It was on the tip of Lessie's tongue to say, 'She'd be better with her two parents, be it in Glasgow or Greenock,' but she held the words back. This crisis was between Ian and Dorothea, and only they could work it out.

'Aye, I'll help you,' she said instead, and Dorothea's lovely blue eyes suddenly sparkled with tears.

'Thank you, Mam,' she said, and hugged Lessie fiercely.

When she was alone again, Lessie fingered the gold leaf brooch, which she wore all the time, and whispered to the empty room, 'Oh, Andrew, my darling, what have you done to our children?'

One thing Lessie refused to do, and that was to move into the Warren house. The thought of being in Andrew's home now that he himself was gone was quite unbearable. Dorothea's argument that it would make things easier as far as Morag was concerned and that it was time Lessie enjoyed a little comfort did nothing to sway her.

'I need to be near the shop, and I'm quite happy in my own wee house. Morag can come here whenever she likes, and there's nothing to stop her staying here now and again.'

Morag was delighted with the new arrangement. To her, being in Gourock was the same as being on holiday. Even attending a new school had a temporary air to it, and she was able to see her beloved gran every day. On most afternoons the housekeeper met her out of school and brought her on the tram to Cathcart Street, where she 'helped' in the shop, then went back to Lessie's house and had her tea. Then either Lessie took her home or she was collected by the housekeeper. Occasionally Dorothea herself came from the refinery in Bank Street to claim her daughter, but more often than not she was too busy.

It was hard work, taking over the reins from Andrew Warren, but as far as Dorothea was concerned this was her chance to prove herself and she was determined not to fail. Through the business contacts she had slowly built up over the years Lessie learned, by dint of a question here, a listening ear there, that her daughter-in-law was giving a good account of herself and winning the grudging admiration of men who had been quite convinced, at the beginning, that sugar-refining was not for a woman.

'I can't see why they should be surprised,' Dorothea said with a grim smile when she heard what they were saying about her. 'After all, it's women who buy sugar and use it, not men. Why shouldn't women deal with the business of refining it too?'

At first she looked so tired and drawn all the time that Lessie fretted about her. But once she settled in at the refinery Dorothea began to bloom. There was no denying that being busy suited her. Her eyes sparkled, her skin glowed, and even her hair seemed to take on more of a red lustre. She moved and spoke with renewed purpose, and Lessie began to see more of Andrew in her than ever before. He would have been proud of his illegitimate daughter, she thought, then wondered what he would have said about what was happening to Dorothea's marriage. She doubted if he would have been happy to know that he had been the unwitting cause of the enforced separation.

269

Ian came down often to visit his wife and daughter, staying in the Gourock house at first; then after a few months he began to stay with Lessie instead.

'I don't feel comfortable in that house,' he told her. 'It's too big for me, too fancy. I'd just as soon be in Cathcart Street. After all, it's where Morag spends a fair amount of her time.'

Dorothea may have blossomed during their time apart, but Ian had not. He looked older, more withdrawn, and a tiny frown, not unlike the frown-lines Lessie had carried since Donald's death, had etched itself between his brows. When they were all together Lessie saw how Dorothea watched him, saw the shadow on the younger woman's face, and wondered each time, with renewed hope, if Dorothea had realised that her marriage meant more to her than her business. After all, she had proved herself. Perhaps it was time for her to install a good manager and go back to being a wife and mother.

Ian, she gradually noticed, tended to avoid meeting his wife's eyes – and his mother's too. He kept his own counsel well, only unbending with his daughter.

'Would you not think of coming back to stay in Greenock?' Lessie asked him on one visit. 'We need doctors just as much here as they do in Glasgow, and you'd be near Dor— near Morag.'

'I like working in the Royal,' he told her at once, snapping the words out. 'There's no reason for me to move. And Morag seems happy enough with the way things are.' There was no more to be said on the subject.

During the winter, bad weather and an increased workload at the hospital meant that his visits became few and far between. When the spring came, the visits stayed at their winter level.

In the summer of 1932 Dorothea went off to Glasgow, asking Lessie to look after Morag in her absence.

'Are you not taking her with you?'

'We've things to talk about, Ian and me,' Dorothea said awkwardly. 'We need to be on our own.'

For three days Lessie waited impatiently, praying that Ian and Dorothea were working out some form of compromise. She loved them equally and she wanted nothing more than to see them both happy. It vexed her that Ian had been so indoctrinated by Murdo, the only father he had known, as far as working wives were concerned. Murdo had been happy enough for her to keep the shop on; indeed, he had loved money too much to think otherwise. It was only when their marriage had soured for him, when he was embittered by his own unemployment and needed to justify his infidelity and eventual desertion, that he had cited the shop as a rival instead of a means of financial support. She wondered what he had said to Ian in the letters he had continued to send, and during his last days, when Ian was with him. Her son had never given her any information and she would have bitten her tongue out rather than ask. Whatever it was, it had been one-sided and unfair, and although she rarely admitted it to herself, she was hurt at Ian's acceptance of it, especially once he matured and became more aware of the complexities of human nature.

Dorothea returned one evening to a rapturous welcome from Morag, who was ready for bed.

'Let me stay one last night,' she clamoured, and her mother laughed and nodded.

'One last night, then. But I want you to come home tomorrow. Daddy's sent you a present. I'll give it to you tomorrow.'

She hugged her daughter, tucked her into the box bed, and read her a story with such an air of serenity that Lessie dared to hope. When Morag had fallen asleep and they were sitting together by the range, the bed curtains drawn, Dorothea said quietly, 'Helene and I are selling the house, Mam.'

'You're going back to Glasgow?'

'No, I'm buying something smaller, more suited to Morag and me. There's a house for sale in Brougham Street, here in Greenock. It has a back garden and it's small enough for the housekeeper to run it on her own.' Keeping her gaze fixed on Lessie's face she went on levelly, 'I'm buying Helene's refinery shares too.'

A chill ran through Lessie. 'And what about Ian?'

'He insists on staying on in Glasgow. He'll not consider moving down here, or living with a businesswoman.' A faint smile touched Dorothea's mouth but not her eyes. 'He doesn't see how a woman can have two loves, her husband and her career, though men do it all the time.'

'Oh, Dorry.'

'Don't ask me to give it all up and go back to him on his own terms, Mam, please.' Dorothea's voice shook and she put a slim hand to her mouth for a moment. The tiny sapphire on the engagement ring Ian had given her glittered in the gaslight. 'I couldn't go back to being a housewife, any more than he could bear to live on my money. Mebbe we're both too proud for our own good. I just know that these past seven months or so I've come alive. I can't give it all up now, not even for—'

In a graceful, fluid movement, she slipped from her chair to her knees on the rug and put her arms about Lessie, her dark bronze head in Lessie's lap.

'I wish women didn't have to make decisions like this,' she said, then her voice broke and Lessie held her as she cried her heart out.

Without saying a word to anyone, Lessie went up to Glasgow on the following Saturday, trying not to remember, as she walked out of Central Station into Hope Street, the last time she had been in the city and the happiness she had carried with her then.

She caught a bus to the end of the road where Andrew had bought a house for his daughter and son-in-law, and was fortunate enough to find Ian in. She had been prepared to camp on the doorstep until his return if the house had been empty.

He came to the door in waistcoat and shirt sleeves, his eyes flaring in astonishment as he saw his mother standing on the step. 'What are you doing here?'

'I've come to talk to you.'

'You're lucky to find me at home. You should have telephoned first.'

'You know fine that I hate telephones. And if I had made myself use one you'd have found some excuse to prevent me coming here,' she told him dryly, going before him into the little living room. Some neatly taped boxes were lined up under the windows and another box, open and half filled with books, stood before a chair. More books were piled close by.

'What's all this?'

'I'm sorry about the mess.' Ian ran a hand through his red hair. 'I'm moving out. The house belongs to Dorothea – she can do as she wants with it.' Then, to forestall the words that were trembling on her lips, he asked, 'Can I get you some tea?'

She nodded, and looked around as he went to the kitchen. The bookshelves were half-empty; some pictures were missing from the walls.

'Ian.' She went through to the kitchen, which bore the unmistakable signs of a house with no mistress.

'I'll be through in a minute, Mam,' he said impatiently, but she was already at the sink, turning on the taps, stacking dirty dishes.

'I'll just do these things first.' She seized the kettle, which had just boiled, and emptied it into the sink then refilled it and handed it back to him. 'Put that on for the tea.'

Twenty minutes later the kitchen was neater than it had been and they were back in the living room, facing each other across a low table as Lessie poured tea.

'Did Dorothea send you?' he wanted to know as she handed him a cup.

'She knows nothing about this. She'd not have let me come if she'd known. Dorry has her pride.'

He nodded, his eyes fixed on the spoon that was circling round and round in his cup.

'It was pride that almost ruined your lives before, Ian; I don't want to see it happen again. Can the two of you not come to some sort of agreement?'

'We've talked and talked about it, and there's no agreement to be reached. I'll not live off my wife.'

'You can earn a good salary in the Greenock Infirmary, and you'd surely not find it hard to get a post there.'

'I like the Royal, I like living in Glasgow. It's a woman's place,' said Ian doggedly, 'to be where her husband's living is.'

'That's nonsense, and it's old-fashioned too. Surely you can see that? And what about wee Morag? Does she not matter at all?'

Colour rose to his face. 'Of course she matters. D'you think I'm happy about being away from her for most of the time? I'll go on seeing her whenever I can. But a child of that age needs its mother more than its father, especially a girl.'

Lessie could see her hopes drifting away. 'So you're just going to let your marriage break up, after all the misery you both went through before you found each other again?'

'We've both changed since then, Mam. I need a wife who believes in me and wants to be with me more than anything else. Dorothea needs—' there was a sudden harsh twist to his mouth, ' – she needs to be free to follow her own dream. I certainly don't think she needs marriage as much as she once thought she did. We married in good faith, Mam; we meant to keep the vows we made. But we've both changed and there's little you or I or Dorothea can do about that. It's all decided – it's over.'

'Not,' said Lessie clearly, vigorously, 'as far as I'm concerned. I don't know what nonsense Murdo put into your head about working wives, but he was wrong.' Ignoring the way her son's mouth suddenly tightened, she surged on. 'Murdo liked money and he'd no objection to getting it from the shop. If I hadnae worked we'd all have starved when he lost his job at the shipyard. There's nothing wrong with Dorry running the refinery if she wants to. Would you rather have her sitting at home growing more and more unhappy? Is that what you want for her? And what would Andrew think of this sorry business? The last thing he had in mind was breaking up your marriage.'

For a moment the cold, implacable expression on Ian's face reminded her disquietingly of the way Davie had looked when she refused to sell him her refinery shares. 'You've had your say, Mam, but it doesn't make any difference to what's happened,' he said, and went over to the bookshelves. 'I've got a lot to do,' he said over his shoulder, lifting a bundle of books down.

'Ian, come back to Greenock with me. Talk to Dorothea again, let me help in any way I can. It's not too late.'

On his knees before the box, he looked up at her. 'You mean she's not told you?'

'She's told me nothing, except that she's staying on in Greenock.'

Ian smiled wryly. 'It was loyal of her to keep quiet, though it means I'm the one who'll have to tell you. I thought you were here because of . . .'

For two pins she would have boxed his ears. 'What are you havering about?'

He got up, sticking his hands into his trouser pockets and fixing his eyes on the floor. 'I'm moving in with someone, Mam,' he told the carpet. 'We were friendly with her and her husband when we came here first. Robert died almost two years ago, and since Dorothea went back to Greenock, Ruth's been a good friend to me. She's got her own house, and she has no interest in a career. She's – I'm in love with her, Mam. So there's no sense in trying to get me and Dorothea back together again. I told you, it's all over.'

30

While her schoolfriends went through all the miseries of growing into womanhood – greasy hair, spots, agonising over a figure that was too plump or too scrawny – Morag Hamilton blossomed like a rose. By the time she reached her fourteenth birthday she was of medium height, slender without being thin, and blessed with a clear creamy skin, glowing red hair cut in a neat, casual bob, and the beautiful violet-blue eyes she had inherited from her maternal grandmother and mother. Even in an unflattering school blazer and knee-length gymslip, with a round-brimmed velour hat held in place by an elastic strap under her chin, Morag was striking.

Throughout the thirties Lessie had watched the girl grow with a mixture of pride and concern; although Morag looked older than her years, there was an emotional vulnerability about her. And despite her happy nature there was a rebellious streak apparent in the girl as she grew older, a reminder of Anna McCauley's disregard for what others might think. If there was any escapade at school, any breach of discipline, Morag was involved, and Lessie lay awake at nights sometimes, worrying in case the girl should one day take a wrong turning and live to regret it.

She had had a great deal to do with her granddaughter over the years, for since her divorce, Dorothea had become more and more involved in the refinery and it had been left to a series of housekeepers and to Lessie herself to see to Morag's upbringing. The girl lacked for nothing as far as material comforts were concerned; she went to the best local school, she had a generous allowance, and she lived in a comfortable home, but she and her mother weren't close.

Dorothea, who had lost weight and taken on a severe, classical beauty as she matured, loved her daughter in her own way but simply didn't have much time to spare her. She had made a good job of running the refinery, proving to herself and to everyone else that a woman could be just as sharp at business as any man. She tended to treat Morag as she treated her employees – with kind, efficient firmness.

With her mother more often than not at the refinery, Morag spent most of her free time in Cathcart Street, either assisting her grandmother in the shop or in the house. It was Lessie who heard all about Morag's hopes and dreams, her worries and her triumphs, the confessions of wrong-doing, the crush Morag developed at thirteen years of age on the new young art teacher. It was Lessie who comforted her when things went wrong and celebrated with her when they went well.

Ian had married Ruth, the widow he had turned to for consolation when Dorothea chose commerce instead of domesticity, and now he lived in contented harmony with her and their three children in Glasgow. Morag was always welcome at his house but as she grew older she chose to see less of her father and stepmother.

'They're so – so cosy,' she told Lessie, her nose wrinkling as they worked together to make the Christmas pudding. She was fourteen and a half years old, and the Christmas pudding ritual, started the first Christmas Dorothea and Ian had spent apart, had become a precious event for both Lessie and Morag. 'Ruth's very kind, but nothing exciting happens in their house. I get bored.'

'What about your brothers and your sister? You enjoy being with them, don't you?'

Morag stirred mixed fruit in with flour. 'They're childish,' she said with lofty disdain. 'The boys are football mad, and the last time I was there Catherine was too busy with her pony to be any fun. It seems to suit Daddy but it's not for me. No wonder Mummy didn't stay with him. I know she's wrapped up in her work, but at least she's enthusiastic about it. And she's much more beautiful than Ruth. Ruth's running to fat.'

'So will you be if you don't stop picking at those sultanas, my girl.'

Morag grinned, took one last handful of fruit, then attacked the stirring of the pudding with relish, scowling down into the mixture, her face closed and her brows knotted as she made a wish. Lessie dusted flour from her hands and washed them, glad that the girl was there to deal with the stiff mixture. Her own hands had lost some of their strength now, and sometimes during the night they ached with rheumatism. It seemed no time at all since she had been wringing out wet clothes over the stone sink in the Vennel, and now and then she railed at the way time had crept up on her and aged her when she was too busy to notice what was going on.

As usual, she spent Christmas with Dorothea and Morag in their comfortable house in Brougham Street. Over the years Dorothea had made several attempts to get Lessie to give up the Cathcart Street house and move in with her, even offering to buy something larger so that Lessie could have a suite of rooms to herself. But Lessie had consistently refused; she loved the little flat that Miss Peden had left her, and it was convenient for the shop where she still spent the greater part of each day.

'Besides,' she told her daughter-in-law, 'I like to be independent. I don't want to be beholden to anyone.'

'You'd still be independent, with your own bedroom and sitting room – and a proper indoor bathroom, not to mention your own kitchen and outside door if you want them. As for being beholden,' Dorothea went on, unconsciously echoing her father's words of so long ago, 'I owe you much more than a home for the rest of your life. I could never have made a success of running the refinery if you hadn't been so understanding and looked after Morag so well for me.'

The housekeeper, a local woman, was spending Christmas with her own family; Dorothea, who hadn't lost her domestic skills, had made the soup and dealt with the turkey and trimmings. Lessie contributed the pudding and Christmas cake, as usual, and Morag's undoubted artistic talent had gone into decorating the house, which was bright with paper chains and bells and a magnificent Nativity centre piece that she had made herself.

Her gifts to her mother and grandmother were framed portraits of themselves, painted in secret from memory. She beamed as she saw the astonishment in their faces.

'Darling, it's wonderful!' Dorothea, elegant in dark green satin trousers with a high-necked cream lace blouse under a small jacket the same colour and material as the trousers, kissed her daughter then went to prop the painting on the mantelshelf, standing back to admire it. Her own fine-boned face looked serenely back at her from a cloudy pearl-grey background; the bronze highlights in her rich dark hair, which was dressed in her usual soft chignon, were just the right shade, as were the long-lashed violet eyes coolly staring out of the canvas.

'I'd no idea that you were so talented,' Dorothea marvelled.

Morag flushed with pleasure. 'Open yours, Gran,' she urged.

The last piece of wrapping paper fell away and Lessie gazed down at a neat rounded face set in a halo of white hair, drawn back and fastened at the back of the head. The mouth was slightly curved in a smile, the face touched liberally with laugh-lines – and two deeply grooved worry-lines between the tidy eyebrows. The hazel eyes that looked out of the portrait were amused, kindly, and yet there was a trace of habitual worry about them that toned with the lines above. In the portrait she wore a dark blue blouse, her favourite, and pinned to the collar, gleaming against the material, was the little autumn leaf brooch.

'What d'you think, Gran?' Morag's voice prompted, then Dorothea's hand, slim and well cared for, the nails tipped with bright red, reached over Lessie's shoulder and lifted the painting.

'This is good too.' She propped it up beside her own. 'In fact, it's excellent. It's so like you, Mam.'

'Is it?'

'Oh yes, Gran. It was easier than Mummy's – I had to have several tries at hers, but I could draw you in the dark with my eyes closed, I know you so well.'

'And you don't know me?' Dorothea's voice was slightly edgy, but Morag seemed quite unaware of the tension.

'You change so much, Mummy, but Gran – well, she's always Gran, isn't she? What d'you think?' she repeated, slightly anxious now, and Lessie fumbled for the right words.

'It's – it's lovely, dear. I just – it's strange, seeing yourself.'

'It's the image of you,' Dorothea assured her, adding, 'Now then, who wants a drink? A small sherry, Mam?'

'Since it's Christmas,' Morag began.

'And since you're fourteen, you'll have ginger wine,' her mother told her.

'But I'm in my fifteenth year, and I look older than I really am. Just a little sherry, Mum.' Their voices rattled on around Lessie, and her portrait gazed down on her from the mantelpiece.

It wasn't until she was back home and had had another look at it that she realised why it had disturbed her so much. It was good, as Dorothea had said. It was like her – a quick glance in the mirror proved that. But it was the portrait of an old woman. A woman with fifty-nine years of hard living behind her – more than half a century. It wasn't, she realised with sharp dismay, the woman Andrew Warren had known and loved. Soon she would be older than he had been the last time they were together.

Lessie sank down onto a chair and her fingers unconsciously groped for the leaf brooch, as they always did in a moment of crisis. Where, she wondered in panic, had the years gone? What had she done with them? It was as though they had been stolen away from her while she was too busy to keep an eye on them. As far as she was concerned she was still the same Lessie who had scrubbed floors to keep herself and Ian in the Vennel. Apart from a touch of rheumatism she was the same Lessie who had left her parents' house eagerly, radiantly, to become Donald Hamilton's wife. Panic stirred in her again as she realised that there was nobody left who remembered that Lessie, with the fair hair and the young face. Nobody except Davie, and she never saw him now, even though he still lived in Newton Street.

Then, mercifully, the panic began to subside as her usual common sense fought its way to the surface to remind her that time affected everyone, not just her, and that there was still plenty of it left. Stiffly, she got up and made a cup of tea, and by the time she climbed into bed, Morag's gift, painted with love, had been hung on a nail hammered into the kitchen wall.

Jess came home for a few days on the following Easter, as beautiful and vivid as ever. Although she was well into her thirties Jess, Lessie thought as she watched her daughter, would never change. She would always be beautiful, confident, crackling with energy. She had been in America on a modelling assignment, travelling on the *Queen Mary*, and arrived laden down with gifts and full of wonderful stories. Morag hung on her every word and after Jess had gone, the girl was in a restless mood and talking of leaving school at the end of the summer term.

'I thought you were staying on and going to art school?' Lessie protested, and Morag shrugged.

'That'll take too long. Aunt Jess started her career by working in a dress shop. I could do the same.'

'Your Aunt Jess had little choice. I couldn't afford to pay for school fees, but your mother can. Why a dress shop, anyway? You don't want to be a model like Jess.'

'No, but I could learn about design, work my way up the way she did. I need to get some experience of life if I'm to be an artist. And Aunt Jess has certainly experienced life.'

'She'll change her mind once she starts work,' Dorothea said when

Lessie appealed to her. 'She'll be glad enough to go back to school by the end of the year. Let her try her wings.'

In June Lessie opened her door to find a young man standing in the close. 'Mrs Carswell? My name's Elder, Colin Elder.'

The name was faintly familiar, but it wasn't until he went on, 'I teach art at your granddaughter's school,' that she could place him as the teacher Morag had had such a crush on over the past year.

He came into the kitchen, hat in hand, and beamed round the small neat room. 'This takes me back – we've a kitchen like this at home.'

'You're not from Greenock, Mr Elder?'

'No, I was brought up in Perth. I live in a boarding house here.' He went over to her portrait. 'This is Morag's work.'

'It was her Christmas gift to me.'

He studied the portrait closely for several moments in silence. Lessie left him to it and poured water from the steaming kettle into the teapot, then took the caddy down from the high mantelshelf and opened it.

'It's good,' Colin Elder said at last, standing back from the picture. 'It's been painted with love, I can see it in every brush stroke.'

'Sit down, Mr Elder. You'll have some tea?'

'Thank you.' He put his hat on the table and watched as she bustled about the kitchen, making tea. 'I hope you don't mind me calling, Mrs Carswell, but I know that Morag's fond of you. She often comes up with some remark of yours in class.' His open young face broadened into a grin. 'In fact, your sensible sayings have often been the saving of me when I was trying to explain things to my class and not making a very good job of it.'

By the time the tea was made and Lessie was seated across the table from him she had decided that she liked Morag's Mr Elder. He was younger than she had expected, with smiling brown eyes and curly brown hair that looked as though it defied any attempt to flatten it. He was dressed casually in a pale blue shirt and a fawn tweed jacket over brown trousers.

When Lessie remarked, as much to herself as to him, 'I always thought that folk judged advancing years by noticing how young the policemen were getting, but it seems to me it's the teachers we should be looking at,' he threw his head back and laughed.

'My mother told me this would happen. She's always fretting about me looking too young for my profession. I'm twenty-four, Mrs Carswell, and this is my first job. But I've not had much trouble in getting my classes to behave themselves and listen to me.'

'From what I hear from Morag you seem to be able to hold their attention without having to shout or threaten. The teachers at the school I attended all seemed to be as old as Methuselah and as crusty as homemade bread,' Lessie started to say, then stopped herself. 'But it's my granddaughter you've come to talk about, not my past.'

His face was suddenly solemn as he leaned across the table, his big square hands clasping his cup. 'She says that she intends to leave school at the end of term.'

279

'Aye. She wants to work in a dress shop and learn something about design from the beginning.'

'She's making a mistake. She's not a designer, you can tell that from the portrait there. I'm told that a teacher – especially an art teacher – is lucky if he gets three or four talented pupils in a lifetime's teaching. I consider myself to be very fortunate to have Morag in my class during my very first year. She's got talent, Mrs Carswell, but she has a lot to learn, too. I've been looking forward to at least another year of working with her, steering her towards art school. I'm not long out of the place myself and I know what they're looking for and how to release it in your granddaughter. Believe me, dress designing's not for her.'

'Her mother thinks she should be left to find that out for herself.'

A frown tucked itself between his brows. 'I know, I went to her before I came to you. Her argument is that Morag can still go to art school once she's got this restlessness out of her soul. But what I'm afraid of is that by that time she'll have taken the wrong road. I want to use that restlessness, Mrs Carswell, to harness it and make it work for Morag. She'd be making a mistake if she left school now. From what I can gather, you might be the one who could influence her.'

'I doubt if I could influence her as much as all that. Morag's got a mind of her own, Mr Elder. You'd have a better chance than me.'

'People of her age tend to do the opposite from what their teachers advise. I'd not want to damage her future by charging in where I'm not welcome.'

'From the way she's been speaking of you these past nine months or more I doubt if you'd be charging in.' Then, as his brown eyes asked a puzzled question, she said with amusement, 'Did you not know she had you on a pedestal, Mr Elder?'

'I did not. Oh, there are some girls who make it obvious – we're warned to expect that and told how to deal with it. But Morag – she's always been too sensible for that. She's mature for her age, downright aloof at times.'

Lessie smiled wryly. 'Not when she's talking about you in this house, I can assure you. Morag's a right mixture at the moment; everyone who knows her sees a different side to her. If I were you, Mr Elder, I'd find the chance to have a wee word with her. Tell her what you've told me, that you'd like to have another year of teaching her and getting her ready for college. I think she'd listen to you.'

When he was leaving, she asked, 'What sort of pictures do you paint, Mr Elder?'

He grinned down at her ruefully. 'I only dabble, Mrs Carswell. I've enough sense to know that my talent's for teaching, not for becoming a famous artist. My pleasure's going to be to see others do what I'd have loved to do myself.'

'Tell Morag that,' said Lessie, and thought to herself when he had gone that her granddaughter was very fortunate to have met up with such a dedicated teacher. She was glad that she had met him, for she'd been slightly worried about the adoration in the girl's eyes whenever she mentioned Mr Elder. Morag was suffering from the lack of a father in her life. Although she still saw Ian, he belonged to his new family now. It was inevitable that the girl should latch on to a male teacher at an age where girls were just as likely to have crushes on the female teachers. Lessie was glad to know that Colin Elder was a sensible, modest young man.

She never found out what the teacher said to Morag; her granddaughter said nothing about any conversation between them. She merely announced, as the summer term drew to a close, that she had decided to stay on at school after all and begin to prepare a portfolio for submission to Glasgow School of Art when the time came.

Morag had grown up against a seething, shifting tapestry; during the thirties so much happened in the world that sometimes it seemed to Lessie as though the globe they lived on had begun to spin faster through the heavens, scattering the wits of its inhabitants as it revolved.

With the death of George V, the decision by the new King Edward VIII to relinquish the throne for the love of an American divorcee, and the subsequent appointment of his quiet young brother as King George VI, Britain found itself with three kings in quick succession during 1936. The country was in a deep industrial depression and that same year, unemployed, hungry and frantic men marched from Jarrow to London to ask for the right to work to support their families. The tick book had come into its own once again in the shop at the corner of Cathcart Street and unemployed men hung around the Greenock streets, their faces grey with worry and becoming more gaunt every week. There had been trouble in Russia and Abyssinia and a war between Japan and China as well as a bloody civil war in Spain, but the most worrying news of all was the rise of a young man named Adolf Hitler in Germany and the subsequent terrorising and imprisonment of Jews in that country.

Reading about shops being looted and helpless, innocent men, women and children attacked in the streets of Germany, Lessie was sharply reminded of Mr Mann and his wife: their frightened faces on the morning she helped them to clean up the mess hooligans had made of their shop in the early days of the war; their poverty when she had sought them out to offer to buy the business; Mr Mann's insistent, bewildered, 'Ve are Sviss!'

Why, she wondered as the stories of atrocities continued to appear in the newspapers, did folk have to treat other folk like that? Was evil a disease that could strike wherever it wanted and never be denied? Why did other nations allow these things to happen and say nothing?

Throughout the thirties, too, the British Government continued to build up the country's defences. Even when Prime Minister Neville Chamberlain waved a scrap of paper and said that Britain and Germany had come to an understanding and there would be 'peace in our time', Lessie found herself doubting the man, much as she wanted to believe him.

'Sometimes,' she told Morag, 'politicians are awful daft. They seem

281

to be playing some sort of game where they have to go by the rules instead of thinking things out for themselves. If they'd only use the brains God gave them they might see what's coming in time enough to do something about it.'

'Don't fret yourself, Gran,' the girl advised her serenely. 'There's nothing folk like us can do about it.'

'Mebbe not, but we're the ones that have to pay for their silly games, every time,' Lessie said with rare gloominess.

31

In September 1939 the German army marched into Poland, and Britain declared war on Germany. Lessie watched, her heart sinking, as the Territorials, their young faces shining with patriotism and determination, marched off to war led by the skirl of the pipes. She had seen it all before, at the beginning of the 1914 war that was supposed to end all wars.

Her younger male assistant, who had started straight from school in the shop as a messenger boy, went off almost at once with the Territorials; the older man had been gassed in the 1914-18 war and was unfit to serve this time. Children scampered off to school with square boxes containing their gas masks looped on string over one shoulder and thumping on the opposite hip. They proudly dragged their new identity discs from beneath their shirt and blouse collars and displayed them in the shop, little realising that the small metal label was intended for identification purposes should they have to be dragged from beneath rubble after an air raid. This war was going to be fought in the air as well as on the ground and at sea, and air raid shelters were being scooped out of back yards, blackout curtains installed, brown paper or tough netting being stuck on windows to prevent glass being blown in when the bombs fell, as fall they must. Greenock was a shipbuilding town and would surely be a target. Some children were bundled off to live in the country, where they were considered to be safer. Brick baffle walls were hurriedly erected at the pavement's edge in front of each tenement close in an attempt to limit damage from bomb blast, causing all sorts of scrapes and bruises at first when children heedlessly scampered out of the closes and rebounded off the walls, or adults bumped into them in the enforced blackout at night now that street lights were forbidden.

'Thank goodness your building's got electric light now,' Dorothea told Lessie. 'At least if it's blitzed you'll not have the danger of escaping gas.'

'You're right,' Lessie said, grateful that her daughter-in-law, normally so sharp, had completely overlooked the fact that some of the other residents in the building had gas cookers. She herself still used the neat, gleaming little range that had been there since Miss Peden's days, and worked as well as when it was new.

Ration books were introduced to quell the rush of panic buying and offset the difficulty of shipping in foodstuffs from abroad, and Lessie spent a great deal of her working day clipping coupons and doling out ridiculously small amounts of butter and margarine to her listed customers. The River Clyde filled with ships, crowding the popular anchorage at the Tail o' the Bank, the deep water area skirting a great sandbank.

Nineteen forty arrived and all at once the town was filled with foreign sailors, predominantly French, young lads brightening the grey streets with the bright red 'toories' on the top of their white caps. The locals and the foreigners eyed each other warily at first across the barricade of two different languages. The local stationers' sold out of French/English phrase books within days, and funny stories of confusions between the incomers and the townspeople swept from one end of Greenock to the other.

After those first apprehensive days the invasion turned out to be friendly, and Scottish hospitality was offered generously to the young men. Dances were held for them and canteens opened for their use when on shore leave. Much against her mother's wishes Morag volunteered to work in one of the canteens after school and at weekends.

'They need people who can speak French, and I can.'

'School French,' Dorothea pointed out disparagingly.

'I can get by, and that's more than most folk can say. Anyway, I want to do something to help,' Morag argued, and her mother eventually shrugged her shoulders and gave way.

As soon as Morag began working at the canteen, her restlessness eased. She might still be a schoolgirl, but now she had something else to do, something that made her feel useful. She was proud of her ability to speak to the sailors in their own language, and Dorothea told Lessie with relief that her school reports were improving and she was doing particularly well in the French class.

At the beginning of April Morag came to Cathcart Street and asked her grandmother diffidently if she could bring a friend to visit.

'A school friend?'

Morag coloured and stared past Lessie's shoulder at one of the wally dugs on the mantelshelf. 'No, it's – he's a French sailor.'

'Oh.'

'He's awful nice, Gran, and he's far away from home and everyone else is asking them home, only my mother wouldn't approve, I know she wouldn't.'

'That's only because you're still so young, lassie.'

Morag's eyes blazed violet fire. 'I'm not saying I want to marry him! He's a friend, that's all, but Mummy wouldn't see it that way. She'd fret about it and think it was wrong and probably make me stop working at—'

'Tuts, girl, I didnae say you couldnae bring him here,' Lessie interrupted. 'Of course you can. Goodness only knows these poor lads need some friends, with their families across the water being threatened by the Germans.'

Morag launched herself across the kitchen and hugged Lessie so

284

hard that she almost took the breath from her. 'Oh, thank you, Gran! I'll invite him to tea next week, will I?'

Georges reminded Lessie strongly of Peter when he shyly followed Morag into the kitchen the following week, his cap clutched in both hands, his eyes flickering nervously around the room. Although Peter's hair was brown and Georges' was fair, although Peter's eyes were grey and Georges' brown, there was the same air of uncertainty, of not belonging, that immediately tugged at her heart.

'Come in, laddie, come in and sit yourself down,' she said briskly, waving one hand at the chairs waiting round the table and making for the simmering kettle. Food and drink made up a universal language.

As the meal progressed the boy slowly lost some of his initial shyness. In the short time he had been in Greenock, anxious to fit in, he had picked up a few English words. He and Morag laughed comfortably together when he said something wrong, or when she made a mistake in her French. He carefully and gently put her right each time and she repeated the correct word or phrase several times, until he nodded smiling approval. They made a good pair, Lessie decided when the meal was over and she sat with her knitting by the range, watching the fair head and the bronze head close together as they studied her one and only photograph album. There was affection between them but it was youthful and natural and she didn't see it as a threat, only something that could be good for the two of them at this time of uncertainty and stress.

'Of course,' she said at once when Morag asked if she could bring Georges again. 'Whenever you like. He'll not be here for long anyway, I expect his ship'll be refitting at the moment.' Then she added cautiously, 'But should you not take him to meet your mother?'

Morag's face set in mutinous lines. 'She'd only insist on inspecting him and questioning him and he'd feel uncomfortable. He likes it here, with you. He says it reminds him of his own home in Tours. I'd as soon leave things as they are. You'll not tell her about him, will you?'

'It's not my business to tell her.'

'Anyway,' said Morag, 'she's so busy these days, it's best to leave her alone.'

Georges came often to Cathcart Street over the next few weeks. He and Lessie found ways of communicating despite the language barrier, and to Morag's amusement Lessie even began to pick up some French words. The three of them spent happy hours working on a large and intricate jigsaw puzzle that Morag brought from her own home, or sat companionably listening to the wireless that Jess had insisted on buying for Lessie the Christmas before war was declared. Sometimes, when music was being played, the young couple pushed back the big table and danced. Watching her granddaughter, seeing her happiness and contentment, Lessie grew to dread the day when Georges had to leave Greenock. He and Morag had already promised to write to each other but even so, life was cruel these days for young folk, and nobody could tell what the future held.

It made her uncomfortable to be aiding Morag behind Dorothea's back, but at the same time it was good to see the girl so contented for once. Although she knew well enough that her daughter-in-law would disapprove of the friendship if she knew of it, Lessie gave permission when Morag asked if she could go with Georges to a Saturday night dance being held in one of the church halls. Dorothea was in Glasgow on business and it had already been agreed that Morag should stay overnight with Lessie.

'But you're to be back here by ten thirty, mind. I cannae have you staying out too late. The Lord knows I'm deceiving your mother enough as it is.'

Morag's cheek was soft against Lessie's. 'I promise, Gran, and thank you!'

On the night of the dance Georges came to collect Morag, his young face solemn with the importance of the occasion. As he and Lessie waited in the kitchen for her, he said awkwardly but earnestly, 'I promise you, madam, zat I come from a good family. My maman teach me to respect young ladies. I respect Morag very much.'

It was clear that he had carefully learned the little speech beforehand, probably from a comrade with a better command of English than Georges himself. Touched, Lessie smiled at him.

'I'm sure you will, laddie. I trust you.'

Then Morag burst into the kitchen, her eyes sparkling, her hair brushed into a gleaming auburn cap about her neat little face, wearing a pretty white crepe blouse and a swinging silky skirt that Lessie knew she had altered herself from some pre-war clothes of her mother's. Looking at the awe and pride on the French boy's face, the way his eyes lit up as he scrambled to his feet, Lessie knew that she could indeed trust him to look after her precious granddaughter.

Morag arrived home at twenty-eight minutes past ten, bringing a waft of cool night air in with her, launching at once into a description of the dances, the music, the people who had been there.

'Where's Georges?' Lessie had two mugs waiting, each with a spoonful of cocoa and a spoonful of her precious sugar in it. She moved the pan of milk, which had been heating slowly at the side of the range, onto the metal plate that covered the fire.

'He had to get back on board. But he walked me right to the door first.' Morag brushed her fingertips across her lips without realising that she was betraying the memory of goodnight kisses.

'In that case I'll have his cocoa. Morag, pet,' Lessie said carefully when their drinks were in front of them and Morag's excited chatter finally began to slow down, 'Georges'll be sailing away soon.'

'I know that.' The happiness was wiped from the girl's face as she slowly stirred her cocoa.

'And you're not sixteen yet.'

'Almost sixteen.'

'Too young to know your own mind.'

Morag took a sip from the mug then put it down. 'Gran, I'm not rushing about like a chicken with its head cut off, falling in love and

286

thinking about the rest of my life. I'm just being happy for now, d'you not see that? Now's all we've got, me and Georges.'

'Aye, lassie.' Lessie reached out and put a hand over her grand-daughter's. 'I know that. I just wondered if you did.'

On the last day of April a dull boom shook the town. Windows rattled in their frames, dogs started barking hysterically, folk rushed to their doors in panic.

It was a half day, so the shop was shut and Lessie was doing some ironing in her kitchen. She set the iron on its heel and ran to the close-mouth to see women and children gathering all up and down the street, and passersby stopped in their tracks, everyone staring anxiously up into the cloudy sky.

Feet pounded on the stairs behind her and two of her neighbours, one clutching a baby in her arms, joined her. 'God help us, it's an air raid!' the girl whimpered, but an older woman out on the pavement said briskly, 'There's no' been ony sirens. Anyway, they'd no' come ower in daylight.'

'Look!' Someone pointed, and they all craned their necks and saw a mushroom-shaped cloud rise slowly above the rooftops.

'It's somethin' doon by the river,' someone said, and another voice chimed in, 'Yin o' the ships – a mine, mebbe?'

'How could the Nazis get a mine intae the Clyde?' someone scoffed. They could hear a clamour from the river now, the frantic blaring of sirens and klaxons, the jangle of a bell as a fire engine or an ambulance raced along a street somewhere. The smoke continued to rise ominously into the sky, the fringes beginning to fuzz as they met the wind, though the body of it remained solid.

'Whatever it was, some poor souls must've copped it,' someone said and Mrs Delaney, who lived above Lessie, crossed herself and whispered, 'God have mercy on them.'

Lessie, watching the smoke towering over the rooftops, felt a shiver run through her, as though someone had walked over her grave.

The clamour of ships' sirens died away, but a few hours later there was another explosion, and again the floor shook beneath Lessie's feet.

All afternoon rumours flew about the town, but by early evening they solidified into something more positive, despite the fact that the stretch of river by the docks had been closed to the public ever since the first explosion. One of the ships anchored at the Tail o' the Bank had blown up. It was understood that a torpedo had slipped from its housing during maintenance work and exploded on contact with the deck. While nearby battleships and oil tankers up-anchored and moved as quickly as possible away from the fiercely burning ship, other boats had gone scuttling out from Albert Harbour to give what aid they could. But there was little anyone could do. Shells stored on the ship had exploded with the heat, and in a few hours she had gone down with heavy loss of life.

Something within Lessie knew without being told that the stricken ship was the *Maille Breze*, the Free French destroyer Georges served on. She waited, expecting Morag to come to her after school, but there was no sign of the girl, and shortly after the second explosion Lessie put on her hat and coat and set off for Dorothea's house. She had just reached the corner of Cathcart Street when Dorothea's car swept in to the kerb beside her and the driver, an elderly man called out of retirement, got out and handed Lessie a letter. Petrol was rationed and most car owners had resigned themselves to keeping their cars off the road until the war was over, but because of the refinery Dorothea was allowed enough fuel to keep her car on the road. Lessie ripped open the envelope, read the few words on the sheet of paper inside, and got into the car.

In the small but elegant house in Brougham Street Dorothea, ashen with worry, came to the door as soon as she heard the car, almost dragging Lessie in. There was a half-empty glass, a packet of cigarettes, a lighter and an ashtray piled with cigarette butts on the little table by Dorothea's favourite chair. As soon as Lessie walked into the room Dorothea lit a fresh cigarette.

'It's Morag, Mam. I can't do a thing with her.' She paced the floor, her slim body taut with worry. 'Her headmistress phoned the refinery this afternoon to say that she had run out of school without asking permission. I worried myself sick for three hours before a policeman brought her home. Apparently she'd been making a nuisance of herself at the hospitals, demanding to know the names of the poor men being brought in from that ship that blew up this afternoon.'

'Where is she?'

'In her room. I wanted to fetch the doctor, but she went hysterical at the very idea. She won't talk to me. Mam, what's going on?'

Lessie took off her coat, noting with vague surprise that she still wore her apron. She sat down and told Dorothea the whole story, making no bones about her own part in it. As Dorothea listened, her face went white with anger, her eyes hardening and the slight scar on her cheek standing out as a streak of rose-pink beneath her carefully applied make-up.

'Morag – and a French sailor? And you allowed this? Condoned it behind my back? Dear God, woman, she's only a child! I credited you with more sense than that!'

'He's – he was a decent lad, Dorothea.' Lessie knew now that Georges must be dead. 'They spent most of their time together in my house.'

'Most of the time? And what about the rest of the time?'

'D'you not trust your own daughter?'

'Not with foreigners! I knew when I let her work at that canteen that there would be trouble, but I'd no idea that her own grandmother would connive at it. She's not sixteen yet!'

'And he was only eighteen. They were both children, both in need of friendship. Can you not see that, Dorothea?'

There was a tense silence. Dorothea stubbed her half-smoked

cigarette viciously into the ashtray. 'Oh, what's the use of arguing about it now? What's done's done. I asked you to come here because I can't get any sense out of her. I thought you might, since the two of you have always been close.' She swung towards the window, though with the blackout curtains fastened securely against the night there was nothing to see. 'You'd best go to her,' she said over her shoulder.

Morag's room was bright and pretty and still heart-rendingly childish. Morag herself was sitting on the edge of her bed, hunched over a battered old teddy bear clutched in her arms. She didn't look up, and her body was rigid and remote when Lessie put her arms about her.

'Morag, lass.'

'He's dead.' The girl's voice was dry, harsh, old. 'I went to the hospitals where they took the wounded but he wasn't anywhere. He's dead.'

'In wartime—'

'He didn't die because of the war!' Morag dragged herself from Lessie's embrace, hurtled to the other end of the room. There was no trace of tears, just a face as white as snow and eyes that burned into Lessie's. The teddy bear, tossed away, rolled beneath the pink-frilled dressing table. 'He died because of an accident! We were going to go for a walk tonight and coming to you afterwards. But now he's dead!' She put her hands to her face then said wonderingly, pitifully, through her fingers, 'How can things go on being the same when people you care about aren't in the world any more?'

Lessie remembered thinking the same thing when Donald and her parents and Thomasina and Anna died. So many people, left behind. Thomasina had been much the same age as Georges. It was cruel, at Morag's age, to suddenly come face to face with death and loss.

'I know what you're going through, lovey. You'd feel better if you'd talk to your mother, let her help.'

'And have her going on at me because I went out with a foreigner?'

'She'd not do that.'

'She'd better not,' Morag said fiercely. 'I'm glad I went out with him. I'm glad we knew each other, and she's not going to make me say any different!'

'I'm glad too. You were a good friend to him just when he needed friends. Morag,' Lessie coaxed, but the girl backed into a corner, shaking her head.

'You can't make it better, Gran. Don't try to pretend that it's like the time I fell off my bike, or the time I lost my coral bracelet. Nothing can make it better, only bringing Georges back. You don't understand!' Her voice rose to a wail. 'How could you understand? You're too old to know what it's like to care for someone and lose them.'

'Stop it!' Without realising what she was doing Lessie stormed across the room and shook the girl by the shoulders. 'D'you think I

289

was always like this? D'you think I was only put on this earth tae be your grandmother? I've been young like you and I've had my hard times just as you will. And I've lost folk that meant more tae me than my own life!' She heard herself going on like a harpie, heard the Vennel accent creeping back into her voice, but couldn't stop the words. Morag's anguish had unlocked sorrows that had been thrust deep down, out of sight but never out of mind. 'This is what life's all about, lassie, and age has little tae dae with it. Losin' folk ye love can hurt as much as fifty-five as it does at fifteen!'

'Why did it have to be him?' Morag's swollen face was reddened and ugly with grief, her mouth twisted. She wrenched herself free with such force that Lessie staggered back and almost fell over a chair. The very air in the room seemed to crackle between grandmother and grand-daughter. 'He was only eighteen! Why should he be dead and some-one as old as you still be alive?'

The words were like a dash of cold water in Lessie's face. She looked into her granddaughter's blazing eyes and knew full well that noth-ing she said at that moment, either in anger or in love, would reach the girl; knew, too, that the warmth that had been between them for fifteen years was over and things would never be the same again.

She turned away and walked out of the room, back to the lounge where Dorothea still paced, another cigarette burning down between slim red-tipped fingers.

'Well?'

'You'll have to be patient with her, Dorry. Let her come to terms with the laddie's death in her own time.' Lessie reached for her coat, which she had laid neatly over the back of a chair. She felt completely exhausted, hollow inside, and raw, as though she had been scrubbed out with a stiff-bristled brush.

'Sit down, Mam,' Dorry said, her voice gentler. 'I'll make us a cup of tea.'

'I'd just as soon get home. I'll walk,' she added as Dorothea went to the door.

'Don't be silly, of course you'll not walk. I told Hamish to wait for you. I'll not risk you breaking your ankle or falling in those dark streets. I've got enough trouble without that.' Dorothea caught her arm as Lessie stumbled. 'Are you all right?'

'I'm fine. Don't fuss me, Dorry,' Lessie said automatically, want-ing only to get back to the safety and comfort of her own home.

By the time she got there she was shivering, as though coming down with the 'flu. When she got inside the door, after fumbling her way through the black close, she took out the little bottle of whisky that she kept in the kitchen cupboard and made herself a hot toddy. The glass rattled against her teeth as she drank; when it was empty she crawled into the box bed fully dressed, unable to face the short jour-ney to her own room.

She fell into sleep without realising it and woke in the early morn-ing to the discomfort of creased clothes and a pillow damp with tears she didn't know she had shed.

She woke to the certain knowledge that she had lost Morag and was alone once more.

32

As the weeks passed more details about the *Maille Breze* came out, bit by bit. About thirty of the French sailors on board had been trapped in the mess deck by a buckled fo'c'sle hatch and all attempts to free them as the fire crept towards them had been in vain. Finally a doctor had lain on the hot metal plates of the upper deck and reached down to the open portholes below with a syringe, injecting a strong sedative into the arms held out desperately from below, trying to ease the young men's final moments. The cries from below had all ceased before the would-be rescuers scrambled clear to save their own lives.

Soon afterwards the fire had reached the magazine near the mess deck and after a final explosion the destroyer had gone down, coming to rest on a sandbank. Her mast reached out above the water, a mute reminder to the people of Greenock, though no reminder was needed, of the youngsters who had met such a cruel end far from their homes.

Lessie hoped against hope that Georges had been among the half-dozen who had died mercifully quickly on deck in the original explosion. She hoped – again without believing it possible – that Morag wouldn't come to hear of the terrible plight of those trapped on the messdeck. She thought of Georges' family, of the 'maman' who had brought him up to be so respectful to young ladies, and wondered if they had heard of his death. But in June when the remnants of the British army were frantically scooped from the beaches of Dunkirk, from the very jaws of the powerful German army that had poured across France and now became its triumphant masters, she thought to herself that the news of Georges' death had probably not had time to reach his parents, and trusted that living as they were now under the German jackboot they took comfort in believing that he, at least, was free and safe.

Just after France fell, Ian enlisted in the Royal Army Medical Corps. He took Ruth and their children from Glasgow to Inverness, where Ruth's sister lived, then came to Greenock to say goodbye to his mother. He had put on weight since his second marriage and there were streaks of grey over his temples.

'Why, Ian? You've already served in one war and you've surely got important work to do in Glasgow,' Lessie said to him as he sipped the cup of tea she'd insisted he drink before he left.

'I'm needed more by the army than the infirmary just now. They can spare me. When I was an orderly I mind standing by many a time watching some poor laddie dying before the surgeon got to him and not able to do a thing to help him. This time I'll be the surgeon, this time I'll know what to do. With any luck I'll see most of them recovering. Anyway,' he gave a short laugh, 'I'm getting a commission. Captain Ian Hamilton. And I can't let Jess have it all her own way. Imagine our Jess, of all people, driving an ambulance! Have you heard from her?'

'Aye, she's the only person I know who can make the blackout and the air raids sound funny.'

'She'll be good for the morale of the poor blighters in her ambulance – mebbe that'll take their minds off the way she drives it.'

'Have you seen Morag and Dorothea?'

'I saw them before I came here. Morag's grown ten years older in as many weeks. I could scarce get a word out of her.'

'You heard why?'

'Aye. Poor lassie, she's too young for such grief.'

'She's a survivor. She'll work it out in her own way, given time.'

'I hope so. Dorothea's looking wonderful; running her own business suits her. I believe,' said Ian thoughtfully, 'that giving her a divorce was the best thing I could have done for her. Marriage was too limiting for her. She turned out to be her father's daughter after all. Mam, you're looking tired. Why don't you go and spend some time in Inverness? Ruth would be glad to see you.'

'I'm fine. And there's the shop to see to.'

Ian gave an impatient wave of the hand. 'Surely the folk that work in it could see to things for you for a wee while. You need a holiday.'

She shook her head. 'I'm not used to holidays.'

'At least think about it.' Then he looked at his watch and a brisk note came into his voice. 'I must go, Mam. I've to be in Glasgow by three.'

'You'll write?'

'Of course I will. Keep in touch with Ruth while I'm gone.'

'Take care, son.' She wished, not for the first time, that the Scots weren't such a dour race. It wasn't the done thing for a mother to hug and kiss a grown son, even when he was going off to war.

'I will,' said Ian, and left her standing alone in her kitchen.

The shop demanded a lot of time and attention, which was just as well because Dorothea was busier than ever and Morag didn't come to Cathcart Street any more. When grandmother and granddaughter met occasionally over Dorothea's tea table, Morag, who had taken the step between childhood and womanhood on the day the French ship exploded, was pleasant enough but as remote as an acquaintance.

'It's not right,' said Dorothea, who had got over her anger with Lessie. 'You were the one who helped her to see this boy behind my back, and now she's punishing you for it. I'm going to have to talk to her.' The two of them were in Dorothea's lounge; after a silent evening meal Morag had left for the canteen, where she had insisted on continuing after Georges' death.

'Leave her, Dorry. Mebbe it's because I was part of their friendship that she can't feel comfortable with me. And she's right, it's hard to understand why old folk are left alive when young folk at the beginning of their lives have to die.'

'That was a terrible thing to say to you.'

'She needed to pass some of her hurt on to someone else. It was too much for her to carry on her own. Leave her,' Lessie said again, her hands busy with her knitting, her voice calm. 'She has to take her own time about things.'

It was a relief to Lessie when Jess came from London for a few days, as fresh and pretty as ever in spite of the London bombings, brightening up the house with her very presence. As always, she turned everything that had happened to her, including ambulance driving during air raids, into an amusing story, though her eyes were shadowed and her lovely face pale with weariness.

On the fourth day of her visit Lessie, who had left her daughter sound asleep when she left for the shop in the morning, came back to find her standing over the range, wrapped in one of Lessie's own aprons. The flat was filled with the appetising smell of liver and bacon and onions. A candle, kept on the mantelshelf for emergencies, burned on the kitchen table, which was set with the best china.

'I thought I'd make a meal for you, for once,' Jess said lightly.

'Where did you get the food? I've not collected my meat ration yet.'

'I managed to coax a little more out of the butcher. You'll have to live on potatoes for the rest of the week, but tonight we dine in style. Take off your coat, I'm going to dish up the soup now.'

'I didnae know you could cook,' Lessie marvelled half an hour later as they spooned up the remains of a rhubarb sponge made from eggless sponge and a handful of rhubarb that Jess had sweet-talked from a neighbour.

'Darling, I can do lots of amazing things these days. The restaurants are pretty awful now, so I've had to learn to fend for myself. And last month a friend who was supposed to give a talk on wartime cookery to a group of housewives went down with laryngitis, so I had to do it for her.'

'You?'

'Don't look so surprised,' Jess reprimanded. 'She wrote it all down for me and I was an absolute riot. I even got interested in it and tried out some of the recipes for myself. They worked very well.' There was a pause before, dropping her gaze and toying with the salt cellar, she said abruptly, 'Mam, I've met someone. His name's Philip – Philip Lorrimer.' Then she added self-mockingly, 'Major Philip Lorrimer, of course. I'd not have settled for anything less than a major.'

'Where is he?'

'In London. We met during an air raid, of all things, and when the all-clear went we just kept on seeing each other. He's based in London at the moment, but,' her fingers released the salt cellar and twined with the fingers of her other hand, 'he'll probably be going away soon.'

'How special is he?'

Jess looked up, her eyes bright with memories and secrets. 'More

295

than anyone else has ever been. I just wanted to tell you. Isn't it ridiculous, falling in love at my age? I'm thirty-eight, for God's sake!'

Andrew's face, his voice, the touch of his lips, suddenly came clearly to Lessie and filled her with longing for him. 'It's not just the young who fall in love, Jess.' She heard a tremor in her voice and wondered if her daughter, normally as sharp as a pin, had heard it too. But Jess was too caught up in the wonder of her own happiness to notice anything.

'And there was me, thinking I'd finally reached the age of common sense.' She made a face, laughed a bit shakily, then said, 'It's bad judgement, isn't it, being footloose and fancy free during peacetime, then falling for someone when there's a war on and nobody knows who's going to survive it.'

'I think that's why people do fall in love during a war – they need a commitment.'

'I just wish it hadn't happened to me. What can I do about it, Mam?'

'Go back to London and to your major and enjoy each other while you can.'

Jess laughed again, reaching out to capture one of Lessie's hands in her own. A tear fell onto their linked fingers and she gave a huge unladylike sniff before saying, 'I knew you'd say something sensible. You always do.'

As the year wore on the list of local war casualties in the *Telegraph* continued to grow. Some of the young men who had gone marching off were back home again, some missing limbs, some blinded or deafened or shell-shocked into a stunned bewildered silence. The Royal Air Force launched offensives against Berlin and Hamburg and Hitler retaliated by sending his own bombers to devastate London. Lessie lay awake at nights fretting over Jess, who continued to drive her ambulance and sent reassuring letters regularly. Once or twice Lessie phoned her; she sounded as cheerful as ever, although her major had been sent overseas.

Coventry was severely damaged by bombing, then Birmingham, then Liverpool. 'They're making their way up towards us,' someone said gloomily in the shop. 'You'll see. They'll not forget about us.'

Nineteen forty-one arrived, marking the close of the first full year of war with no sign of the early ending that had been confidently prophesied fifteen months earlier. The sirens still sounded in Greenock, but not often. Twice a stick of bombs, possibly from some plane shedding the last of its load before heading for home, landed in the town, but there was no full-scale attack.

When the sirens wailed their eerie warning to the town one moonlit night in March, Lessie, who had been sitting alone listening to the radio, switched it off and listened anxiously for the sound of aircraft engines. She could hear the occasional dull thud as the anti-aircraft guns on the hills above the town and across the river began to fire, but that was all. She put the lights out, went into the coal-black hall, moving with the ease of someone who has lived in the same place for so long that even a blackout can't do more than blunt the edge of familiarity, and pulled on her coat before slipping out of the door.

'Who's there?' a familiar voice barked from the closemouth.

'It's me, Mr Delaney, Lessie Carswell.'

The man made room for her and together they stared up at the moon floating serenely in a cloudless sky. Searchlights prodded their long fingers up from the ground, sweeping back and forth, and the guns thudded in the hills. There was the faint drone of massed engines from above, but although Lessie narrowed her eyes she couldn't make out any planes.

'They're high,' her neighbour said. 'Passing by overhead. They're after some other poor bugger tonight, if you'll pardon the language, Mrs Carswell.'

The throb of aircraft engines died away, the guns fell silent, the lights were switched off. They could hear other guns firing, further away.

'The all-clear'll go in a minute,' Mr Delaney said, and nodded his satisfaction as he was proved right within minutes. 'We can get to our beds now. It's not our turn. Not yet.'

The bombers had been making for Clydebank, a shipbuilding town further up the river, close to Glasgow. They returned to their target on the following night, like a dog returning to a buried bone, and by the time they had finished with it the town had been appallingly and ruthlessly ravaged, with hundreds of 'Bankies' dead or wounded. Only a handful of houses had escaped without any damage.

In May the enemy planes returned, this time unleashing their savagery on Greenock while Lessie crouched in a makeshift cave comprised of two upended armchairs pushed against the big kitchen table. Holding a cushion tightly over each ear to try to keep out the worst of the continuous, terrifying din, she recited the multiplication table at the top of her voice, then went on to the poems she had learned at school, nursery rhymes, street songs, songs she had heard on the radio; anything that came into her head, anything that would take her mind off the whistling noises of the bombs coming down, and the way the floor shook beneath her with each one that fell.

It was a long, clamorous night, filled with the throbbing of heavy German bombers, the dull thud of anti-aircraft guns, the high-pitched whistle of bombs coming down, then the crash of their arrival. The building surely couldn't stand up to such punishment, Lessie thought, and was instantly reminded of the floors above her, poised to give way and crush her.

'Don't be daft!' she ordered herself in a shaky voice, and found some comfort in summoning Andrew's memory to keep her company. The thought of him, and her great need for him at that moment, brought tears, but at least they were tears of grief and not of fear.

Finally, exhausted, she fell into a doze and was jolted awake by a fist thundering on the door. Confused and startled, thinking at first that she was in her bed, she bumped her head on the underside of the table when she tried to get up.

'Mrs Carswell! Are you in there?'

She shook her head hard to clear it and managed to fumble her way out from beneath the table, clutching at the torch when her hand found its familiar shape.

'I'm coming!' she yelled as Mr Delaney's fist started assaulting her door again. Still dazed with sleep she collided with the coatstand which went down with a clatter, and at last reached the door, waiting until he was inside before switching on her torch. 'Has the all-clear gone?'

'Five minutes ago. Did ye no' hear it?'

'I must have fallen asleep.'

'Asleep? You're a cool yin,' he said admiringly, then, 'Are ye all right? Yer voice is awful hoarse.'

'I think I've got a summer cold coming on,' lied Lessie, feeling her cheeks grow hot. It would never do to let him know that she had been sitting all alone under her own table singing to herself. She reached for the light switch, but nothing happened.

'I think they got the power station,' Mr Delaney said. 'God, that wis a bad night! We're lucky tae have survived it. If ye're sure ye're all right, Mrs Carswell, I'll get away tae my bed. It'll be a busy day tomorrow.'

Dorothea, as smart as ever in spite of a night without sleep, arrived in Cathcart Street while Lessie was finishing off her morning cup of tea.

'It's terrible,' she said as soon as she walked in. 'The whole town – they're still putting the fires out and trying to find missing folk. Mam, I was worried sick about you! You'll have to come to us tonight.'

'I'll do nothing of the kind. If I'm going to die I'd as soon die in my own house, among my own possessions.'

'But they might come back. They bombed Clydebank for two nights. Mam, will you listen to sense for once?'

'I'm not in my dotage, Dorry, so don't speak to me like that,' Lessie snapped. She had a headache and there was a tender lump on her skull where she had collided with the table when Mr Delaney had wakened her abruptly after the raid. 'I've got a shop to run, and as long as it's standing I'll be here to see that it opens on time in the mornings. I'm not going to let Adolf Hitler get in the way of my work.'

All morning customers filed into the shop, dazed with shock and lack of sleep, adding their own contribution to an ever-growing list of death and injuries and damage. The shipyards, the prime target, had been badly hit. The Westburn sugar refinery had been damaged and at the height of the blitz melted sugar had been seen running down the gutters. The distillery had received a direct hit early in the raid, and the inferno caused by about three million gallons of whisky catching fire had attracted the bombers back to that area, which was almost flattened. The incendiaries, one woman reported in wonder, had looked like flaming fire falling out of the sky, and people scrambling to the hills behind the town for shelter away from burning buildings had been machine-gunned by low-flying German planes.

In a tenement building in Dunlop Street the blast from an exploding bomb had dragged the feathers from an unfortunate canary sitting in its cage in a close where its owner had trusted in the baffle wall to protect her and her pet from the bombing.

In the afternoon Lessie left the shop to her assistants and went to have a look for herself. Glass crunched under her feet and the air was still heavy with the reek of smoke and charred wood and cloth, mingled with the sweet caramel tang of burned sugar and the reek of whisky. In some places shop windows had been blown out and tins and boxes were still strewn over the pavement. The pavement in front of a painter and decorator's smashed window was a magnificent rainbow of brilliant colours where the tins had burst and their contents run together. Here and there smoke still trickled sullenly from a gaping window or a battered roof; parts of the pavements were roped off because of the danger of falling masonry.

People stood and stared in disbelief, or picked among the ruins of a tenement, searching for any possessions that might be intact and worth salvaging. Water arced from hoses into buildings that still smouldered; men worked in one street she passed to shore up a building that was in danger of sliding into the abyss where its neighbour had stood only the day before. Lessie looked at it all, appalled, wondering what possessed folk to do such terrible things to each other.

Since the beginning of the war an old shopping bag had served as Lessie's emergency holdall. Each night she filled it with a box containing her important papers, a torch, a clean handkerchief, candles, matches, some first aid essentials, a box of biscuits and a flask of hot tea. She was stoppering the flask on the night after the raid when Morag came to the door, slipping into the hall as soon as the door opened wide enough. The power was still off and, in the light of the candle Lessie carried in a saucer of water, Morag's hair gleamed like a polished chestnut beneath her woollen beret.

'Gran, I've come to take you to Brougham Street.'

'I told your mother—'

'I know you did, but you've got to come!' The girl's thin face was determined. 'I'll not have you here all alone.'

'Does Dorothea know where you are?'

'I've been at the canteen. I sent a message to tell her I was coming to fetch you.'

'But Morag—'

'Gran, please!'

Lessie hesitated, but only for a moment. It was the first time in over a year, since the young French sailor's death, that Morag had made a move towards her. The girl's concern brought a lump to her throat.

'All right. I'll just fetch my bag and my—'

The familiar banshee wail of the siren cut across the words, and they stared at each other in horror before Lessie said briskly, 'It looks as though we're both going to have to say here, lassie.'

'But you don't have a shelter.'

Lessie drew her granddaughter into the kitchen. 'We'll manage fine without one. The other folk in the building go to Mrs McBeth's house across the close, but I'm happier here. Give me a hand—'

Together they dragged the two armchairs into position in the centre of the kitchen and upended them so that they formed a solid wall between the table and the window, to give protection from flying glass if the window should be blown in. Lessie scooped back the curtains across the alcove bed, brought out armfuls of pillows and blankets, and tossed them under the table together with her emergency bag, then fetched an extra torch. The siren was still sending out its urgent warning and there were other sounds, too, now – the thump of the guns, the ominous broken drone of hundreds of big heavy planes reaching the end of their long journey.

'Under the table with you, lassie.' Lessie anchored two quilts to the top of the table with the coal scuttle, the pouffe and two stools, so that they hung down like a curtain.

'It's cosy in here,' Morag said from beneath the table. 'Cosier than our garden shelter at home.'

'I spent a lot of time designing it,' Lessie said, and was rewarded with a soft giggle. She blew out the candles and crawled in beside Morag, puffing as she went. 'Dear God, I'm getting too stiff and too old for this sort of nonsense!'

Morag's hands reached out for her, drew her down onto a nest of pillows and blankets. 'You're not too old,' she said fiercely. 'Gran, I'm sorry I said that you were.'

'Wheesht, lassie. Don't fret yourself about that. I am old, there's no getting away from that.'

'But it wasn't fair of me to say it,' Morag said with a gulp. 'It wasn't your fault – what happened to Georges. I should have—'

The floor vibrated and the windows rattled as a bomb exploded somewhere close. Morag screamed and Lessie held her closer, switching on one of the torches with her free hand, illuminating their snug little shelter. 'It's all right, pet, you're all right.'

Morag's eyes were huge and brilliant in the torchlight. 'It s-sounds so loud. You don't hear them so loud in our shelter.'

'Noise cannae hurt you.'

They sat for a while, listening. Tonight was going to be just as bad as last night. The bombs were coming down thick and fast. She thought of Dorothea, who must be worried sick about Morag.

'Gran,' Morag asked at last, tentatively, 'that night that Georges – that the ship blew up – you said that losing someone was as bad at fifty-five as at fifteen. Did you . . .?'

Her voice died away into an inquisitive silence. For a moment the raid was forgotten as Lessie floundered for the right words. For years she had longed to tell someone about Andrew, to be free to talk about him. But once it was shared, a secret was no longer a secret. Even in the telling it could lose some of its magic. And anyway, Morag was too young as yet to hear that particular secret.

'Don't you be so nosy, miss,' she said at last, and Morag giggled again.

'Does that mean you're not telling?'

'One day, mebbe, when we're both older.'

The aircraft continued to drone overhead, wave after wave of them, and there were muffled explosions, mercifully far away. Heavy booted feet thundered by the window, then the floor shook again. That bomb had landed quite near to Cathcart Street, Lessie thought, tightening her arms protectively about her granddaughter.

'Are you scared, Gran?'

'A wee bit. I'll tell you one thing,' Lessie said wryly, 'I'll never tread on a cockroach again, not now I know what it's like to be cowering on the floor, never knowing when a big boot's going to land on you. When I think of the cockroaches I killed in the very first house I lived in after I was married . . .'

The bombs fell and she talked on, about Donald and about Ian's babyhood and about the people who had lived in the street, talking herself hoarse to keep the girl's attention away from the death that was being flung down on them from the night skies.

Then suddenly the world was wrenched apart by a crash that shook Lessie's teeth in her head. She and Morag flew into each other's arms and the girl's screams of terror corkscrewed through her ears. The floor thundered beneath them then calmed as there was a great rending, roaring noise from a short distance away. The noise faded at last, giving way to an agitated tinkling over by the mantelshelf, where the wally dugs and the clock and a little pair of matched vases stood. For a moment there was silence before Morag said shakily, tears and laughter in her voice, 'We're still alive! Gran, we're all right!'

'Of course we're all right. We'll always be all right.' The torch had fallen off its perch on the top of Lessie's emergency bag and was shining its beam uselessly up at the underside of the sturdy table. She rescued it and lifted a corner of the quilt. The room looked its usual self.

'It couldnae have been this building,' she said in relief. Then, sharply, struck by a terrible thought. 'Morag, which direction d'you think the noise came from?'

'That way, I think.'

'The shop. Dear God, what's happened to my shop?'

'Gran!'

Without stopping to think Lessie scrambled out from under the table and got to her feet, fumbling in the darkness for the door. 'Stay there, Morag. I have to go and see if anything's happened to the shop.'

'Gran!'

As she reached the hall there was another explosion, too far away to do more than make the building vibrate. The front door opened and Lessie scrambled out into the close, which was erratically lit by flashes of light and an ominous dull glow reflecting against the inside of the baffle wall.

She reached the closemouth, almost running into the temporary brick baffle wall, bringing herself up in time, using it to steady herself, straining her eyes towards the corner where flames were beginning to lick greedily up from the ground. It must have been the shop that time!

'Gran!' Morag said breathlessly, snatching for her and finding her. From above came a menacing whistling noise. Folk who had been outside during raids spoke of the whistling sound the bombs made as they fell.

'Get back into the house, Morag!'

The whistling cut out; there was a pause, as though the world was holding its breath, then it really did split apart. Somebody or something gave Lessie a hefty shove in the chest and she went staggering back, reaching out in search of something to catch onto, in search of Morag. But there was nothing but a deep black well with no more noise, and no bottom to it.

33

The shop was gone, and so was the tenement she had lived in for most of her life. She was lucky to be alive, they told her in the hospital. Running out just before the bomb fell at the back of the building, she had been caught by the blast and thrown back against the brick baffle wall, sustaining concussion and severe bruising, but no broken bones.

Morag, behind her, had been thrown clear of the wall and had escaped with scratches and bruises. 'Oh, Gran,' she wept when she and Dorothea came into the hospital ward, crammed with blitz victims, 'I thought you were dead! I thought we'd lost you!'

'You'll have to work harder than that to lose me,' Lessie whispered, and summoned up a smile. Talking and smiling were hard work; all she wanted to do was to lie still and not have to think, or even be. Her hand lay in Morag's warm clasp, and she could scarcely find the energy to return the pressure of the girl's fingers.

'They found your bag, still there under the table,' Dorothea told her.

'The shop?'

'It's gone, Mam. Most of Cathcart Street went last night.' So had poor Mrs Delaney, but Dorothea kept that to herself for the time being. 'You'll be out of here in a couple of days, then you'll come to stay with us, Mam. There's plenty of room.'

She was lucky, Lessie thought when they had gone, lucky to have family, to have somewhere to go. She should be grateful, but she only felt tired, and very old. She had never felt old before. It was a frightening sensation.

Mercifully, the enemy planes didn't return and she was able to sleep that night, a confused sleep that had her battling enormous cockroaches in the Vennel one moment, with Ian, tied into a chair with a scarf, contentedly gumming away at a sugared crust, and in the shop the next minute, dealing with a continuous queue of customers. Mam was there, and Da, and Thomasina filling a paper poke from the sweetie jar, and Peter, pale and silent. And Anna, who blurred and changed into Dorothea, who glowered at Lessie with her beautiful violet eyes and said, 'He was only eighteen! Why should he be dead and someone as old as you be alive?'

She woke with a start to find herself in the quiet, dimly lit ward, and tossed and turned until the lights went on and the nurses' heels clicked up the long crowded ward to start preparing their patients for the day.

The cuts and bruises healed but the fire that had blazed at the core of Lessie's being for sixty-two years had been quenched on the second night of the blitz. She sat in the comfortable lounge of Dorothea's house, or in the garden if the weather was good, and couldn't be bothered to think about her future. One day she would have to stir herself, but each time she said so Dorothea replied firmly, 'You've done your bit, Mam. You've raised three of us and worked all your life. You deserve a bit of mollycoddling.' And Lessie was content to accept her decree.

Morag spent a lot of time with her grandmother, pathetically anxious to make up for the rift that had been between them for a year. She and Lessie went out for walks by the Clyde, worked on a jigsaw, played cards together. Morag chattered on about school and her work in the canteen, and she painted Lessie again, a replacement for the picture that had been destroyed in the blitz. For the sittings Lessie wore the little autumn leaf brooch, which had been in the emergency bag rescued from the tenement ruins. Looking at the picture when it was completed, then into the mirror, she saw that although this time she had sat for the painting, Morag had again worked from memory, and turned out an almost perfect replica of the original, depicting her grandmother as she had been before the blitz. The woman in the painting was serene, with the hint of a smile in her eyes and at the corners of her mouth; the woman who looked back at Lessie from the mirror was years older, with the humour and the strength gone from her face.

Occasionally she woke in the night or the early morning, wondering what had happened to her. Never in her life had she been so helpless and hopeless, she told herself, recalling her mother's favourite criticism. A neighbour who didn't work every hour of the day to keep herself and her house and her family clean and decent had always been dismissed by Barbara Kirkwood as 'helpless and hopeless'. Not worth fretting over. What would her mother think of her now, Lessie wondered, and knew that she should start taking control of her life. But not yet; later maybe, when the war was over and they all knew what lay ahead of them. For now, she hadn't the energy. Adolf Hitler, it seemed, had got the better of her after all. Perhaps Dorry was right, perhaps she had reached the age where she should just give in and sit back and enjoy the rest of her life. Not that she was enjoying any of it at the moment. She was just drifting, like one of those big silvery barrage balloons that had been put up to foil enemy aircraft.

Day followed day and summer gave way to early autumn. The invincible German battleship *Bismark* was sunk and the Germans invaded Russia. In October Lessie's sense of duty made her rouse herself and pay her annual visit to Anna's grave. Morag accompanied her, and Dorothea insisted on sending them in the car. Without it, Lessie could never have managed the long driveway from the gate to where the first of the gravestones stood. At the top of the drive they left the car and Morag took her grandmother's arm, accommodating her long strides to suit Lessie's slower, shorter steps. It was a grey day with a chill wind blowing in from the river. In addition to her thick school coat, Morag wore a dark blue woollen beret pulled down over her bright hair and a long matching scarf looped about her neck. Lessie's shopping bag hung over her arm and bumped against her hip with every step; a large bunch of chrysanthemums picked from Dorothea's garden nodded their lush bright heads over the top of the bag.

They took a path to the left and visited Andrew's grave first; he and his wife lay beneath a handsome marble stone, one of several marking the graves of other Warrens, including Frank, who had died so ignominiously in Anna McCauley's bed in the Vennel. There was no grave for Martin, who had been buried in France, but his name and the years of his birth and death were on his parents' stone.

Morag took the jug they had brought to fetch water from the stand-pipe and watched as Lessie arranged flowers in the urn that stood at the foot of the stone.

'I don't remember him, but Mummy says we got on very well together. I wish he'd lived long enough for me to get to know him properly.'

'So do I,' said Lessie, getting to her feet slowly.

Anna's grave was some distance away, near the wall. As they walked towards it Lessie suddenly noticed a sturdily built man standing motionless before it, grey head bowed.

'Morag, take the jug over and fetch some more water, will you?' she asked quickly, shaken out of the lethargy that had become her constant companion since the blitz, and went on alone towards the man, who didn't lift his head as she neared him. It was only when she stopped by his side and said, 'Hello, Davie,' that he looked up.

'Lessie?' He had aged a great deal since she had last seen him, but then so had she. His hair was completely grey now, as grey as his cold and piercing eyes, and all the lines of his square face dragged down. There was nothing left of the good-looking, laughing young man who had shared her home in the Vennel.

'I wondered who left them every year,' Lessie said, nodding at the bunch of crimson roses lying on the grass that covered Anna McCauley.

His jaw twitched but he only said, 'How are you?' His voice was harsh and stiff, as though it wasn't used much for conversation.

'Well enough. And you?'

'I heard you'd lost the house and the shop in the blitz.'

'I'm living with Dorry just now.'

'I heard,' said Davie, then turned his head sharply as Morag, carefully balancing the jug of water, appeared at the end of the path. 'Who's that?'

'My granddaughter.' And Anna's, she was going to add, but something stopped her. Perhaps it wasn't a good idea to interest Davie in Morag – not if he still retained his obsession with Anna. Looking at the roses, Lessie knew that he did.

'I'll say good day then,' he said, and swung round on his heel, walking away from the approaching girl, striding out as though anxious to escape from them both.

'Who was that?' Morag wanted to know in her turn as she knelt by the grave, drawing her gloves off with her teeth so that she could pour the water carefully from the jug into the urn Lessie had put on the grave on the first anniversary of Anna's death.

'Someone your grandmother Anna and I used to know, long ago. Put the flowers into the water for me, will you? And the roses too.' Lessie handed over the chrysanthemums and watched as Morag's slim fingers arranged them, working among the brilliant blooms with a deft, sure touch. All at once she felt very tired, and anxious to get back to the safety and comfort of Dorothea's house.

Lessie could just make out Davie, between the tombstones, leaving the cemetery. 'Next time round I'll make sure things'll be different for him – for us all,' she thought, then remembered with a pang that there would be no next time round; life only happened once, and some mistakes couldn't be undone.

'Imagine roses in October. They must have been growing in a sheltered spot.' Morag's hand reached out for them.

'Be careful,' Lessie said, her eyes on the gate. 'Be careful. Roses have thorns.'

The ringing of the phone in the hall woke Lessie from an afternoon nap in her chair by the sitting-room window. She hadn't had a phone in her house or even in the shop, and the jangling bell always made her jump. Looking at the clock she was appalled to find that she had slept two hours away since coming back from the cemetery. The sky outside had been grey when she dozed off, but now there was a shaft of sunlight lying across the carpet, stretching almost to her feet, and when she got up stiffly and followed it to the window she saw that the clouds had rolled back and the sky was blue.

The phone had stopped ringing; Dorothea's voice, clear and decisive, floated from the hall. 'She's resting and I don't want to disturb her. Yes, of course she's fine, just worn out with everything that's happened, that's all. She was out this morning and when she came back she was so tired that I didn't even have the heart to waken her for her lunch. Look Jess, you're not supposed to use the phone for long chats just now, or haven't they told you that in London? When she wakens I'll tell—'

'Is that Jess?'

There was a pause, then Dorothea called back, 'Yes, Mam. She's only phoning to ask after you.'

'Tell her I'm coming,' Lessie said, then muttered irritably under her breath as her legs, stiff from inaction, refused to carry her across the room quickly enough. In the hall Dorothea, her immaculately made-up face disapproving, held the receiver out to her.

'Did the phone waken you? I though it would.'

'Jess?' Lessie hated telephones, and was never sure how loudly she should talk into the receiver. Jess's voice, with its usual undercurrent of laughter, travelled blithely across the miles between London and Greenock.

306

'Mam? How are you?'

'Never mind how I am, how are you?'

'I'm fine. Why shouldn't I—' There was a silence, as though some-one had just clapped a hand over Jess's mouth, then a sudden gasp before she said, the laughter gone, 'Oh Mam, Philip's missing. Some-where in Africa. Mam,' said Jess, her voice broken, 'I can't bear it, not on my own. I want to . . . Can I come home?'

'Of course you can, pet. Right away.'

There was a huge inelegant sniff and a choke from the other end of the line before Jess said, 'I'll not be able to get away for another three weeks, but I just needed to know that it's all right. I know Dorry's house won't be big enough for us all, but if you could find a place for me to stay, somewhere near you . . .'

'I'll find somewhere. Just come as soon as you can.'

'I'll let you know the date. Oh, Mam,' said Jess with a shaky laugh, 'falling in love's hellish, isn't it?'

'Not always,' said Lessie, reaching out to her daughter with her voice instead of her arms. 'Just sometimes.'

'She's coming to Greenock, isn't she?' Dorothea asked when the receiver had been replaced.

'Philip's missing. She needs to be with her own folk.'

Dorothea's brows knotted. 'I'm sorry for Jess, but even so, Mam, you're not strong enough to cope with this sort of thing.'

'Nonsense,' said Lessie firmly. Someone needed her again; for the first time since babyhood Jess needed her. 'Nonsense,' she repeated, and her mind, rusty from disuse over the past six months, began to crank into action.

'I could mebbe borrow a camp bed from someone, if you don't mind sharing with her,' Dorothea offered.

'You've done enough, Dorry. It's time I got myself sorted out.' Lessie looked round the room for her handbag and found it stuffed down the side of the chair she usually sat in. She claimed it then made for the door.

Dorothea followed her out into the hall. 'Mother, where are you going?'

'To the housing people,' said Lessie, one arm in the sleeve of her coat. 'I'm surely entitled to a wee place now that I've been bombed out.'

'But—'

'I need to have somewhere of my own for when Jess comes home. If she's had no good news by then she'll take a lot of looking after.'

'Mam, you're not fit to start house-hunting and worrying about Jess.'

'I'm perfectly fit. You've been good to me, Dorry, but it's time I got on with my own life.' The coat was on now and Lessie was but-toning it, remembering the way small Jess used to stand stoically, her face screwed up with boredom, while her coat was buttoned for her.

'But—'

'Leave her alone, Mother,' Morag said from the kitchen door where she stood, a potato in one hand and a knife in the other. 'Gran knows what she's doing.'

'I'll be back by teatime, Dorry.'

'At least let me send for the car!'

'I've got two good legs. It's time they started doing some work again.'

'Can I come with you, Gran?'

'If you want.'

Morag thrust the potato and the knife at her mother, snatched her jacket from its hook, and hurried after Lessie, who was opening the gate. She offered her arm and Lessie was glad to take it.

'A room and kitchen would do me fine,' she said as the two of them, close-linked, set off. 'Jess won't be able to stay for long. Mebbe I'll look out for another corner shop when she's gone away again – just a wee one would do.'

'There's sure to be something, Gran.' Morag's voice was enthusiastic, happy. The blood began to surge through Lessie and creaking muscles began to stretch. She drew a deep breath, felt the autumn air flood her lungs, and thought with pleasure of the challenge that lay ahead. It would be good to have a place of her own again, and perhaps a business to occupy her energies.

It would all take time but, God willing, she had enough. There was always tomorrow, she told herself as she and Morag, shoulders touching, turned the corner.

There was mebbe even next year.

34

The chill, grey November wind cutting its way in from the river sent crisp packets and bus tickets whisking among the people standing on a stretch of waste ground alongside Lamont's shipyard. It was 1968 and the new Cunard liner the *Queen Elizabeth II*, recently arrived from John Brown's yard in Clydebank to be fitted out in Greenock, was attracting crowds of sightseers.

Morag Elder kicked away a sheet of newspaper, greasy with the memory of fish suppers, that was making amorous advances to her left ankle, buried her hands deep into the pockets of her thick jacket, and looked round anxiously for James and Elizabeth. Spotting them through the crowd, standing together, gaping up at the magnificent bulk of the liner in the dry dock a short distance away, she felt free to do a bit of gawping herself.

Product of the Clyde, where the finest shipbuilders in the world could be found, the ship was a sight worth the seeing. She soared up from the cradle that supported her massive keel, challenging the sky, looming above the streets and houses. From this angle, her bows flaring out overhead, it was impossible to see the magnificent white superstructure and the men working there, poised halfway between heaven and earth.

The Elders – Colin, Morag and their two younger children – had driven over from their home in Glasgow, taking the road over the hills so as to get the best possible first sighting of the new liner. And what a sight it had been. Even James and Elizabeth, wrangling in the back seat, had gasped then fallen silent as the ship came into sight below them, its bulk turning Greenock into a toy town.

'If she fell, Mum, she'd crush the whole town!' James had said at last, in an awed voice.

'She wouldn't fall, would she, Mum?' his thirteen-year-old sister had asked, her voice tense.

'Of course not. They can't afford to let something as beautiful and as costly as that just fall over,' Colin scoffed.

'If she did, she'd not land on Gran's house, would she? Not on Gran and Malcolm?' Elizabeth had had little time for her elder brother when he was at home, but now he was out of the house and living in Greenock with their grandmother her fondness for him had grown by leaps and bounds.

'We-ell . . .' James, who was about to put his name down for a mathematics course at Glasgow University, started measuring distances with his hands, then had the sense to fall silent when Morag screwed herself about in the driving seat and glared at him. But the damage had been done and it had taken a full five minutes after they finally found somewhere to park the car to convince timorous Elizabeth that it was safe to venture near the enormous ship.

'She is a queen, isn't she?' Morag marvelled. 'She knows fine and well that we've all come to pay homage. She looks as though she's graciously holding court.'

'She's fantastic.' There was awe in her husband's voice, then sudden bitterness. 'I just wish they'd had more tact than to name her Elizabeth the Second.'

It was a sore point with many Scots. Only their famous Clydeside yards had been good enough to entrust with this new ship and her older sisters, the *Queen Elizabeth* and the *Queen Mary*. But their pride had been soured by the naming of the liner. The first Elizabeth had been ruler of England alone; the current monarch was in actual fact the first Queen Elizabeth of Great Britain, not the second.

'They did say that it meant second to the old liner, not to the Queen.'

'Aye, and you can believe that if you like!' Colin grunted. She moved closer, slipping her hand into the crook of his elbow. After a moment he relaxed and grinned down at her. Although he was in his mid-fifties and there was more grey than brown in his hair, his face was still open and youthful. 'Okay, love, I'm not going to start doing my Scottish Nationalist bit today. It's not the ship's fault that she's been caught up in a row.' He craned his neck. 'Did you ever see such beautiful lines? Think of the craftmanship that went into making that, Morag. They've got a lot to be proud of, these men.'

The wind gusted, bringing with it a fine smirr of rain. Morag, who had considered her soft green sweater and navy trousers and heavy jacket adequate when she left the house, shivered. She dug into her pocket and took out the deep lilac silk scarf Colin had given her for her last birthday, her forty-fourth. He had bought it because, he said, it matched the colour of her eyes. As she tied it about her throat, Elizabeth, finding the mighty liner just too much to take in, sought out her parents and announced that she was hungry.

'We're not due at your mother's for another forty-five minutes, and you know how the matriarch hates folk to land on her before she's ready,' Colin said as the four of them eased their way out of the crowd and back to the car.

'We'll go somewhere else first, then.' Morag unlocked the driver's door, tipped the seat forward to let her son and daughter get into the back, then got in herself and leaned across to open the passenger door. Colin preferred not to drive if he could avoid it; he had been invalided out of the Second World War with a smashed right arm, and although twenty-five years had passed since then and he could use it fairly easily, it tended to ache if he drove for too long. It had put paid once and for all to any hopes he might still have had of progressing as an artist himself, but he was content enough to teach, and immensely proud of his wife, who had, with his support and encouragement, become a successful and well-known artist. He loved to tell people that he had been the first to recognise her potential, in those long-ago innocent days when she had been a pupil in his art class in Greenock.

The rain had only been an empty threat; the windscreen was clear as Morag drove further into Greenock then turned the car up the hill, into a residential area. 'She loves me,' James's amazingly deep singing voice boomed from the back seat, and Elizabeth at once joined in, harmonising with practised skill, 'Yeah, yeah, yeah!'

The interior of the car was comfortably warm after the chill of the dockside. Morag, who was a Beatles fan herself, hummed along with her children and noticed that there was a streak of blue paint down the side of her right forefinger. It had taken her two hours to spot it; it would take her mother, always elegant despite her sixty-seven years, two seconds.

In the back seat James and Elizabeth had started squabbling again. Morag turned into Newton Street, drew in to the side of the road and switched off the engine. She could have taken the car to the top of Lyle Hill but it would do them good to walk. 'Everybody out.'

'Mum! We've only just got in!' With exaggerated groans the children – she would have to stop thinking of them as children, Morag realised with a pang, they were both teenagers now – struggled out of the back seat, making heavy weather of it. She waited, swinging the car keys from the blue painted finger.

'Straight on up the hill.' She snatched a swift glance at herself in the wing mirror as she bent to lock the car door. She had been too busy finishing a commissioned painting to go to the hairdresser for a few weeks and her coppery red hair, which had grown long enough to swing about her face and annoy her while she was working, was tucked beneath a restraining fabric band. She pulled the band off and let her hair swing free.

Colin had waited for her. He took her hand and pushed their linked fingers deep into the pocket of his duffle coat. 'Think of the money in this street alone,' he said, nodding at the large houses lining both sides, most of them well back from the pavement and hidden from curious eyes by trees or shrubbery.

'They were built by people who made their fortunes in the area – or retired here, where they could look down over the Clyde.'

'Like him, poor soul,' Colin murmured as they halted to let a middle-aged woman in a navy coat and hat emerge from a gate a few feet in front of them, pushing a wheelchair. She gave them a slight nod of thanks and began to wheel her charge, a very old man muffled in rugs and scarves, round them and along the pavement. Smiling down at the man in the chair, Morag met a pair of chilly grey eyes set beneath thick white brows. The eyes suddenly widened, held hers for a few seconds in an intense, almost intimate stare. The yellow-white moustache fluttered but the mouth beneath it was only capable of making inarticulate sounds. A gloved hand fluttered like a wounded

311

bird trying to fly, then subsided helplessly back onto the rug that covered his knees.

'Yes dear, that's right,' the woman said with automatic and impersonal cheerfulness as she pushed the chair past them. Morag was left with the strange feeling that the old man had recognised her – or thought that he had recognised her.

'Newton Street,' she said thoughtfully as she and Colin, still linked, walked on. 'I remember Gran talking about a brother who lived here, but I don't think I met him. He was a recluse and they didn't have any contact with each other. He wasn't at her funeral.'

'A skeleton in the family cupboard?'

'I don't know. He was very rich, I'm sure she said that.' She shivered, then said decisively, 'He must be dead by now. Gran was seventy-one when she died, and that was eighteen years ago.'

'You've got an amazing family,' Colin said, not for the first time. 'You keep telling me that they all sprang from modest beginnings, yet your grandmother amassed a fair amount of money just by running corner shops and your mother's wealthy. Not to mention your Aunt Jess being Lady Lorrimer down in London.'

'That was only because Uncle Philip was knighted for his services as a Member of Parliament.'

'And now you spring another wealthy relative on me. I wonder who he left all his money to?' Colin mused as they toiled up the hill after James and Elizabeth. 'Some fortunate cats' home, no doubt.'

By the time they reached the top of the hill James had left the road and scrambled up to the highest point, calling to his father to come and see the liner far below. While Colin went to join him Elizabeth slipped a hand into her mother's and together they walked along to the huge white stone anchor on its plinth. Elizabeth went through the gate in the low fence and began to translate the French inscription on the plinth, brows knotted the way her father's did when he was trying to work something out. 'To the – memory of—'

'—the sailors of the Free French navy.' Morag's French was still good. 'The French sailors who came here during the war, and died before it was over.'

'Were there a lot of them?'

'A lot. All of them young and far away from home.' Her fingers strayed to the little gold and diamond autumn leaf brooch that had once belonged to her grandmother. The second portrait she had painted of Lessie Carswell wearing it hung on the studio wall of her Glasgow home. She and Colin had moved out of their rented tenement flat and bought their roomy house when Malcolm was three years old, using the money Morag had inherited from Lessie to pay for the house and for the studio Morag had had built in the garden. Nobody, least of all Morag's mother Dorothea, had had any idea until after her death that Lessie Carswell had amassed so much money by a mixture of thrift, good business sense, and an amazingly shrewd knowledge of the intricacies of investment.

Morag's red hair whipped about her face as she walked to the front of the monument, hands thrust deep into her pockets, to look down over Cardwell Bay and the Clyde. Lessie had lived to be a great-grandmother and had been proud of Malcolm, now being groomed by Dorothea to take over the sugar refinery. She had died quietly one day in her armchair in the small flat behind the corner shop she owned a few streets away from Cathcart Street, and had never known James and Elizabeth, or how well Morag herself had done. On the other hand, perhaps she did know. Probably she did, Morag thought, because nothing had ever slipped by her. She wondered for the umpteenth time what her grandmother had meant when she spoke about loving and losing being hard at any age. Morag had never found out after all; that was a secret that Lessie had kept to the end.

Her stomach rumbled, reminding her that time was passing and they were due soon at her mother's house for tea. They would all be together again for a few hours – Dorothea and Colin and Malcolm and James and Elizabeth. Then there would be a lazy weekend and on Monday she would start the task of preparing for her next exhibition.

She turned, her eyes on the memorial. So many years had passed, but Georges was still young, unchanged, though not as clear in her mind as he once had been.

'I'm hungry,' said James, arriving in a whirl of arms and legs. His father was only a few yards behind him.

'We all are.' Morag held out a hand to her daughter. 'Coming, love?'